Corinn _____ om Sarah
Lawrence College in 2016. Her stories have appeared in *Night*
_____ *Knee-Jerk*, and *Pithead Chapel*, among other publications.
_____ is her first novel.

indecent

CORINNE SULLIVAN

ONE PLACE. MANY STORIES

HQ
An imprint of HarperCollins*Publishers* Ltd
1 London Bridge Street
London SE1 9GF

This paperback edition 2018

1
First published in Great Britain by
HQ, an imprint of HarperCollins*Publishers* Ltd 2018

ISBN: 978-0-00-824478-1

For Mickey

ONE

THERE HAD BEEN NO MAJOR INCIDENTS—AT LEAST, NOTHING OF the sort I imagined could happen my first week at Vandenberg School for Boys (no salmonella outbreak, no still-lit cigarette imprudently disposed in a wastebasket, no menacingly quiet freshman with a handgun). Then I caught Christopher Jordan with his hand down his pants. I didn't mean to see it. I certainly didn't want to see it. But I saw it nevertheless: the flaxen-haired second year from Roanoke, prostrate and panting on his twin bed.

Beating the monkey—that's what the Vandenberg boys called it. The first time I'd heard that term used there—"Dude, I beat the monkey every night to those tit pics Cassie sent me," said one guy to his friend two spots before me in the chicken-fajita line—I was brought back to Camp Barbara Anne, to lying in my bottom bunk and spotting the Magic Marker sketch of a penis and testicles on the bedpost (two bulging eyes and a big long nose, I'd initially thought) and recognizing it distantly as something I'd heard about, something I should know about but would probably never fully grasp. As I've spent the majority of my life pretending to understand things I do not—Jackson Pollock, 401(k) plans, Buddhism, euthanasia—the sight of Christopher Jordan beating the monkey just reminded me once more how little I understood.

I'd asked Kip once if he did it a lot. He'd said, "Imogene. I'm a guy," accompanied by a look that said *duh*.

The rock music screaming through the door of Christopher Jordan's fourth-story single room in Slone House had made me stop to knock—it was quiet hours, after all. My co-apprentice Rajah Patel was supposed to accompany whatever girl was assigned to dorm rounds each night (the injustice of being the sole male apprentice, I suppose), but we'd decided instead to split up the building by floors—he one and two, I three and four—to get the job done quickly. I'd been too relieved to be on my own to worry about bending the rules. I never knew what to say to Raj; his gaze was too intense, as though he could see right through your clothes and maybe even your skin, too, and he seemed able to provide only unwelcome facts and opinions. On the first day I met him, he gestured to my face and said, "Did you know freckles are really just bunches of melanocytes that become darker when exposed to the sun?" I said, "Oh," feeling then that every already-abhorred freckle now bulged from my face like pulsating skin pustules.

I had already been up and down the hall of the third floor, passing by half-ajar doors behind which I could see the golden heads of boys bent over desks composing essays or poring through textbooks. One guy—bless him!—fiddled with a chess board, playing against an invisible opponent. My heart swelled for each and every one of them, for the uniform shirts pressed and hanging on the back of their desk chairs for tomorrow, for the sticks of Tom's of Maine deodorant and bottles of Drakkar Noir cologne and tubes of acne cream cluttering their dressers, for the patchouli-and-sweat-and-gardenias smell of boy wafting from each room.

I couldn't hear Christopher Jordan's response to my knock, if there even was one, and I only opened the door a crack (*no stepping foot into a student's dormitory room*), but that was enough. As though stunned by a camera shutter, I stared, immobilized by the sight of him in the small gash of light from his bedside table lamp, his brutish grunts, the sound like a plastic spoon churning a thick batter—no, a plunger unclogging a stalwart toilet—still audible above the awful metallic shriek of his music. He caught my eye before I could catch myself, before I could even realize what I was seeing. "Whoops" I heard myself say, as I would if I'd accidentally stepped on someone's shoes from behind or tripped going up the stairs. *Whoops!* It's a word I'd never will myself to say but somehow always manages to emerge from my parted lips in moments of surprised indignity.

"Mother—*Jesus*!" He jumped as if he'd been shocked by an electrical outlet and slapped a pillow over his lap. "Don't you know how to fucking kn—"

"I'm sorry. I'm so sorry . . ."

In the dim light, his eyes were coin slots, his mouth a jeering sliver. Authority shifted.

"Who the fuck are you anyway?"

"I—" I was six years older than him, yet not feeling nearly old enough. "If you could just turn down . . ."

Christopher Jordan smiled the smile of a boy—a *man*—who probably knew the words to say to get a girl to undress. "Sure thing." He reached over to his desk and adjusted the volume on his laptop, pillow still balanced precariously on his lap. "Better?"

I couldn't speak; I nodded instead.

"Would you mind shutting the door behind you?"

I shut the door behind me. Before I had even taken a few steps away, I could hear that he was at it again. As I continued on, I fixed my gaze on the emergency exit door at the end of the hallway, afraid of what else I might see.

Raj met me outside the building. "All good?" he asked.

I nodded. I feared that if I opened my mouth, I might've admitted that I had irrevocably fucked up within my first week at Vandenberg, proving to myself and everyone else that I didn't belong there. Either that, or I'd puke.

— — —

Dorm rounds was just one of the daily duties I began in that first week. (That first week—how long ago it seems!) Other duties included supervising study period, monitoring the dining hall, helping to coach the varsity lacrosse team, and acting as the Honors History assistant teacher for first years—first years, that's what freshmen were called, like it was Hogwarts.

Study period was easy. Sometimes the first years would laugh and poke each other over their open biology textbooks, but just give them a hard stare—their balls would shrivel like leaves, and they'd shut the fuck up. At least that's what Chapin said, though it certainly hadn't worked on Christopher Jordan.

Dining hall duty was also mostly benign. I had to make sure no one stole an extra serving of French fries or banana pudding and that the trays were cleared before they were stacked in the dish room. Rumor had it among the apprentices that a few years ago, a couple of second years had started a food fight, splattering creamed corn and broccoli casserole—Thursday's dinner special—on the mahogany-paneled walls and twenty-foot-high Palladian windows. I hoped that wouldn't happen when I was on duty.

My first lacrosse practice was the day before the Christopher Jordan incident. It was tradition for the older boys to attempt to pants the newcomers to the team—the "virgins"—as they ran around the field with their sticks. A slight third year named Clarence Howell got his pants ripped down by team captain Duggar Robinson as they ran an overhead shooting drill. He wore a pair of grayish briefs, which set the other boys howling and made me feel strangely sad.

The best part of that week was chapel. On that first Sunday—as they did on the first Sunday of every new semester—the boys donned suit jackets and ties and filed into Morris Chapel, first years in the front and fourth years in the back. (*We're nondenominational,* the Vandenberg pamphlets all boasted. *We are a spiritual campus, not a religious one.*) From the sidewall bench under the stained-glass windows, I watched as the Chosen Boy from each class—selected carefully by the faculty members each August based on leadership, scholarship, and philanthropy—strode solemnly up the center aisle towards the pulpit with a lit candle in his hand. (When I asked Kip if he'd ever been a Chosen Boy, he said they'd asked him his sophomore year and he'd turned them down. He then proceeded to cackle for a solid minute; I'm still not sure whether it was a joke.) They stood in order from youngest to the oldest, from the baby-faced schoolboy in front to the muscled mammoth trailing the pack, an ages-and-stages development chart from the boys' edition of *Our Bodies, Ourselves.* Not a whisper or a vibrating cell phone was to be heard. They lined up before Dean Harvey, headmaster of Vandenberg School for Boys, with their candles flickering beneath their chins.

Dean Harvey spoke, his voice a ringing bell through the rafters. His hanging jowls jiggled like a bloodhound's, but the blue eyes behind his glasses were clear and wise. "Do you seek to integrate intellectual excellence with moral commitment, to concern yourself with mind as well as character, to value knowledge and transcendent values above all else?"

"Oh yes, oh yes we do," the four boys chorused back obediently.

He raised his eyes to the room and spread his arms. "And how about you, pupils of Vandenberg?"

With the groaning of benches and rustling of jacket sleeves, the boys all stood and sang, in almost perfect unison, "Oh yes, oh yes we do."

I mouthed the words with them, feeling pride and love swell inside me, feeling as though my heart might beat out of my chest.

— — —

On my walk alone back to the Hovelina House—Raj slept in a single room in Perkins Hall, a fourth-years' dormitory—I mentally rehearsed the story. Yeah, so I opened the door—just so I could ask him to turn down his music, you know—and there he was, masturbating! Like he was brushing his teeth! I thought maybe if I said the story out loud it would become funny, a joke. Maybe my stomach would untwist from its knots.

"Imogene!" I heard ReeAnn cry as soon as my key turned in the lock. She sat at the kitchen table reading a book on the lifestyle and habits of Parisian women, her pudgy pink face eager as a department store makeup consultant. "How was rounds duty?" ReeAnn Finkelstein, in the few days I had known her at that point, seemed to always want to know how things were. How was my run this morning? How had I slept last night? How would I like to try her new Maximizing High Volume Lip Plumper?

"Okay," I said, deciding in that moment that I wasn't going to tell the story, now or ever.

"Okay!" she parroted, nodding, grinning.

I tried to smile back. My lips stuck to my teeth. "I have work to do."

The Hovel, a renovated old horse barn tucked behind the administrative building, had been the home of all of the Vandenberg teaching apprentices for the last dozen years. ReeAnn, Chapin, and I slept upstairs, while Babs Lawrence (a vegan and a Christian whose alopecia forced her to wear a horrible thick-banged human-hair wig) and the Woods twins (who owned a collective fifty pairs of Tory Burch shoes and weighed a collective one hundred and eighty pounds) had bedrooms downstairs. I headed up the back stairwell, and on the way to my bedroom, I passed by the open door of Chapin's room. She lay sprawled on her paisley-print comforter, texting with her phone held above her face. Soft acoustic music crooned from the laptop at the foot of her bed. I paused in the doorframe.

"Hi, Imogene." She didn't look away from her phone as she said this.

Around Chapin Dunn, I was struck dumb, like a boy with a crush. She wasn't what I would consider beautiful; her nose was long and severe, her frame bony and curveless, her dark hair styleless and often unwashed in a knot on top of her head. Her brows were overgrown, her nails little stubs, her clothes seemingly thrift-store castoffs. But unlike me, who felt the need to apologize for everything—ingrown hairs on my legs, eating a second cookie after dinner, the splotchy brown birthmark on my hipbone that Kip would nickname the Cheetah Spot—Chapin was unapologetic. Plus, her dad was some hedge fund honcho; being moneyed made everything she did permissible.

"Did you have a nice day, Imogene." This came out in a yawn, less a question than an obligation.

"Yeah, it was fine."

"Glad to hear it." A beat of silence followed. She finally turned to face me, one thick brow raised in an *anything-else-I-can-do-for-you* manner.

I hesitated, then took a step into her bedroom. "I have a question."

She reached down with her big toe, its nail painted an electric green, and changed the song on her computer. She sat up and turned to me curiously.

"Have you ever seen or heard anything . . . *inappropriate,* you know, being around all these boys?"

Chapin smiled, a secret smile that wasn't for me, but rather for some unseen audience. I felt sure she was looking at the spot between my eyebrows, the spot where that morning there'd been the telltale tender bump of an impending pimple, a bump that I'd picked and poked and then coated with my little pot of beige cover up. "Imogene," she said. "We're twenty-two-year-old women surrounded by a bunch of fourteen-to eighteen-year-old boys. Inappropriate things are bound to happen."

I choked up a laugh.

"You haven't spent much time around guys."

She wasn't asking; Chapin knew. I shrugged, then nodded because she was right. I didn't have any brothers, and all of my male cousins lived in Wisconsin and were already in their thirties. My dad wasn't exactly the paradigm of young masculinity; he wore fleece house slippers and spent his mornings watching birds through a pair of binoculars on the back deck. Even in high school I never had any guy friends. Having realized I was awkward at a young age, I had retreated early on to the chorus room to be among the girls who were similarly challenged in determining what to do with their hands or faces when boys were around. In college I may have begun to kiss them and touch them (always sedated with liquor, always feeling like a made-for-TV-movie actress, always pretending their hairy chests and hard buttocks and probing appendages were part of an exhibit in a strange science museum), but they were just bodies; there was nothing, I'd come to realize, as impersonal as a body.

And yet, the only way I could handle touching someone else's body was to pretend I wasn't in my own.

I could see the next question forming on her lips, the question that had been asked by my parents, by my younger sister Joni, by my academic advisor at Buffalo State, by my friends, by my nosy neighbor Mrs. Harrington, by myself as I flipped through the Vandenberg catalogs and stared out my window and watched the neighborhood boys curse and shove one another and scramble after a soccer ball in the street—*Why this? Why Vandenberg? Why now?*

It's a great opportunity, I would tell them.

The truth: I didn't want to teach girls. I'd visited a few coed independent schools in Westchester and Connecticut during my application process, sitting dully in the back of the classrooms like a potted plant, and I'd watched. I stared as the female students tucked golden hair behind ears adorned with diamond studs and crossed bony ankles beneath their desks. They sat poised and pouting like grown women, though some hadn't even developed breasts yet. Sometimes I caught the eyes of the girls in the mirrors of their compacts or the reflections of their cell phone screens—always primping, always keeping tabs on each other, on themselves—and I could tell without even speaking to them what they thought of me: *Poor. Timid. Plain.* I feared them, those privileged girls. I hated what I saw in their gaze, hated how small they made me feel.

But the male students on these visits: They never made me feel small. When I checked into the main office at one school, the secretary asked her student intern if he would mind leading me to the classroom, and he stood and smiled at me and said, "This beautiful woman? Not in the least bit," and suddenly I was transported to an alternate universe, one in which I was back in high school but cool, coveted. I liked the ease in the boys' bodies as they sauntered through the halls and settled loosely in their chairs. And I liked that when they looked at me, they didn't see unfashionable shoes or flat hair but instead a person, a woman—maybe even an attractive one.

— — —

Vandenberg School for Boys, founded in Scarsdale, New York, in 1913, was steeped in honor, tradition, and many, many rules. Vandenberg boys were expected to dress in navy blue or gray dress slacks, white or powder blue dress shirts with a tie, solid black footwear, and the uniform school sweater or school blazer. Vandenberg boys were expected to be clean-shaven and neatly groomed, with nails cut in neat half moons and hair in no danger of festering into that reprehensible mop-like surfer style. For all intents and purposes, Vandenberg boys appeared as deferential as geishas, each one striding purposefully about campus with a thirst for knowledge and a golden halo hovering above his perfectly coiffed head.

And in that first week of school, I believed it. To me, each boy seemed more capable and charismatic than the last—future heads of State, surgeon generals, chief executive officers. The boys shimmered like imposing bronze statues, laughed and posed and grinned like models on the cover of a brochure. They held doors for one another, said "thank you" to the cafeteria ladies, and engaged their professors in stimulating (yet respectful) debates. Sure, there were vestiges of indiscretion—cigarette butts stubbed out behind the gymnasium, empty beer cans crushed on the running trail, giant phalluses carved into picnic tables and scrawled on the desks in the back of the classrooms—but as far as I could discern, Vandenberg boys were an exceptional breed.

"Above all, you must remember that these boys are little shits," Janice McNally-Barnes informed us on our first day of orientation. She was the head of the apprenticeship program, making her our supervisor for the next year. "They may act civilized, sweet even, but don't trust them. Let your guard down, and these kids will eat you alive."

We sat in a semicircle around her in the library conference room, Meggy Woods on my left, her skinny legs crossed over themselves twice, and ReeAnn on my right, working an enormous wad of gum between her molars. Both stiffened in their chairs with this final statement. Chapin, sitting across from me, checked her watch.

Ms. McNally-Barnes was a squat, indelicate woman with a bulbous nose and even bigger mouth. She lived in White Plains with her partner where they bred dairy goats. She'd worked at Vandenberg for seventeen years now and, according to her, she would take raising a goat over one of these boys any day. I'd already known, when she called in May to accept me to the program, that she was not someone to cross.

"This program is not for everyone," she'd said, "and I need to be assured that you won't disappoint us, Imogene." Weighty pause. "Are you going to disappoint us?"

"I won't disappoint you." I felt I was signing myself over to her in blood.

Begun in 1987, the Teacher Apprenticeship Program at Vandenberg School for Boys was a model for independent schools. The one-year program was for recent college graduates who wanted to develop the skills needed to be boarding-school teachers, combining training with residential life experience. Apprentices worked closely with seasoned mentor-teachers and Ms. McNally-Barnes to prepare and teach lessons as well as to support and manage their students' academic, emotional, and social well-being, supplementing the experience by coaching, running an after-school club, or tutoring. After the year was up, the expectation for apprentices was to pursue a master's degree in teaching and to become head teachers in classrooms of their own. Apprentices were also expected to serve as role models for the Vandenberg community, a fact that seemed strange to me since, with the exception of Raj, we were all girls—which was reflective of the nature of the teaching profession. Raj was only the third male in the history of the program. He saw this as a point of pride rather than considering, as I did, the reason why there were so few.

Ms. McNally-Barnes handed out a thick packet entitled VANDEN-BERG SCHOOL FOR BOYS: THE TEACHER APPRENTICE GUIDE. Apprentices, they called us, like we were learning how to cobble shoes or mend fences.

"This will be your Bible," she said. "Stick to this, and you'll do alright."

We all had previous teaching experience. For the last four years while I was in college I had worked at different elementary schools throughout the Buffalo Public School District. I knew how to make lesson plans. I could teach long division and administer a spelling test and explain the difference between mitosis and meiosis. I learned to play handball at recess and how to make friendship bracelets. I'd even been a finalist for The Most Promising Young Teacher in the Buffalo Area award, the most prestigious honor I have ever (almost) earned and maybe ever will. The girls in the classrooms would look at me with big, dewy eyes that provided more validation than any award.

But when it came time to apply for jobs after graduation, I realized I didn't want to teach elementary school, nor did I want to be in the public school system anymore. I didn't want to wear a school ID on a lanyard around my neck and lead lines to the cafeteria and ask students to use quiet voices in the hall. I didn't want to stay in a world where my students weren't sure whether they needed to use the rest-room, much less who they were, and where kids outnumbered books two-to-one. In the break room of the school where I taught during my last year of college, Mrs. Mlynarski, the science teacher who had been there since before I was born, took me aside. "Public school is going to shit," she wheezed. "It's all about closing the achievement gap and coddling mixed with chronic, purposeful underfunding." I told her I had gone to public school, realizing as I did so that I wasn't refuting her point as much as stating a fact. "But wouldn't you have rather been somewhere else?" she pushed. "Don't you still wish you were somewhere better?"

Yes, I told her. And a few days later, I submitted my resume to Vandenberg.

Ms. McNally-Barnes settled herself on a desk, her supple stom-ach spilling like risen dough over her waistband, and continued. "Having appropriate student-apprentice relationships is essential to maintaining your authority," she said. "There has been trouble here, in the past, with young women not knowing where to draw the line. Dean Harvey has tried in the past to ban female apprentices from the program, but you know: Only so many guys want to grow up to be teachers."

Raj, sitting barefoot and cross-legged in his chair, sat up straighter. "And I'm happy to act as representative for that underutilized talent pool." His sneakers and socks lay in a crumpled pile under his chair, and I turned away from the sight of his naked feet, as though he was openly picking food out of his teeth. Every time Ms. McNally-Barnes referred to us pointedly as "ladies and *gentleman*" he grinned widely, happy for the attention and for the novelty of being constantly differentiated.

Ms. McNally-Barnes pointed grimly to the packet on my lap. "Don't let these boys think that you're their friend. Never let them think they have a shot at a romantic relationship with you, oh no. The minute they stop seeing you as an apprentice and start seeing you as a woman, you're in trouble."

ReeAnn had taken out a notebook and was scribbling furiously. I peeked over at the page. APPROPRIATE CORRESPONDENCE ONLY, she wrote. Then, underlined twice: APPRENTICE, NOT WOMAN.

There were certain rules we had to abide by, Ms. McNally-Barnes explained: No stepping foot into a student's dormitory room. No touching the students in any way. No allowing the students into your personal residence. No texting, calling, or messaging with any of the students, and emails were only appropriate if they were related to an academic matter. No relationships outside that of student and apprentice.

"I assume these rules all apply to me, too?" Raj asked, drawing attention to his maleness once more.

"These rules apply to everyone," Ms. McNally-Barnes said, and I felt certain as she said these words that she was looking right at me.

— — —

Even after the Christopher Jordan incident, I thought I would do all right. The incident had been a small mishap—I stored it away in the same place as the memory of wetting my pants on the school bus in fourth grade and of vomiting outside the Town Houses my sophomore year at Buffalo State after trying weed for the first (and only) time. It wouldn't be until I told Kip about the incident that the shame would dissipate. "That's fucking hilarious," he'd say, and I'd realize that this is why we share things—to transform those memories into tidy stories that are no longer ours alone to carry.

The night before my first class, I sat at my desk and planned a lesson. According to the course description given to me by my supervising professor Dr. Duvall—call me Dale, he had said in his email— the aim of Honors World History at Vandenberg was "to acquire a greater understanding of how geography along with cultural institutions and beliefs shape the evolution of human societies, tracing the development of civilization from the Neolithic Revolution to the Age of Industrialization." I would begin my first lecture by defining culture and explaining how the development of tools influenced the culture of early humans. I would show them on a world map the sites where the remains of various hominid species and early humans had been found. I debated whether I would be able to talk about the distinguishing physical characteristics of *Homo habilis, Homo sapiens,* and—most titillating of all—*Homo erectus* without the class dissolving into laughter.

Of course, I wouldn't be teaching entirely on my own yet, not for a few more weeks. I wished I could be more excited. Teaching is what I wanted to do after all; teaching is what I was supposedly good at. But instead I felt a strange sense of dread, one that felt larger and more threatening than simply standing before a classroom of teenage boys.

I lay my outfit out on my bed, a pale pink ruffled blouse I had purchased the month before from a department store—loose fitting, high in the neckline, consciously conservative—and a pair of shapeless gray slacks. Downstairs, Babs, ReeAnn, and the Woods twins were watching a TV show they all liked, something about random men and women being paired up to train a puppy together. I thought about bringing the outfit downstairs for the girls to approve. I could hold it up and joke: *What do you guys think, too revealing?* Maybe I could even watch the show with them for a little while. But I'd already washed my face, and I didn't feel like covering it up with makeup again. Laughter rolled up the stairs, grating as a car crash, and I felt tired. I crawled into my bed, letting the outfit slip to the floor.

Through the wall behind my headboard, I could hear Chapin talking on the phone, her voice gravelly and soft and the words indistinct. I wondered how many people she'd slept with. I thought about calling my mom; I imagined her back home in Lockport in her gray terrycloth robe with the holes in the elbows, drinking a mug of Sleepytime Tea in front of the evening news with my dad snoring next to her and the TV volume turned up too loud. My mom and dad had waited to have children until later in life and now, as an eternal stay-at-home mom and a retired support services technician with high school diplomas, my parents simply wanted to rest. That involved attending the occasional Lockport town meeting, providing key lime pies for bake sale fundraisers, and never touching one another (a fact that didn't strike me as strange until I started watching PG-13 movies and saw the way men and women in love were supposed to behave). I already knew what my mom would say: *Put yourself out there. You're going to do great. Everything is going to be okay.*

I crossed the room to get the notes from my desk and returned to my bed. I sat against the headboard, the covers pulled up over my lap, an invalid awaiting visiting hours. "Welcome to Honors World History," I said to the room. "I am your teacher, Miss Abney."

— — —

It rained the next day, a cold damning rain, and the boys tracked wet footprints up the stairs and into the halls of the academic buildings. My hair was a crown of frizz around my face, and my ballet flats squelched with each step. "You must be Imogene," said Call-Me-Dale when I walked into the classroom, coming around his desk to greet me.

I took his hand. "Nice to meet you, Dr.—"

"Dale."

"Dale, right. Dale."

Dale was tall and angular, with long, thinning hair pulled back into a ponytail, wild eyes, and a wide grin. He could have been thirty-five or fifty-five. He bounced on his heels as I set down my bag, a little kid with a secret or a full bladder.

"Now, Imogene, that's an interesting name. Are you named for the daughter of King Cymbeline?"

He grinned as he asked this. I felt bad letting him down. "I'm sorry, who?"

His grin persisted. "Shakespeare's *Cymbeline*. Imogen is the princess of Britain, known for her moral purity, unable to be seduced by Iachimo, who bets he can woo 'any lady in the world.'"

My skin felt hot. "Oh. No, I think my parents just liked the name."

"Well, that's fine, just fine. It's a lovely name." He winked, and I felt a *thump* between my legs; attraction was still sometimes indistinguishable from discomfort for me. "Now, Imogene. Tell me how excited you are."

"Um—"

"It's thrilling, isn't it?" Dale swept his hand around the classroom, to the four neat rows of desks with hinged tops that lifted to store students' books inside and the beautiful vintage world map that took up almost the entire back wall and the enormous bay windows streaming light from the courtyard. "Being here, at one of the most prestigious preparatory institutes in the nation, helping to shape the young minds of the future. It's really something."

It occurred to me that Dale might be gay, and perhaps that he was on drugs as well. It didn't matter to me; I felt I loved him already nevertheless. This was a bad habit of mine, falling in love. A few days before, on my morning run through town, I had spent the better part of a mile trailing a guy with yellow running shorts, keeping just a few paces behind him. He had impossibly long, wiry legs and feathered brown hair, and I matched my pace to his until he suddenly veered off the path into the woods. I imagined us going on runs together in the morning, panting beside one another as we jogged through town, until we finally stopped at our favorite coffee shop to get egg sandwiches and kiss. On weeknights we'd lie in my narrow bed, legs entangled, and watch classic films (he'd been a film major in college, I decided, a Hitchcock aficionado), and on the weekends we'd go into the city to see art exhibits and eat ethnic food we'd never even heard of but wanted to try, and we'd take goofy pictures of ourselves that would hang in the West Village apartment we'd move into together to remind us, always, of how we first began.

I never even saw his face.

"Yeah," I agreed. "It is really something."

The bell rang for third period, and the boys began to filter into the classroom. The first few entered in silence, choosing desks near the front. As the clock ticked towards the start of class, the rest of the boys filtered through the doorframe, chatting and laughing but still respectfully hushed. I watched as they settled in like eggs in a carton, so charmed that I nearly missed the exchange between the last two to enter.

"Sack slap!" jeered one boy as he whacked his friend up between his legs with an open palm. His friend doubled over as the slapper slid into the last available seat in the back row. "Dammit, Marco," the friend scowled. It stunned me, this childishness; I hadn't been there long enough to know that the boys I'd seen in the pages of the pamphlet—the boys I'd imagined marching in orderly lines and quietly sipping their soup—did not actually exist, at least not outside the eye of teacher supervision. I glanced at Dale; he hadn't noticed the exchange, or at least willfully refused to see it. The behavior wasn't hidden from me, however; I felt cool to not illicit censor, as though I was part of the joke.

"Greetings, gentlemen." Dale took his place at the podium in the front of the room. "Welcome to Honors World History. Welcome to Vandenberg. Welcome to the first day of the rest of your lives."

Someone let out a half-hearted *whoop!* from the back of the class.

"I am Dr. Duvall"—only I, the fellow adult, could call him Dale—"and I will be leading you this semester with the help of my assistant, Miss Abney."

"Hello, Miss Abney," a guy with a pink-and-green polka-dot tie intoned by the windows. His voice was mocking, insular.

I gave a timid wave to the classroom. These were not the susceptible, open faces of the elementary school students I was used to. One of the boys had a dark shadow of stubble on his chin. Another had an angry blotch of boils on his forehead. I'd wanted this, students old enough to reflect and respond rather than parrot back memorized information like trained dogs, but I'd forgotten that I was a subject they would reflect upon and respond to as well. Before the boys' condemnatory eyes I felt as authoritative as a cup of plain yogurt.

Dale launched into a monologue about his career as a commercial artist, his experience in the military as a parachutist, his chihuahua/dachshund hybrid—a "Chiweenie"—named Maxine. The speech was craftily nonchalant, spoken as though off-the-cuff—I could tell he had been doing this, earning the respect of adolescent boys, for longer than he let on. He cursed in places—*how cool, a teacher who says 'fuck!'*—and made theatrical pauses in others. He commanded the class like someone accustomed to praise.

As Dale weaved through the aisles passing out syllabi, I unzipped my rain jacket (realizing just then that I had never taken it off) and set it on the floor by his desk. I'd printed out world maps for the boys to mark with famous early hominid finds and their locations—Dale had said he would allow me ten minutes at the end of each of his lectures to do an activity with the students—but the printouts had become crinkled in my book bag. Shame tightened my throat—for my wrinkled papers, for my squeaky shoes, for my frizzy hair, for my inability to command this room and to shape the young minds of the future.

"Hey, Dale?" I asked, hesitantly at first and then louder, "Dale?"

He turned to face me, halfway down the third row. The boy in the polka-dot tie turned to his friend beside him and waggled his brows. *"Dale?"*

"Yes, Miss Abney?" The pointedness with which he said my name made me think that perhaps "Dale" was not how he was to be addressed in front of the students. The room shifted to face me, fifteen scathing sets of eyes.

"Can I run down to the copy room? It seems that, um . . ." I held up one of my crinkled worksheets like an apology.

"Of course, of course." His grin returned, and with it I felt a rush of relief. Everything was going to be okay.

I collected my papers and squeaked down the hall. In the copy room, I smoothed the least-wrinkled sheet out on the photocopier screen and pressed the right buttons. The machine whirred to life. As the warm papers slid into the tray, I looked up and met my reflection in the window above the copier, checking to make sure my blemishes were still buried beneath makeup. I slid a hand over the frizz in my hair, the wrinkles in my blouse and noticed, as I did so, that my wet rain jacket had made my blouse go sheer, and that the outline of my sensible beige bra was on display for all to see, having become visible through the fabric.

I returned to the classroom and zipped my rain jacket back over my shirt. I took Dale—Dr. Duvall—aside to ask if I could just spend the day observing, as I wasn't feeling quite ready to lead a lesson just yet. I spent the rest of the hour—dripping, useless—on a chair in the corner, while the boys cast sidelong glances at me, all of us wondering what exactly I was doing there.

TWO

I USED TO DREAM OF BOARDING SCHOOL. I'M NOT SURE WHAT first put the idea into my head—maybe it was *Villette* or *A Separate Peace,* or all those *Facts of Life* reruns I watched—but at some point in the year before high school, the family computer became my portal to the best boarding schools on the East Coast. Choate Rosemary Hall, Phillips Exeter Academy, the Hotchkiss School. I spent hours poring over their websites, their names as familiar as friends. "It's homework," I told my parents, to justify the amount of time I spent before the screen; afterwards, I'd delete my search history. I clicked the buttons that said, Yes, I'm interested, and thick, glossy catalogues arrived at my house, which I pulled from the mailbox and hid under my bed. I turned the pages slowly at night, studying the images with the squirming guilt and pleasure that an illicit top-shelf magazine might provide, dreaming of secret societies, four-poster beds, pranks and friendships and matching cotton nightgowns. I imagined every girl in the pictures—pretty girls studying bubbling beakers in laboratories and running up and down lacrosse fields—was me. Or, rather, the me I could be.

There was nothing wrong with the public high school in Lockport. My best friends Jaylen and Stephanie would be there, as well as everyone else I'd attended school with since kindergarten. I knew better, too, than to make my parents privy to my fantasies. I'd once idly mentioned boarding school to my dad, and he scoffed like he did whenever he caught me watching reality TV or reading *People* magazine. But still, after I slipped under my sheets with my catalogues, I imagined myself in a plaid skirt and a navy wool blazer with a school crest embroidered on it, walking down flagstone paths between imposing ivy-covered buildings with my fellow blazer-wearing peers.

The therapist I'd seen throughout high school for my skin-picking problem asked me once why I wanted to go away. "Why not the private Catholic school down the road?" she asked. Somewhere I could still wear a uniform but stay at home with my family. I told her there was no money for the private Catholic school, that my dad—like several other dads in Lockport—was suffering the consequences of budget cutbacks at Rural/Metro, and therapy was just about the only luxury we could afford. Then she asked if I'd ever applied for scholarships, and I told her all the scholarships were for prodigies and minorities, spoken-word poets and trombone players and first-generation Americans, that it was the extraordinary and unique that were rewarded free tuition, not the slightly-above-average.

"Then why wish for boarding school?" she still wanted to know.

Because, I explained, when you wish for something, you wish for the best thing, and nothing could be better than being away from the people you'd known your whole life—the people who'd defined and judged and limited you and would continue to do so until you escaped. Because when it came to wishing, practicality wasn't a consideration.

But once high school began, the fantasies faded. I took up lacrosse and sat on the bench. I dressed like the other girls dressed and didn't raise my hand in class and minded my own business. I didn't date, and I went to school dances with paper decorations and girls who wore the same three dresses from the one dress boutique in town, and I patiently waited for my life to begin.

— — —

Even by my first Saturday at Vandenberg, a week after my arrival and the day of the first varsity lacrosse game, I thought my luck would change. When I walked through the forty-acre campus that first week—past Morris Chapel, the Marshall Huffman Library, all the cherry trees and stone archways and Tudor-style buildings reflecting in Silver Lake—I sometimes felt the overwhelming urge to cry; how lucky I was! How lucky we all were! I thought of the high school in Lockport, with its cracked vinyl tiles, its sloppy joes, its leaking toilets and dirty windows and slow insipid students who pushed past me in the hall without a second glance.

At Vandenberg, every last faucet and doorknob gleamed with possibility.

That Saturday, we were playing against Brunswick School in Greenwich. We rode the twenty minutes there on a bus driven by the head lacrosse coach, Larry, a balding divorcée with acne scars and a chipped front tooth who was probably teased by boys like the ones on his team when he was in high school. When I'd first been assigned to be his assistant lacrosse coach, he'd asked, "You any good?"

"I did a camp at the Buffalo Lacrosse Academy the summers after freshman and sophomore year," I said.

"I didn't ask that."

"I'm going to try to be as helpful as I can."

He grunted.

The boys, led by team captain Duggar Robinson, were taking turns punching each other in the gut to determine their "sex noise." The stocky goalie, known only as Rollo, made an oafish "oof!" when Duggar punched him, and raucous laughter resulted. This was different than the quiet exchange in the classroom; this was flagrant, aggressive.

Instead of being cool enough to understand, I'd been pegged as meek enough to disregard.

"Rollo, what do the girls think when you bust a nut in them and do that shit?" one of the guys near the front demanded.

Rollo got up on his knees and thrust his crotch a few times into the back of his seat. "I dunno, Baxter. Your mom seemed to like it just fine last night."

The other guys bellowed their approval. Sitting alone near the front of the bus, I couldn't help but smile, too, as sequestered as I was. Their laughter was infectious.

"Hey, Coach Imogene!" Baxter poked me across the aisle with the end of his lacrosse stick. "Hey, what's your sex noise?"

The guys roared now. Larry narrowed his eyes at them through the rearview mirror.

"Let's find out, shall we?" Duggar stood and swept towards me up the aisle. With his blond curls, Roman nose, and 60's-style square-frame glasses, he was beyond reproach; Larry didn't bat an eye.

I thought, suddenly, of Jared Hoffman from high school. Jared was black and wore diamond studs in his earlobes, and he was one of the few people at the school that excited me. We sat next to each other in AP Spanish, and sometimes he would reach across the aisle to grab my hand, caressing it with his thumb. On Valentine's Day, he brought all the girls in class, including the teacher, a pink carnation. When he handed me my flower, he winked. It didn't matter to me that he'd winked at every other girl, too, including the teacher—I felt sure there was something meaningful behind the wink he'd directed at me. He included a note with my flower, slipped onto my desk: *Go out with me sometime, Imogene.* I still wonder if he meant it. At times I thought I'd love Jared Hoffman forever, even after my body sagged and swelled and my hair turned gray. According to his profile page, Jared was at Johns Hopkins getting his medical degree. I wondered what it was like to know the world would never say no to you.

Duggar leaned against the back of my seat. His eyebrows were black, incongruous with his golden head, and nearly met in an impenitent tuft above his crooked nose. Those brows, if anything, made him even more handsome and frightening. "Stand up, Coach Imogene."

I looked to the rearview mirror, hoping to meet Larry's eyes, but he concentrated on the road, uninterested. I knew I had to say no. I imagined myself narrowing my eyes and snarling, "Back to your seat, Duggar," like I imagined Chapin would. Or I could even joke with him: "Like hell I'm going to let you punch me!" Funny and authoritative. Cool and under control. But under Duggar's cold glare, I simply stared up at him, struck stupid. Duggar had nearly a foot on me, and a rush of sweat flooded my armpits.

"You're really going to punch a girl, Robinson?"

"Please, Rollo." Duggar flashed his teeth, his eyes still on me. "You know me better than that." Then he turned back to me. "I guess you don't have to stand up for this."

He wound back his arm. I stiffened. The fist propelled towards me and, just as it was about to make contact with my stomach, I flinched and let out a tiny yelp, like a dog that had its tail stepped on.

"See? Didn't even have to touch her." Duggar patted my shoulder. "You're a good sport, Squeak."

Larry's eyes finally flicked up into the rearview mirror. "Siddown!" he barked, a one-word command that seemed embarrassingly directed at me as much as Duggar, even though I knew it wasn't, even though I wasn't even standing up. Larry didn't seem to notice the punch. Larry didn't seem to realize how unwise it was to leave me alone with them back there.

I slid down into my seat, mortified, defeated. It wasn't until Rollo called from the back, "Hey, Squeak, how's about asking Sergeant Larry to turn up the tunes?" that I realized that Squeak was my new nickname.

— — —

Vandenberg sent me stacks of catalogues after I accepted the job. The glossy pages provided the facts I needed to familiarize myself with— Vandenberg School for Boys is the oldest nonmilitary all-male boarding school in the United States. The school has an enrollment of 150 students. Tuition is $46,000 a year—but what I was most interested in were the pictures. *Attractive* wasn't the first word that had come to my mind to describe the young men pictured performing on stage, reading in the quad, shaking hands with state officials; what I thought, instead, was *special*. It was more than pedigree, or good breeding, or any of those vague, aristocratic terms that seemed only to be understood by those who had it (and more apt, to me, for dog shows). What the Vandenberg boys had, I'd finally decided, was exemption. Freedom from liability or failure.

Lockport didn't have old money, or new money, or much money at all. The closest thing my high school had to aristocracy was Melanie Hoffman, who boasted a BMW and two real Gucci bags thanks to the chain of drug stores her father owned. My knowledge of galas and debutantes and high teas came from Jane Austen and the Brontës. In the first week of classes, when Chapin nodded to a student walking by and whispered to me, "Paris Hilton's cousin," I immediately reached for my phone to take a picture, and she slapped it out of my hand, snarling, "This isn't Disney World, Imogene." Vandenberg boys fascinated me, and I studied and dissected them like characters from a reality show. They were formidable and foreign. It seemed impossible that I could belong to it all, that such fine young men could be mine.

In their suit jackets and ties, the students seemed less like boys and more like men, informed and opinioned and—more than likely—experienced. Their smiles spoke of privilege that I had never known, and it wasn't because they attended a school with nine athletic fields, a 100-acre nature laboratory, and one of the world's most important collections of early American art. It wasn't even because they attended an institution that comprised the bedrock of an earlier American establishment, with alumni including Astors, Vanderbilts, Tafts, and Kennedys.

It was because they were given a uniform that assured their place in the world: that place being The Very Top.

— — —

The game was going well, up until Clarence Howell—the skinny third year who had his pants pulled down during our first practice—broke his nose. We were up by two when a Brunswick attacker's swinging stick met with poor Clarence's face mask. The snap was audible, the blood everywhere. The referee blew his whistle, and Larry and I ran out onto the field.

"You alright, Howell?"

Clarence removed his helmet and looked up at Larry, blood bubbling from his nostrils. "I don't think so, Coach."

"Should I call an ambulance?" I pulled my phone from my back pocket. "I mean, we should call an ambulance, right?" I looked at Clarence. His hands were clasped over his face, blood leaking through his fingers. Embarrassingly, I felt myself starting to tear.

Larry grunted, though whether it was in agreement or because of some phlegm stuck in his throat I wasn't sure, and then he squinted at me. "Are you crying?"

"No." It came out more indignant than I intended.

Over his clasped hands, Clarence's eyes were wide and desperate.

"Well, go on," Larry said.

I dialed with shaky hands. Soon enough, Clarence Howell and I were sitting in an ambulance, on our way to Greenwich Hospital.

We sat in silence side by side, me looking out the window, Clarence holding a thick cloth towel up to his gushing face. In this close proximity, I could smell the sweat that had dried on his skin, salty and endearing. It was my first time alone with one of the students, my first time deliberating how I was supposed to talk to them. It felt silly to ask where he was from and how he liked school with blood gushing from his face. Every once in a while he snuffled, adjusting the towel. It was not a time for small talk, I decided. We were on a mission. I used this logic to justify my disinclination to speak.

Clarence surprised me by speaking first.

"It's probably for the best anyways."

I turned to look at him. "Sorry?"

He lowered the towel, his mouth sticky with dried red blood. "I said, it's probably for the best anyways. You know"—he gestured to his nose—"this."

"Why do you say that?"

"C'mon, Imo—er, Coach Imogene."

"Imogene is fine."

"Okay. Imogene. You can tell that the other boys don't really like me, right?"

It was obvious to me then the way it hadn't been before—the way the back of his neck was always scruffy and unshaven, the way he was afraid to look anyone in the eye, his dirty shoelaces and his cheap nylon shorts and the haggard backpack he carried around with a pencil sticking through the hole in the bottom. There was a reason the other boys didn't like him, and it wasn't because his breath smelled like tuna fish and he sometimes got distracted during practice by a leaf floating through the air or the tweet of a bird.

He didn't come from their world.

"Well, do you like playing lacrosse?"

Clarence nodded and wiped his mouth on his sleeve.

"Then you shouldn't worry about what those other guys think. You should just enjoy it."

He squinted at me, considering. "How old are you?"

"Twenty-two."

"Really?"

"Why? How old did you think I was?"

"I dunno . . ."

"C'mon, how old? Twenty-five? Thirty?" I shoved his knee. Something about the touch felt unnatural, flirtatious even, and I quickly drew back my hand. *No touching the students in any way.*

His eyes flickered, and red blossomed up his neck. "My age."

"But why would—"

"You just—the way you let Duggar boss you around on the bus . . ." He looked down at his shoes.

"Do you all think that?" My tone, again, was unexpectedly indignant, unrecognizable.

"Sorry," he told his shoes.

"It's okay." I felt my anger release; it wasn't him I was angry at, after all. "I don't exactly fit in here either, you know. This whole world, it's new to me." I hesitated. "So maybe . . . maybe we can sort of figure it out together." I wasn't sure what I was offering him, only that I felt the need to offer him something. I felt strangely responsible—not because I had denied him a new backpack and a trust fund and the easy confidence that comes with money—but because, knowing he'd been denied those things, I could no longer regard him without pity. Even I, the lowly teaching apprentice, had used him unthinkingly as a scapegoat for my frustration; I couldn't imagine how the other boys used him.

Clarence looked up at me. "Like friends?"

I felt a little sick suddenly, as though I'd been caught in a lie. "Yeah. Sure."

"You're nice, Imogene." He said this mechanically, without surprise, as factual as his being on scholarship. Imogene Abney: Nice.

"You're nice, too, Clarence."

He grinned widely, and then put his hand to his nose. "Ow." But he kept looking at me.

The ambulance stopped; we had arrived at the hospital. An EMT came around and opened the back door. Clarence stood. He turned and looked back at me with a hangdog smile. "Come with me?"

I imagined us sitting together in the waiting room, perhaps for hours. I was already feeling regretful about offering my friendship— what else might I thoughtlessly promise him in that time? "I need to get back to campus," I said. "I'm sorry." Clarence looked as though he might cry. The EMT called me a cab. As I rode back to Vandenberg, I wondered how it was that, being around a bunch of high school boys, I felt younger than ever.

— — —

Chapin spent most of her nights out. I'd never joined her—of course, I'd never been asked to—but I desperately wanted to know where she went. Sometimes she brought guys back; I would hear her headboard beat steadily again the wall, her breathless screeching—"Oh, god! Oh, Christ!" When I'd pass by her open bedroom door the next day, she'd smile blithely from her bed, where she'd be reading a magazine or watching TV on her laptop. "Hello, Imogene," she'd sigh, not caring, and perhaps not even wondering, if I had heard her the night before.

On one of these nights, the Sunday after the Clarence Howell fiasco, I felt a pang in my stomach, a punch to the gut, which I recognized as agonizing loneliness. All that first week, ReeAnn, Babs, and the Woods twins tried to include me: "Imogene, I baked some brownies, do you want one?" "Hey, Imogene, we're doing facemasks and having a movie marathon tonight, you in?" It wasn't that I didn't want to join; it was that, from the very beginning—even though they were strangers to one another as much as I was to them—I felt left out. It was as though a secret meeting had taken place without me, one during which the other girls had compared interests and traded stories and created inside jokes, all the things that happen naturally over time but seem to happen without my notice in the course of a week. Even on the third night—when we skipped the dining hall and made pasta together and Meggy took one of the almost-cooked strands of linguine and dangled it between her legs and the other girls laughed like it was the funniest thing they'd ever seen—even then I didn't belong. Of course, it was impossible to say whether the pasta bit was a previously established joke, or if I just didn't find it funny like they did.

I wasn't comfortable, like they were, hanging out in the living room braless under a T-shirt and scrubbed free of makeup. It didn't matter that they were all doing it—that the Woods twins had perpetually hard nipples under their sheer tank tops and that Babs would even wear her retainer to watch TV at night. I wasn't ready to expose my spotted face and pointy breasts to them—to anyone—and knew that to join them at night still made up and fully dressed would only invite more scrutiny.

With Chapin they had never bothered; girls like Chapin didn't need an invitation and wouldn't join in even if she had one.

Downstairs, ReeAnn and Babs and the Woods twins were watching that show they liked, the one about the mismatched couples and the puppies.

"Oh my god, did you see that?" I heard ReeAnn shriek. "The dog just peed everywhere!"

I tried to open a book and distract myself—*Old School* by Tobias Wolff, one of my favorites. "You felt a depth of ease in certain boys," I read, "their innate, affable assurance that they would not have to struggle for a place in the world; that is already reserved for them." The pang grew worse, radiating down my legs and shooting out through my fingertips until I felt I would burst out of my skin.

The door opened and closed downstairs. A voice greeted the others—a male voice. It was Raj. I heard the clink of a bottle on a table, a cheer from the girls. A cabinet creaked open in the kitchen and glasses were passed around—wine glasses, I could tell. "Let's play a game!" one of the Woods yelped. (I couldn't yet tell their voices apart.)

"Where's Imogene?" Raj asked. He knew better than to inquire about Chapin's whereabouts.

Babs gave a response I couldn't hear. I opened up my bedroom door. Perhaps it was the novelty of Raj being around—he rarely hung out at the Hovel—or the lure of intoxication to placate the anxiety I felt in these sorts of situations, but I found myself creeping down the steps and suddenly standing before the others in the kitchen.

"Imogene!" ReeAnn cried, as though I were back from the dead. I was relieved to see that she wasn't yet in her pajamas. She retrieved an extra glass for me, and I joined them at the table. The others smiled at me, and the smooth dry smell of Merlot wafted to my nostrils. "Did you know that 'Merlot' translates to 'young blackbird' in French?" Raj volunteered as he handed me my full glass, and I thought, maybe I was wrong. Maybe I did belong here.

Raj pulled out a deck of cards and said we would play a game he invented called "Give a Question, Take a Question." If the player selected a black card, he or she would pose a question to the group. If the player selected a red card, anyone in the group could ask that player a question—"The dirtier the better," said Raj. The girls giggled, and I considered Raj, trying to decide if he was cute. The idea of him having sexual experience made him unexpectedly alluring.

Twenty minutes and nine rounds later, we were all on our second glass of wine except for Babs, who drank water ("I don't drink," she announced piously; none of us were surprised). We'd learned that ReeAnn once gave a hand job in the back row of a movie theater, that Babs kissed two girls one summer at Bible camp ("But I'm not gay!"), and that the craziest place Raj had ever had sex was in a Starbucks bathroom. My head felt light and fizzy, a balloon barely tethered by its string. Though I'd drunk in college, I'd never been able to hold my liquor; after a strong drink or two I often found myself smiling for no reason and paying compliments to strangers, one time even dancing with my eyes closed in the corner of the party with my cup held triumphantly above my head, entranced by the music.

Sometimes it scared me how much I enjoyed drinking, how much

I enjoyed feeling more myself and less myself at once. Sometimes, when I started drinking, I feared I'd never want to stop.

I looked around the table at my fellow apprentices and felt sure, in that moment, that I loved them all. Several times Raj turned and smiled right at me, and I smiled back. He was cute, I decided. I wondered what the girl he'd had sex with at Starbucks looked like.

Maggie Woods selected a black card and smiled devilishly. "Have you ever had anal sex and, if not, would you?" she asked the group.

Babs squealed in disgust. ReeAnn shrugged and said, "I haven't, but I'd be open to it." Meggy Woods said, "One time, but he promised it was an accident." By the time Raj said, "I don't know, are we talking about me giving or receiving here?," my teeth chattered I was laughing so hard. Why had I never realized how funny they all were?

"What about you, Imogene?" Maggie asked, and everyone turned towards me. I hesitated. "I haven't," I said finally, "but if the guy really wanted to, I'd probably let him."

I'd meant to make them laugh, but no one did. Maggie refilled her glass and nudged me. "Your turn, Imogene."

I picked the card on top of the deck, hoping it was a black card so I could ask something funny and redeem myself from whatever I had said before that was wrong. It was red.

"Ooh, Imogene!" everyone howled. I knew I wasn't the only one who was drunk.

"I have a question for you," Raj said. The sureness of his voice made us turn to him in curiosity. "Have you ever hooked up with a guy of color?"

My face felt hot. The others eyed me expectantly. I felt certain this time that there was only one way to answer this question.

"Yes, in high school. I dated a guy named Jared Hoffman who was black. He's at Johns Hopkins for med school now." I brought my glass to my lips to keep from grinning. My pulse raced. I was never a good liar.

Raj's foot grazed against mine under the table. It was bare, I could tell, but I didn't feel disgust; I felt a bit giddy.

Raj picked a card. "Red again," he said, slapping the card upright on the table.

If I had been someone else, or perhaps if I had drunk a few more glasses of wine, I could have asked what I wanted to: "Would you ever hook up with me?" And maybe he would smile, and take my hand, and the girls would clap and howl like a TV audience as Raj and I made our way upstairs to my bedroom, where we would lie down in my bed and he'd slip his tongue between my lips and his hand between my legs—

"Do you think you and your girlfriend are going to get married?" Babs asked this.

Raj shrugged. "Honestly, I think I just might be with the girl I'm going to spend the rest of my life with."

The girls sighed happily, and I clutched the edge of the table. The room was spinning. He had a girlfriend. A girlfriend he was probably going to marry.

"You okay, Imogene?" ReeAnn asked.

I realized then that I was standing. "Yeah. I just realized—um, I need to call my mom, I think."

Everyone stared at me. I wondered if I was wrong, and no one else was drunk, because it seemed to me that I was the only one who didn't know what was going on.

"Okay," she said, with the wariness you use when you're humoring someone who's drunker than you.

I grabbed my coat off the hook, opened the back door, and tumbled into the night.

— — —

I thought about walking around Silver Lake. It felt cinematic, romantic even—a girl walking along the edge of the water on a warm

September night, hair blowing, hands in her jacket pockets, head turned to the sky above. I imagined the boys high up in dorm rooms looking out their windows into the night and seeing me, wondering, *Who's that? Where is she going?*

But the lake was two and a half miles around, and I was tired and, though considerably sobered up now that I was walking, still a little drunk. In the distance, I heard the uninhibited laughter of boys who had never known failure and probably never would. I followed it. Between Slone House, a third-years' dorm, and Perkins Hall for fourth years, a rope was strung a foot above the ground between two trees. Around it stood three boys, their shirts untucked and sleeves rolled up and impish grins on their faces.

"Dude, try it again," said one, a gruff redhead with thick forearms that bulged through his shirtsleeves.

The boy beside him—super thin and Asian—snorted. "Pussy's going to blow it."

"Prepare to be amazed, gentlemen."

I couldn't see the source of the last voice, but it was clear and light, the voice of someone delivering a speech. I crouched in the shadow of Perkins and peeked around the corner.

He was neither tall nor short, with skinny limbs and a messy mop of inky black hair, trimmed enough to be within Vandenberg regulations, but long enough to demonstrate that he kept it so reluctantly. His face was coated in a thick layer of stubble, and he had unbuttoned the first few buttons on his shirt, revealing a shock of wiry black hair on his chest. As his friends and I looked on, he stepped up onto the rope, using the tree trunk for support. Then, ever so carefully, he released the tree, spread his slender arms, and began to make his way to the other side.

He bit his lip, eyes glued to his feet. His friends watched in reverent silence. He wobbled once, and I gasped aloud, but he regained his balance and continued on. Once he got close, he reached his arms in front of him for the opposite tree, a wobbly child reaching for his mother. Once his hands touched the tree, he wrapped one arm around it and pumped his other fist in the air. "Fuck yeah!" He pointed at the Asian guy. "In your face, Park!"

His friends applauded. I released my breath.

"Well done, dickhole." Park reached into his pocket and pulled out a beer—my heart seized at the sight of it, the alarm in my head blaring: Alcohol! In the hands of minors!—which he tossed to his friend. The friend caught it in one hand and lifted the pull-tab with a hiss. After a long chug, the leader belched a response:

"FuckyouguysIrock."

It was gross, but unapologetic in its grossness; the noisy release of gas—rude or embarrassing or immature in any other circumstance—was made cool, funny, because it came from him. I liked watching him, I realized; there was something about the way he held himself and the way the other boys regarded him that made me unable to look away. It was clear he was the chosen one, the leader, the one who made the rules. The one who got the girls and charmed the teachers and would never be wanting for friends. To me, there was nothing quite as attractive as being able to trick other people into believing you were.

"Shit, dude, it's late." The redhead held up his watch. "We still need to study for trig."

"Alright, Skeat. Don't get your thong in a bunch." The leader brought his beer to his lips, downed the rest in two chugs, and tossed the empty can into the bushes. "Let's go."

After the three of them disappeared through the back door of Perkins, I snuck out from behind the dorm and went around scooping up the empty cans. I felt somehow that I would get in trouble if I didn't, that this was my responsibility.

"Need help?"

I jumped. It was Raj, approaching from the direction of the Hovel.

"What are you doing here?"

He gestured to the building. "I live here."

"Right." I deposited the cans into the trash barrel beside Perkins.

I scrambled to think of a reasonable excuse for why I was there, but he didn't seem to need one.

"Tonight was fun."

"Yeah, it was a lot of fun. Thanks for coming over."

"I'm just glad you joined us." He looked up at the sky. "A lot less stars out here than at home," he said, speaking more to the sky than to me. "It's due to light pollution, you know. It's a direct cause of wasting our light sources."

"There are a lot of stars in India?"

He looked at me, confused. "No. Indiana."

"Oh."

He opened the front door, stuck half his body inside. My head was still a bit foggy, and I thought for a moment that he might be inviting me to his room.

"My grandparents are from Pakistan," he said.

"Oh," I said again.

"Goodnight, Imogene." He gave me a sad sort of smile and closed the door behind him.

— — —

By the time I returned to the Hovel, everyone was in bed. Our dirty glasses sat in the sink, and I washed them each by hand and put them away as a sort of apology, though for what I wasn't exactly sure. Upstairs, Chapin's door was ajar, her bed empty. I felt the sense of missing out on something better, and I realized then why I never wanted to hang out with the other girls: Chapin had rejected them, so I was, too. I couldn't decide if I would rather be lumped with them in Chapin's mind—one of the boring girls, the plain girls—or considered separate, yet still alone.

In my room, I opened my laptop and I looked up Raj's profile page. We weren't friends on the site yet, but it felt awkward to send a friend request now—the window of opportunity for sending one had already closed. His girlfriend was lanky and freckle-faced, with dirty blonde hair and a small gap between her front teeth. Besides the gap in her teeth, and the few inches of height she appeared to have on Raj judging from his photos, she actually looked a bit like me. *But I'm prettier,* I thought, startling myself; I'd always considered myself cute enough, but unexceptional. Never pretty. It must have been the wine.

After perusing his profile a bit more, I looked up the Vandenberg School roster. The roster was divided by dormitory, and I clicked on the link for Perkins Hall. I found Maxwell Park first. The accompanying photo showed him smirking at the camera, looking as though he knew something dirty about the photographer's wife. Samuel Keating I spotted next, his red hair combed back in neat grooves and his mouth set in a small O-shape, the look of being caught off guard. With little to go off of, the leader was the hardest to find, but once I spotted his photo I couldn't believe I had missed it before. He was unmistakable. His suit jacket was wrinkled, his face scruffy, and he was laughing, his mouth wide open and eyes nearly closed. Adam Kipling, the text beneath the photo read.

I thought of the rope, still suspended between the two trees. If they had left it hanging there, it meant that they planned to return.

THREE

and a week before my fourteenth birthday, I heard the rumor about Stephanie and the blowjob. I had only the vaguest idea of what a blowjob was; I pictured a girl inflating a guy's penis with her mouth and then, like the balloon man who sometimes came to my youth group meetings at the rec center when I was a kid, bending and twisting it into all sorts of shapes—a dog! A snake! A flower! What I did know was that, according to Jaylen, Stephanie had given one to Jason Stern's older brother Keith in her basement the weekend before.

Jaylen and Stephanie had been my best friends since third grade. When I got my period at the mall and the sanitary napkin dispenser in the restroom was out of order, Jaylen and Stephanie sat outside the bathroom stall to help me guide in my first tampon. When Stephanie's hamster died, Jaylen decorated a tiny wooden box from the craft store for Chip's coffin, and I played my recorder for Chip's backyard funeral (a slow, sad rendition of Hot Cross Buns, the only song I could play). At almost fourteen, I hadn't even yet kissed a boy (I'd lied when I told my friends I kissed Bobby McCoy in the teachers' lounge), and now Stephanie supposedly had done stuff, things I couldn't even describe or imagine or understand, with someone three years older.

"Is it true?" I asked her after school one day. I remember crying. Stephanie thought I was jealous. I didn't have the words to explain what I really felt: a profound sense of betrayal.

She was getting books out of her locker, and she turned to look at me. "Is what true?" She'd recently started wearing eyeliner; it looked like thick black rings around her eyes.

The TV shows I'd watched growing up made me believe that best friends were bound by unspoken understanding, a telekinetic power mysterious to outsiders. "*You* know."

Stephanie stared at me blankly. My therapist would later suggest that TV had made my expectations unrealistic, but then, and even after, I would believe that my friendships had failed to live up to my expectations.

"Did you really give Keith a—" I lowered my voice, "—b-l-o-w . . ."

She sighed with an impatience I'd never had directed at me by anyone besides my mom. "This is why I can't tell you these things."

Things? I wondered, what else was I not privy to?

"You're immature, Imogene. You make a big deal out of everything."

I wondered, were these two faults related?

Then—the worst part—she put her hand on my shoulder and smiled, pityingly. "Your time will come," she said, "and when it does, you'll understand."

I wondered, *Understand what? What is it that I need to understand?*

— — —

Dean Harvey called assembly before classes on Monday to announce that our joint theater program with Baylor Academy, Vandenberg's sister school, would be cancelled until further notice. Rehearsals had just begun for *Oklahoma!* the Thursday before, but due to "unforeseen circumstances," we would no longer be collaborating with the girls of Baylor for our productions. We sat in the chapel, and the groans of the boys reverberated up to the ceiling.

"Good luck trying to get any fags to join theater now," a second year sitting near me whispered to his friend. I was the only person within earshot, and I wondered if he knew I could hear him or, like the boy who grabbed his friend's scrotum in the classroom on my first day, he thought of me as someone who could be privy to misbehavior, cool enough to *get it*.

"Good luck trying to get *laid* now," his friend replied under his breath.

It wouldn't be until later that night that Babs would tell me what had happened: a first year was found in the prop closet back stage with his pants around his ankles, a Baylor girl kneeling before him performing—Babs reddened here and leaned in to mouth the words too horrible to speak aloud—*oral sex*. I felt a mix of pride, for having more sexual experience than Babs—at least I could allude to oral sex without blushing seven shades of pink—and shame, for knowing that a fourteen-year-old girl had done what I had only attempted to do once—with Zeke Maloney in college—before embarrassment forced me to stop after just a minute.

"What's the big deal?" Zeke had asked me. "It's just a dick."

It's only a mountain, I'd thought. I wondered what this girl had thought, what my old friend Stephanie had thought, when they kneeled before that strange, insistent appendage.

My head ached dully from last night's wine. The girls didn't comment on my sudden departure the night before, but the feeling I'd had sitting around the table just hours before had dissipated. Their voices felt too loud, their faces too eager, their gestures fraught and uncoordinated. I could tell ReeAnn had overheard the conversation between the two boys near us as well, and she tried to smile at me conspiringly. I managed a grimace. Even Raj had lost all appeal for me overnight; as soon as he kicked off his shoes and folded his bare feet under himself on the bench, I inched away. It wasn't that his feet smelled bad; I was repelled by their startling nakedness. (*Inappropriate,* I thought suddenly. *Arrogant.*) In doing so, I moved closer to Chapin, who sat with her back flat against the wall, her hands folded in her lap, her eyes blank. I sat back and assumed a similar pose: cool, unperturbed. Then I spotted Adam Kipling.

He sat in the back row between his redheaded friend Skeat and a tall black guy I'd seen around campus a few times before. Adam's eyes were closed and his tie loose as he tapped a rhythm with his palms on the back of the bench in front of him. A teacher came by to tap his shoulder and shake her head at him and he assumed a look of appropriate contrition, but as soon as she walked away his drumming continued. *He is unembarrassable,* I realized in wonder; the embarrassment that he was supposed to have felt as the receiver of scolding seemed entirely absorbed by me, the mere bystander, instead.

After revealing that *Timon of Athens* would be the new winter production and tryouts would be held that night, Dean Harvey rang his bell on the pulpit, and the boys were dismissed.

I watched as Adam Kipling stood and swung his book bag over his shoulder.

"What are you looking at?" asked ReeAnn, following my line of vision.

I turned away. "Nothing."

Her shoulders slumped almost imperceptibly. I'd disappointed her.

As I followed her and the other apprentices towards the chapel door, I chanced another look. The tall black guy was telling a story, gesticulating wildly, and Adam Kipling was laughing, his head thrown back and shoulders shaking, looking just like he did in his ID photo. I wished I were closer, so I could hear what his laugh sounded like.

— — —

I prepared a ten-minute bit on the history of animal domestication for the end of Dale's lecture that day. After the disaster that was my first class, I'd been improving day by day; by Thursday of that first week my hands had stopped shaking violently every time I stood at the podium, and by Friday I'd even worked up the nerve to call a few of the boys by name, which seemed to both startle and please them.

Dale asked to meet with me fifteen minutes before class to go over my lesson, and after assembly, I headed to his classroom and knocked on the door. Through the glass panel I could see him sitting at his desk bent over papers. He raised his head and motioned for me to come in with an eagerly beckoning hand.

"Imogene! Hello, hello!"

Dale's hair was loose around his shoulders, wispy and limp as a toddler's. His grin was manic as ever, the grin of someone who had just downed a pot of coffee or an amphetamine. I sat in the chair facing his desk and attempted to return a smile of equal enthusiasm.

"So? How has your first week been?"

I shrugged one shoulder. "Um. Interesting."

He threw back his head and barked a full-bodied laugh. "Interesting. What a wonderful word."

"It's been great, really. Just—"

"A learning experience."

"Yes," I agreed. "A learning experience."

He leaned towards me over the desk, propping his chin in his hands. I reflexively backed away; I hated anyone being too close to my face. "I began teaching at Vandenberg nine years ago after I finished my doctorate. And I'm going to tell you the truth, Imogene. These boys, they scared the shit out of me. They're shrewd, they're exacting, and given the opportunity, they're scarily influential. Because we're not just talking about your average high school guys here. We're talking about the most well-read, well-bred high school boys out there."

I thought of the boys I'd gone to high school with in Lockport, the ones who always had the first pick of players on their kickball team in gym class and of dates for the prom. The ones who doused themselves in Axe body spray and revved the engines of their souped-up secondhand cars in the parking lot for attention. Dale was right; I'd been scared of those boys then, but not one of them would have stood a chance against a Vandenberg boy.

"Never let them see you falter, Imogene," Dale continued. "Remember, you're in control in this classroom. Don't let them forget it."

"I just—" I returned for a moment to the bus, to Duggar Robinson telling me stand, so confident that I would submit. "How do you get them to like you?"

Dale bobbed his head in his hands, considering. "Yes, being liked is nice, isn't it? I wasn't quite the most popular boy in my class back in high school, so it's definitely nice to be liked. But to be frank, Imogene, it doesn't matter if you're well liked here or not."

My palms felt sweaty, and I swiped them across my thighs under the desk. I kept myself from saying *but it does*.

"What matters is that you're respected."

I nodded, wishing I agreed.

"Now, let's see that lesson."

After the bell for third period rang, I stood before the class and talked about the earliest known evidence of a domesticated dog, a jawbone found in a cave in Iraq and dated to about 12,000 years ago. I talked about selective breeding, about how the gray wolf evolved into the modern canine. The boys seemed interested and asked questions, wondering how man taught the wolf to be submissive, to be subdued, to obey the will of a master. It wasn't until one of the boys in the back raised his hand and asked (to the delight of his friends) what the men did to the wolves that couldn't be tamed that I realized the joke—they had made an unspoken agreement that the wolves were women.

"Gentlemen, please." Dale made a settle-down motion from his desk.

I feigned ignorance to the joke. "The tamer wolves were more likely to survive and evolve into dogs," I admitted. "But, the wolf was also domesticated at a time when humans weren't very tolerant of carnivorous competitors. Humans were already successful hunters without wolves, and wolves don't exactly like to share."

"So why do we even need them?" the same boy from the back called. His friends snickered.

"More than likely, it was the wolves that approached humans, not the other way around. The ability of dogs to read human gestures is remarkable, and with this ability, having these protodogs on a hunt gave people an advantage over those who didn't."

"So you're saying the wolves tamed us," Dale volunteered. I glanced at him and he winked. I felt faint from gratitude and—perhaps something else?

I turned back to the class. "Dogs may even have been the catalyst for our civilization."

Nobody protested. The bell rang, and as the boys collected their books, I turned towards the chalkboard to hide my grin, feeling as though I had just won something.

— — —

Clarence was feeling well enough to watch lacrosse practice that afternoon. He sat next to me on the wooden bench facing the practice field, a white splint taped over the bridge of his nose.

"How are you doing?" I asked. I felt a little awkward, having not talked to him since depositing him at the hospital, but I knew not to talk to him would only make the situation more uncomfortable.

"Okay," he said, his voice dolefully nasal. "The doctor said there shouldn't be any change in the size or shape of my nose."

"That's good."

"My cousin, he broke his nose playing hockey three different times when he was in high school. He never even saw a doctor. He's got this big bump in his nose now."

I searched Clarence's face for a hint as to what my reaction should be. "Yikes."

"I didn't want a bump in my nose. I'm glad I won't have one."

"You should be. You have a nice nose."

Clarence grinned widely and then put a hand to his splint. "Ow."

We turned to watch the boys running drills up and down the field. While waiting his turn in line, Duggar stuck his stick between his legs and rhythmically thrust his hips forward, poking Baxter in the back.

"Coach, Duggar is poking me with his shaft," Baxter called.

Larry groaned. "Robinson, stop poking Baxter with your shaft."

Clarence took out a notebook and started doodling. I peeked over his shoulder to see what he was drawing. On the page was a massively muscular Mexican luchador poised for a fight, his fists held up in front of his bare chest and his eyes narrowed behind his mask.

"That's really good."

Clarence jumped and shut the notebook.

"Whoops, sorry. I didn't mean—"

"It's nothing. It's stupid."

We turned back to the field. After a moment, Clarence turned to face me again.

"His name's El Músculo. He's just this character I draw sometimes."

"That's cool. Are there others?"

Clarence nodded, and he smiled shyly as he flipped through his notebook and showed me a few of the other characters he'd invented. A skinny masked man with a gun slung over each shoulder and a sly grin, a spandex-clad woman with hair that flowed past her waist and enormous breasts. Larry blew his whistle; practice was over.

"Do you want one?" Clarence asked.

"Oh, no, that's—"

"Here." Clarence flipped to a finished drawing of El Músculo and ripped out the page, which he then handed to me. "Take it."

I held the drawing in my hand. "Thank you."

The boys ran off the field to the locker rooms. I turned to slip Clarence's drawing into my bag and felt someone standing behind me. I turned around to find Duggar, his eyes magnified behind his goggles.

"Hey, Squeak," he said, "how about you spend less time flirting with your boyfriend and more time watching the practice?"

I looked at Clarence. He'd busied himself with packing up his backpack, his eyes unwilling to meet mine. I turned back to Duggar and his bug-eyed stare, feeling like a sample beneath a microscope, his to poke and pick apart and eventually throw away. The thrill of my afternoon victory drained away; before Duggar, I was fourteen again, unsure of myself, unsure of anything.

— — —

I waited until a few days after my fourteen birthday party, which Stephanie left early from to hang out with Keith Stern (she'd told me she had a dentist appointment her mom couldn't reschedule), to confront her. I waited until before gym class, when the locker room was nearly empty, to stand by her gym locker and say, "You've changed."

"For gym class?" It wasn't clear whether this was a joke or a communication failure. Stephanie reached up to the top shelf for her sneakers. She'd purposely ordered her gym shirt a size too small, so that when she raised her arms a strip of her stomach showed.

"I mean, you're different than the person I used to know." This was more than likely a line I'd taken from a TV show. Ruth Walter was the only one left in the locker room, and she watched us from the sinks excitedly.

"Having a boyfriend doesn't make me different, Imogene." She squatted to lace up her sneakers.

I fought an urge to stomp my foot, to slam a locker door, to somehow express the frustration I was feeling with an ineffable blast of sound. "Yes, it does! They change everything!" I knew, by they, I did not mean boyfriends; I meant boys.

Ruth crept towards the door.

"I just want things to be like they used to," I said.

She shrugged, locked her locker door. "Well, they're not." And then, smiling sadly, as though I was Ruth Walter rather than the girl who helped her bury her hamster, "Sorry."

But we stayed friends through high school, Stephanie, Jaylen, and me. Even after Stephanie gave Keith Stern a blowjob, even after Jaylen started sneaking vodka into her morning coffee, even after we stopped having Friday night sleepovers and their bedrooms no longer felt as familiar to me as my own. Even after Stephanie and Jaylen got boyfriends and I began spending too much time in front of a magnified mirror, examining my skin.

What changed was what I then understood: that you could never know what people were capable of, even yourself.

— — —

ReeAnn asked me how lacrosse practice had been after I returned to the Hovel, and I immediately thought, *she knows*. The cartoon drawing from Clarence still sitting in my bag felt like an admission of guilt—though really I had nothing to be guilty of—and I excused myself upstairs to my room, where I folded the picture into a tiny square and slid it into my desk drawer.

Had I flirted with Clarence? Had I led him to believe that he had a chance with me, that I could become his girlfriend? Was that just Duggar talking, or had Clarence told his teammates his own imagined version of the afternoon in the ambulance? I replayed the scene in my mind. Had I done anything to encourage him? No, the thought was ridiculous. Clarence was a kid, the little brother I'd never had. All I'd wanted was for him to feel less alone.

I took out the drawing again and smoothed it out on my desk. He'd signed the drawing in the corner of the page with his cramped boyish scrawl. It wasn't fear of getting into trouble I felt; I was almost sure I wasn't in the wrong. It was fear of being judged. I'd seen the look in Duggar's eyes when he'd sneered the word *boyfriend*. It was disdain, not because I had maybe flirted with a student, but because I had maybe flirted with someone who wasn't cool.

"What's that?"

I looked up. Chapin stood in the doorway. Her hair was braided messily down her shoulder, loose pieces framing her fox-like face, and her bitten nails were painted blood red. She nodded towards the cartoon drawing on my desk.

"Nothing." I flipped it over, then flipped it back again. "Something one of my students gave me."

"Fucking adorable." She stepped into my room and took the drawing from my desk. She'd never been inside my room before; none of the girls had. I felt intensely aware of the period stain on my sheets and the stretched-out cotton underwear in my drawers, things she couldn't even see but that I knew were there nevertheless. I was forever surprised by how comfortable the other girls were around one another. The other day, I'd walked into the living room to find Babs clipping her toenails at the coffee table while she watched the news. The Woods twins often peed with the bathroom door open and would ask you how your day was as you walked by, peering out at you from the toilet seat as casually as though they were sitting at the kitchen table. ReeAnn even once left a used sanitary pad spread open on the top of the upstairs bathroom trash barrel (I knew it couldn't have been Chapin's, so it must have been hers), her dried blood laid bare. I was so horrified (and so worried that Chapin might think it was mine) that I took the trash out right then, disposing of the evidence.

Maybe I'd once been this comfortable around Jaylen and Stephanie—we'd fart and burp and change our clothes in front of one another—but that had been years ago, long before I finally revealed to my mother the crusted-over mess of skin hidden beneath my newly-chopped bangs and was sent to therapy, long before I learned the consequence of relinquishing privacy.

"Who's Clarence Howell?" Chapin asked, studying the drawing.

"A third year. He's on the lacrosse team." I paused, and then added, "I took him to the hospital after he broke his nose."

"*El Músculo*." She smiled and set the drawing back on my desk. "Careful, Imogene. Sounds like someone has a crush."

She knows, I thought. "He doesn't," I said.

Her smile persisted, infuriating in its certainty. "Just be careful, that's all."

I crumbled the drawing into a ball and stuffed it deep into the trash.

— — —

At dinner the next night, I was distracted by the sight of Christopher Jordan and accidentally agreed to the game night ReeAnn had proposed for later on. It was a late dinner for us, nearly nine, having spent the greater part of the afternoon making lesson plans and grading papers together. We did these no-nonsense tasks together—working, grading, eating—not because we had to, but because it felt safer to stick together sometimes, us against them, apprentices against students. Even Chapin joined us for every meal without fail. We always sat at a table in the back of the dining hall, which usually afforded us privacy, but tonight Christopher Jordan the Monkey Beater and his friends had settled with their trays at the next table over—straight from sports practice, judging from the way their hair was plastered to their foreheads in wet strands. I kept my eyes on my plate, focused on cutting my meatloaf into cube-shaped bites.

"Can we play *Friends* Scene It?" ReeAnn asked. "My mom just sent it to me in the mail."

Raj nodded. "I'm in."

The Woods twins were tossing their lettuce leaves and trying to distract us from the fact that they weren't eating. "We're so good at that game," said Meggy.

Maggie bobbled her too-big head on her skinny neck. "Yeah, we practically grew up watching that show."

Babs sniffed. "My parents didn't let me watch television."

Chapin was busy building a tower out of her mashed potatoes and didn't respond.

Christopher Jordan looked up as he chewed his meatloaf and caught my eye. He gave me a closed-mouth grin, his cheeks bulging, and waggled his fingers.

Chapin followed my gaze. "Is that your lover?" she hissed.

The other girls and Raj swiveled in their seats to look.

A rush of sweat flooded my armpits. "I have to go," I decided, and I stood.

"Where are you going?" asked ReeAnn.

"I have to—"

"Call your mom again?" Babs smirked. *I would never be friends with these people,* I thought, *not really.*

"Check my mail," I lied.

"Sure."

"Will you be back for game night?" ReeAnn pressed.

"Yeah." I grabbed my tray and headed towards the doors.

I knew already where I was going, had been secretly planning it all day, but I'll never admit it.

FOUR

IN HIGH SCHOOL, I DECIDED I WOULD GO TO COLUMBIA UNIVERSITY, and it was not just because Jared Hoffman, my high school crush, once expressed an interest in applying. To me, it was the best school, just as 115 pounds was the ideal weight (I'd read it in a book once—the main character, a "beautiful, waif-like girl" as the narrator described her, was 115 pounds) and seventeen years old was the most popular age to lose your virginity (I'd read this on a let's-talk-about-sex forum I'd stumbled upon online, though I wouldn't lose my own until several years after that age). Why Columbia, I'm not sure, but I cemented its name in my mind as the best school, the perfect school.

I didn't imagine a transformation would take place. I didn't imagine any sort of fairy-tale reinvention or the kind of incontestable change people from high school would see in pictures on social media and talk about with wonder—"Have you seen Imogene lately? My god!" Or, at least, I never could have articulated having these desires.

But I did imagine that, by going to what I imagined to be the best school, I'd become better. That confidence could be siphoned from imposing buildings and golden-haired legacies. That an acceptance could grant a new identity, that of a girl with skin that didn't need to be covered and a body that didn't induce shame, whom no one knew came from a blue-collar family and had never kissed a guy. A girl who wanted to be noticed.

— — —

In one of those rare moments in life that work out as they should, Adam Kipling and his friends had returned. Skeat was trying his luck this time, and he took two wobbly, lunging steps before he pitched off the side onto the ground. I resisted the urge to spring out from my hiding spot behind Perkins to help him, but his friends were laughing.

"You fat fuck," Park cackled.

Skeat pushed himself off the ground with a groan. "Let's see you do it then, you skinny motherfucker."

Adam Kipling watched with his hands stuck in his pockets, amused.

He seemed like the embodiment of a buoyant male presence I lacked in my life, the sort of jokey, arrogant, entitled boy who everyone loves and hates in equal amounts. The kind of boy who, I imagined, would make even a trip to the grocery store into some grand adventure, would make every moment lighter and funnier, would make you feel lighter and funnier yourself. Squatting there in the grass by Perkins, watching Adam Kipling sling insults and take jabs, I couldn't help but smile; I felt part of the joke, even if he didn't know it.

Later on I'd confess my stakeout to Kip, and he would laugh, telling me what I did was weird, fucked up. I should have been relieved that Kip thought it more funny than freaky, but still his reaction disappointed me, as though what I'd done was voyeuristic rather than merely curious, somehow more wrong than I meant it to be.

Park pulled a cigarette out of his pocket. "Whatever, jerkoff."

Without prelude, Adam began to chant. "*Tug it, tease it, slug it, squeeze it—*"

His friends chanted their response in unison. *"Jerk, jerk, jerk it off!"*

"*Stroke it, pat it, beat it, bat it—*"

"Jerk, jerk, jerk it off!"

The boys did not laugh afterwards or even acknowledge the interlude; they continued as though the moment had not been broken, the chant apparently as routine to them as their insults. Adam leaned back against a tree. Skeat bent to brush the dirt off his knees. I felt witness to a secret handshake or a complicated door knock, something you might miss if you blinked, and even if you did catch it, would never be able to recreate yourself. It was immature, and I felt hearing it should have made me feel disappointed in Adam, in all the boys of Vandenberg, but I didn't. Like when I caught notes passed in class and overheard the lewd whispers in chapel, it tickled me somehow that the boys of Vandenberg weren't nearly as prim and straight as they appeared in the pamphlets. I was witness to this secret side of the student body, this darker side, and it was as exciting as the celebrity tabloid magazines I leafed through at the grocery store—actors scooping dog shit from the sidewalk, starlets with cellulite.

Park brought his still-unlit cigarette to his lips. As he went to light it, his eyes caught mine, and he jumped.

"Whoops!" I stood, brushing off my knees. "Oh. I'm sorry. I—" My hands shook. I felt culpable, though I wasn't quite sure of what. They stared at me, as though waiting for me to perform, and I turned to walk away.

"Hey, hold up." I knew it was Adam Kipling who spoke. It felt strange knowing his voice when he didn't even know my name; perhaps that's what I felt guilty of, of knowing too much. I heard him jog up behind me.

I faced him and found myself at eye-level with his lips. "I'm sorry," I said again.

"Why are you sorry?"

"I didn't mean—"

"Have you ever done parkour?"

"Done what?"

"Parkour. You try to get from point A to point B in the most efficient way possible, using only your body and your surroundings for momentum." Gone was the belching boy I'd seen last night and even the singer of the jerk-off song from moments before; he stood before me poised and sure, a parents' dream.

"Dude, how is this parkour then?" interjected Skeat. "Like, how in the fuck is crossing a rope the most efficient way to get between two trees? Couldn't you just, I don't know, walk?"

"Shut up, Skeat. My brother's in the parkour club at Yale, and they do this all the time." Adam Kipling turned to face me again. "Want to try?"

"What?"

"Try it. Going across the rope."

"I'll fall!"

"No, you won't."

We stared at each other. I was making a decision greater than deciding to cross the rope, and we both knew it. To join them would be to shrug off my authority, to close the gap between rank and age and sex. To fail as a Vandenberg School for Boys Teaching Apprentice. But in crossing the rope, I would be one of them, however briefly. I hesitated a moment. Then I held out my hand.

He took it with surprising force. My heart seized. I couldn't remember the last time someone held my hand. He led me to the rope. "Climb on." I did. He steadied me as I shimmied up the tree trunk, and then he took my right hand in both of his. "Ready? I'm going to lead you across."

Together, we edged from one tree to the other. He gripped my hand tightly, offering words of encouragement along the way. "You're doing just fine. You've got this." His hands were warm and soft and damp with sweat. Strangely, I didn't fear for a moment he would let me go, that he would fail me. I didn't even hear Skeat or Park; for all I knew they had left, and it was just the two of us. I just kept my eyes on the toes of my sneakers, putting one foot in front of the other, hovering precariously above the ground below. The rope was slack, not rigidly taut as a tightrope would be, and it stretched and swayed beneath me like a long narrow waterbed. I closed my eyes. I was walking on water—no, on air.

"Stop. Hey, stop."

My eyes popped open. I had nearly walked into the opposite tree. I looked down at him. "You did it!" he said. He grinned wildly.

Using my free hand, I held on to the tree and stepped back onto the ground. It wasn't the dizzying relief I usually felt descending from heights; I felt powerful. I laughed, perplexed and unsteady from the ridiculousness of the moment, and we stared at each other, wondering what was supposed to happen next.

He made the first move. "Adam Kipling," he said, offering his hand. "But just call me Kip."

I took his hand, resisting the impulse to say, *I know*. "Imogene Abney."

"Now, Imogene," he started, mock serious. Park and Skeat snickered behind him. I wished my name were something other than Imogene, and that my fleece zip-up didn't have dried ketchup on the front pocket. "I can't help but inquire as to how a female wound up on the campus of an all-male institution at this hour on a school night. Are you on the run, or are we safe?"

I could have lied. Maybe, that night, I could've been anyone I wanted to be. Maybe I'd never have to see him again—but I wanted to. The words spilled out before I could stop them.

"I live here, actually. I'm, well, kind of a teacher here, actually."

Kip's mouth opened slightly before he regained his composure. I'd caught him, the unflappable Adam Kipling, off guard.

"In that case, then," he said, recovered, "may I walk you to your sleeping quarters?"

— — —

Even while earning mediocre test scores (I'd be too distracted by the loud wobbling of my desk when I used my eraser and the fear that I was bothering my neighbors and the certainty that everyone was looking at me, all while the clock ticked away) and failing to participate in extracurricular activities (I had no interest in Spanish Club or Environmental Club, much less making new friends), I held onto Columbia University like a secret, a candy hidden under my tongue. I was smart—I got all A's—and I would be the first Abney to go to college; I wanted to believe that the right person would see that. When I presented my list of potential colleges to my guidance counselor, she said, "Ambitious." It didn't matter that we both knew what she meant was *impossible;* my desire was strong enough to circumvent reality.

For my college admissions essay, I wrote about my pubescent boarding school dreams. I spoke of my longing for the best resources, the best faculty, the best education. And when my rejection letter from Columbia arrived, I cried—I didn't realize, until that moment, that I'd truly believed that I would be accepted.

Buffalo State covered three-quarters of my tuition, and so that is where I went. I wondered if they knew—as Columbia had more than likely known—that my dream of attending boarding school was never about the education.

— — —

As Kip and I walked through the dark, I thought of a dozen questions I could ask him—*Where are you from? How do you like it here?* Even, lamely, *Aren't you afraid of getting in trouble staying out so late?*

Any banal question I could ask Kip would be a joke, a comically deliberate attempt to skirt around the issue at hand. It would be to compliment another woman's dress at a funeral. Kip was a student, and I was a teacher. How was I supposed to address him—like a kid in my charge, or like a guy who was only really a few years younger than me? I knew I didn't want to make polite conversation; I wanted to impress him. Right now, it didn't matter where either of us was from.

I was glad it was dark. I always felt more comfortable in the dark.

Kip spoke first. "So. The Hovel, huh?"

I glanced at him to gauge his expression. I decided it was one of amusement. "What's wrong with the Hovel?"

He shrugged. "It's nice, I guess. If you don't mind the smell of horse."

He wasn't my student, I decided. It would feel foolish to talk to him like he was. "Hey, it doesn't smell like shit!"

"I didn't say horse shit. I just said horse."

I paused, considering. "How would you know, anyway?"

"Oh, believe me. I know."

"You're lying."

"Wanna bet?"

We were passing Silver Lake now. Kip stopped, so I stopped, too. I was torn between the desire to keep moving towards the Hovel and the need to look as cool and unperturbed as Kip seemed. He cleared his throat and bent his face down towards mine, eyes wide and serious. I pressed my lips together and tried to remember the last time I brushed my teeth.

"Two years ago, I was a second year . . ."

So he's a fourth year, I thought.

". . . and there was this teaching apprentice—I forget her name—who loved to party. All the other apprentices were apparently really boring, so she started having these little social gatherings for a select few guys, including yours truly."

"Naturally." His candor was infectious, but I still felt uneasy. *No allowing the students into your personal residence.*

"Naturally. So we would go over on Friday nights to the Hovel after the other apprentice girls had gone to sleep, and we'd drink a little, smoke a little . . ."

"Oh, c'mon." I imagined a younger Kip stretched out on the bed of an ethereal blonde creature, all lips and lashes and long skinny limbs. The sort of girl who would leave lipstick stains on the joint she passed from her puffy lips to Kip's, a girl who would wear colorful lacy bras instead of practical beige ones like mine.

He spread his arms out in protest. "What, you don't believe me?"

It must have been quiet hours by then; the campus around us was eerily still, and Kip's voice echoed across the lake. Without thinking, I shushed him.

"Did you just shush me?"

"Sorry."

"You say sorry a lot." Kip looped his arm through mine and tugged me along. My looped arm tensed from my shoulder through my fingertips, but if he could feel my tension, he didn't acknowledge it. "Point of the story being, I've spent a fair amount of time in the Hovel, and it smells like horse."

"It does not." The more I tried to relax, the more rigid my body became. He squeezed my arm tighter in his; it was becoming apparent to me that he sensed my discomfort, and that he enjoyed causing it.

"It does, too."

I could see the Hovel up ahead. I cast a sidelong glance at Kip again. His lips curled faintly, his chin in the air. Something needed to be said.

"Hey, Adam—"

He furrowed his brow. "Kip. Just Kip."

"Kip—"

We reached the back door. He released my arm and gave a theatrical bow. "Your sleeping quarters, my ladyship."

I didn't want to like him; I wanted to resent his affected gallantry, his swaggering sureness. He was a caricature of a prep school boy, a cocktail of charm and condescension. The walk back to the Hovel had felt divorced from time and suspended in space; I'd felt drunk, though under the influence of nothing but the strangeness of the night's events. But standing on my doorstep, exposed in the light from the kitchen, I was sober, liable. I was relieved when he immediately turned to go.

"'Night, Teacher." He waved his arm over his head as though heading out on a yearlong voyage at sea and started to walk back into the dark.

I hesitated, then called out to his retreating form. "I shouldn't have let you walk me home."

Kip turned, studied me. "Why's that?"

"Students aren't allowed here."

He looked up at the sky, seeming to contemplate his answer, but then he just shrugged. "If you say so," he said.

I stood by the back door, watching him walk away, until he disappeared.

— — —

Raj, ReeAnn, Babs, and the Woods twins were playing *Friends* Scene It when I returned. They turned to look at me.

"Imogene!" ReeAnn beckoned me into the room. "We're just getting started."

"Give me a minute," I said, and I climbed up the stairs two at a time with no intention of coming back down.

I checked my email first. I had a message from Dale. *Awesome lesson today,* he said. *You're really doing great work.* He signed his name with a smiley emoticon.

Then I pulled up the Vandenberg School roster.

I wanted to look up his profile page, but that felt like an invasion. He wasn't Raj, a coworker, an equal; he was a student. Those pictures and messages posted on his page were not for me to see. So I stuck to the roster. I studied his wrinkled jacket, his open laughing mouth. I wished the roster gave more information than just his name.

"Imogene? You okay up there?" I heard ReeAnn call.

This was wrong. I shouldn't be thinking about anyone his age this way—a high school student. At the school where I taught. I wasn't even sure what I wanted him to be. A friend? A—I was embarrassed to even say this word in my own head—*lover?* I felt sick at the thought. I wasn't in high school anymore; I was too old to imagine anything would happen just because I wanted it to. I was too old for him.

I opened up my email again, reread the message from Dale. Then, I composed a message to Ms. McNally-Barnes.

There are some issues that have come up recently. Are you available anytime tomorrow to speak with me?

I sent the message and closed my laptop. Then I joined the other apprentices downstairs. This was what I was supposed to be doing. These were the people who were supposed to be my friends.

— — —

Ms. McNally-Barnes smiled at me when I entered her office the next day. Purplish lipstick stained her front tooth, and I pretended not to notice. "Dr. Duvall told me you're doing good work," she said, and I smiled back at her because I loved being one of the good ones. I may never have been the best, may not have been Columbia material, but I'd always been good—the good influence, the good guest, the good student, the good daughter. I never tired of hearing about my goodness; without that reassurance, I might think I wasn't any good at all.

I sat across from her at her desk.

"Everything else going well? Those little shits aren't giving you a hard time?"

I laughed hesitantly, a laugh that wasn't my own, because I never knew what else to do when adults cursed in front of me. "No, no, they aren't. My students have been great."

"And the other apprentices? Everything going well with them?"

"Yeah, they're all great."

She raised her eyebrow questioningly.

I shifted in my chair. "You see, I've been having difficulties with a student outside of my class."

"What sort of difficulties?"

"He, well . . . His behavior towards me has been inappropriate for a student."

Ms. McNally-Barnes opened a notebook on her desk and clicked open a pen. "What's his name?"

"Duggar Robinson. He's a fourth year on the lacrosse team. The captain, actually."

She nodded and scribbled down the name. I sat on my hands to keep them from shaking. A rhyme from childhood played in my head. *Tattle Tale! Go to jail! Hang your britches on a nail!*

"Imogene?"

I looked up at Ms. McNally-Barnes, realizing I had missed a question. "Sorry?"

"I said, what sort of inappropriate behavior has he displayed?"

"He just . . . He doesn't treat me with the respect he shows Coach Larry." It occurred to me then that Duggar didn't exactly treat Larry with any respect either and that, perhaps, Duggar Robinson was not the kind of boy to show respect for anything.

Ms. McNally-Barnes looked tired. "I need some specifics, Imogene."

"He talks back to me. And one time he punched me in the stomach."

"He what?"

"Well, he didn't exactly punch me. He pretended to." I hesitated, my face burning. "It was a game the boys were playing. To find out their sex noises."

"Sex noises?" She said this the way one might say "foot fetish," and I wished I had never walked into her office. It was as terrible as the first time I'd seen my therapist in high school, when I'd had to try to explain why I picked and prodded at my pores until my face was ruined, until I felt sick with myself but unable to stop.

"It was just . . . inappropriate," I concluded lamely. *Inappropriate.* Back in college I'd learned about a psychological phenomenon called semantic saturation, in which the repetition of a word causes it to temporarily lose meaning. *Inappropriate.*

"Alright." She scribbled another note. "I'll be sure to talk to Larry about this. Thank you for bringing this to my attention, Imogene. It's important to speak up when these sorts of things happen. You never want to find yourself too involved to get out."

Feeling emboldened, I said, "Actually, there's one other thing."

"Yes?"

"There's another student who I think might have a crush on me."

She clicked open her pen again. "And his name?"

"Clarence Howell. A third year on the team."

"Has he acted inappropriately towards you as well?"

"Not exactly. His behavior has just seemed to suggest . . ." I trailed off, feeling stupid once again.

"Imogene." Ms. McNally-Barnes leaned over her desk towards me conspiringly. "A teenage boy will fall for anything with hair and a pair of breasts."

I never thought I could be made so uncomfortable by this, by the acknowledgement of my breasts by a relative stranger.

"Hell, I'm pretty sure half the boys at this school have a crush on me!" Ms. McNally-Barnes cackled, showing that smudge of purple on her tooth again, and I thanked her for her time before quickly excusing myself from her office.

— — —

Before lacrosse practice began the next day, Coach Larry called us in for a huddle. Clarence had gotten the cast removed from his nose, but the bridge was still bruised a purplish-blue. He glanced at me from across the circle, and I looked away guiltily.

"It has come to my attention that some of you boys have been acting inappropriately," Larry began, and my stomach churned. That word again. No, this couldn't be how he handled the situation. Not like this, not in front of everyone.

The boys stared at him blankly, wondering where this was going.

"Every teacher and apprentice in this school deserves to be treated with your upmost respect," Larry continued. "They are your superiors, regardless of age, regardless of sex." A bit of spittle sprayed between his teeth with the emphasis of this final word. I was embarrassed for him, that he didn't even realize that the word he'd meant to say was *utmost*. "This includes me, and this includes Coach Imogene."

Clarence's gaze probed me like a finger, but I refused to look.

"Aw." Duggar put a hand to his heart. "We respect you, Coach."

"Then act like it, you entitled little shit."

Duggar's mouth fell open, and the other boys shifted uncomfortably, half laughing, half nervous that they were next.

Larry grinned. I could see his teenage self, finally vindicated. "In fact, why don't you run a few laps, Robinson? Show me just how much you respect me and Coach Imogene."

Duggar stared a moment, ready to argue, before he turned on his heel and took off around the field.

"And if I hear of any more disrespect from you," Larry called after him, "you better believe that captainship can be revoked!"

That practice, I ran a defensive drill as Larry supervised. I heard myself yelling, "Let's go, let's go!" in a voice I didn't know I possessed. I called Duggar by his last name, and he didn't talk back. I ignored Clarence, though I could feel his eyes from where he sat on the bench behind me. When I blew my whistle—I'd never utilized my whistle before—a couple of the boys even jumped.

Something had shifted, too imperceptible to name, but taking

Kip's hand and crossing the rope no longer felt irredeemable. I wanted Ms. McNally-Barnes to like me. I wanted Larry to like me. I wanted to prove to everyone—to the boys, to myself—that I was worthy of a position at Vandenberg. That I was worthy of a position of authority.

That afternoon on the lacrosse field, for the first time since I had arrived at Vandenberg School for Boys, I felt in control.

FIVE

DARBY LI HAD BEEN RANDOMLY ASSIGNED MY ROOMMATE THE summer before our freshman year at Buffalo State, and when I looked up her profile page, I was terrified. She was beautiful, the kind of beautiful you couldn't fake with professional photographs and manufactured confidence. With her gray eyes and thick dark hair and caramel-colored skin (the product of a Chinese father and a Jamaican mother), she was the poster child for palatable exoticism—the kind of exoticism I secretly longed for. She was from Soho, I discovered, daughter of a curator and visual artist. She'd attended an elite all-girls private school where they wore plaid kilts and knee-high socks with loafers.

I didn't think I belonged at Buffalo State, but I knew that Darby didn't; it was a mistake, a mix-up, and I almost wished Buffalo had paired me with a plump homebody from Upstate, someone unobtrusive and safe. Darby and I would never be friends, I decided, not because I was plain and white—plenty of her friends were white, it appeared, though none could be described as plain—but because my life was without distinction. During freshman orientation, when we were asked to say a "Fun Fact" about ourselves, I volunteered that I played the flute until tenth grade, a fact that elicited blank stares and a sympathetic pat on the wrist from the girl on my right.

But strangely, miraculously, Darby Li and I became friends. Darby had just broken up with her boyfriend of three years—heir to an enormous mattress fortune and possessor of a tiny prick, as Darby informed me—and she was looking to go wild. I had never done anything wild in my life, and the feverish energy in Darby's eyes excited me. Within the first month of college, Darby had taught me about everything from handles and pregames to hookups and blackouts. Darby was the one who orchestrated my first real kiss: with a junior named Paul at a party in her brother's apartment. Darby was the one who urged me to dance with Jonah Davis from my Communicating Nonverbal Messages lecture at the freshman Halloween bash, which later led to my first real hookup. "What would you do without me?" Darby often asked me. "I'm not sure," I would answer quite truthfully.

I even trusted Darby enough to let her see me without my makeup, to see the naked, spotted face that I disguised everyday. "You can't even see it," she'd assured me as I fussed over a raised blemish on my chin or my forehead, something that left a beige-colored protuberance under my makeup that became the only thing I saw when I looked in the mirror. Assurance was the kindest thing she could have offered me.

I knew why I liked Darby—her beauty, her frantic energy, her ability to repel culpability and embarrassment and shame and all the burdens of those who did not possess her unique beauty—but I could never be sure why she liked me. Perhaps she found me funny, or loyal, or kind. Perhaps she enjoyed my company on all those nights we hiked barefoot back to campus, our heels in our hands and our heads floating somewhere up above our bodies.

But more than likely, even if she did grow to like me for me, our friendship began as a project. Corrupting me gave Darby a thrill, and I was so grateful for her attention that I willingly allowed her to do it.

— — —

I didn't mean to think about Adam Kipling. But it seemed anytime I entered the dining hall, or walked around campus, or performed dorm rounds in Perkins Hall—pausing by each door, wondering if I might catch his voice or get a hint as to what door he slept behind—I was on the lookout. I wasn't even sure what I would do if I saw him. I was more curious to see what he would do if he saw me.

Tuesday night in the dining hall, I thought I spotted him across the room by the salad bar, thought I saw him look at me and even raise his hand in greeting. But I was so sure I imagined it that I didn't look back at the salad bar for the rest of dinner.

I hardly knew anything about him. His name. A cursory physical description: black moppish hair, skinny arms, eyes that got squinty when he grinned. Much of what I'd learn about him would come later, and mostly from Chapin. "Distant descendent of the Rothschilds," she'd tell me, which didn't mean anything to me beyond "Jewish." His father a moneylender, his mother a former member of the Royal Ballet. They owned properties in Hingham, Kennebunk, and Naples (both Florida and Italy). Kip's childhood best friend was the prince of Lesotho.

But despite how little I knew, I still revisited the night between the trees again and again, the memory growing in urgency. How had he known it was okay to hold my hand so tightly? What made him sure that he could walk me back to my dorm room? As far as I could see, he hadn't stopped to question any move he'd made that night, the way I would have at his age, the way I still did now. He was certain about everything, and his certainty kept me from retroactively questioning the night's strangeness. He had been meant to be there, and so had I. And I wanted to see him again, if only to confirm there was a reason he continued to linger.

I imagined scenes. I pictured us running into each other somewhere away from campus—maybe running, an early-morning reunion on the trail I traced each morning through town—and him stopping and tugging his earbuds from his ears and saying, *Hey, it's you,* his face bright with sweat and recognition. He'd jog alongside me, knowing I wouldn't mind. He'd probably even challenge me to a race; from what little I'd seen of him that first night, I felt certain that was something he would do.

I'd come to savor the afternoons I spent supervising study period. From the sweeping bay windows of the Marshall Huffman Library's third-floor classroom, the campus was spread out before me like a map. Sitting at my teacher's desk in the front of the room, I felt at once more removed from and closer to Vandenberg than ever, the world below me far off yet contained within that window frame, only the sounds of scratching pencils and the assured ticking of the clock on the wall for company. I spent my hours looking out over the bent heads of the students at their desks, watching all those boys milling silently about below, looking for that familiar mess of dark hair. That Wednesday afternoon, I felt sure that if I concentrated hard enough, he would appear eventually, a dark blot on the map, an answer to a question.

"Imogene!"

I startled. Raj stood at my elbow, grinning down at me. I hadn't even heard him come into the room.

"What are you doing here?"

He grabbed a chair from the corner of the room and brought it over to my desk. "Grading some essays. I'm bored though."

I'd never understand the person who sought out the company of others in boredom, who felt certain that other people could eradicate the tedium of everyday life. I was far more comfortable with tedium than I was with posturing and forcing conversation. I was at my most comfortable, it seemed, when I was alone.

"Entertain me?" he asked, a pathetic plea, and I desperately wanted him to leave.

I gestured to the working students, some of them peeking up at us curiously. "I don't want to distract them," I whispered, knowing full well they welcomed distraction.

He took a notebook from his bag and jotted something down. Then, he passed the notebook to me along the desk.

Then we'll talk like this.

Okay, I wrote.

Raj and I had had limited contact since the weekend. I wondered if he understood what had transpired between us, if he was even aware that something had transpired. I suspected sometimes that I experienced things much differently than other people did.

He passed back the notebook. *You are in a room that is completely bricked in on all four sides, including the ceiling and floor,* he had written. *You have nothing but a mirror and a wooden table in the room with you. How do you get out?*

I raised my eyebrows at him. "What?" I mouthed.

"It's a riddle," he mouthed back.

I'd never understood riddles. I didn't care if the chicken or the egg came first, or why it even mattered.

I don't know, I wrote.

He scribbled his answer and passed the book back.

You look in the mirror, and you see what you saw. You take the saw, and you cut the table in half. Two halves make a whole, and you climb out of the hole.

How was I supposed to have gotten that?

I thought everyone knew that one.

Not me, I guess.

I'm sorry for the other day.

My heart clenched. *For what?* I wrote.

It's okay that you didn't know I was Pakistani. I didn't mean to seem offended.

I hesitated, and he snatched the notebook back from me and added another note before handing it back.

India and Pakistan were once one nation before the partition of British India in 1947.

I didn't know that, I wrote back.

That's okay.

Do you have any more riddles?

He read my note and smiled, accepting my apology, and then he began to scribble furiously. *Maybe we could be friends,* I thought. I looked over his head at the world outside. The leaves were beginning to turn, and several boys sported peacoats and scarves over their uniforms. The flash of a long red scarf trailing in the wind caught my eye. It was attached to a spindly body with a mass of dark hair. I followed the figure until it disappeared from sight, not caring if it was Kip or not, knowing it didn't really matter.

— — —

Darby and I stayed out all night one time. It was a Thursday in our freshman year, and I had stats homework to finish and a class at nine the next morning, but Darby promised we would have fun so I agreed to go. We used the fake IDs Darby had secured us (I was Sandra Lee McNatt, a bright-eyed blonde from El Paso, Texas) to get into Cubby's in downtown Buffalo, a place where many of the seniors went on Thursday nights. I was nervous. I'd never seen so many bodies crammed into so small a space, elbows and hands and mouths everywhere, and I didn't recognize a single face. I felt anchored by the glossy head of my roommate as she tugged me through that crowd of elbows and hands and mouths; she was the reason I was there, the reason I was anyone at all.

And it was fun. The later it got, and the more alcohol I consumed, the more comfortable I felt, easing into that crowd of bodies like a warm bath. That night, I was Sandra Lee McNatt. Or no, maybe I was still Imogene Abney, just an Imogene Abney who felt pretty in her strappy tank top and cool talking to the cute boy with the elfin ears and crooked smile from her stats class, and later kissing him, not caring who was looking, not caring what would transpire the next Tuesday in stats, just knowing it felt good in that moment.

We ended the night at a diner down the street. I tried not to make a habit of eating after dinner, much less at four in the morning, but it felt okay as long as Darby was doing it, too. I ordered a stack of pancakes, which I smothered in so much syrup it dripped off the edge of the plate. I couldn't remember the last time I'd felt so hungry.

"This is why you just have to do things, Imogene." Darby pointed her fork at me, her mouth full of challah French toast. She was drunk, I could tell, and her raven hair stuck to her face in sweaty strands, but she was still beautiful.

"Do things?"

"Do the things you want to do."

I dragged a giant bite of pancake through the puddle of syrup on my plate and shoved it between my lips, sweet golden goo dribbling down my chin.

"Do all the things you want to do, or you'll just regret it. That's what I think."

I nodded. Then we lowered our mouths to our plates and ate like we hadn't eaten in years, ravenously, rapaciously, until our plates were empty and our mouths sticky and our stomachs heavy and swollen but satisfied.

Living with Darby, I noticed things about her that no one else would, though it took me some time to see them. It wasn't until halfway through freshman year that I noticed the pudgy roll of fat that spilled over the waistband of her jeans. It didn't occur to me for a while, either, that she had a habit of chewing with her mouth open. The difference between Darby and me however: She wasn't sorry about her roll of fat or her open mouth chewing. She didn't even seem to notice these things about herself, much less feel the need to apologize for them. Every time she slipped on a tight T-shirt or dress, her roll of fat protruding under the fabric, I'd feel a mix of admiration for her confidence and anger that she didn't feel the need to hide herself, that her roll of fat didn't make her hate herself, even a little bit.

— — —

Chapin knocked on my door Thursday night. She stood on the other side wearing a cheetah-print romper, leather ankle boots, and dark red lipstick, her hair piled in a messy sprout on the top of her head like a cartoon character. "Let's go out," she said.

I can't remember if I agreed—more likely Chapin already knew the answer would be yes—and within a moment she was pushing hangers aside in my closet. I stood and watched her dumbly, wearing slippers and Buffalo State sweatpants.

She held out a purple corset dress my sister Joni bought me for my twenty-second birthday, having mistaken me for someone else. "Wear this."

"Okay." I took the hanger from her and headed towards the door.

"You can change in front of me."

"Okay," I repeated. I pulled off my T-shirt, under which I wore a simple cotton bra, and stepped out of my sweatpants. She watched me with an intensity I felt sure I wasn't imagining. I tried to appear as cool as possible as I slipped the dress from the hanger and pulled it over my polka-dot underwear.

Chapin shook her head. "You can't wear a bra with that dress."

I unclasped my bra and slipped it over my head. It felt strange, my bare breasts bobbing unbound in the top of the dress.

Now she nodded. "You look good."

I walked over to the mirror, inspected my reflection, then smiled. I did look good.

Chapin called a cab, and we rode together to the Scarsdale Metro-North station. She had brought along a water bottle of vodka and Sprite, and we split it between us on the way. I knew better than to ask where we were going. Chapin paid for the cab, as well as for my train ticket, and I didn't protest.

Once we were on the train, the water bottle now empty and no longer able to provide a diversion, I struggled to think of something to say. Chapin leaned back against her seat, her lids heavy. Why didn't she feel this compulsion to fill the silence that I felt?

"This will be my first time into the city since we've been here."

Chapin smiled blandly, didn't respond.

"I think the last time I was in the city was to see *The Lion King* with my parents and my sister. And that was probably four, five years ago." I paused, thinking. "Yeah, Joni still had braces then so that must have been five years ago." My tongue already felt a little heavy from the drink in the cab. "I really like the city. It just feels like anything can happen there, you know?" I didn't like the city. I was in constant conflict between the person I was and the person I thought might work better given the situation.

Chapin still hadn't responded. I looked over at her to make sure she hadn't fallen asleep. She hadn't; she smiled at me mischievously. "Let's play a game."

"Okay," I said.

She stood and slid over me on the seat so that she sat on the outside. Then, she pulled one of the straps of her romper down her shoulder so that nearly the entire cup of her red bra was exposed. Her chest was emaciated, her collarbone jutting out and the cup of her bra unmistakably empty. It was difficult not to stare. She didn't care about her lack of breasts; strangely, I felt suddenly self-conscious, weird and large and old, for having any breasts at all.

"Keep count," she said.

"What—"

The train made its first stop, and passengers stood to exit. Chapin pressed her lips together and stared straight ahead; she looked so deliberately innocent I wouldn't have been surprised if she began to whistle. After three passing men paused to openly stare at Chapin's exposed bra, I understood what I was supposed to be counting. Once the train pulled away, she adjusted her strap and asked me, "How many?"

"Nine," I said.

She stood and slid back into the inside of the seat. "Your turn."

"But—" The older woman across the aisle was glaring at us, so I lowered my voice. "But I'm not wearing a bra."

"Stand up."

She was more persuasive than Duggar Robinson on the bus, if that was possible. I stood, and she hiked the hem of my purple dress up around my waist, exposing my polka-dot panties. "Chapin!" I instinctively reached to pull the dress back down.

She forced me back into my seat. "Almost at the next stop."

I sat, helpless, feeling naked with my underwear in direct contact with the seat. We pulled into the stop. I stared directly into the seat before me, feigning Chapin's same obliviousness. After we'd pulled away and I'd tugged down my dress, I couldn't help but ask. "How many?"

"Thirteen," she said. "Nice."

The woman across the aisle shook her head in disgust and looked out her window. I wished I could explain to her that this wasn't me.

Chapin slid back over me. "My turn again."

She was so like my old roommate Darby, yet so unlike her at the same time. Darby I wanted to be, but Chapin I simply wanted not to fear. She grinned wildly, and the game continued all the way to Grand Central.

— — —

At the station, I was amazed, as I always was, by the sheer amount of people there were. Where had they all come from? Where were they all going? I was definitely a little drunk.

"C'mon." Chapin took my hand and yanked me along. We got in a cab (it was understood that she would pay again), and she directed the driver to an address, stated with the confidence of her home address. She leaned against her seat with that same sleepy-eyed look she had on the train, and I did the same, trying to sink as comfortably as she could into silence.

The club was dark and hot, like the inside of a mouth. Chapin bought us two drinks at the bar, something that tasted sour and potent. As she sipped, Chapin peered around, assuming a practiced expression of blasé but open to amusement.

It didn't take long for two men to approach us. They appeared to be in their early-30s, and they wore the kind of thick-framed glasses that I'd only recently realized were supposed to be cool. They weren't unattractive so much as unremarkable; I wasn't sure I could describe them even as they stood before me. Perhaps I was drunker than I thought.

"I'm Mark. This is Mike," one of the guys said by way of introduction. He had an accent—ambiguous, European.

"Maeve." Chapin held out her hand. I was confused until I realized this was her new name.

"Mona," I said, following her cue.

"*Moan*-ah," Mike repeated, wiggling his eyebrows. Chapin giggled, and I did, too. They were goofy, European, harmless. I swallowed the discomfort fighting its way out and forced myself to relax.

Mark paired off with Chapin, and I was left with Mike. I wasn't sure how and when this was decided. Mike grabbed my hips and rocked them back and forth. I'd been to clubs before, had danced with men before, but I'd never been to a club *this* clubby, had never danced with a man *this* manly.

I thought to ask him what he did for work, or where he was from, but I saw that Chapin was silent, sipping her drink and rocking to the beat Mark had set. Be comfortable with the silence, I told myself. I closed my eyes, felt the pulsating bass. I was Mona; I wore dresses without bras and didn't feel obligated to entertain others.

The night went on. Mark and Mike bought us another round of

drinks, and then another. Mark and Mike faced Chapin and I towards each other, and we danced together, laughing, as though there weren't a stranger behind each of us gripping our hips and grinding his crotch into our ass. I felt the inevitable stiffening and prodding from behind, and I felt guilty and excited and embarrassed for having inspired his arousal. I wanted to hide it so no one else could see. I wanted to hold it in my hand. Soon enough we were swiveled around, facing our respective partners. Mark and Chapin began to make out, so when Mike leaned in to kiss me, I let him. His tongue was thick and insistent. By the end of the night, Mike and I were holding hands.

"We should go home soon, Mona," Chapin said, holding up an imaginary wristwatch.

Mike put his mouth to my ear. "Come home with me."

I imagined waking up the next day at Mike's place. He'd roll over in bed and look at me, his face creased from sleep, and say, "Some night, huh?" And we'd laugh together, at the ridiculousness of it all. I'd tell him my name was really Imogene, and he'd say, "Imogene. That's much better than *Moan*-ah."

"We're going home," Chapin insisted.

She led me to the door, and I waved goodbye to Mike—or was that Mark? They were both waving goodbye, both already interchangeable in my memory.

In the cab on the way to Grand Central, Chapin closed her eyes, and I thought this time she might actually be asleep. After a few minutes, she spoke.

"Those guys were gross."

"Yeah," I agreed.

Her eyes were still closed, but she looked sad. I might have just been imagining it. Chapin was silent for the rest of the trip home, and once we'd returned to the Hovel, she said only, "Goodnight, Imogene," before climbing the stairs and closing her bedroom door.

— — —

I couldn't concentrate in Honors World History that day. The boys were fidgety because it was Friday and it was warm outside, and it didn't help that I was massively hungover from the night before. I gave a ten-minute lesson on the earliest agricultural methods and machines, listing various tools and placing them on a timeline, and then I gazed out the window for the duration of Dale's lecture. I planned the rest of my afternoon: I would take a long nap. Later, I would order a pizza, watch some TV. I would think about nothing.

After class, I went to the mailroom. In my mailbox, I had a letter from my Noni, which enclosed a check for ten dollars; a menu for a local Chinese restaurant; and a piece of notebook paper folded into quarters. I stuffed the envelope and the menu into my bag. The note contained only a phone number and a brief message: *Hey, text me sometime.* Absurdly, for a moment, I imagined it was Jared Hoffman from high school, before I remembered he was becoming a medical doctor at Johns Hopkins and had undoubtedly forgotten who I was. Then, for another horrible moment, I imagined it was from Clarence. I held the paper in my hand like a secret as I walked back to the Hovel. I didn't allow myself to imagine whom else the note could possibly be from.

Chapin was in the kitchen eating carrot sticks when I came home. "Hello, Imogene," she said.

"Hey." I set my bag down and leaned on the counter next to her, feeling emboldened by the night before. "Are you as hungover as I am?"

"I don't get hungover," she said. She chomped down on a carrot.

"Oh."

She turned and started up the stairs, crunching the carrot between her teeth. I wondered if all of last night had been a dream, if I had even left my room, if anything that I thought had happened had happened at all.

— — —

I lay restless in bed for nearly an hour before I reached for the piece of paper, folded next to me on my nightstand. The handwriting was cramped and slanted, undoubtedly a boy's. I picked up my phone, punched in the number. Who is this? I texted.

When a response didn't come within a few minutes, I picked up my book. After twenty minutes, I put down the book and looked up the number's 781 area code online. I learned that area code 781 covered most of the Boston suburbs along Route 128 and about two-thirds of the South Shore of Massachusetts.

The other apprentices were all back from class by then. I caught snippets of their conversation.

"—*so* nice out—"

"—have a picnic or something—"

"—get drinks at that place with the outdoor patio tonight—"

I turned back to my book. An almost violent irritation coursed through me. I thought, perhaps, it was just a product of my hangover. I wondered if I should feign sleep, or simply pretend not to be home.

The laughter and chatting continued a little longer, inaudible, before I heard the opening and closing of the front door and then silence. I dropped the book, peeked down the stairs. They were all gone. They'd left, and they hadn't invited me along.

I returned to my room, fighting an embarrassing urge to cry. Could it still be considered a loss if it was something I hadn't even wanted? I was thinking about calling my mom when my phone vibrated. It was the unknown number, as I knew it would be.

I'm hurt. I thought we had a moment the other night.

I felt dizzy. My phone vibrated again.

Don't tell me you've forgotten about me already.

I don't think I know who this is.

A few minutes passed, and then a reply. I think you do. Before I could even think, another vibration. I waved to you the other night in the dining hall. Another. Why didn't you wave back?

I didn't have to ask, but I did anyway. Adam?

Yeah?

I was glad to be sitting; it suddenly felt difficult to breathe. *No texting, calling, or messaging with any of the students, and emails were only appropriate if they were related to an academic matter.*

Hello.

Hi.

This was wrong, so obviously, recognizably wrong. I began to reply. I'm sorry, I can't—I stopped, deleted everything I'd typed. It was better, I decided, to not say anything.

I turned my phone facedown on my nightstand. It buzzed, and then again, and then one more time a few minutes later. I waited until I was sure he was done before I looked.

First, You think you shouldn't be talking to me.

Then, You're probably right.

Finally, I just want to know more about you.

SIX

WHEN I SAW MY FIRST PENIS, I WAS EIGHTEEN YEARS OLD AND dressed as an olive branch, a costume I thought would be clever but really just earned me several confused looks. After dancing at the freshman Halloween bash for the better part of two hours with Jonah Davis, who sat in front of me in my Communicating Nonverbal Messages lecture (we had never acknowledged each other before and still wouldn't after), he asked me to come back to his room, and I said yes. Darby hooked up with boys all the time. My first real kiss had only been three weeks before, at a party in Darby's brother's apartment with the junior named Paul who told me I was beautiful, who bit my lip and pawed at my breasts in front of everyone. But as we kissed, my hands shook and I felt that *thump* between my legs that told me I was ready for more than just kissing. I thought he might become my first boyfriend, too, and I felt sick when I saw him cupping the ass of a longhaired Indian girl an hour later. Kisses mean nothing, I realized. Kisses are as disposable as old gum and banana peels.

Jonah Davis was dressed as a pirate, and once we started making out on his bed I felt the fly of his silky black pants expand and harden beneath me, poking my belly impatiently.

"You can touch it," he said. His drawn-on mustache was smeared above his lip and also, as I would discover later when I looked in the mirror above the bathroom sink, on my chin.

He drew my hand close to him and guided it down the front of his pants. My fingers curled around something warm and fleshy and rubbery, and when he eased his pants down to his knobby knees, I saw it: the Magic Marker sketch from my Camp Barbara Anne bedpost incarnate, a clam without a shell, so vulnerable and pink I wanted to laugh and cry at once.

I was exposed soon enough as well; my shirt and bra on the floor, my skirt pulled up, my ladybug-print panties pulled down. I'd always been the type to change my clothes in the bathroom stall before gym class, never imagining I could lie nearly naked with a stranger. How easy it was, I thought, to show those vulnerable, pink parts of ourselves to someone when we know that person will never ask or expect anything else of us. When he thrust his finger inside of me, I winced and wondered, is this it? And after I peed later and saw blood, I didn't feel irrevocably changed, as I imagined I might, but instead vaguely disappointed, as I hadn't even realized what was happening as it happened. I'd missed it.

"Fingering doesn't count," Darby told me, but still I wanted to ask her, *Then what does count?*

It was okay that I hadn't lost it in high school. It would have been nice to have been entered for the first time, tenderly and sweetly, by the object of some sixteen-year-old romance, clutching each other in my childhood twin bed, the feeling of fitting our bodies together so thrilling we would wonder how we could do anything else ever again. But of course, with no High School Sweetheart there had been no High School Sweetheart Sex.

And it was okay to enter college a virgin, too. As Darby assured me, some guys were into that, virgins. The idea of conquest, of pillaging lands. If the subject came up, I was Waiting For The Right Person. By junior year, I was Waiting For Something I Wouldn't Regret. But by senior year, when Zeke Maloney from down the hall asked if I wanted to just fuck already (we'd been doing everything but for three weekends by that point), I decided I was Ready To Just Fuck Already, and I said yes. Zeke Maloney liked to chew tobacco and spit the juice into strangers' Solo cups at parties. As Zeke Maloney pumped inside of me, his breath hot and labored in my ear, I thought, once again, *Is this it?*

"This is okay," I said, more to myself than to him. "This isn't so bad. This is okay." Each pump felt like stabbing a shovel into still-frozen ground.

"God, you're tight," he grunted, and I imagined him stretching my body like pizza dough, no, like the waistband of a pair of childhood pajamas over the years, distending it wider and wider until it was barely recognizable.

We slept together two more times, and then I saw him kissing another girl at a bar. I confronted him via text message.

We were just kissing, he replied. And I never said you and I were exclusive.

Sex means nothing, I decided. Sex is just as disposable as kisses, which were, apparently, just as disposable as me.

— — —

The third years were taking a field trip that Saturday to Hook Mountain for a hawk watch. Field trips were an integral part of the Vandenberg curriculum—a chance for the students to briefly emerge from what was commonly known as the "Vandenberg Bubble," but also, more notably, a chance for Vandenberg to present its students to the larger Westchester community as the fruitful products of an esteemed institution. The week before, under the care of the Woods twins, Babs, and Chapin, the first years had taken a trip to the art museum in Katonah. Three boys had been placed on disciplinary probation for taking pictures of themselves with Roy Lichtenstein's *Beach Scene with Starfish,* which apparently features several nude female comic book characters. For the Hook Mountain trip, ReeAnn, Raj, and I were assigned to chaperone, and I hoped all the boys would stay out of trouble, at least for that day.

At eight o'clock that morning, the boys boarded two buses dressed in sturdy shoes and khakis rather than their usual blazers and ties. I'd assumed, perhaps immaturely, that ReeAnn and I would sit next to each other on the bus; we were the only girls on the trip, and didn't that mean we were expected to stick together? I was running late, having forgotten my water bottle in my room, and when I finally boarded the bus, I saw that ReeAnn was already sitting next to Raj, the two of them watching a video on Raj's phone. I was reminded of how my old best friends Stephanie and Jaylen and I used to rotate who sat next to whom on the bus, and how in the eighth grade Stephanie and Jaylen began sitting next to each other every day, forcing me to become seat partners with Mary Elizabeth, a sixth-grader who wore pilgrim dresses.

As I passed down the aisle, I waved to ReeAnn and Raj in a way I hoped appeared indifferent and peered around for an empty seat. A few rows behind ReeAnn and Raj sat Clarence Howell, scribbling in his notebook, his ratty backpack on the seat beside him. He wore binoculars around his neck, and his hair didn't appear to have been washed in the last week. I approached him.

"Is this seat taken?"

He looked up, startled, and moved his backpack to the floor. I sat. Our mutual loserdom sat between us like a stench, and I wanted desperately to dispel it. Finally, I asked, "Draw anything new lately?"

"Not really." He closed the notebook and slid it into his backpack. He met my eyes warily.

"Your nose looks better."

He put his hand to his nose. "Thanks?" he said, the question mark tacked on like an afterthought.

The supervising teacher, Susanne Moore, who taught third-year anatomy, boarded the bus. "We'll be leaving in just a minute," she announced. "Chaperones, a headcount please."

I stood and counted along with ReeAnn and Raj. "Thirty-nine," they announced in almost perfect unison. "Thirty-nine," I echoed. I'd gotten thirty-eight on my count.

The bus pulled out from the school lot. Clarence was still watching me.

"I'm glad you did it," he said.

I was startled by the lack of prelude. "Did what?"

"That you told on Duggar."

I grimaced at that word, told, and he noticed.

"Well, not *told*. Reported him, I guess."

"Yeah?"

"Yeah. He's been different."

Duggar Robinson had been different since the day after my meeting with Ms. McNally-Barnes. He was quieter, sullen, avoided my eye. So were, I'd noticed, most of the other boys on the team. It made me feel at once powerful and lonely.

"I feel like the team doesn't like me anymore," I said, hating how childish I sounded.

"That's not true."

"Then why doesn't anyone talk to me?"

Clarence hesitated. "I guess . . . some of us aren't really sure how to talk to you."

"Why?"

"Because you're not just, like, a coach. You're . . ." He shifted uncomfortably in his seat. "I don't know."

My mind compiled a list of ways he could potentially end that sentence—twenty-two, a girl, a woman, maybe even pretty—but none felt quite right. Nothing could fill the void that gaped between Clarence Howell and me.

Quietly, Clarence added, "We still like you though. I still like you."

"Good," I said.

The changing leaves and green expanse of Westchester rolled past the window behind Clarence. I nudged his arm. "Want to hear a riddle?"

"Okay."

"Okay. So you're in a room that's all bricked in, like even the ceiling and floor, and you have a saw—no, a table and—what else is it? A mirror! And . . ." I trailed off. "I'm not telling this right."

Clarence smiled. "You look in the mirror, and you see what you saw. You take the saw, and you cut the table in half. Two halves make a whole, and you climb out of the hole."

"How did you know that?"

He shrugged. "I thought everyone knew that one."

— — —

After the first time Zeke Maloney and I had sex, I was sure everyone could see it. When I bought my breakfast the morning after, the dining hall worker who spooned a lump of scrambled eggs onto my plate pursed her lips reproachfully. When I walked through the quad back to my dorm, a group of freshmen looked over at me and laughed. When my mom came to pick me up from school the following weekend (I was going home to celebrate my sister Joni's seventeenth birthday), and I sat in the passenger seat of our minivan and she swept my hair out of my eyes and smiled sadly and said, "You look different," I felt so sure she knew that I nearly cried.

What's more, they all knew it had been with someone who didn't love me. Someone who I waved to without saying hello when I saw him around campus. Someone who (as I discovered one time when he lost his phone under my bed and asked me to call it) had entered me into his contacts as "Imojean" because he didn't even know how to spell my name. Perhaps Zeke told everyone. Or perhaps, made too uncomfortable by the little squeaks of pain I'd made and by the quarter-sized bloodstain I left on the bed, he told no one. Whether those few nights I'd spent with Zeke Maloney were private or not, I knew my first time hadn't been what I wanted and felt convinced everyone could at least see that.

— — —

Clarence and I fell into comfortable silence after a little while, him doodling in his notebook, me looking past him out the window and thinking about Kip. After his last text, I'd saved his number as a contact in my phone: Adam Kipling. Then I deleted it. Then I deleted all of his messages. But still, I'd slipped my phone into my back pocket this morning so I could feel if it vibrated.

I just want to know more about you.

What could Adam Kipling possibly want to know about me? I studied my reflection in the window: limp hair, freckled nose, collarbones jutting from shoulders. Perhaps if I had a distinctive haircut, or an eyebrow piecing, or ethnic ambiguity, I'd understand. But as I was now, there was nothing to indicate that I had a story to tell. As I was now, what was there to know?

What I wanted to know more about was him. I ran through the facts I'd already collected, stored in my memory like little trinkets or trading cards: He was from the suburbs of Boston, the South Shore. He had an older brother who went to Yale. He liked to smoke and drink and break rules. He was charismatic and strange.

I wondered once who he'd be if he'd gone to my high school, but it was impossible to imagine him stepping out of a flashy foreign car in the parking lot, strutting through the dirty halls in a woolen blazer and rugby-stripe tie. I didn't need to know his family's net worth to know Kip was wealthy, and like most of the boys I'd encountered at Vandenberg, his wealth was inextricable from his person. Kip was money, and everything that came along with it: a thick shiny watch and straight teeth and confidence that he exuded through his loose limbs, his laugh. I couldn't be sure if I wanted to be with him or if I wanted to be him. I couldn't even be sure that the person that had been infecting my thoughts was the boy who'd walked me home or a Tobias Wolff creation.

The bus drove over a pothole and tossed us momentarily from our seats. I felt a vibration and pulled my phone from my back pocket. No new messages. I was imagining things.

Soon enough we arrived at Hook Mountain. Tim Ludd, the hiking guide—a bespeckled man with a limp who didn't look like he could make his way up a flight of stairs, much less a mountain—handed out pamphlets with pictures of the birds we'd likely spot today: red-shouldered hawks, broad-winged hawks, sharp-shinned hawks, bald eagles.

"Aren't bald eagles, like, extinct?" one of the boys near the back of the group called out.

"Though it was on the brink of extirpation in the late twentieth century, the bald eagle is no longer even on the list of endangered and threatened wildlife," Tim Ludd explained.

"So they're real?"

The guide peered out warily, searching for the source of the voice. "Yes, they are very real."

"So we'll see one today?"

"Well, there is no guarantee on any given hike that—"

"I won't believe they're real until I see one."

Tim Ludd sighed. "Well then." When he was sixteen, being sixteen must have meant a very different thing than it did now.

The boys were split into four groups, one led by Ms. Moore and one for each of the chaperones. My group, which included Clarence Howell and, to my horror, Christopher Jordan, was last in the pack. With Tim Ludd leading the way and keeping an impressively quick pace, we started to make our way up Breakneck Ridge.

I wasn't sure what I was expected to do as the guide for my group. Tim Ludd was so far off that we could barely make him out, never mind hear him, and so the boys took to talking amongst themselves,

88   CORINNE SULLIVAN

which was fine with me. The air was crisp and invigorating, and the Hudson Highlands spooled out beneath us like an autumnal movie set. I thought, suddenly, that I could be anyone, be anything; it's strange what pretty things can make us feel.

"Look, a bird!" one of the boys in my group called.

We turned our heads to the sky. Clarence peered through his binoculars.

"What is that, Miss Abney?"

"Um." I consulted my pamphlet. The bird was a speck in the sky, with no discernible identifying features. "A hawk."

None of the boys responded, but I saw Clarence smile behind his binoculars. Clarence and I could be friends, I decided. He could grow out of his crush, and I could be his big sister. Instead of stilted and strange and full of insinuation—like my relationships with the other boys seemed—my relationship with Clarence could actually be appropriate, normal.

We stopped to eat after an hour and a half, and ReeAnn, Raj, and I helped pass out the brown-bag lunches the dining hall staff had prepared for us. "This smells like bologna," one of the boys sneered as I handed him his bag. "I don't eat cold cuts," said another. Once all the bags were distributed, I sat with ReeAnn and Raj at one of the picnic tables.

"Having fun?" ReeAnn asked me.

"Yeah," I said. "This is actually really cool." The sandwich in my bag was turkey, and I hungrily took a bite.

"This would be cooler if I wasn't so hungover," Raj said. ReeAnn laughed, affirmation of their shared affliction. They both had pushed their sandwiches aside, untouched; I wondered if sandwiches were now uncool, and when exactly that had happened. I threw away my own, half-eaten.

The hike began again. Far up ahead, it sounded as though Tim Ludd was trying to lead Ms. Moore's group in song, and a few of the boys joined him in mocking falsettos.

"Where are all the fuck-ing birds?" a boy sang behind me to the tune of their song.

I marched on ahead, ignoring the boys.

There was a burst of laughter behind me.

"Dude, try to piss on the rabbit!" someone hollered.

I spun around. Christopher Jordan stood facing out on the edge of the mountain, feet spread apart and pants unbuttoned, the world spread out before him in the triangle between his legs.

I could have pretended not to see it. It would have been easy, and less uncomfortable for everyone, for me to ignore it. But the word burst out of me anyway: "Hey," and when it was ignored, again, louder. "HEY!"

Christopher Jordan turned around to look at me, startled yet somehow unembarrassed. "Yeah?"

"Pull them up. Right now." My mouth was moving, but this wasn't my voice, this wasn't me. My hands shook violently.

He stared at me, uncertain. "But I have to take a leak."

"I SAID PULL THEM UP."

The other boys gawked. Christopher Jordan zipped up his pants and turned around. Then, in an attempt to save face, "Not what she said last time."

His friends howled and the blood rushed to my face. These boys had the maturity of fourteen-year-olds—no, twelve-year-olds! They would never act like this in front of Ms. Moore, or Tim Ludd, or even ReeAnn or Raj or any of the other apprentices. (I'd asked Babs once how often she found gum under the desks in study hall and she'd replied, puzzled, "But students aren't allowed to chew gum on campus.") It was me, only me, who was subject to this harassment. And though I once thought it was acceptance, I now saw it for what it was: exploitation. For a moment, I hated every last one of them.

"Look!"

The boys ahead were scrambling to the side of the mountain and pointing up towards the sky. The discomfort of the moment before temporarily forgotten, my group rushed on to see what the commotion was about.

"A bald eagle! They're real!"

The boys pulled out their phones to snap pictures. I couldn't take my eyes away. If I went to take a picture, I might miss it.

"Do you want to look?"

I turned. Clarence stood at my elbow, offering up his binoculars. I took them and smiled, then peered through the eyeholes. I watched the eagle circle up ahead, beautiful, unreal, until it finally circled out of sight.

— — —

We did another headcount before we boarded the bus, and this time, ReeAnn, Raj, and I all got thirty-eight. After a flustered search of the attendance list and a call to the student services office, Ms. Moore discovered that Freddie Finnerty had never boarded the bus that morning; he'd slept through his alarm and missed the whole trip. There had been forty-eight students on Bus One all along.

The brief panic seemed to sap whatever energy remained, and the bus ride home was unnervingly quiet. The smell of dried sweat hung in the air, and some of the boys were slumped against the windows, mouths open in sleep. Their vulnerability made me want to forgive them, but I couldn't, not yet. I was angry with the boys, angry at Raj and ReeAnn for being wrong on the first head count, angry with myself for being so quick to give in when I knew I was right.

I'd spent most of my life feeling too young, but right then, for the first time, I felt startlingly, achingly old. I wondered, How old was the Adam Kipling in my mind? Certainly he wasn't just a year older than the boys who dozed around me, twitching and snoring like restless puppies. Next to me, Clarence worked on a drawing of his spandex-clad character, shading in her enormous breasts with complete absorption. He chewed on the thumbnail of his free hand and, for a moment, he appeared to be sucking his thumb. I looked out the window past him and thought of Kip as I dozed off.

I couldn't tell you what I dreamed of as I slept, but I know it was of him. Him and his mouth, open and laughing.

Next thing I knew, Clarence was nudging me. "We're back."

"Oh," I said, jerking from sleep. I stifled a yawn and pulled out my phone to check the time. I had one new text message, a number with a 781 area code. It felt at once obvious and fortuitous, inevitable and preternatural.

— — —

I didn't want to look at the text message until I'd returned to my room. What a thrilling affliction a secret was. Throughout dinner, the phone sat in my back pocket, a wrapped present, a time bomb. As ReeAnn and Raj recounted the day and the bald eagle sighting to the rest of the apprentices, I concentrated on my macaroni and cheese. I wasn't sure what my face might reveal, but I imagined it carried something resembling guilt. I told myself that I was excited by the novelty, not the person. I told myself that as long as I didn't read the message, I wasn't complicit. I told myself that I hadn't asked for this to happen.

Back in my room, I finally opened the text.

Hey there, Imogene, it said.

My first thought: *He knows how to spell my name.*

My next thought: *This is wrong.*

With shaking hands, I composed my reply. You can't text me anymore, Adam.

His reply took a while to come. Okay, it said.

Okay. It was over. Okay. I set my phone on my nightstand and took a few deep breaths. But it wasn't relief I felt—I couldn't put a word to the twisting feeling in my stomach, but it wasn't relief.

It didn't come to me until the middle of the night, when I crept down the hall to pee. Perched on the toilet seat, the stream of my urination the only sound shattering the stillness of the Hovel, what I felt was disappointment.

I knew then that the shame in having lost my virginity to Zeke Maloney wasn't because he didn't love me; it was because he mumbled and had blotchy skin and shaved his head so close that patches of his scalp showed through the dark stubble. I was embarrassed to be tied with him because I knew—or at least liked to believe—that I was capable of having better, of having someone charming and clever and—I hated myself for thinking this but I thought it all the same—*rich*. Someone like Adam Kipling. I thought again of Raj's girlfriend.

But I'm prettier.

— — —

ReeAnn, Raj, and I were summoned to Ms. McNally-Barnes' office on Sunday afternoon. She offered us a donut from the open box on her desk, and she smiled and asked us about the field trip, but we all knew why we were there—we had let her down.

After a few minutes of the kind of agonizing idle conversation that's used to delay the ugliness of truth, Ms. McNally-Barnes laced her fingers on her desk and leaned forward, a pose I interpreted as "getting down to business."

"Ms. Moore told me what happened," she said.

Raj paused mid-chew, powdered sugar on his lips, his expression that of a dog who just peed on the carpet. ReeAnn looked as though she might cry.

"I told you all when you took on this job that it would come with accountability," she continued. She, too, had powdered sugar on her lips, and I concentrated instead on the space beside her right ear. "You're not just responsible for teaching the students here. If a student gets left behind, that's your responsibility as well."

I nodded, attempting to appear contrite. I wanted to say, *but it wasn't my fault.*

"They may be little shits, but that's why it's your job to keep them from screwing up as often as possible."

"And I guess we can't really do that if we screw up first," Raj said with a grin.

Ms. McNally-Barnes frowned. He had misinterpreted her candor for exoneration. "No, you cannot. Don't let it happen again."

I felt nauseous. I tried to meet her eye, but she refused to meet mine. This wasn't how it was supposed to be; I was the good influence, the good guest, the good student, the good daughter, the good apprentice. I tried to recall a time I'd ever been chastised like this in my life, and all I could think of was a sleepover at Jaylen's house in seventh grade, when we'd snuck out to meet up with some boys who lived down the street, and Jaylen's mother caught us coming back in and called my and Stephanie's mothers to come pick us up. I hadn't even wanted to go meet up with those boys; I'd wanted to play gin rummy and eat tortilla chips with melted cheese.

"Okay?" Ms. McNally-Barnes gave us a stern look, but her voice was softer; we would be forgiven, just not yet.

"Okay," we echoed, a trio of obedient school children.

On the walk back to the Hovel—ReeAnn and Raj had gone to the dining hall to get some lunch, but I said I wasn't hungry—the relief I'd expected to feel last night finally washed over me. Watching out for Kip, thinking about Kip, texting with Kip—none of it was acceptable. Extracting myself from the situation was the best thing I could have done to assure I remained as I always had been, and how I always wished to be: good.

What I didn't expect was for Kip to be sitting on the back stoop of the Hovel when I arrived. I froze when I spotted him. He stood and waved. "Hi."

"Adam," I said dumbly, more confirmation than greeting.

"You said not to text you."

I remained frozen. "Yes."

"So." He shrugged. "Here I am."

SEVEN

MY SURPRISE AT SEEING KIP OUTSIDE THE HOVEL WAS TOO GREAT to formulate a reaction. When my parents threw me a surprise party for my fourteenth birthday, gathering my Aunt Carol and Uncle Fred and cousin Anastasia and Noni and Joni in the living room with balloons and streamers and a vanilla sheet cake from the local A&P, I'd been similarly dumbstruck. I'd walked in from lacrosse practice to find them all waiting, eager and grinning, and I'd stared at them, waiting for a cue. What was my line? What was my motivation? Who was my character?

With Kip, I struggled only a few moments before deciding on, "They can't see you."

"Who are they?"

Who was I? A teacher. A figure of authority. "Anyone," I said.

"Then perhaps we should go inside."

No. No, no, no. "No," I said.

"I just want some water. Then I'll go."

"I can bring you a glass," I said. "Out here."

He raised his eyebrows. "Really?"

"Really what?"

"Really, you won't let me come inside for one minute?" He stepped closer to me. "What do you think I'm going to do? Ransack your drawers?"

Ransack. I'd never heard anyone use the word in earnest, and a childish giggle threatened to spew from my lips. His face was so close to mine I felt cross-eyed from looking at him. He knew I wouldn't put into words what I was actually afraid he might do, and I knew to protest any more would only make me look absurd. "Just for a minute."

He nodded solemnly. "Just for a minute."

I unlocked the door and led him inside. The kitchen was empty; everyone else was at lunch. He sat at the kitchen table and watched as I took a glass from the cabinet and filled it at the sink. I handed him the glass, and he gulped it down in two chugs.

"Ah." Kip swiped the back of his hand across his mouth for emphasis. "Thanks."

I stood above him. I had a small blemish on my forehead, almost healed, and I untucked the hair behind my ear so it fell into my face in a way that I hoped appeared casual. "Why are you here?"

"This is nice." He held his empty glass up to the light. "Do they give you all these or did you have to bring your own?" He refused to meet my eye.

"They gave them to us."

"That's nice. What about the table and couches?" He tapped the lip of the glass lightly on the table, and I heard the clink of glass falling to the floor. "Oops. Chipped it a little." He set it back on the table, unconcerned.

My hands were shaking. I clasped them together above my navel like I had a stomachache, which I feared I might have soon. "Adam?" It sounded too much like a question.

"It's been a while since I was last here, but it looks pretty much the same. Except for that." He pointed to the cross Babs had hung above the sink. "That's new."

I tried again. "Adam."

He finally turned to look at me.

My hands released each other, and I forced them down by my sides. "You can't be here."

"Why not?" His eyes did not have their usual mischievous glimmer. He seemed legitimately puzzled as to why his presence there could possibly be unwanted.

"Because," I said. My voice, which I wished to make authoritative, sounded instead teasing, flirtatious.

"Do you want me to leave then?"

I didn't, but I couldn't say so. I shrugged.

"So maybe I can stay then, just for a little bit."

I didn't protest. "Do you want more water?" I asked.

He shook his head no. His eyes were on my face, looking for an answer even though I didn't know the question.

"Do you want to go to your room?" he asked finally.

So that was the question. I picked up his chipped glass and placed it in the sink, avoiding his eyes. When I turned around, he had his hand extended towards me, and I thought, for a strange moment, that he was going to shake my hand goodbye. But his hand was palm up, an offer.

"C'mon," he said. It wasn't playful, or pleading, or even exasperated; it was the matter-of-fact command of someone who knew what was going to happen next. It was the confidence from the night he took my hand, walked me home. It infuriated me.

"No," I said. He lowered his hand, and I repeated, more certain of myself, "No."

His mouth tightened—he looked defeated, maybe even angry—but then just as quickly neutralized. "If you say so," he said, just as he had the night we met, when I first reminded him that I was a teacher and he was a student. He gently pushed in his chair—I thought ridiculously for a moment that he might throw it against the wall, make some sort of scene—and then smiled at me, a perfect gentleman. "Thank you for the refreshment."

He let himself out. I plucked his glass from the sink and wrapped it in several layers of paper towels and shoved it all to the bottom of the trash bin until you couldn't even see it.

— — —

The summer before starting at Vandenberg, I took a beginner's rock-climbing class with my sister, Joni. Having already secured employment at Vandenberg back in May, after finishing college, the summer at home in Lockport lazed before me, strange and unstructured. I scrambled eggs in the morning (I never slept past eight-thirty) and ate them on the back porch, watching my dad watching the birds. After, I settled in the hammock with a book. I dozed and woke up sweating and disoriented, the angry red indentation of crisscrossing ropes welting my face and arms. At night, I watched TV with my parents, the canned sitcom laughter like gunshots. I wondered if, as you got older, life slowly became less interesting, or if you just stopped caring to do anything about it.

My mom encouraged me to call up my friends from high school. What's Jaylen up to these days? Or how about Stephanie? Jaylen had dropped out of SUNY Purchase after one semester and was then running a business out of her parents' garage, making novelty knitted animal hats and selling her mother's prescription pills to high schoolers. Stephanie had failed her nursing exam three times and was living above a convenience store with a twenty-eight-year-old beatboxer. (I'd found this all out through a combination of social media sites and Joni.) I told my mom that Jaylen and Stephanie were never really my friends.

"You need to let people in, Imogene," she said.

"I try," I promised. "I really, really do."

She said that if I wasn't going to make an effort with my friends, then I should at least make an effort with my younger sister.

Joni has lavender-tinted hair and a tiny silver nose ring that she pierced herself with a safety pin and that my dad hates. Her body is soft and shapely, her breasts full in a way mine never will be. After I left for Vandenberg, she went off to Hunter College, studying to become a writer. She told me once that I was the least interesting person she'd ever met. She never got pimples.

The rock-climbing class was my mom's idea. The recreation center downtown had just installed a new rock-climbing wall, and she thought it would be a nice way for us to connect—that was her word, connect. So every Monday and Thursday I drove Joni and myself there in our shared Ford Saturn, grappling for a way to make her see me as someone other than her tedious older sister.

Our instructor's name was B.K., and he had shaggy red hair and the whitest teeth I'd ever seen. B.K. and Joni connected without issue—she nodded appreciatively at his Dirty Projectors T-shirt, he nicknamed her Grape because of her hair. Once, belaying the rope from below, I noticed B.K.'s eyes studying the curve of Joni's ass in her spandex shorts as she scaled the wall. B.K. had graduated from Buffalo State two years ahead of me. I didn't have the nerve until our second-to-last lesson to point out that he had sat in front of me in the comparative literature class I'd taken my sophomore year. "That's right," he said, nodding vaguely. He was too kind to admit that he didn't remember.

He was also kind enough to wait until the end of the summer to ask Joni out. He would take the train into the city to visit her on weekends, up until November when she met her current boyfriend Alex, a silent Canadian. Joni and I never spoke about him, or us, or that summer; we both knew how shameful it was to be jealous of one's younger sister.

I never made it to the top of the rock wall. The farthest I'd ever made it was three-quarters of the way before I felt I might pass out and begged B.K. to please, please let me down. I was cautious, anxious—being so far off the ground was unnatural to me. By the end of the summer, I wished—as I had many times before—that I could be more like Joni. She never seemed afraid to take risks. She never seemed afraid to fall.

— — —

Even though I'd done nothing wrong with Kip, I still spent the next few days jumpy, nervous. When I walked into the bathroom one morning to find Meggy brushing her teeth, I screamed. "What are you on?" she asked, spitting toothpaste into the sink. Around campus, I feared running into him—Kip—but still looked for him everywhere. I told myself it was precautionary; I couldn't admit to myself that I was dying to see him again.

ReeAnn remarked that it seemed as though we were missing glasses. I stole one from the dining hall, where there were identical glasses, wrapping it in a dinner napkin and carrying it home in my purse to replace in secret later.

It was the week of the college fair at Vandenberg, where the third years would attempt to charm (or, depending on the wealth and legacy of the student, be wooed by) a representative from an Ivy League or a Might-As-Well-Be-Ivy-League institution, thus ensuring themselves a spot at their choice school before applications were even rolled out the following year. It took place in the gymnasium, the bleachers pushed back and the racks of balls rolled away to make room for the many tables set up around the room. Harvard, Yale, Columbia, Dartmouth, Williams, Amherst—I ticked off the banners strung from each table in my head, like A-list celebrities on the red carpet. Babs appreciatively pointed out the stand for Rice University, her alma mater, and Chapin went over to talk to the representative from Princeton, who was a friend of her father's. Looking around, I realized I was the only apprentice whose college wasn't represented. Where's the Buffalo State table? I thought of joking, but I suspected that this would elicit more pity than laughter. Self-deprecation, my standby, wasn't as well received there as it was pre-Vandenberg.

ReeAnn and I were instructed to stand by the main entrance to hand out flyers to students as they entered. Each of the colleges represented was listed on the page, along with its respective alumni or faculty representative—Vanderbilt University, Jonathan English, Methodist clergyman; Northwestern University, Johanna Griffin (Ph.D.), history professor and graduate school dean; Cornell University, Michael Chen (Rhodes Scholar), former U.S. Commissioner of Education.

"Doesn't this make you miss applying for college?" asked ReeAnn.

I replied with a noncommittal nod.

At ten, the boys swarmed the room in a sea of suits. Hair was slicked back, loafers were freshly shined, and every hand grasped a folder with twenty copies of updated résumés. I could only imagine the credentials these boys boasted—a summer volunteering at a Mongolian orphanage, a student internship with Ernst & Young, a prize-winning essay on the Objectivist philosophy in Ayn Rand's *Atlas Shrugged*. A few of the boys looked nervous—one standing near the door flipped through a stack of flash cards, which I read over his shoulder: "Speak slowly and clearly," said one. "Make eye contact and shake with a firm grip," said the next—but most appeared quietly confident, imperturbable. They'd been primed for this moment their whole lives. They couldn't possibly fail.

I was glad to be by the door, away from the action. The lights in the gym were too bright, like spotlights, and my skin felt damp and shiny under their glare. The exposure made me feel sick. I wondered idly where Kip would apply before I remembered that he was a Vandenberg senior, that his decision had probably been made months ago. I felt myself looking for him despite knowing he wasn't there. At one point, I could have sworn I felt Chapin eyeing me from her station at the refreshment table, but when I looked towards her, she was busy pouring Dean Harvey a cup of coffee.

I spotted Clarence Howell over by the table for Johns Hopkins. He wore a wrinkled gray suit jacket, cuffed at the wrists so it didn't hang past his hands—his father's, I figured. His face was tomato red as he spoke to the rep, and he seemed to be addressing the woman's shoes. I felt culpable just watching; he felt like my responsibility somehow. I should have prepared him better. I imagined returning to the woman later, after Clarence left, maybe telling her about his being on the lacrosse team, his art skills, how kind he was, but I knew none of that would make a difference. The injustice felt glaring; none of it mattered. Nothing he or I did mattered.

I don't know why I ever thought it was my responsibility to take care of Clarence Howell. We were too much alike, him and me— poor and unsure and ill-equipped to be here. I didn't have anything of use to offer.

ReeAnn watched the boys with a mother's pride. "I'm excited for these boys. They all have such amazing futures ahead of them. Aren't you excited for them?"

"Yeah." Christopher Jordan had entered my line of vision at the UPenn table, grinning assuredly and shaking the hand of the man standing at the table—the same hand, I couldn't help but think, he'd probably used to beat the monkey the night before. "Yeah, I am."

— — —

I left the fair early, feigning cramps, and when I saw Kip sitting once again on my doorstep, it felt like a product of my will, as though I'd been thinking of him so often that I'd drawn him to my door. His chin was in his hands and his backpack at his feet, as though a parent had forgotten to pick him up after school.

"What are you doing here?"

He stood. "Waiting for you."

"Why? How did you know I'd even come home? And what if—?" I stopped myself; he wasn't listening, was too busy unzipping his backpack. He didn't plan ahead, I reminded myself; he didn't need to take precautions.

"I stole a new glass for you, but . . ." He held out his open backpack, sheepish; I didn't need to look to know it had broken. "Whoopsie."

Whoopsie. I tried to fight my smile. I wanted to tell him I'd wrapped my stolen glass in a stolen napkin, but I knew better than to admit this indiscretion to a student. "I came home because I'm not feeling well. Everyone else will be home soon."

He blinked at me, as though wondering what any of this had to do with him. Finally he asked, "What hurts?"

I didn't understand the question until he stepped forward and put his hand on my forehead. His hand was cool, strangely dry.

"Your head?" His hand moved to my stomach, and my body went rigid. "How about here?"

"Cramps," I almost whispered.

His hand moved south, right above my pelvic bone. "Here?"

Everyone would be home soon. My head felt thick with panic, my groin fluttering madly beneath his unmoving hand.

"Can I come inside?" he asked, just like last time.

"Okay." It came out a squeak. He retracted his hand, and I reminded myself to breathe. I wiped my hands on my jeans, fiddled with a button on my shirt. I said it again, steadier. "Okay."

He let himself inside. He moved right past the kitchen, right for the stairs. I opened my mouth to protest, to forbid him, but instead I followed. I was letting him do this because the other apprentices might return soon, and he couldn't be seen in the kitchen, I decided. I was letting him do this because it would be rude not to let him stay, just for a little bit.

Upstairs, Kip walked a slow circle around my room, scanning the titles in my bookshelf, glancing furtively at the papers on my desk, touching the small ballerina figurine on my bureau from my recently deceased Great Aunt Betty, who didn't know me well enough to not give me a ballerina figurine. I watched him nervously, ready to defend or explain anything that might be construed as weird. "Neat," he said.

"Thank you." I wasn't sure whether he meant in the sense of coolness or cleanliness. I stood watching him, unsure of myself in my own bedroom. Having him there was like seeing a teacher in the grocery store—no, like a celebrity step out of the TV screen.

"This isn't what I expected." He set the figurine down and looked at me.

"My room?"

"Yeah."

"What had you expected?" The flirtation was back; it was unimaginable that he had thought anything of me.

"I don't know. It's just . . . plain."

"Oh."

"Not in a bad way," Kip said quickly, sensing my disappointment. He was still across the room; we faced off like sparring partners. "It just doesn't seem like you."

I had no idea what a room that seemed like me would look like. I didn't have a favorite movie or band, nothing I felt compelled to display on a poster. There was no one color I loved; the purple-and-pink-striped reversible bedspread my mom had purchased for me because it was on sale, the plain white walls were as bare as they had been when I moved in. I didn't have photos. My bedroom, just like my childhood bedroom, was nothing like my sister Joni's: twinkle lights strung from the ceiling, records hung on the wall, every inch of blank space colored with the essence of Joni.

"Is this where she slept?" I asked it on a whim, playing at casual. Truth was I'd been thinking about her a lot: the other apprentice, the one Kip had so offhandedly mentioned the first night we spoke.

Kip didn't follow the way I thought he might. "Who?"

"The girl. The other apprentice you used to hang out with be . . ." I let the explanation trail off. It was too soon to say, *before me.*

"Oh. Kaya."

"I thought you couldn't remember her name."

He laughed. He was at my window, flicking the blinds open and closed. "Relax. She was whatever. I haven't talked to her in forever."

I wasn't sure how long forever was to him, or what whatever was to him. I wasn't sure why I felt suddenly angry, almost violently so, towards a girl who'd done nothing to me.

"Hey, Imogene?"

I felt a rush of warmth at the sound of my name from his mouth.

"There is a reason I'm here."

"Okay." I watched him shift from foot to foot, unnerved by his nervousness. The Kip I knew—in my mind, at least—was never nervous.

"Can I do something?" He snapped the blinds closed and released the cord, a decision.

I imagined my heart pounding madly out of my chest and through my T-shirt like a cartoon character's would. I knew exactly what would happen. I'd always known—from the moment I saw him on my front step, before that even—what would happen. "Sure."

He crossed the room towards me, licking his lips in a way that seemed more like a nervous tic than a threat. He reached out and put his hands on my hips, preparation for a slow dance. He leaned in and put his mouth to mine.

No relationships outside that of student and apprentice.

No, I thought. No, no, no. But still I allowed his wet tongue to slip between my lips, my mouth to open and let him in.

He was Joni's age. He was the age of my baby sister. But thinking back to the summer before—to her soft womanly curves and practiced flirtation—my sister was not that young anymore.

— — —

I walked in on her once, Joni, with B.K. the rock-climbing instructor. It was a week before we would leave for New York—me for Vandenberg and her for freshman year at Hunter—and I'd gone into her room without knocking, looking for a book of mine that I'd lent to her but I'm sure she never read. They were in bed, Joni's knees spread, B.K.'s orange shag of hair resting on her navel, slurps and grunts and other inhuman sounds that couldn't possibly belong to them (were these sounds borrowed? Imitated? Innate?) somehow brought to existence with their mouths. I'd never seen pornography, had never watched two people engaged in such erotic intimacy. I'd never once considered my sister—though she'd had boyfriends before—as sexual. I'd stared before silently shutting the door. I'd never be able to forget the sounds I heard my sister make, another damning secret for me to keep.

With Zeke Maloney, I was silent. With Zeke Maloney, I found myself looking at his roommate's posters on the wall or the crumbled pile of socks in his closet or the distant lights winking outside his window and sometimes forgetting there was a body on top of mine.

— — —

Kip and I had been kissing for what felt like hours but was probably minutes when the front door opened. I'd slipped into a strange floating place—a place where walls surged and shuddered and the floor shifted up and down, a place where it didn't seem odd to hold someone you didn't know and kiss them (Who was this person? When did he get there?) as long as it felt good—but the familiar sound jolted me into disquieting consciousness.

"Whoops!" I pulled away and stumbled backwards onto my bed. Kip sat down next to me, taking it as invitation, and reached for my face. I let him plant two more kisses on my lips before I pulled away again.

"What's up?" he asked.

"Someone's back."

We sat quietly, listening. A cabinet opened and closed in the kitchen. A plate clattered into the sink. Then I heard the click of heels approaching the stairs.

"Chapin," I whispered.

"Is that the really skinny one with the—" He gestured to the top of his head, making a circle with his hands, "—hair thing?"

I nodded. I felt pleased that we apprentices were known by the boys, identifiable like celebrities, as well as by the fact that Kip's description of Chapin was less than erotic. Perhaps Chapin was not as beautiful as I thought she was, or rather, as I thought others thought she was.

The heels clicked up the stairs. I turned to look at Kip to find that he was already looking at me. We stared at each other, our faces so close I could see every eyelash and every dark scruffy hair above his upper lip. I thought suddenly of the angry red blemish that had appeared on my chin the night before—the one that I'd carefully concealed with foundation and a makeup brush hours before that had no doubt become smudged and exposed with all the kissing—and put my fingers to my bottom lip. His hand rested on my hip, and he drummed his fingers slowly.

Chapin's footsteps reached the top of the stairs. "What should I do?" I asked, not sure why I thought Kip would have the answer but desperate enough to ask. I could think of nothing but that hand.

He grinned, amused. "What can you do?"

Her bedroom door opened and closed.

"Should you leave?" I was asking questions I knew the answer to, but didn't want to answer myself. I was stalling because Adam Kipling sat on my bed with his hand on my hip.

He raised a brow. "Should I?"

"Should you?" I giggled.

"But should I?"

"I don't know, should you?"

Music played through the wall. Kip pulled me back on the bed, back into the strange floating place, and we continued kissing, his tongue pushing once more into my mouth, his hands in my hair then down my arms then around my back. Kissing! I'd never noticed how odd it was, had never been so conscious of it before—the slurping–sucking exchange between two eager mouths wanting to feel something and say nothing.

A toilet flushed, and I shot up, reawakened. The sink turned on and off, and then Chapin padded past my room on the way back to her own. Kip tried to pull me back down and I flinched, surprising us both.

"What's—?"

My stomach churned. I imagined the doorknob turning, the other apprentices' horrified faces waiting on the other side. What was I doing? What the *fuck* was I doing? "You need to go."

"She can't hear us." Kip tugged lightly on my arm.

"No, Adam. You have to go."

He dropped my arm, his brows creased in confusion and—was that hurt?

I tried to smile, tried to soften the blow, but my stomach was twisting itself into queasy knots, the stomachache I'd felt coming on earlier finally materializing. "I'm sorry."

"It's cool." Kip had recovered, smiling easily back. Then, again, almost to himself, "It's cool."

"I'm sorry," I repeated. I felt fresh off a spinning ride at the fair, my head a pinwheel, my feet struggling to plant themselves in a straight line on the ground.

He reached out to touch my arm and then stopped, sticking the hand into his pocket instead. He got up and started towards the door.

"Just be sure to be—"

"Quiet. Yeah. I will be."

We smiled at each other, willing the discomfort to pass.

"So long," he said.

"So long."

He crept down the stairs and out the door, so stealthily I wouldn't have heard him if I hadn't been listening for it, and then I crawled under my sheets. Dizziness overwhelmed me. I lay there for only a few minutes before I had to sit up and reach for my trashcan, where I retched until I shook from the effort.

— — —

I didn't leave my bed for three days. I woke up later that evening dozy and disoriented, the room nearly dark and my head so thick and heavy I could barely lift it off my pillow. When I didn't come to dinner, ReeAnn brought me two slices of toast and a banana, which sat untouched on my nightstand until the toast crumbled and the banana browned. I emailed Dale and Coach Larry the next morning to let them know I wouldn't be in class or at practice, a task that exhausted me into another daylong slumber. I slept off and on for the rest of the day, getting up only once to pee and stumbling down the hall clutching the wall as though attacked by a spell of vertigo. Another time I woke, I conducted an online search for "Kaya apprentice Vandenberg" to no results, and I wondered, strangely, for the first time, whether Kaya ever even existed. The day slipped into the night, which slipped into the next day, and I slept the sleep of the dead, dreamless and undisturbed.

When I finally rose that third night, feeling drugged, feeling as though I'd stepped out of a time machine or a rocket ship, out of another world entirely, I was unsurprised yet still disappointed to find that the world had gone on without me. It was October. The girls were downstairs watching TV, laughing. The banana on my nightstand was soft and mushy and inedible.

I reached for my phone and checked my messages. Twelve new texts, all from the same familiar number. Without reading any, I deleted them one by one.

EIGHT

I KEPT UP WITH MY MORNING RUNS, EVEN AS THE WEATHER cooled and I was forced to bundle in extra layers before going out the door. The cold was coming on faster than any fall I could remember, quick and careless as disease, and I felt scared, though of what, I couldn't say. I'd wear spandex leggings and thick socks and a yellow wool hat with a pom-pom on top, not caring all that much if I looked ridiculous. This was my favorite time of day on campus, when it was nearly empty, and I could get away with wearing just a little makeup. On the running trail, I encountered only a few professors and the rare student who was up at this hour, and we would nod to each other in early-morning-runner solidarity. The Running Club, I dubbed this group in my head. I wondered if the other runners recognized me from day to day, their fellow member, the girl with the yellow pom-pom hat. I liked to think that they did.

I still looked out for Kip, even though my perception of him had shifted slightly, and I didn't think of him as an early-morning runner anymore. I just wanted to see him. More accurately, I wanted him to see me. A runner, an early bird. I wanted him to see different sides of me, to wonder what else I could be.

During my cool down, I always walked past Perkins Hall, the fourth-years' dorm. I looked up to the window on the end of the third floor, a window I'd arbitrarily decided was his (and, as I'd later learn, wasn't). I watched for a slit of light between the curtains, a flit of a shadow, a hint of life.

— — —

I met with Dale in his office for my midsemester evaluation that Friday. I thought it would just be the two of us until Ms. McNally-Barnes burst through the door a few minutes after me, combing through her hair with her fingers and apologizing for her tardiness. Dale and I had been discussing nice weather anticipated for this weekend, and I felt myself stiffen when she sat down beside me. It seemed now less like an evaluation and more like an intervention.

"So things seem to be going very well for you, Imogene," said Dale, bobbling his head. "I can see you gaining confidence in the classroom. The boys really seem to be responding to you, too."

I nodded, unsure whether "thank you" was in order.

"You need to work on projecting your voice at times, but the content of your lectures is always spot on. You're always prepared for lessons, even when you're under the weather." He paused and leaned forward. "How are you feeling, by the way? You seem to be feeling much better."

Ms. McNally-Barnes looked at me curiously.

Were they plotting together to catch me in my lie? Dale's eyes were warm and concerned, without misgiving. I took a deep breath, steadying myself. "Yes, much better." I paused and then added, "I think it was the flu. I hear it's been going around. It's that time of year, you know."

Dale and Ms. McNally-Barnes nodded in assent.

"But I'm feeling much better."

"Well, that's good to hear!" Dale beamed at Ms. McNally-Barnes and me from across the desk. "Other than that, it seems this semester is going quite well."

Ms. McNally-Barnes shifted in her seat and cleared her throat, a prelude to an interjection, and I froze, knowing already what she would say.

"That, and the incident with the field trip." She pursed her lips and smiled at me knowingly, a reprimand fit for a small child. Hot shame washed over me, itchy and unbearable. I hated her in that moment. Out of the corner of my eye I could see Dale raise his eyebrows curiously, but he didn't ask for explanation. I thanked him silently.

"But that's all in the past now." She patted my shoulder, and I tried not to flinch.

Dale nodded, hoping to edge the uncomfortable moment along.

"I think we're all set then." Ms. McNally-Barnes clasped her soft hands together, then pushed off from her thighs to stand. "Well done, Imogene."

Dale continued nodding, a bobble head on a dashboard.

But the meeting had soured. I left with a nagging feeling, a little bug bite in a hard-to-reach place that I kept forgetting the source of throughout the rest of the day but that kept returning in searing, insatiable bursts: I didn't belong there, and they were beginning to notice.

Worse still: Kip didn't belong in my head but he was there, and I couldn't make him leave. I wasn't sure I wanted to either.

— — —

As short-lived as my romance with Zeke Maloney was, I liked to think it was something more. Once, in conversation with ReeAnn, I'd said, "My ex was obsessed with those Marvel Comics movies." It didn't matter that this fact was based entirely upon the sole Fantastic Four poster that hung from his dorm-room wall. That word, "ex," slid out so readily that I'd nearly fooled myself.

I'd felt—imagined or not—like I knew his roommate, Todd, and the girl Zeke was rumored to have been hooking up with for a few weeks during freshman year, Brittany, and his ex-girlfriend from the crew team that I knew he had lost his virginity to. I felt like I knew them the same way I knew what sneakers Zeke always wore (blue and silver Nikes with white laces) and what his favorite TV show was (*The Sopranos*, according to his profile page) and the way I could pick his laugh out of a crowded dining hall, braying and hiccupy like a goat's.

After I saw Zeke make out with that other girl at the bar, after I knew for sure that it—whatever "it" was we had—was really over, I tried not to talk to my old roommate Darby about Zeke (I wished I could constantly). But when I did, I would try to sound offhand, casual: yeah, we used to hook up, but it was whatever. It's over now.

But Darby knew, and I knew, that it was not whatever. I'm not entirely sure I was ever attracted to Zeke Maloney, or if I even liked him. What I felt certain about—because we both listened to the Arctic Monkeys and talked about maybe seeing them in concert together, and because I'd listened to his snores and snuffles the one time I'd spent the night, and because he had taken my virginity—was that he was the first great love of my life.

After the second time that Zeke Maloney and I had sex, we took a shower together. He suggested it, and I hesitated; I was okay with my body—skinny, small-breasted, narrow-hipped, not exemplary but not unappealing—but the idea of being stark naked with Zeke in the pitiless light of the bathroom rather than under the bedroom's cover of darkness was terrifying. "It will be fun," he promised. I slipped out of bed and felt for two towels in my closet, which we wrapped around our bodies before making our way to the bathroom down the hall.

He let his towel drop first, and as he turned on the shower tap I studied his body in the light: his burly chest and slightly paunchy tummy, the muscular curve of his glutes, the dark hair sprouting from his toes, his still-erect penis—how gratifying it was, to know that erection was for me. I let my towel drop, too, and stepped into the hot spray behind him. Standing in the dirty ceramic tub where dozens of naked feet had stood before us, he pulled me into the clump of matted hair that was his chest. I closed my eyes as he ran his hands over my back, his fingertips soft and curious.

After the shower, we stood side-by-side before the bathroom mirror, still dripping and wrapped in our towels. My mascara ran in tracks down my face, and our hair was plastered to our faces in wet strands. It was one of the rare days when my skin was blemish-free, and I felt invulnerable. He smiled, and I began to laugh, and for the first time we felt like friends.

"I should take a picture of this," he said.

I knew he was joking, but I wish he had. I wanted some way to preserve that moment, to preserve us, so that it still felt real in the morning, when I woke up alone with my hair dried funny from sleeping on it wet. So that we felt like something I hadn't just made up in my head.

— — —

The weekend after my evaluation, I barely left my room. I read ahead in the textbooks and worked on lesson plans for Dale's Honors History class. I watched lacrosse videos online and devised new practice drills for the team. I graded the Honors History midterm papers and wrote a page of critiques on the back of each essay, my handwriting tiny and illegible and frantic. Though it was one of the last warm weekends of the fall, when ReeAnn knocked on my door on Saturday to ask if I wanted to join her and the others on a trip into town, I said I had too much work to do. An afternoon of lunch and shopping felt so idle, wasteful. Those were activities for someone who had accomplished something; I'd done nothing yet to deserve idle time.

I decided, too, to start taking my morning runs more seriously. I ordered an expensive new pair of running sneakers online. I created running music playlists. When I pumped down the trails, I pushed myself harder than I'd ever pushed myself before. I sweat. I ached. With each step, I imagined my muscles tightening, my soft limbs becoming hard and firm and strong. I imagined a crowd cheering me on, my fellow Running Club members watching in awe as I ran faster and farther each day. Sometimes I imagined I was running to something, sometimes from something; that something always changed.

I tried not to think about Kip. Or, rather, I actively tried to think about other things—lesson plans, making more of an effort with the other apprentices, the feel of my arms swinging and feet thumping on the path—so that there would be no room for thinking about Kip, so that he was squeezed out of my mind like a passenger from an overcrowded subway, forced to wait until later, until there might be space for him.

— — —

When I went downstairs to make a sandwich Sunday night, Chapin sat at the kitchen table, a rarity. She was painting her nails cotton candy blue, and as I hadn't emerged from my room or reapplied my makeup since my morning run, the sight of another person startled me.

"Imogene," she said without looking up. "Hi."

I thought about turning around and returning up the stairs, such was my aversion to interaction right then, but my hunger and my fear of looking strange kept me from leaving. I pulled a loaf of bread and a jar of Nutella from the cabinet.

"Nutella sandwich?" She scrunched her nose in a way that seemed to imply *weird* or maybe even *gross*.

I nodded. I hated when people noted my quirks ("Why are you always biting the insides of your cheeks?"), my purchases ("New shirt? What's the occasion?"), and especially my diet. Food choices felt so personal, so embarrassing. If a guy were to ever ask me to dinner, I'd have to whisper my order into the waiter's ear and eat my dinner in the kitchen. Better yet, we'd avoid eating, skipping the stomach-gurgling, breath-morphing, stuck-in-teeth grotesqueness of food altogether. I worked hard enough to keep my appearance in check without having to worry about my anxieties and ulterior motives and guilty pleasures becoming a public display.

I spread Nutella on both pieces of bread, stuck them together, and cut the sandwich diagonally down the middle. Chapin watched carefully. I fought the urge to shield the sandwich with my body.

"So are you going to tell me who was in your room the other day?"

My stomach clenched. Usually I licked the knife after I was through, but instead I stuck it in the sink to avoid grossing Chapin out further. I lingered at the sink, clenching the counter, unable to look at her. She'd heard us, I realized. She'd heard Kip and me. Just when I'd begun to relax, to feel safe again, the foolishness of what I'd done hit me in a sickening wave.

"Well?"

I could feel her eyes on me, and I turned. "It was no one."

She smirked. "Was it your secret admirer? El Músculo?"

Clarence. I tried to imagine kissing him; it felt like as much of a perversion as kissing the Power Ranger–obsessed neighbor kid I used to babysit. My little brother. "No. No, definitely not."

"But it was someone."

Her gaze undressed me, less sexual than inquisitorial, and it left me feeling both vulnerable and flattered. Chapin honestly wanted to know. My lips curved into a stupid grin against my will. Because even as I was reminded how careless I'd been, it occurred to me, too, that I wasn't sorry I'd done it.

"C'mon, Imogene. You can tell me."

And for a moment, I thought I could. We could keep this secret together, Chapin and I. That's why we share things, right? To share the burden. To legitimatize excitement. "There was someone in my room the other day," I started. If I told her, then maybe we could really become friends.

She raised a thick brow, urging me on.

But the lie took over before my desire to divulge could stop it. "It was Raj."

Chapin frowned. "Doesn't he have a girlfriend?"

I shrugged. Was I to plead ignorance? Act the role of the callous vixen? I hadn't planned this out. My regret was immediate and painful.

"Interesting." Her probing gaze went dead, suggesting she found the information anything but. She returned to her nails, and as I turned to leave she added, "You really shouldn't fuck with your skin so much. You're going to get scars."

I returned to my bedroom with my Nutella sandwich, but I no longer had an appetite. It unnerved me to know that I'd been watched so clearly—my worst fear confirmed—and that the things I thought I'd successfully concealed were actually right on the surface, exposed, like graying underpants hung from a clotheslines for all the world to see.

— — —

I'd been working on a lesson plan about the rise of the great civilizations in Egypt, Mesopotamia, China, and India, but after talking to Chapin I couldn't concentrate. I ripped my sandwich into bits and ate it piece by piece, no longer even hungry. The nagging feeling I'd had after my meeting with Dale and Ms. McNally-Barnes returned, only this time I recognized that feeling as disappointment. Was it because I desperately wanted to be able to tell Chapin—to tell anyone—this exciting new development in my life, the thrill of which fueled my morning runs and motivated my new work ethic and—though I'd never admit it—compelled me into vigilance all day so that I might get a glimpse, just one, of the boy who had chosen me?

Or was it because my phone had been silent for the past few days, with no word from the guy who had perhaps not chosen me after all?

I stood from my desk and overturned my wastebasket, where I'd deposited the shredded remains of the note with his number a few days before. Post-Its and index cards and balled-up tissues scattered the rug, and I dug through the pile with my hands. Anytime I found a ripped-up shred of paper I put it aside, but the task wasn't an easy one; my wastebasket was filled with dozens of ripped shreds, the result of a not-altogether-irrational fear of someone (Chapin, most likely) snooping through my trash—even though, up until a week ago, I'd never had anything important to hide. After attempting to piece together several different shreds, I finally admitted defeat and returned all the contents to the wastebasket. It was entirely up to Adam Kipling as to whether this . . . whatever it was would continue—but then again, hadn't it always been entirely up to him?

I remained on the floor for another few minutes before I finally grabbed my coat and headed for the door, pausing only for a moment at the bathroom mirror to make sure my makeup hadn't been sweated off or rubbed away since the last time I checked.

Chapin still sat at the kitchen table. "I'll be back," I told her.

"O-kay," she sang back, skeptical or uninterested or perhaps not even listening.

— — —

It was too cold for Kip and his friends to spend their nights outside between the trees anymore, but I looked there anyway. I thought about the first night we spoke, his infectious smile, the feel of my smaller hand in his larger one.

I went inside Perkins Hall and knocked on the first door to the left, which I knew from ReeAnn was Raj's.

He answered the door shirtless, wearing only a pair of slouchy gray sweatpants. I stared at the dark tuft of hair that led from his belly button to down under the elastic waistband of his pants, feeling as though I'd walked in on him naked. He stared at me. "Imogene. What are you doing here?"

I forced my eyes away from his navel and up to his face. "Hi. Sorry. It's late." The initiative that led me to Raj's door was now decomposing, silly seeming. Like sobering up, all that was left was embarrassment, heavy and pungent as a wet towel.

Raj scratched his head. "Are you on rounds duty?"

"No, I . . ." I hesitated, biting the insides of my cheeks. "Do you have a list of all the residents in the hall and their room numbers?"

"Yeah, yeah I should have one somewhere. Why?"

"One of my students. I need to give him something."

"Don't you teach first years?"

I clasped my hands together to keep them from visibly shaking. "I mean, one of my lacrosse students. From the lacrosse team."

He continued to stare. "You can't email it to him? Or give it to him at practice tomorrow?"

I shook my head. "He really needs it tonight, I think."

"I don't know, Imogene. I don't think this is a good idea."

He reminded me then of my high school guidance counselor, looking disapprovingly over my list of prospective colleges. Was there anything quite as demoralizing as having one's dreams dashed by a trusted consultant? Perhaps this is why it was better not to share things at all; we expect others to support us, to reinforce us, to tell us we are deserving and good and right, when really we're just giving others the power to expose our rose-tinted fantasies to the harsh light of reality. I opened my mouth to apologize or excuse myself, but instead I squeaked out a single word: "Please."

Raj stared at me searchingly for a moment longer and then sighed. "Okay. Just . . . be quick, alright?"

I nodded, and I waited in the doorway as he retrieved the list from his desk drawer. I scanned it quickly and handed it back to him.

"Got it?"

I nodded. "Thanks."

As soon as he closed his door, I turned to the stairwell.

— — —

This is what I'd imagined: he'd be alone, working on a paper at his desk, when I knocked. He'd answer the door and smile, unsurprised by my appearance. He'd take my hand and pull me in, right over to his bed, where our mouths would meet and his body would wrap around mine and I'd know for certain that the Sunday before was more than just an already fleeting memory.

What I didn't imagine was that his redheaded friend Skeat would answer the door instead. He only opened it a crack, poking his pink face out. "Hey?" he said, more question than greeting.

"Who is it?" I heard Kip ask behind the mostly-closed door.

Skeat ignored him, his eyes still on me. Finally recognition slid over his face. "You're that girl."

"I—"

The door opened fully, revealing Kip with his hand on the knob and his friend Park sitting on the bed behind him. The three of them stared at me.

"Is the music too loud?" Skeat finally asked.

"What?" It was only then that I noticed the tiny hum of classic rock coming from a set of speakers on Kip's desk. "Oh, no. It's fine." I tried to meet Kip's eyes, but he looked away. He hadn't told his friends about me. I was that girl, as in that girl who spied on them weeks ago, not Kip's girl. I felt a strange mix of relief and disappointment. Mostly disappointment, it took me a minute to decide.

Skeat tapped his fingers on the door. "So . . ."

Kip's eyes were still focused on the floor.

"I think I have the wrong room," I said. I stepped back and looked up at the number beside the door. "Yeah, wrong room. Sorry."

I hurried away before Skeat had even closed the door, but didn't get far enough away not to hear him mutter, "Fucking weird."

— — —

It was over. It was nothing. I rammed my hands deep in my pockets and quickened my pace, distancing myself from that room, from that humiliation, from that person. I was a conquest too embarrassing to even tell his friends about. The cold night air snapped at my face when I pushed open the door, and I let out an involuntary gasp. I would not cry. I was a teacher, for Christ's sake, an adult. I was too old to still believe that people wouldn't disappoint me.

My phone buzzed in my pocket, and I quickly retrieved it, my hand having already been curled around it in the pathetic hope that such a thing would happen. The blue square of my phone's screen lit up the dark.

Give me 5.

I stared at it, uncomprehending, before shoving the phone back in my pocket. How powerful it felt to ignore him, even while my head flooded with dizzying warmth, rendering me wobble-kneed and disoriented as a drunk.

The phone buzzed again. Wait for me.

I slowed my pace, tried to breathe. I was caught in the undertow, simultaneously pulled back and pushed forward, unsure what was up or down, what was the surface and what was further darkness. I hated my excitement.

I had nearly reached the Hovel when I heard the heavy footsteps behind me. He was running. His loafers galloped and crunched through the fallen leaves, and when I turned, I saw him, hair flying off his forehead, cheeks red, tie loose and flapping over his shoulder like a scarf. He slowed when he saw me, and by the time he approached me he was walking, barely panting, as though he'd ambled the whole way over.

"Hello," he said, as casual as his walk.

"Hi," I said, matching his coolness.

He took my hand and pulled me through the back door and together, in unspoken agreement, we flew up the stairs to my bedroom.

NINE

KIP'S HANDS WERE COLD WHEN HE SLID THEM UNDERNEATH MY sweater. His hands explored my stomach and squeezed my hips and massaged the tiny indentations in my lower back, like I was clay beneath him. Anytime his face pulled away, I pushed mine forward, insistent, my mouth drawing his back in. I kissed him until my eyes crossed beneath closed lids. I kissed him until the pressure of his body on mine seemed to push me through the sheets and the mattress onto the floor and further still. I kissed him until I felt weary and sad and almost thankful to be done so that I could start reimaging it all in privacy. Chapin wasn't home, had deserted her spot at the kitchen table and left her bedroom closed and dark before we returned, but I don't think I would have cared if she weren't. I wanted her to hear, I think. I wanted her to listen, as I had listened to her, for her to know that she wasn't the only one who could coax a boy into her bedroom.

"You really like kissing," he noted.

"Yes," I said, an apology.

He lifted the hem of my sweater and stuck his head beneath. I jumped in surprise.

"Adam?"

His breath was hot on my chest and the rough hair on his chin tickled my skin. I felt the soft poke of his nose in my armpit, first snuffling and then inhaling deeply.

"What are you doing?" I laughed, too perplexed to even be embarrassed about the proximity of his face to my underarm. He snuffled with a dog's insistence, his head bulging from underneath the cotton fabric like an alien baby. I didn't care that the sweater would be ruined.

He finally emerged, face flushed and grinning. "Pheromones," he said.

"What?"

"It's like an animal attraction."

"I know that, but—"

Kip rolled off of me and propped his head on his hand, stretched out like a centerfold. He could feel comfortable in a soup kitchen, on a red carpet, naked under a spotlight, the kind of comfortable that made me wonder if I had ever felt comfortable before. I wanted to crawl inside his skin like he had crawled under my sweater, just to see what that kind of ease felt like.

"You know you're into a girl if you're into the smell of her pits."

His comfortableness, as always, was infectious. He emboldened me. "Well?"

"Well what?"

"Well, are you into mine?"

He laughed, his mouth a glorious chasm. "I'm into you," he said.

"You didn't text me all week." I don't know who spoke those words, whiny and shameless, but it couldn't have been me.

He stared at me. "Yeah . . . ?"

"Why not?"

He blinked. "You didn't text me."

I hadn't realized I could. I was his choice; it had never occurred to me that he could be mine. I tried on flirtation. "Is that permission?"

Kip furrowed his brow. I appeared to be speaking in tongues, my words incomprehensible once they left my mouth. Were we having the same conversation? Had he not learned his lines from the movie I had cast us in—*The Illicit Affair,* starring Imogene Abney and Adam Kipling? Or was it me who was reading from the wrong script? "You don't need my permission to do anything," he said.

Then he took me by the wrist and guided me towards the pitched tent in his pants, and he let me feel for myself how into me he was.

— — —

I went on a date over the summer before Vandenberg, the first date I'd ever been on, really. His name was Robert. He was a teller at Lockport Federal Credit Union and had graduated from Rochester two years before I graduated from Buffalo State. He asked me to lunch, and I said yes because it didn't occur to me to say no.

I can't remember what we talked about. I can't remember where we ate, or what we ate, or what he looked like. When I returned home and my mom asked me if the date had gone well, I said I didn't know.

What I remember was looking at the people around me. I remember thinking, I am on a date, and they all know it. The waitress, the maître d', the woman at the coat check. How thrilling it was to be a girl sitting across the table from a guy, a part of a pair, a person whom someone else had chosen to spend a meal with.

Most thrilling of all: I could add him to my list. Jared Hoffman from high school, Paul the junior from Darby's brother's party, Jonah Davis from Communicating Nonverbal Messages, Zeke Maloney from down the hall, Robert from the bank. Guys who had passed through my life, however fleetingly, but for a few months or an afternoon had chosen me. Had been mine.

And now there was Adam Kipling, from Vandenberg School for Boys.

— — —

The time that passed after that first real hookup with Adam Kipling was just that: passing time. I stepped out of the shower the next day unsure if I'd washed my hair or even my body. Food passed between my lips perfunctorily, tastelessly. Hours passed as I sat in study hall or on the side of the lacrosse field or at my desk, unmoving, maybe even unblinking, and thinking of nothing but him and the next time I would be with him. I replayed our interactions. I conjured his face. I felt myself under my blankets at night, imagining my hands were his. It was the fluttery insatiability of a new relationship—yes, relationship, I had finally decided, that is what this was. It was the exhilaration of learning someone new.

Already, less than twenty-four hours since Kip had crept down the stairs and out the back door of the Hovel after finally leaving my bed, none of it felt real, like sand slipping between my fingers. I needed to see him during the day, I decided—walking around campus, flesh and blood and dark curls of hair—to know this wasn't all a figment of my imagination. I needed to see him upright and animated, a body moving through space rather than the dark, amorphous warmth that lay itself on me and put its mouth to mine. I needed him to see me and to smile and say, *Hey, Imogene,* to acknowledge me before day turned to night and we transformed into different people. I looked for him and saw him everywhere and nowhere.

Dale noticed my distraction, and he pulled me aside Monday after class.

"Is everything alright, Imogene?"

And I assured him that it was, that everything was more than alright, that things had never felt so right.

"Just be sure to remember that midterms are coming up."

And I nodded and smiled, the reproach only stinging slightly, the strains and anxieties of everyday life as easy to shake as water droplets.

I finally searched for Kip's profile page. He had been tagged in 2,056 photos. I looked at every single one.

— — —

After lacrosse practice on Tuesday (where I'd been so distracted I'd tripped over a spare stick and blanked on Clarence's name when I tried to call him out on a missed pass), I had just returned to my room when Chapin appeared at the door. She wore a silver lamé jumper under a cropped leather jacket and hoop earrings big enough to stick my hand through. "Drinks," she said.

"Sorry?"

"We're getting drinks." Chapin made a beeline for my closet and flipped through the hangers.

"But—" After another day of perpetual inattention, of not knowing whether I'd washed my hair or eaten, or where exactly I was going or supposed to be, of thinking of Kip everywhere and seeing him nowhere, I'd finally decided that I would text Kip first. I would say, *Come over,* nothing more. I'd get to feel his arms and his chest and the certainty, for another night, that he was real, that he was mine. I was even thinking I might be ready for him to slip beneath my waistband, where two nights before his eager fingers had been hinting. The plan was made, fizzy bubbles of anticipation rising in my belly at the thought of it. I couldn't back out now.

"You don't have anything to wear." Chapin turned to face me, hands on hips.

"The thing is . . ." My face was still damp from practice, and the thought of doing my makeup all over again was exhausting. "I actually don't think I can go."

"You can wear something of mine." Chapin bulldozed through my words, relentless. She smiled with closed lips; I had no choice. I wondered if it would be possible to keep that day's makeup and dab off the perspiration, to salvage the work I'd already done once that day.

"Might want to wash your face, too," Chapin called over her shoulder as she padded down the hall to her closet. "You look sweaty."

— — —

An hour later, Chapin and I were flying through the dark towards New York City, my body squeezed into Chapin's too-tight bandage dress and my own denim jacket, which I'd worn much to Chapin's chagrin. She had brought along a mixed drink for the ride and already I could feel its sedative effects. My mind felt cool and viscous, a wiggly bowl of Jell-O. I turned and studied Chapin's profile, the changing scenery streaking behind her in a blur. Her eyes were closed and her lips were curled, as though she was thinking of something funny and didn't plan on sharing. I was glad to be with her then, away from Vandenberg, away from the hot confines of my room and my thoughts. Perhaps this would give me the clarity I needed. Or perhaps I just needed some alcohol to soften the lights and turn time to liquid. It really did scare me, how much I enjoyed the feeling of slipping into drunkenness, of slipping out of my head to float around in space. Sometimes I never wanted to return.

We went for drinks at a place Chapin knew; the neighborhood or the street or even the name of the restaurant I couldn't have said. We sat at the bar and she ordered us two bright pink drinks that came in cocktail glasses with an orange wedge perched on the edge. The music was loud and angry. Chapin drained half her drink, returned it to the bar, and then stared at me.

"What?" I pursed my lips together and ran my tongue over my teeth, searching for stray food.

She had the same amused half-smile from the train. "You're not fucking Raj."

It took me a moment to remember that "fucking" was also an action. "How—?"

"I asked him." She picked up her drink again, holding the stem of the glass between two skinny fingers.

"What?" My body felt cold and feverish at once. How would I ever explain this to him? "What did he say?"

"He just seemed confused. He said you guys barely even talked."

For some reason, this hurt more than the exposure of my lie.

She stared at me expectantly. "So?"

"So what?" I picked up my untouched drink and took a sip. It tasted like liquid Jolly Ranchers.

"So who are you really fucking?"

I closed my eyes and tipped the drink back into my mouth. I realized then that I'd known, the moment she appeared in my doorway, that this was where the night would lead. I'd known that she wanted to know, and that she'd eventually convince me to tell her, and I'd gone with her anyway. I wanted Chapin to know. Or, at least, I wanted Chapin to want to know. I had something she didn't: a secret, equal parts exhilarating and agonizing. But what would be more satisfying, to share or to deny?

I placed my drink on the bar, nearly empty. "Hmm," I said.

Her big eyes bulged. She was growing impatient. "Are you seriously not going to tell me?"

My head was filled with cotton. "I don't know."

Chapin waved over the bartender. Two more drinks appeared.

"You trying to liquor me up?" I joked. My tongue was suddenly too big for my mouth and words came out mangled.

She pouted and sipped her drink.

A thought occurred to me. "Why do you want to know so bad?"

Chapin considered this. "The same reason you want to tell me," she concluded. Her face softened. "I like you, Imogene. Seriously. I have fun with you. I want to be friends with you."

My chest thudded erratically. Chapin Dunn wanted to be friends with me! And I realized, with amazing clarity, that she was right—I did want to tell her. I wanted to romanticize every interaction in the retelling, to dissect each nuance. I wanted someone else to make sense of it all. I needed Chapin to make it real. "If I tell you . . ." I started cautiously. I spoke slowly. It felt important to hide the fact that I was drunk.

Chapin nodded solemnly. "I won't tell anyone."

"Do you promise?"

"Jesus, Imogene, yeah, I promise."

"Because he pursued me. You have to know that, that he came on to me and that's how it happened."

"What, is he a teacher?"

"No." I looked down at my lap, trying to hide my smile. Saying the words felt like taking a dive. "A student."

She blinked. "Oh my god." She laughed, amused, surprised, contemptuous. She put her hand to her mouth, saying everything, nothing. "Please tell me that he's at least—"

I nodded. "A fourth year. Yeah. He is."

"Name?"

"Kip. Adam Kipling." And with those words, there was no turning back. I tried my best to swallow my unease at her reaction. I clinked my drink against Chapin's without invitation, sloshing a little onto the hem on my borrowed dress, and drank until my head drifted up to the ceiling.

— — —

We didn't talk much on the ride home. We were lost in our own private thoughts. Her silence unnerved me. My head still felt waterlogged, but regret was creeping in. It would be better if we were talking. If we were talking, I wouldn't have to worry about what she was thinking.

My phone was in my hand. He hadn't texted. I felt self-righteous, for having been out, for not having been in my bedroom waiting to hear from him. He didn't know that, of course, but I still had that satisfaction.

Back on campus, Chapin headed towards the Hovel, and I told her I would see her later.

"What?" She looked suddenly like a little girl, her jumper shapeless on her slight frame. "Where are you going?"

"I'll be back later," I said. I intended for this to sound suggestive, but it sounded more like a question, expectant of approval. I waited for her to return a conspiring smile.

She frowned. "Okay." I felt myself deflate; I'd let down, and maybe even lost, the confidante I'd gained just an hour before. But that wouldn't stop me. I'm not even sure what could.

I was halfway to Perkins Hall before I knew that I'd decided to go there hours earlier. I'd planned the whole night ahead of time and neglected to fill myself in.

— — —

I remembered where Kip's dorm room was. I slipped off my heels at the front door of Perkins and slithered up the stairs, a performance of stealth. I put my ear to his door—silent. I knocked once, and then twice, and waited.

He opened the door, bleary-eyed and unsurprised. I wondered what time it was.

"Hi," he said.

"May I come in?" *Mother May I*. I cringed at my misstep, tried to hold onto the liquored confidence that had led me there.

He opened the door wider and made a grand sweeping gesture. I padded inside and deposited my heels on the floor. Then I took in his room.

The walls were sparse and orderly—a banner from a Hingham sailing regatta, framed album covers (The Who, Red Hot Chili Peppers, The Rolling Stones), a poster of the London Eye. His desk was empty save for an open laptop and speakers. Three pairs of shoes (loafers, sneakers, boat shoes) made a neat row along the edge of his bed. A soccer ball sat in his closet, which was free from clutter. I wasn't sure exactly what I had expected—baseball cards? Race car memorabilia? Ashtrays and pipes? Even his few pairs of jeans, all dark wash and expensive-looking, hung from hangers among the khakis and suit pants in his closet. It looked like a picture from a catalogue. It looked uninhabited.

"Welcome." He kissed me hard on the mouth and tangoed me backwards onto his bed, a move that felt at once effortless and choreographed. I nearly stumbled, but he held me steady. He propped me up against his pillows and set about clearing the books from his bed.

"This isn't what I expected." It was an echo of an earlier conversation, the same words he'd said to me when he'd first seen my bedroom. I smiled at him hopefully, but he didn't seem to recognize his own words. After a pause I added, "You hang up your jeans."

He leaned over me to switch off the lamp on his bedside table. "Don't you?"

We kissed frantically, desperately, talking through each other in senseless circles between kisses.

"Are your walls thin?"

"I like your dress."

"Like, can you ever hear the people next door?"

"You never wear anything like this."

"Did I wake you up? Were you sleeping?"

"How do you take it off?"

Then I was naked, and so was he. I don't remember it happening; I just suddenly realized that all my skin touched all of his. He realized the same moment I did, as though we were both waking from a dream.

"You're naked."

"Yeah."

"I like it."

He nosed his way into my underarm and inhaled deeply. He planted a line of tiny soft kisses, starting at the crown of my head and working his way down to my chin. He paused, his chin on my chest, and looked up at me like a question. I hoped he couldn't see up my nose.

"Do you . . ." Kip turned his face left, then right, and planted a kiss on each of my nipples. It tickled, and I laughed.

"Do I . . . ?"

He batted at my left breast with his hand, bouncing it up and down, his eyes still on me. "You know," he said.

"Do you want to?"

"Only if you do."

"Have you . . . ?"

"A few girls. You?"

"One guy. A couple times." I paused. I didn't want to ask it, but the question pressed against my lips, threatening to spew out like vomit. "Did you with Kaya?"

He drew back, and my body stiffened with horror. I'd ruined the moment. I'd ruined everything. "What is your obsession with Kaya?"

"I just . . ." I couldn't stop thinking about her, the ethereal blond creature I'd designed in my mind, the apprentice who'd invited Kip into her bedroom before me. Who was she? What was she after? Kip would have been a second year at the time. That relationship—whatever relationship they had—felt far removed from my own relationship with Kip, and yet it plagued me all the same. There was something wrong with it. *Fucked up.* Nothing felt wrong about what I was doing, but still I somehow needed Kip's reassurance that it was okay, that what we were doing was okay. "Never mind." I peeked up at him, channeling coquette. "I want to be with you."

"Okay. So . . ." His hand was off my breast. A finger slipped inside of me. We smiled goofy, embarrassed smiles. Yes, he had done this before.

"Yeah, okay."

"Cool."

He reached into the top drawer in his bedside table. In the pale moonlight of the window, his body looked gaunt, fragile. It occurred to me suddenly that he might be skinnier than me. I reached up and petted the furry pelt of his chest.

"Don't hate on the chest hair."

"I like chest hair."

He pulled aside the sheets, and got onto his knees, his sheathed hard-on poised to take over the world. His smile cut through the dark. I'm going to have sex with Adam Kipling, I thought suddenly, lucidly.

"Are you ready?" he said.

"I am," I said.

TEN

MY OLD HOOKUP ZEKE MALONEY SPENT THE SUMMER AFTER graduation bartending in Rockaway Beach. I know this not because he told me, but because I saw pictures online. Natalie Dawkins, who I eventually concluded to be his new girlfriend, tagged several photos of him throughout the summer—pretending to drink a giant bottle of whiskey behind the bar, lazing on a towel at the beach. Natalie Dawkins had thick bangs and a crooked nose. I decided that I hated her.

Zeke and I hadn't spoken since the previous March, but still that summer I thought about him. I replayed our interactions. I imagined new ones. I planned out what I would say if I were to ever see him again.

Rockaway Beach wasn't far. I could have driven there to see him if I wanted to. I could have shown up at Bungalow (yet another fact of his life gleaned from his profile rather than him) while he was working. I didn't want a relationship with him, I was pretty certain of that, but what I did want was acknowledgment that what had transpired between us mattered.

You were with me, I would say. You were inside of me. You won't forget that, will you? You can't forget that. You can't forget me.

I never did go to see him, of course. Those kinds of things only happen in movies.

— — —

Kip lay on top of me for a while after he finished, his heart knocking frantically against my chest, breathing as though he'd just run a race. My legs were propped up on either side of his skinny body, bent into triangles. I wished to wind them around his back like ropes, hold him tight against me until his heart slowed and even after that. My arms lay useless at my sides. I wasn't sure yet of the rules; could I still touch him after it was over? And how was I supposed to touch him?

He put his mouth to my neck. "Was that good?" he asked, speaking into my skin.

"Yeah." Static buzzed in my ears. I hadn't known it was possible to feel so good.

"You didn't make any noise." His face was still buried in my neck, his words muffled.

"Sorry?"

He lifted his head. His hair stuck up in all directions; sex hair, I thought with a thrill. "I said, you didn't make noise."

"Should I have?"

He furrowed his thick brows and regarded at me with unfamiliar intensity. "You should if you want to." He paused, reconsidered. "I should make you feel like you need to. Like, feel so good that you can't help but to."

He delivered this so seriously, with intensity I hadn't even known he possessed—intensity I hadn't thought him capable of—that laughing felt wrong, even profane. "Oh," I said.

"Has anyone ever made you come, Imogene?"

"I don't know," I said.

He grinned, and I realized, with a flush of embarrassment, that this of course meant that no one ever had. "You're a sweetheart," he said.

He nestled his face back into my neck. His breathing slowed; after a few minutes, I wondered if he had fallen asleep. His breath tickled my ear. He was a giant sack, with pointy ribs and coils of scratchy black fur on his chest. I thought again of wrapping my arms around his back, prone and useless as I was beneath him, but I was too afraid to wake him. If he woke, it would end.

But it had to end. We couldn't wake like this, our sticky sweat-dried bodies stuck together like two slabs of deli meat, my toxic mouth in such close proximity to his nose, my makeup a beige smear on his pillow and spotty skin exposed. We couldn't wake like this, because that would mean we had spent the night together, rather than simply joining our bodies in the wee hours of the morning when the line between dream world and reality is so fuzzy that nothing you do really counts anyway. Not to mention I was also developing an urgent need to pee.

It didn't occur to me at the time the most pressing reason why I could not stay—that I'd be caught.

"Adam," I whispered to the back of his sleeping head. And, when he didn't answer, louder: "Adam!"

He snorted back into consciousness. "Huh?"

"I have to go."

He shook his head, his scruff tickling my neck.

"No, Adam, I really should go."

He rolled silently off my body. I felt newly naked and cold and desperate to see his face, but it was turned towards his wall. I scooted to the edge of his bed and reached for my clothes. I'd slid one leg into my underwear when suddenly Kip clutched me from behind. He bit my earlobe.

"I'm going to make you come, Imogene," he said. Then, just as quickly, he turned back to the wall and slipped under his covers. By the time I'd dressed, he appeared to be fast asleep once again.

Me, I thought as I walked across the dead campus. He wanted to make me come. He wanted to make it good for me. *Me.*

— — —

I slept the whole next day, waking in brief dazed respites to the sound of the rain battering overhead. I could hear voices downstairs, their shouts and laughter mingling with my dreams.

"Your turn, Meggy."

"Hey, what about me?"

"Oops, sorry, Raj. Go for it."

Raj. I thought of his reaction to Chapin's question about our relationship, how he'd said we barely even talked. I actually couldn't remember the last time we'd spoken; I couldn't remember the last time I'd spoken to any of them. We were no longer a pack, grading our papers together, eating meals together. I ate alone in my bedroom. I slinked around the Hovel when everyone else was asleep. A few days before, I'd seen Babs a few paces ahead of me as I left Dale's classroom, and I'd actually stopped, crouching down to idly rifle through my book bag until enough distance stretched between Babs and me that I wouldn't be obligated to talk to her.

More accurately, they were still a pack; I just wasn't a part of it. Perhaps I knew they were the kind of girls who would invite me into their fold if only I made the effort, but it felt better to pretend that I'd done all I could, to bask in self-pity rather than to try.

My phone, tucked beside me in bed, was my silent companion. I willed his name to appear on my screen. Kip, Kip, Kip. *He's still sleeping,* I told myself. Then later, *He's studying.* And over and over I slipped back into sleep, revisiting the night I'd spent with Kip in my dreams.

When a crack of thunder pulled me from sleep at a little past one in the morning and I reached over automatically to check my phone, I finally had a message waiting for me: Come over. It had been sent two minutes before; it was fate. Without a moment of hesitation, I slipped a bra under my T-shirt, pulled on a pair of yoga pants from the floor, and tiptoed to the bathroom to brush my teeth. My eyes were bright, my cheeks flushed, and the few spots I'd had the day before had faded, almost disappeared. I'd never woken from sleep looking this . . . was radiant the right word? Yes, radiant.

Then I sped across campus—dodging puddles, avoiding light, the rain drenching me in heavy, cold sheets—through the door of Perkins and up the stairs. Before I'd even fully awoken, I stood before Adam Kipling's door, hair stuck to my face in dripping clumps, my hands shaking—from nerves, from cold, from the thrill—but ready nevertheless.

"Come in," came his voice from within. I hadn't even knocked yet. I hadn't even texted him back to say I would come.

I opened the door. He lay naked on top of his sheets, hands laced behind his head, grinning.

"You're wet," he said.

I nodded. He had a knack for stating the obvious.

"Take off your clothes," he said.

He coolly watched me undress. His eyes followed me as I crossed the room towards him. He scooted over and patted the space next to him on the bed. And then, feeling as though only a few minutes had passed since our bodies were last stuck together, he pulled my face towards his and sucked me in.

— — —

The days that followed continued the same. The rain persisted, tireless and indifferent. The study period for midterms began that Monday, and the boys filled the library armed with books and notebooks, prepared to catch up on all that they had slept through throughout the semester in five days—though of course they would all still pass. Without any classes to teach or papers to grade, I slept away the days, thinking and dreaming of nothing but Kip, until I was summoned again to his room by night.

After we'd have sex—Bang? Fuck? Make love? I still wasn't quite sure what kind of sex it was we were having—I'd make a map of his body. I'd trace it with my fingers, catalog it in my mind—the irritated bumps under his jaw, the pink jagged scar on his left elbow, his dry bony knees. He was frank about his body, talking about it like it was a something hanging on the wall, open for discussion. "My nipples are different sizes," he said once. And, another time, "I have no butt. And it's hairy, too. Look."

And I looked, though of course I had before. I loved his nearly nonexistent glutes, flat and sunken in like deflated balloons and covered, like the rest of his body, in thick dark hair. I loved his bumps, his scars, the bones jutting from his skinny frame. He was the most captivating combination: objectively good-looking, yet not so untouchably attractive that he couldn't be had. He wasn't a movie star or model, in an airbrushed stratosphere all his own and worshiped from below; he was there, walking among the rest of us, as attractive and desirable as he was real and flawed.

We didn't talk about my body like we did his; after having sex (Banging? Fucking? Making love?) I usually found a way to slip back beneath the sheets, to hug my arms around my chest, to find some way to cover up my nakedness. I didn't feel the way about my body as I did the skin of my face—wanting to hide it, willing eyes away from it—but it still didn't feel right to have it studied in the clinical way I took in his. It wasn't until Sunday night, the night before midterms would begin and after the sixth time we'd had sex (Banged? Fucked? Made love?) that he even acknowledged my body.

"You know, Imogene," he said, sitting up in his bed, legs spread and half-soft penis flopped between them as though it were the most natural thing in the world, "you have a really nice body."

"Do I?" I said.

He pulled me up onto my knees, propped me on his lap. He ran his hands down my sides and over my hips, looking at my body—

no, *leering* at my body—as though it was his own, as though he owned it. The thought excited me.

"Yes," he said, "you do."

"Thanks."

He laughed. "You're a sweetheart."

And then before I had to leave we did it again—whatever *it* was—and for the first time I felt it—the big It, the pulse, the spark—that compelled me to clamp my knees together and force from my throat a single helpless moan.

I was deep in sex—drugged, stunned. I'd never felt less like myself, and I couldn't get enough. But with each postcoital contemplation of Kip's bedroom ceiling, I knew I was getting deeper into something else. It would be ridiculous to call it love, but nothing else seemed to fit, except perhaps fear. Yes, I was afraid. I was deeply afraid.

— — —

I overslept the next day (despite sleeping all day, my overnight trysts had left me exhausted) and met up with the other apprentices in the dining hall unkempt and unshowered, with only time to paint over my blemishes with cover-up. I felt betrayed that none of them had woken me up, but then again, why should they have? I wasn't a part of them anymore. They didn't owe me anything.

I slopped oatmeal into a bowl and started towards their table. I couldn't decide where, strategically, would be the best place to sit: Raj I hadn't seen or spoken to since Chapin had exposed to him my cover story, and Chapin hadn't acknowledged me since I told her the truth. I suspected she was angry that I had gone to Kip's that night, that my desire to see him had superseded my desire for her consent. I chose a seat on the end, next to ReeAnn, who always seemed like a safe bet. I felt every head turn towards me. I stared down into my bowl. I hadn't done anything, I told myself. I had no reason for feeling guilty.

"Hey, stranger!" ReeAnn said. "Long time no see."

I forced a closed-mouth smile and swallowed a mouthful of oatmeal. "Yeah, I know," I said. "Hi."

She persisted. "Where have you been?"

Her face was open and friendly, her questions innocuous. Relax, I told myself. "I've been busy, just really busy." I nodded for emphasis. "Just trying to catch up on everything."

"I totally know what you mean. Grad apps are kicking my ass."

I kept nodding, even while my heart clenched. I'd forgotten about the impending Master's program deadlines. I'd forgotten that things were still expected of me.

"What programs are you applying to?"

"I'm, um, torn between a few. Just working on general stuff right now."

ReeAnn's enthusiasm was indefatigable. "Totally, totally."

"Are you guys talking about grad apps already?" Babs turned to us from ReeAnn's other side. I felt a little flicker of hope. "I was working on mine until three this morning. I can't even think about them again until I've had two cups of coffee." My hope was quickly extinguished.

Table conversation turned to Master's programs, with even Chapin looking up from her phone to join in. I concentrated on my oatmeal. The boys began to filter in, flipping through notecards and chattering nervously as they waited in line for bacon and eggs. Though Kip rarely made it to breakfast and my back was to the room, I felt the heat of the boys' presence—of his potential presence—regardless. I took deep breaths and scooped mouthful after mouthful of too-hot goop into my mouth, fighting off the creeping feeling of terror as talk of the future swelled past.

— — —

After breakfast, we left for our classrooms, where exams would be distributed and the boys would have two hours to go off and complete them on their own. When I'd first heard about the system at lacrosse practice one September afternoon, I had thought it strange that the boys would be allowed to take their exams without any sort of supervision. "Doesn't everyone just use their books?" I asked Clarence. He shook his head and said that would be cheating. "But I'm sure people do it anyway," I said. He shook his head and said that everyone signed a waiver saying that they, under no circumstances, would use reading materials or other resources. "But what about the internet? Or their friends?" He shook his head and said those counted as other resources. "But c'mon. Not everyone must take that seriously." Duggar overheard and answered for Clarence: "You don't get it, Squeak. No one cheats here. End of story."

In Dale's room, most of the boys already sat at their desks, spending a few last minutes with their notes, ready to dash once exams were distributed. Dale sprung towards the door as soon as I entered, so quickly I couldn't tell where he'd come from.

"Miss Abney," he said with his usual manic grin. Then, his voice hushed, "Where are the exams?"

I blinked at him, wondering if he had misplaced them. "Sorry?"

"The exams, the midterm exams." Dale ran his hand through his thin gray hair, his eyes popping out of his head, his manic grin seemingly stuck on his face. "Did you not see my email this morning? Or last night? Or all this week?"

My oatmeal churned sickeningly in my stomach. "Um . . ." Email. I'd forgotten about email. I'd forgotten that I had a job, that I had parents and a sister, little other than my name and what it felt like to have Adam Kipling on top of me.

"I asked you to get a draft to me by Friday." He tilted his head and stared at me, as though just realizing some horrible truth. "Apprentices always write the exams, Imogene. You knew that, right? You wrote it, didn't you?"

"Um." This had to be a nightmare. There's no way I could have forgotten something so essential.

"Imogene?"

"Um. It seems as though I . . . Um, the thing is . . ." My eyes were filling with tears. No, I couldn't. Nothing would be more disgraceful than crying in that moment.

Dale sighed. "You don't have it."

I shook my head.

"You didn't even do it."

I shook my head again, feeling a tear slip down my cheek.

Dale turned to the class who, I then realized, had already been watching us curiously. "Class," he said. "Take out your notebooks and write down the following questions. Okay? Number one."

I turned towards the board and swiped a hand under my eye while Dale continued with his questions. I couldn't look at them. Even though they were first years, I was sure they all knew—I had failed to do over the course of half a semester what Dale was now doing off the top of his head. Perhaps he had already prepared those questions, having expected me to fail. More likely, I'd just failed to complete what should have been a very easy task.

As the boys filed out of the room, Dale laid a hand on my shoulder, and the unexpectedness of his touch made me jump. "Imogene," he said, "what's going on?" I had expected anger, but his voice was soft. He was concerned; that was worse than anger.

"I'm sorry." The tears continued to slip from my eyes, out of my control now. "I'm really sorry."

He handed me the tissue box from his desk, and a sob burst from my chest. He hurried to the door to shut it before my crying could escape into the hallway. Then he pushed me gently towards the chair before his desk.

"Imogene," he said, sitting on top of the desk in front of me, "tell me what's going on with you."

I clutched the tissue box in my hands without taking one, trying to slow my breath. "I'm sorry. I just . . . have a lot going on right now."

He shook his head mournfully. I wondered what he thought that meant. Dying grandparents? Dying parents? Dead dog? This sympathy was unexpected, and it encouraged me.

"I'll be better next week, I promise. It's just been a . . . weird week."

"We've all been there," Dale said. He reached out to touch my shoulder again. He had to lean forward off of his desk to do this, and his touch felt strange. His hair hung over his face as he smiled at me. I tugged a tissue from the box and blew my nose to keep from looking at him.

"Um." I held the soiled tissue in my hand and peeked back up. "Are you going to tell Ms. McNally-Barnes about this?"

"Hmm." He furrowed his brow, a pantomime of thinking hard, the pressure of his hand on my shoulder becoming increasingly uncomfortable. "You know what? I should, but I'm not going to. Because shit happens, you know?"

I nodded. I felt dizzy from all that had happened in the last few minutes.

"Just know, Imogene." Dale's stare became intense, reminding me strangely of Kip's when he'd told me he wanted to make me come. "Just know you can always come to me if you need to talk. About anything."

"Okay," I said. I desperately wanted to throw away the tissue in my hand, as well as for him to release my shoulder.

"Okay." He smiled and returned to his perch on the desk, my shoulder finally free from his grasp. "Go get some rest. We'll talk later."

"Okay," I repeated. I handed him back his box of tissues and headed for the door. I looked back after I'd opened it to find he was watching me leave; I forced a smile and shut the door behind me.

– – –

I spent another full day in bed. I imagined that the mattress had begun to take the mold of my body, an Imogene-shaped well permanently printed in its foam. How did anyone ever get out of bed? I wondered. Forget our obligations, our jobs—why would we ever leave the comfort of this thing that knows our bodies so well? I knew I should check my email—who knew what other messages I could have in my inbox waiting for me?—and return that call to my mom that she had made three days before, but instead I drew my shades and burrowed deep under my blankets. I would deal with it all after I'd had some rest. That's what I needed, according to Dale—some rest.

After dozing off and on for a few hours, my phone buzzed. I was surprised to see it was Kip—what could he want from me in the middle of the day?

Studying sucks.

I stared at his message for a moment, puzzled, before replying. Isn't that what you were supposed to be doing all last week?

Probably. A minute later, I was a little preoccupied with other things, though.

I grinned. Looking for a study break?

I wish. If I don't get through this trig stuff I'm fucked for tomorrow.

I felt deflated. If he didn't want to have sex with me, then what did he want?

My phone buzzed again. I've been in the library since 7am. Bored as fuck. Hope your day is going better.

He just wanted to talk. He'd texted me, not because he wanted something from me, but because he'd been thinking of me. My day might actually have yours beat as far as shittiness goes.

Oh yeah? Tell me about it.

Under my nest of blankets, sinking ever deeper into my mattress, Kip and I continued to talk into the afternoon.

ELEVEN

MEGGY AND MAGGIE WOULD TURN 23 THAT WEDNESDAY AND SO, with repeated encouragement from ReeAnn, I joined her and the other apprentices out for a birthday dinner that Tuesday night. The Woods twins chose a Mexican restaurant in downtown Scarsdale, a loud, obtrusive place with bright sugary drinks and plastic tablecloths and complimentary bowls of chips and salsa on every table. Mariachi droned through the speakers, and my head ached.

Chapin wasn't present—not that her absence ever necessitated remark—but everyone else, even the usually sour Babs, was in high spirits. ReeAnn sat to my right, with Babs beside her, and Raj was sandwiched between the twins across the table. ReeAnn took out her phone for a picture, and Raj slung his arms around the Woods's skinny bodies, their three faces pressed tight together. "Dude, cilantro in your teeth," Babs said, pointing. Raj bared his teeth and leaned over the table. "Lick it out for me?" They all howled. ReeAnn turned to me still laughing, welcoming me to join in on the fun. I hated that I could tell she felt sorry for me.

Six goblets filled to the brim with Pepto-pink frozen margarita appeared. "Drink!" Maggie commanded. Their five heads bowed to meet their colorful straws, even Babs, who apparently no longer abstained from drinking. I followed suit, and the icy thickness shot a painful blast to my temples. When I raised my head again, everyone was smiling at me, though whether their smiles were friendly or wary, I couldn't decide. If they were willing to pretend I hadn't spent the past two weeks shut up in my bedroom, then I was, too.

Conversation floated between grad apps, midterm exam grading, and a drunken night the five of them had shared at a bar the weekend before. I sucked up my drink and did my best to play my role. "Yeah, just about done." "Yeah, totally a pain." "Yeah, too bad I missed out. I'll be there next time." I was working on my second drink when Raj materialized at my elbow, having dragged over a chair from an unoccupied table nearby.

"Rajy," Meggy pouted. "Where are you going?"

He pointed at me. "Going to catch up with Imogene for a sec."

"Okay," I said, realizing as I did that a response wasn't expected of me.

He turned to me. "Hello." He still had a bit of cilantro in his teeth; I caught a flash of green as he spoke. I gave a furtive look around the table to make sure nobody was still paying attention to this unexpected seat rearrangement. He noticed. "Don't worry, it's cool," he said.

"Okay." I tried to look cool.

"So." He leaned back in his seat. "What's up?"

A simple question that could spawn a million answers. "Not much."

He smiled past me for an unseen TV audience. These girls liked him, his being male a fun anomaly, and their attention made him cocky. I had a strange desire to see him taken down a peg, by cooler girls, or better yet by cooler guys, by anyone who could see right through the fabricated confidence his sole maleness among unhip girls allowed him. "Okay. Listen. Chapin told me what you told her, about us . . ." He lowered his voice and waggled his brows. ". . . you know. Hooking up."

"Okay." My margarita gurgled unhappily in my stomach. Okay was the only word that seemed safe anymore.

"I just . . . I have a girlfriend, you know?"

I nodded. Nodding was okay, too.

"And I thought it was weird, especially since we haven't hung out in a long time, you and me. Like, why would Imogene say that when we don't even hang out? And then I thought, well, maybe we should hang out more often."

Nod, nod, nod.

"I don't know. It's like, ever since she told me . . ." He smiled, suddenly sheepish. "I guess I've just been thinking. About you."

I stopped nodding.

"Not like that," he said quickly. "Just . . . thinking."

"Do we have a birthday in the house?" a voice sang from behind. We turned and watched as a group of waiters spilled out of the kitchen, one wielding a giant slice of chocolate cake and another a vihuela. Raj turned back to me as they started in on *Feliz Cumpelaños*.

"So let's hang out sometime soon."

"Okay." I was back to my standby response.

He flashed another smile and returned to his seat between the twins. I peered down into my drink and sucked it up until I could see the bottom of the glass.

— — —

Kip finished his exams that Thursday afternoon, and late on Thursday night, he invited me over. It was almost two in the morning, and I had just taken off my bra and slipped into bed, resigned at last to the fact that I wouldn't be hearing from him that night. When my phone vibrated with a message notification, I leapt from my covers. I was at his door a few minutes later, an emergency official reporting for duty.

He kissed me before he'd even fully opened the door. "Hi," he said. We smiled goofily at each other. We hadn't been together since the Sunday before.

After scooping me up and carrying me to his bed, he clawed at my clothes. I helped him off with my shirt and pants, eager to comply. Once I was naked, he knelt before me, rubbing my thighs. I resisted the urge to cover myself.

"Wow," he said. He squeezed my thighs tight. "Wow, wow, wow."

"Hey. You, too." I reached down and tugged at his shirt.

He stood, stumbling a bit, and unlatched his belt. His pants and boxers crumbled around his ankles. We both looked down at his penis, which hung flaccid between his pale legs. "Uh-oh." He flicked it with his finger and it swung, a useless pendulum. "Uh-oh, SpaghettiOs."

It was then that I realized he was wasted.

"You okay?"

Kip grinned guiltily at me, a kid with his hand caught in the cookie jar, and sat next to me on the bed. He buried his face between my breasts. "Help me, Teach. I'm fucked up."

Teach. I inhaled sharply, inadvertently. "Please don't call me that."

"What, Teach?" Kip's head lolled, his neck failing to hold it up. "Short for Teacher."

"I know. I don't like it."

"Teacher. Apprentice. Whatever the fuck you are."

I dug my nails into my palms. I had thought it unspoken that we wouldn't address my title. It felt like a taunt coming from his mouth then, or a threat. He's drunk, I reminded myself. He doesn't know what he's saying. "How much did you have to drink?"

He shrugged, head still firmly pressed into my chest. "Too much. Too much to get it up." He giggled at the near rhyme and sang this line again in a girlish falsetto. *"Too much to get it up."* He paused and grabbed himself. "And too much Adderall. Which makes my dick go, *pfft*." He blew a raspberry and released his penis, letting it swing downwards again.

"Well, that would do it."

Newly energized, he sat up and looked at me with wide eyes. "You can do something." He laid his hand on the back of my head and pressed it downward, urging me towards his lap. "Use your magical mouth to make me magically hard."

I knew I should have been annoyed, angry even, but I wasn't. I didn't like this Kip, but I liked seeing him without his edge, without his cool. It felt raw and vulnerable, private. Seeing him this way was like being let in on a secret, and I felt special, even as Kip pushed me single-mindedly towards his crotch.

I slipped to the floor, crouched on my knees. I didn't feel like I had kneeling before Zeke Maloney's insistent appendage; I felt older. I felt more capable. Kip stroked my hair and mumbled appreciatively, but we both knew the effort was in vain. Eventually he pulled me up and hugged me into his chest, and we fell together back into his pillows. I kissed his face. He was mine to take care of, mine to make better. He'd never seemed sweeter to me.

"Let's just talk," he said. His eyes were barely slits.

"Okay."

"Tell me about yourself, Imogene."

"What do you want to know?"

"I don't know. Anything."

Why is it that when someone asked me about myself I could never think of a thing to say? Anyone could be from Lockport. Anyone could have a younger sister. Anyone could have gone to Buffalo State. I was anyone, no one. I spotted a Yale pennant hanging by his closet, one I didn't remember from before. I nodded to it. "Is that new?"

"Hmm?" He opened his eyes, shut them again. "Oh. Yeah."

"Is that where you want to go?"

He nodded. "That's the plan."

"That's where your brother goes." I said it before I could stop myself. He was quiet for a moment and then, perhaps deciding he had told me this piece of information himself and forgotten, he let the moment pass.

"Where my dad went, too. And grandfather."

"Wow."

"I want to sail there."

I thought I might have misheard him. "As opposed to driving?"

"No. Sail *there*. Like, when I'm there. On the sailing team." He paused, then added for clarification, "I sail."

And then, without further prompting, eyes still closed, he began to talk—a monologue that didn't necessitate an audience but that I listened to every word of nevertheless. He talked about growing up on the water in Hingham, about sailing with his father and brother, about his boat, *The Orion*. He smiled as he talked, and I smiled to hear him talk about something with such passion. *We're talking,* I thought. We'd moved on from our bodies, from sex. He turned to look at me, and his eyes bore into mine with sudden startling intensity, and I realized, like a blow to the head, that losing him would destroy me. I couldn't say when that became true any more than I could stop it from being true.

"I'll take you there sometime," he said.

"Where?"

"Home. To Hingham. I'll take you out on *The Orion*."

"Really? Me?"

Kip opened his eyes, bloodshot and beautiful. He didn't love me, I knew that. But he felt something for me. He felt something close to what I did, or else I wouldn't know to feel that way myself. I was his mirror, after all. I hadn't, and wouldn't have, given him any more than he gave me. I closed my eyes, relaxed into those thoughts. He burrowed his head into my lap and spoke into the valley between my legs. "You," he said. "You, you, you."

— — —

Dale asked me to meet him in his classroom Friday morning to start grading midterms, and having left Kip's room only hours before, all I could think of on my walk across campus was returning to my bed afterwards to sleep. Dale grinned when I entered his room. His hair was pulled back into a wispy ponytail, as it had been when I first met him, and he'd untucked his shirt.

"Imogene," he said, gesturing to the stack of papers on his desk. "Welcome to my hell." I thought maybe the strangeness of earlier in the week had all been in my head.

He divided the midterms into two stacks and pulled a chair over to his side of the desk.

"Want me to sit over there?"

Dale patted the chair. "That's what it's for."

I circled around the desk to join him. He slid me a stack of papers. Our knees touched under the desk, and I jerked away.

"Now, Imogene." Dale tapped my stack with his finger. "What I'm looking for with these answers is clarity and conciseness. You'll be able to tell if they know their shit." His fingernail was a little long; everything about him seemed to need a little trimming. I wondered if he was married.

"Okay," I said.

"Here are some guidelines as to what I'm looking for." He handed me another sheet of paper printed with bullet points. "Just let me know if you have any questions. I'll be right here." He laughed at his own joke, and he was close enough that I could feel his breath, hot but not offensive.

I nodded, unsure as to whether my own breath would offend.

For a while we worked in silence. Dale stood a few minutes in to turn on a radio by the window, and hearing the slinky drumbeats of reggae from the speakers surprised me. I thought to comment but decided against it, not sure what I would say if I did. I'd finished grading one exam and half of another before Dale began to hum and then sing, bobbing his head and shoulders along with the music, all the while still marking the test paper before him with his red pen. I kept my eyes to the desk. Was he performing for me? Looking for praise, for laughter, for me to join in? I wished it were clearer sometimes what kind of response others wanted.

Dale saved me from having to guess. "Like this?"

"Sorry?"

"Reggae. Ever listen to it?"

"Oh. No, not really. Or, I guess, not at all."

He laughed. "It's cool, isn't it?" He scribbled a B on top of a test paper and began on the next. *"Chill."* He emphasized this last word, making it clear this wasn't part of his vernacular, that he was assuming the speech of his students.

I responded with the smile I knew this time he was seeking, feeling strangely disappointed in him. I turned back to my test paper in the hopes of discouraging further conversation.

But he wasn't to be discouraged just yet. "This is also the perfect music to . . ."

I looked at him, wondering why he'd stopped. He had his thumb and index finger pinched together by his lips, and he sucked in and then blew an invisible stream of smoke into the air.

I blinked at him dumbly.

"Right." He seemed suddenly embarrassed. He'd told a foolproof joke to the wrong audience. He ran a hand over his ponytail. "Right. You wouldn't do that. You're a good girl, right?"

"I guess so." I was having that uncertainty again, that one I'd had the first time I spoke to Kip when he walked me back to my room. What was allowed here, in the space between our ages, our stations? What rules were suspended outside of school hours?

"Did you ever read *Cymbeline*? Princess Imogen was virtuous, unable to be wooed."

I felt too tired to remind Dale that he had told me this before, and that no, I still hadn't read the story of my namesake. "Yeah, yeah, I have."

He smiled at me. I stared back. The room felt airless. After a moment, I turned back to my stack of test papers. I could still feel his eyes on me.

"So what's going on, Imogene?"

I turned back to him reluctantly. "What do you mean?"

"You've just seemed so . . . distracted lately. I just want to make sure everything is okay."

I wondered if I could pretend to have to leave, if I could ask to grade my exam papers back at home alone. "I'm sorry again about the midterms. I don't know how—"

He waved this away with his hand. "Water under the bridge. I just need to make sure everything is okay with *you*."

Sweat beaded up on the back of my neck. "Um . . ."

"Because you can talk to me. I'm not just your advisor in the classroom, remember. I'm here to help you."

His eyes bugged out of his head, and I found it impossible to look anywhere else. "No, no, really, I'm just—"

And then I felt it: his hand—heavy and thick-fingered and threatening, a man's hand—on my thigh, a place I instinctively knew it did not belong. His fingertips pressed through my jeans. I froze. I'd always had a fantasy of making a scene—of a man trying to grab me from behind in the street or getting too handsy in a crowded room, and me shouting, "Hands off, asshole!" or "Touch me again and I'll knee you in the balls!" or, most satisfying of all, a triumphant "Fuck you!" I'd always liked to believe that, given the opportunity, I'd be able to fight rather than take flight, that I possessed in me some untapped strength that needed only the necessary urging to emerge like hot lava. But when Dale put his hand on my thigh, fingers curled towards my crotch, I didn't say a word. Scenes were too uncomfortable, too embarrassing. How easy it was to simply let the moment pass.

"Whatever it is, you can tell me, okay?" He gave my thigh a squeeze. "Okay?"

His prodding informed me the question wasn't rhetorical. "Okay."

"Good." Dale released my thigh. "Now we should get back to work, shouldn't we?"

I nodded, grateful. The reggae music continued to play. I stared intently at the top exam in my stack, but I could no longer concentrate. My thigh tingled where his hand had been. I was wondering—as I had been more and more often it seemed—when every interaction I had at Vandenberg became so fraught.

— — —

I spent the next three nights with Kip, and then another night a few nights after that, and then again, and again. He always texted me—that had begun to feel like a certainty, not something I ever had to initiate myself. I loved the thrill of being woken from near sleep by the buzzing of my phone. I loved the thrill of being summoned by Adam Kipling. I applied new makeup before I went to bed, always ready.

My running training was paying off. Though my late-night rendezvous had left me too tired to wake early for runs anymore, I challenged myself each night to see how quickly I could reach Kip's door. I leapt over branches, scurried between trees, took stairs two at a time. It wasn't even the fear of being seen; that I no longer felt, if I'd ever felt it at all. It was simply that I couldn't seem to reach Kip quickly enough. One night I arrived at Kip's door in less than two minutes. "What, do you sleep with your sneakers on?" he'd asked. "Were you hiding outside my dorm?" I just laughed. We were beyond playing it cool. We wanted each other—desperately, madly—and we no longer had to pretend like we didn't.

The sex was never the same. Kip would turn me on my stomach, on my side, up against a wall, bent over a chair, on the floor on my knees. I was his to shape and bend, and the greatest thrill for him was to discover what would make me come. "This is so fun," he'd say. "You like everything!" He declared that I was experiencing a Sexual Renaissance. I said that made him my Renaissance Man. He stroked his chest hair and said, "Man, huh?," and I corrected myself—he was only a Renaissance Boy—and he pinned me to his bed and nuzzled his nose into my armpits until I was shaking with silent laughter and begging him to stop.

We kept as quiet as we could. We kissed sloppily and moaned into each other's open mouths. I bit down on his pillows to keep from yelping. When his bedsprings squeaked, I laughed and he shushed me and we slowed our thrusting and I wondered sometimes, secretly, if maybe I wanted to be heard.

And afterwards, we always talked. He held me to his chest and told me stories about sailing, about Park and Skeat, about his mom and dad and brother. I encouraged him; I wanted to know everything about him. I was reluctant to leave, and he clung to me tightly and said, "You can't leave! You're mine!," but I always returned to my room before the sun rose for the next day. No matter how many times it happened, no matter how little time passed between leaving his bedroom and waking in my own, those first few moments of consciousness were always muddled with uncertainty, with wondering if perhaps I had imagined it all.

I'm thinking about you, he'd text me during the day. I never stop thinking about you, I'd want to reply.

As I prepared to leave for Kip's room that Saturday night, the day after my strange interaction with Dale, I received a text message from Raj. I wasn't even sure how he had gotten my number or when exactly I had obtained his. I meant what I said about us hanging soon, he said. I closed the message without answering, something for me to deal with later. I couldn't imagine spending time with anyone but Kip. All my energy, all my wit—it was invested entirely in Kip.

— — —

I woke on Monday morning to the sound of a note slipping beneath my door. It was a sheet of loose-leaf paper, folded into the shape of origami lips. From my bed I watched the note materialize under the door and listened for the soft pad of footsteps down the stairs. Then I slipped from my bed and retrieved the message.

Within its elaborate folds, Chapin had only written a single sentence: *Is he 18?*

I stared at it a moment, then refolded the folds, restoring the paper lips to their original shape. Then I tore it all to shreds.

TWELVE

AS WAS BECOMING CUSTOM, I BEGAN THE NEXT WEEK RUNNING late, and I slipped into my seat for the first assembly after midterms right before the great oak doors of Morris Chapel were shut. Ree-Ann offered me a smile, and Raj glanced at me uncertainly. I felt a twinge of guilt, remembering I had yet to answer his text. I glanced down the row of apprentices to Chapin, who sat on the opposite end. She sat staring forward, head resting up against the wall, seemingly unaware that I had even arrived.

Dean Harvey ascended the pulpit and leaned into the microphone, jowls jiggling. "Good morning, pupils of Vandenberg, and congratulations on the completion of your midterms."

A cheer rose from the boys, but a tepid one, polite; even the most rambunctious among them felt the inviolability of Chapel. I looked, as always, for Kip. It didn't take me long to spot him; he was repeatedly spanking Park on the butt while Park adamantly ignored him, all of it subtle enough to avoid the detection of anyone not already watching. I wondered how Kip had done on his exams; I hadn't even thought to ask him. It was as easy to forget why he was at Vandenberg as it was to forget why I was.

Dean Harvey segued into the usual announcements: coat-and-glove drive for a local homeless shelter, Drama Club bake sale ("Fags!" I heard a guy hiss to his friend), and the approaching lacrosse team state finals. Dean Harvey even had Duggar Robinson and Coach Larry come to the front of the chapel to give a little wave and encourage the boys to sign up for the school shuttle going upstate for the game. I was relieved to have not been called up, too, in front of all those people, in front of Kip, but after the moment had passed, the lack of acknowledgement left a sting.

"Lastly, the announcement you've all been waiting for." Dean Harvey's lips curled into a grin as he paused, milking the crowd. "The date of the All Hallows' Eve Ball with the ladies of Baylor Academy."

With that, the boys dared a more disruptive response. Two first years from my history class clasped a hand over their mouths and smashed their faces together, pretending to make out. Kip began whacking both Park and Skeat on their butts, alternating between the two in balanced rhythm. I'd always assumed an all-boys boarding school would foster an environment of hypermasculinity and intensely performed manhood, but instead I found something almost homoerotic about the boys' interactions, all the touching and fondling they did in play. The irony of their celebration for the coed dance amused me; perhaps they feared for themselves in this male-only domain, seizing any opportunity they could to assert their unquestionable heterosexuality.

Whispers about the All Hallows' Eve Ball began soon after the first of October, referred to among the boys only as the Ball. At lacrosse practice, I overheard Duggar tell the other boys about how the captain from the year before had snuck onto the snack table a bowl of sour worms soaked in vodka. In study hall, I watched two boys pore over a photo list of Baylor first years they had printed out from online, ranking them from hottest to least hot. The Ball committee appointed a specific theme each year—Carnaval or Victorian or Monte Carlo—but from the pictures I'd seen archived in the library, each theme translated to masquerade masks and costumes as scandalous as the students could get away with without appearing overtly sexual. Rumor had it the Ball was almost cancelled because of the Drama Club scandal earlier in the year, but to everyone's delight, the administration appeared to have turned a blind eye.

"Gentlemen, please." Dean Harvey made a settle-down motion with his hands. When this did not suffice, he rang the bell kept on the pulpit, and like Pavlov's dogs, the boys were instantly silenced. "More details are to follow in the coming week, but let it be known now that proper decorum will be expected of each and every one of you." He gave the room a stern glance. "Understand?"

The boys responded in typical chapel fashion: "Oh yes, oh yes we do."

— — —

Chapin fell into step with me as we filed out of chapel towards the dining hall. "So?" she asked as way of greeting.

I turned to her. She looked even skinnier than usual, her eyes and cheekbones and jawline jutting from her face cartoonishly. I felt irrationally envious. "So what?"

"So is he?"

Chapin knew I had read her note, and she knew she didn't have to reference it for me to understand the question. I looked around to see if the other apprentices were listening; Raj appeared to be telling a story, his hands gesticulating wildly, and none of the girls were paying Chapin and me any mind. "What does it matter?"

She smirked. "I'll take that as a no."

I felt a sudden pinch of irritation, a band tightened around my head. "No, no, that's not a no. It's a it doesn't matter."

"Do you even know?"

I didn't answer. I turned away.

"Do you?" Her voice was shrill now; a few boys walking ahead of us turned around to look.

"Chapin," I hissed.

"Well." She lowered her voice again, leaned in. "Either way, you're in the clear. The age of consent in New York is seventeen. I looked it up."

The invisible band squeezed tight around my temples, and I felt dizzy, unable to think. I began to hurry forward, hoping to leave her behind, to catch up with the other apprentices and make this conversation end, but I stopped instead. She stopped as well, and the people behind continued around us in a steady stream.

"Why are you doing this?" I asked.

"Doing what?"

"*This.*" I threw my hands up, searching for the right words. "Making me feel like I'm doing something wrong."

She shrugged. "Just trying to help. Isn't that why you told me in the first place?"

I didn't answer, and she started to walk away. But I couldn't let her leave.

"Chapin!"

She turned around, raised a brow.

"I—" I wanted her to tell me it was okay. I wanted approval. But I didn't know how to say that, so I just stared at her, hoping she'd understand.

She walked back over to me. "Why do you like him, Imogene?"

I continued to stare. I imagined, briefly, the three of us hanging out—Chapin, Kip, and me. Other than the night we met, Kip and I had never interacted around anyone else. I thought about the times when I'd see Zeke Maloney out at parties in college, how he'd dodge away when I approached and not appear again until later that night in my bed. "Why do you like him?" Darby would ask me. "He treats you like shit." Kip wouldn't do that, I knew. He'd put his arm around me. He wouldn't be afraid to stand close, to let others see. Maybe, seeing us together, Chapin could see what I saw, too.

But that would never happen. Not there, not in that world.

"Just think about it," Chapin said. With that, she continued on to the dining hall, leaving me behind.

— — —

Dale had emailed me the night before to let me know he wasn't feeling well and that I should spend class going over the exam questions. The message was curt, simply signed "D." I was relieved not to see him. I'd decided he was unmarried; I'd never seen a ring. I pictured his apartment—a dirty ring around the tub, crusty dishes in the sink, an unmade bed with dingy sheets. Dale eating out of a plastic container in front of the TV, potato salad or tuna fish, something prepackaged he'd picked up at the grocery store on his way home. Barefoot in sweatpants, openly picking his nose, no one around to impress. Before I'd thought his touch might interest me, but all it had done was scare me—not so much in a threatening way, but because of what getting involved with a man his age would mean. I didn't want any part of that apartment, of the man living in it.

At lacrosse practice that afternoon, Coach Larry was in a particularly bad mood. He growled at every missed pass, incessantly reminding the team about the upcoming finals. I'd always considered him unlike Dale in that way, not caring whether the boys liked him or not, but perhaps he cared more than I thought; perhaps the realization that the boys would never like him—that good humor or funny jokes could never compensate for his chipped front tooth and sallow skin and swollen belly, for all the cruel ways in which time had separated him from them—is what made him so bitter.

"Hey, Squeak!" Duggar called out to me at one point, his newfound respect for me having long ago faded. "Did you get Larry synced up on your cycle or something?"

I was glad, I realized, that they regarded me as a girl rather than a teacher, someone they didn't need or care to respect. I wasn't grouped with Larry and Dale, those who had gone over the hill and were too far gone to relate to anymore. I was, if not a friend, an equal. They still considered me to possess the puerility, the incapability, the free pass that was youth.

"Where's Clarence?" I asked Duggar after practice, not realizing until then that he'd been missing.

He laughed. "You serious? He got kicked off the team a week ago. Didn't you know?"

"Oh," I said. I felt my stomach twist, not so much because of his disgraceful removal from the team, but because I hadn't even noticed it. "Right."

Duggar threw his bag over his shoulder and laughed again; he knew I was lying. "Think you'd know when your own boyfriend gets the boot." He headed towards the locker rooms.

"That's inappropriate!" I shouted at his retreating back.

Duggar looked back over his shoulder, confused at my sudden anger. "Relax, Squeak," he said. "It's a joke."

— — —

After showering, I had a text message waiting for me from Raj. You get my text this weekend? he'd asked.

No, I didn't, I replied. My phone's been weird lately. Lying, I'd found, was becoming easier and easier for me, an almost instinctive reaction.

That's okay. I just said that we need to hang out soon.

Yeah, definitely.

So when should we?

I hesitated, caught off guard by his persistence. I don't know. Maybe this weekend?

Okay, cool. I'll hold you to it.

I didn't answer. My phone vibrated again a moment later and I looked at the screen, expecting another message from Raj. But it was Kip.

Listen to this song, it said. He included a link to a webpage.

I followed the link and turned up the volume. The song, called "For Luna," was strange and beautiful, filled with unidentifiable percussion sounds and nonsensical vocal wails all while a synthesizer moaned in the background.

What is this?

Rabbit Foot. Just discovered them. Do you like it?

I love it.

Cool. Listen to this one. He sent another link.

I listened. And while it played, I thought of Chapin's question, as I had been all day. Why did I like Adam Kipling? I thought of the face he made when he came, his eyes bugging out and mouth in a perfect round "O" like a fish on land gasping for air, the way he let it take over his whole body without ever holding back. The way he kissed with his eyes open, and how they'd stare back at me, unblinking, unashamed, whenever I opened my own. The way he pretended my nipples were buttons and would poke them with his finger and go, "Boop-boop!" I thought how serious he'd become when he told stories about being on *The Orion*, about the jeans hanging, neat and crisp, in his closet, about the way he stuck his face into my armpits and sneakers and inhaled deeply like it was the loveliest smell in the world. Over the weekend, he'd asked me when my last period was, and he marked it on his calendar with a red dot—so he could keep track, he said. He'd also made up a dance—after he came, he'd jumped to his feet, put his hands on his hips, and shook back and forth to make his penis swing. He called me sweetheart. He never once made a comment about my skin. He never wanted me to leave. He'd sent me this song just because he thought I would like it.

But it was more than all that, I knew. It was what Kip represented, what being in a relationship with someone like Kip meant. He was elite. He was smart and sure and special. And of all the girls he could have made laugh, all the girls he could have thought about throughout the day and slept next to at night, all the girls he could take sailing and call his sweetheart—he had picked me. He felt something for me. He felt, I was sure, the same thing I did, that yet-unnamable feeling that was so precious and tenuous and frightening.

There was never a simple answer to attraction, I decided. It was a series of looks and touches, of small, strange exchanges. It was private and inexplicable, something an outsider could never try to understand, something you rarely even understood yourself.

— — —

Apprentices were part of the Ball committee, and we met for the first time in the library conference room on Wednesday to determine that year's theme. Dean Harvey hadn't been able to make it, as he had a meeting with the Board of Trustees, and the two other faculty members on the committee—the French professor and the drama director—both made excuses to leave a few minutes in, so the planning was left to the seven of us. Chapin had grinned and waved at me the moment she entered the room, and as soon as she sat down next to me she asked about my day.

"It was fine," I said.

"I'm glad," she said.

Chapin, I decided, was someone whom I'd never understand, and I had a feeling she liked it that way.

Meggy and Maggie had already created a list of themes in advance—"We love coming up with theme party ideas," Meggy had explained.

Maggie started at the top of the list. "Moulin Rouge."

"Boring," Chapin said.

Everyone turned to her. No one had ever heard her express an opinion before, negative or otherwise.

"Okay." Maggie moved on to the next item. "Arabian Nights?"

"Unoriginal."

Babs and ReeAnn exchanged glances. Meggy looked confused, while Maggie just looked pissed. "Okay, then," said Maggie. "Do you have any ideas?"

"Zombies."

"For a Halloween dance? Yeah, that's real original."

"Hey." Raj, sitting next to me, poked my shoulder.

"What's up?" I whispered back.

He gestured to Maggie and Chapin, who were still arguing. "Shit's getting tense."

"That's why I never get involved in this stuff."

"Me neither."

We sat in silence for a minute, listening to them fight.

"So," said Raj finally. "What are we going to do this weekend when we hang out?"

I wished he'd stop bringing that up. It was as though he knew I had no intention of hanging out with him and wanted me to admit it. "I don't know. What did you have in mind?"

"I don't know. What do you usually do when you hang out with people?"

He was staring at me. I laughed nervously. "Just . . . hang out, I guess."

"We could go out to dinner and to the movies. Or order in food and watch a movie."

He was so close I could see his pores. "Raj . . ." I started.

"We broke up."

"What?"

"Me and my girlfriend. We're not dating anymore. If that's what you're thinking."

"These aren't dumb themes!" Maggie was screeching behind him. "We spent a long time coming up with these!"

"So think about what you want to do this weekend," Raj said.

I nodded dumbly. I didn't know what could be said.

"*Star Wars*!" Chapin volunteered.

Maggie groaned.

After another hour of squabbling and finally deciding on *A Midsummer Night's Dream*—an idea proposed by ReeAnn and agreed upon by both Chapin and Maggie—Chapin caught up with me outside the library. "Hi," she said, still with the same friendliness from before.

"Hello," I replied, still wary. "What was that in there?"

"What was what?"

"That whole thing with you and Maggie. I didn't think you would care about that kind of thing."

Chapin frowned. "I care about everything," she said. I couldn't tell if she was joking or not. We walked in silence a moment before she spoke again. "I met your boyfriend."

The band that had been tightened around my head all week finally snapped. "What?"

"Adam Kipling. I met him."

"Why? How?"

She seemed amused by my panic. "I wanted to see what he looked like, so I got a copy of his schedule from the office and went by his trig class today."

"How did you know which one he was?"

"Because I yelled 'Adam' as I walked by and waited to see who would respond. He's cute."

Infuriation at her carelessness, wild jealousy, embarrassed pride—I felt so many things at once that I wasn't sure what reaction to settle on. I gaped at her instead.

"Don't worry. I'm not going to do anything about it." She looked back at the other apprentices trailing behind us, and I looked back, too. Raj was eyeing us curiously. She turned back to me. "I just wanted to see."

"Okay."

She heard the uncertainty in my voice. "Imogene. I meant it when

I said I wanted to be your friend." She smiled toothily, an imitation of a smile. "Don't you know you can trust me?"

And once again, she was right. I wanted to trust her. Having her as a confidante was the only way I'd be able to trust myself.

— — —

I hadn't heard from him since Monday, when he sent me the Rabbit Foot music, so I did what I hadn't done in a very long time and texted Kip first. How's it going? I set my phone on the nightstand by my bed and waited.

I'd been listening to Rabbit Foot nonstop. While I waited for him to reply, I opened my laptop and played the first track on their album, which I'd downloaded Monday night. "For Luna" started in, soft and hypnotizing. Every song reminded me of him, but especially "For Luna." I listened to the first song play, and then the second, and then the third. I picked up my phone and checked its screen, wondering if I'd missed his reply. The screen was blank. I set it down and lay back in my bed.

After the entire album had played and he still hadn't replied, I began to panic. I picked up my phone. There was no rule against calling him, but I knew I couldn't. I thought of texting him again, but that seemed a bit desperate. He had to have a reason for not texting me back—he was at the movies, or meeting with a study group, or had fallen asleep after dinner and had yet to wake up. I thought of more potential reasons as the album started again on the first track. His phone was dead and he couldn't find the charger. He was having a long phone call with his brother or his parents. Someone in his family had died and he'd turned off his phone to grieve undisturbed. He'd fallen down the stairs of Perkins and lay crumpled at the bottom, alone, blood spilling from his open head.

I texted him again. What are you up to tonight?

His reply came twenty minutes later. Sorry. I was busy. Come over later.

I lay back against the pillows, relieved, but also a bit annoyed, though I wasn't sure why. It wasn't until after the album finished the second time that I figured it out: ever since things had begun with Kip, I hadn't let my phone leave my sight for even a moment, as I always wanted to be prepared for the possibility—for the hope, for the expectation—that his name would appear on its screen. I was always ready to answer.

— — —

He wasn't smiling when he answered the door. "Hi," he said, mouth barely moving.

"Hi?" I looked at him uncertainly and then, desperate to make things right—wanting to right some wrong I wasn't even sure I'd committed—I leaned in to kiss the hard line of his mouth. He turned at the last moment. The kiss landed on the bristly angle of his jaw. He turned back into the room, and I followed him, shutting the door behind me.

"What's up?" I asked. My head felt thick with panic. I tried to make the question sound light, casual, rather than accusatory.

"Nothing." He lay back against his pillows, face turned to the ceiling.

I kicked off my shoes and sat carefully on the edge of the bed. I'd never been good at sudden changes in mood. When my old friend Jaylen's parents divorced in eighth grade, I avoided her for a month. When my mom's Aunt Betty died, I brought her breakfast in bed for a week, brought her fresh flowers, and never once asked how she was feeling. I didn't know how to offer words of comfort; to me, things were as bad as they seemed—Jaylen's parents would never love each other again, if they ever did; my mom's Aunt Betty would never wake up—and I didn't have the conviction to pretend otherwise.

Others' despondency drew me in. I glanced at Kip. I was afraid to touch him; I didn't know this Kip.

We sat without talking for a few minutes, him staring at the ceiling, me sitting beside him, before I finally spoke. "Should I go?"

He didn't answer. I turned to look at him.

"Kip?"

He smiled slightly. "You called me Kip. You never do that."

"Oh. Yeah, I guess not."

"I like it."

He still did not move. His arms were crossed over his chest. I got up from the bed slowly, afraid to spoil the small moment of warmth calling him "Kip" had created. I slid on one shoe and picked up the other.

"What are you doing?"

I heard his sheets rustle behind me as he stood up from his bed. "I don't know," I said. "I feel like maybe I should go."

"Why?"

I looked at him, hesitating. His brows were scrunched angrily above his nose. He reached out, took the shoe from my hand, and threw it across the room. It banged loudly against the opposite wall, causing me to jump, and fell to the floor. I stared at it. I felt, for the first time, not the fear of falling too fast, but the fear of falling for someone I maybe didn't know at all.

"I should go." I started towards my shoe, but he grabbed my wrist. "No."

"Kip, what do you—"

"Stay." He looked at me pleadingly, drew me towards him. "Stay."

I let him pull me back onto the bed; I couldn't say no. He curled his body around my back and wrapped his hands around my waist. It was a relief to have him touch me, to feel forgiven for whatever misdeed I had or hadn't committed, but I was uncomfortable nevertheless. Even if he wanted me to stay, I wanted to leave. This Kip was a stranger.

He put his mouth to my neck and blew a wet raspberry. He rolled me around to face him and put his nose to mine. "I'm sorry." He had liquor on his breath.

"It's okay."

Kip kissed my lips. "You're a sweetheart."

I drew back slightly; having his face so close to mine made me dizzy. "Why do you always say that?"

"What?"

"'You're a sweetheart.' Why do you say that?"

He looked confused. "Because you are."

"I'm not." The anger I hadn't felt when he didn't answer my text, when he told me to come over rather than ask, when he was cold with me, when he threw my shoe—all that anger was bubbling up now. Perhaps it was the sourness of his breath on my face or the constriction of his arms; perhaps the disappointment of an evening not going as planned, of seeing an unfamiliar and unwelcome side of a person I thought I knew. "I'm not a sweetheart. I'm not all that nice, or friendly, or considerate. When you say that, I feel like you don't know me."

I thought this might make him angry again, and I was nervous for a moment. But, surprisingly, he laughed.

"What?" I asked, and when he continued to laugh, I asked again, "*What?*"

"You. You take everything so seriously." He kissed me. "It's just a thing I say." He kissed me again. "Okay?"

"Okay," I said. I thought to ask, *Did you call Kaya a sweetheart?* but I didn't feel like making trouble. I asked instead, softly, gently, "What's going on with you tonight?"

"It's nothing."

"You can tell me." I took his hand, squeezed it. "You've been drinking."

"Yeah." He pulled me closer. He began kissing me. I pulled back.

"You know you can talk to me, right?" I searched his eyes desperately, looking for something I recognized.

"It's just . . ." He trailed off, let out a big puff of breath. "School stuff. You know."

"Okay," I said, as though I did know. I wanted to push, to get more, but I knew better than to think I was getting any more than that tonight. He wants to, I assured myself. Just not now. Not at this moment.

"Okay," he said back. His smile was almost shy. Something had opened up between us, and even if he wasn't ready to totally open up yet, I was willing to wait.

We began to kiss harder, and he slid his hands beneath the waistband of my pants, and all of the evening's earlier unpleasantness was brushed under the bed, to be dealt with later.

THIRTEEN

DALE RETURNED TO CLASS AFTER HIS SICK DAY LOOKING WORN and tired. I knew I was supposed to ask him if he was feeling better, but inviting unnecessary conversation seemed like a mistake. I offered him shy smiles instead, and he gave me the same. We didn't talk at all, really, unless it was required, until he asked me to stay after class on Friday. I approached his desk cautiously, timidly, unsure what he could have to say.

He gave me his usual grin, but it was strained, a half-watt attempt. "How are you?"

We were both standing, facing off on opposite sides of the desk, and it felt odd. "I'm good," I said.

"Monday went alright?"

I nodded.

He sat finally, and feeling even stranger standing above him, I sat as well.

"Listen." He ran his hand over his ponytail, a nervous habit I'd noticed. "I wanted to talk to you. About last Friday."

I laced my hands so tightly in my lap that my knuckles turned white. I didn't want to think about his hand on my leg, and I certainly did not want to talk about it.

"If I . . ." Dale didn't want to be having this conversation either. "If I did or said anything to make you uncomfortable last week . . ."

"Oh, no," I said immediately. I would say anything to end this. "No, no, definitely—"

"No, really. I feel I may have overstepped my bounds. I'm . . ." He hesitated. "I've only been here a few years. I'm still not used to working with young women. I'm not sure how to talk to them, to be honest, or how I'm supposed to talk to them. To you."

"Oh."

"Especially . . ." He paused again, and I clasped my fingers so hard I feared they might snap. "Especially young women who look like you."

"Um . . ."

"Goddamn it." Dale buried his face in his hands. "Goddamn it. I'm sorry, Imogene." He looked up at me and attempted another smile. "Go. Have a nice weekend. I'll see you on Monday."

"Right." I stood warily. "You, too."

His face was still frozen in its half-smile as I shut the door behind me. On my walk back to the Hovel, I imagined his apartment again, the dark dank place I'd given him in my mind. I imagined him lying in bed—perhaps the sound of a siren wailing from outside the window—and his dick in his hand, him thinking about me. The thought gave me pleasure that I didn't understand.

— — —

As I might have predicted, Raj wasn't prepared to let me get out of our date so easily. When I returned home from my meeting with Dale, I had a list of options for the evening waiting on my phone.

There are three or four good movies playing at the theater. Or we can go into the city to see this comedy show I've heard about. Or we can always just do drinks here or in the city if you're not up for a show. What are you thinking for dinner? There's that Italian place by the train station, or the Mexican place we went to for the twins' birthday, or if we go into the city . . .

I surprised myself by thinking, maybe I should go. Would it be so bad? I opened my laptop and looked at his profile page, scrolling through his pictures. It seemed a long time ago that I'd been attracted to him; I couldn't even remember what I had once seen. All I could see now was enlarged pores, cilantro in his teeth, bare feet folded up on his lap. I imagined him coming to the Hovel to pick me up in a button-down shirt—wrinkled, too big, the armpits already dampened with sweat—and steeped in pharmacy-brand cologne. Everyone would come out of their rooms to "ooh!" and take pictures and say, "Have fun, kids!" What if he brought me flowers? I would have to put them in water before we left, stick them in a drinking glass because we had no vases, watch them droop and brown and stink on the counter all week until I finally had to throw them away. What if he tried to hold my hand as we walked to the train? It would be sticky and wet, and everyone passing by would know that we were together, at least for the night, and I'd have to hold it until mutual discomfort allowed us to let go. And what would happen after? Not just the possibility of an attempted kiss or an invitation to his room, but when I returned to the Hovel, when everyone asked, "How did it go?" and sliced my privacy, my sacred privacy, into six even pieces and passed it around on paper plates.

I texted Raj back. I'm so sorry. My advisor has been sick all week and I think I caught whatever he has. I'm not going to be able to make it out tonight.

He responded almost instantly. That sucks! Want me to bring you anything? Think you'll be better by tomorrow?

No, I don't need anything, but thank you. And maybe. I'll let you know.

I knew already that I would not be better by the next day. I knew I would not be going out with Raj, the next day or ever.

— — —

Perhaps I willed it upon myself—or it was brought on by guilt for having lied—but that Friday night I actually began to feel sick. I lay swaddled in my bed—my refuge, my cave—and felt hot and then cold and then achy all over and strangely self-righteous because, whether my symptoms were imagined or not, I felt I had not told a lie. I hadn't heard from Kip since Wednesday, since I witnessed his inexplicable moodiness, and he slipped in and out of my fevered dreams. He was lying beside me, stroking my hair. He was on top of me, lifting my shirt, kissing my collarbone. When I woke, sweat-soaked, near midnight and checked my phone, it didn't feel possible that the last text sent between us had been two nights ago. It took me a few minutes to shake off sleep and realize he hadn't been there at all.

I texted him. Where are you? I didn't expect a reply right away, but I thought one would come.

I stayed in bed the whole next day. My sheets were beginning to stink. I thought about washing them, about collecting the dirty dishes that had been accumulating in my room and picking up the soiled clothes scattered on my rug and opening up the curtains and making the whole room bright and fresh and clean again, but I was too tired. There was comfort in darkness, in filth. I sank into it like a warm bath. When the afternoon rolled around and Raj texted me— How are you feeling today?—I answered without a second thought.

Still sick. I'm sorry.

Raj didn't answer. My hair was slick with grease, and I hadn't changed my clothes since Friday morning. The already-setting sun made me want to cry. I curled up and pulled the blankets over my head, waiting—though for what exactly, I couldn't say.

— — —

I waited until everyone else had gone to bed—or, in the case of Chapin, had disappeared for the evening—before I showered. I turned the water temperature as hot as it would go and scoured my skin. Once I'd combed out my hair and changed into a clean pair of clothes, I texted Kip, the same message as the night before: Where are you?

Ten minutes passed without an answer before I began to cry. I sat on my bed, put my face between my knees, and sobbed without restraint. I sobbed until the floor spun beneath my feet and my throat felt dry, my sobs becoming indulgent imitations of sobs. And after I exhausted myself and was rubbing my aching eyes, the screen of my phone lit up like a sign. Come over, he said.

I crossed the room and looked at myself in the mirror above my bureau. My eyes were already swollen, my face slack and spotted. I was scared by what I saw. I was scared of the power I'd allowed someone else to have over me. But I knew just as well that I was powerless to resist. I slid my feet into my sneakers without untying them, splashed some water on my face in the bathroom, and reapplied concealer over the constellation of blemishes on my forehead before heading out the door.

He had been waiting for me, and he opened the door before I was halfway down the hall. "Greetings," he said.

I took a deep breath to steady myself. "Hi."

He squinted at me in the dark. "What's wrong with your face?"

"I was sick."

"Nothing contagious, right?" He pulled me inside his room and shut the door. "Fuck it. I don't care." He kissed me. I smelled liquor on his breath—gin this time.

"I'm feeling better."

"I said I don't care." He scooped me up like a baby and deposited me on his bed.

"You sure?"

He unbuttoned my jeans and slid them off, along with my underwear, in one swift movement. "I'm sure I have a boner."

I felt ridiculous for having cried earlier. I felt ridiculous for having thought Kip would just disappear.

He left the light on, and from beneath him I watched him make love to me, watched him pump himself in and out of me, until he finally climaxed in that oxygen-deprived fish gasp that I'd come to love so much, eyes bulged and staring as if to say, "Can you feel this, too? Can you?"

I didn't—I wouldn't—mention the text he hadn't answered the night before, and he didn't mention it either. He surprised me, instead, by mentioning the lacrosse state finals game.

"You guys ready for tomorrow?"

It took me a moment to figure out what he was referring to. "How did you know I coached?" I asked.

He twined his bare leg around mine. "Don't you?"

"I do, but how—"

"I'm going to come watch."

"You are?"

He ran his foot up and down my leg. I'd never had anyone's toes on my body before, but I didn't mind his. "Yeah."

"Do you have friends on the team?"

"No."

"Then why—"

"Because maybe I want to see you." He poked me in the knee with his big toe. "That okay?"

"Yeah. Yeah, of course it is." I paused and, feeling encouraged, I said, "You've been drinking again."

A flicker of irritation crossed his face, but just as quickly disappeared into a grin. "You going to tell on me?"

"I'm just worried about you."

"You shouldn't be." He paused, searched my face, and then added, "It's just school stuff. Really."

"Please tell me." I was begging, and I hated myself for it.

Kip propped himself up on his elbow. "Why do you care so much?"

"Because I care about you." The words came out before I could hesitate. Even while my heart pounded, awaiting response, I felt proud of my boldness.

He stared at me too long before saying, "I care about you, too, Imogene."

"You're just saying that."

Irritation clouded his face again, and then passed. "No, I'm not." His face softened and he touched my arm. "I want to talk to you, I really do. And I want you to talk to me. I'm just so sleepy right now."

Sleepy—with one word, so cloyingly babyish and yet said so coolly, Kip had pulled me back in. I was his again. "Really?"

He kissed my head. "Yes, really," he said, and I believed him. He pulled me into the damp nest of his chest hair, and as he fell asleep I matched my breathing with his, our bodies swelling and retracting together in slow, even waves.

— — —

I woke to light flooding through his curtains. I rubbed my eyes and looked at the clock on his nightstand. It was almost eight o'clock.

"Fuck!" I flew from his bed and onto my hands and knees to collect my clothes from the floor. He turned over and watched me in half-asleep confusion.

"What's up?"

"I fell asleep! I didn't mean to stay."

He rolled back over. "It's cool," he said, voice muffled in his pillow.

I lay on my back to tug my jeans over my thighs. "Shit, shit, shit." Kip was breathing steadily, seemingly already back to sleep. Once I'd tugged on my shirt and jacket and forced my shoes back on my feet, I approached Kip's bed. I wanted to kiss him, but instead I pulled his comforter up to his chin and tucked it around his skinny shoulders. He smiled; he was awake. "I'll see you later?" I whispered.

"Mm hmm." His eyes were still closed. I tiptoed to the door and shut it behind me as slowly as I could to not make a sound.

The hall was empty. I crept down the stairwell and towards the front door, not believing my luck that no one was yet awake. That is, until Raj stepped out of his room, dressed for a run. We paused for a horrible second, staring at each other, until I spoke.

"I didn't know you were a runner."

He blinked at me. "What are you doing here? What—why were you upstairs?"

"Um." Alarms blared in my head. It felt possible that I would get sick on the floor between us. "The lacrosse game. I had to get something to one of the players. I had—his jersey! I had to give it to him. The game is today."

His face was impassive. My panic felt as obvious as a stain. "You feeling better?" he asked.

"Yeah! Yeah, I'm feeling much better. Sorry again about this weekend." I thought to offer the next weekend, to redeem myself somehow, but I couldn't bring myself to do it.

"You shouldn't be here." He zipped up his jacket. "You can't just go to their rooms."

I wondered why he said "their," not "his," before I remembered that, to Raj, there was no "his." There were the boys, and then there were the apprentices. Them versus us. He didn't see them as different people, capable of different things. He didn't know there was just one person whose room I was interested in entering. "I know, I know, I'm sorry. I really—"

"I'll see you later." He turned and walked out the door. I leaned up against the wall for a moment to slow my breath before I followed him out.

— — —

When I boarded the bus for the game an hour later, I was surprised to see Clarence sitting in the first row of seats. His hair was curled over his ears, desperately in need of a trim, and he gazed blankly out the window, seemingly unaware of where he even was.

I sat down next to him. "Hi there."

He jumped.

"How are you? I haven't seen you in a while."

He turned to look at me, something between confusion and anger in his eyes. "That's because I'm not on the team anymore."

"Oh." I didn't expect that response from him, didn't even think him capable of such a response.

"You knew that, right? That I'm not on the team?"

"Yeah, of course. I'm sorry that happened."

Clarence turned back to the window. I felt guilty, but not for the reason he probably thought. Back in the beginning of the semester, I had promised Clarence something—guidance? Comfort? Friendship? I still wasn't sure exactly what—and I had failed to deliver on that promise. I'd let my brother down. Worse still, I wasn't the outsider that he was anymore; I'd been accepted and he hadn't, and I could never promise him that that would change.

"Really, Clarence, I had no idea that Larry was going to do that. I would have stopped him. I really would have."

He seemed to soften a bit at this. "It's okay," he said. "I wasn't very good."

"Of course you were!"

He looked at me and smiled. "No, I wasn't."

I smiled back and didn't respond; to protest again would be a lie.

He pulled out his notebook and a pencil as the other boys began to board the bus. As Duggar passed he pursed his lips and smacked two wet kisses in our direction. We both ignored him.

"So," I said as the bus pulled from the lot. "Why . . . Um, did you just come . . . ?"

"I wanted to watch." He didn't look up from his notebook as he drew. It was tilted away from me so I couldn't see what he was drawing. "Coach Larry said I could come with the team."

"That's great. That's really nice of you."

Clarence shrugged and continued to draw.

I lay my head back against the seat and thought back to the field trip to Hook Mountain for the hawk watch. How much had changed since then. How much Adam Kipling had changed everything. I must have dozed off because the next time I opened my eyes, we had arrived.

"Imogene?" Clarence said as the boys began to collect their bags.

"Yeah?"

"I didn't just come to watch the game, you know." He tucked his notebook away into his bag. I thought he might have been drawing me something, and I was disappointed that he didn't have anything to give to me. It wasn't until the team was warming up and I caught a glimpse of Clarence in the crowd, chin in his hands, that I wondered why else he had come to the game, if that reason could possibly be me. With surprising sadness, I concluded that I didn't know Clarence Howell at all, not really.

The boys lost the game 3-1. Duggar broke his stick over his knee and the boys were too afraid of Larry to speak for the whole ride home. I'd kept scanning the crowd the whole game, but I knew before the first half even ended that he hadn't come. Kip hadn't ever been planning to come, and I felt like a fucking idiot for thinking he actually might.

— — —

The All Hallows' Eve Ball was held that Friday in the dining hall, and the apprentices were given the day off to decorate. Babs and ReeAnn took an early trip to the store to buy paper lanterns and streamers and strings of lights. Meggy and Maggie went to the costume store for fairy wings and flower crowns—even for Raj, who was more than happy to comply. "Do I look pretty?" he asked, flapping around the room with his new accessories. The girls howled. I concentrated on untangling the lights, which spooled around me in twisted knots.

Raj hadn't spoken to me all week, and judging from the coldness of the other girls, he'd also told them about my refusal to go on our date—though how much he'd told them, I couldn't be sure. Why did disinterest have to be cruel? And why should I feel that I owed Raj anything? I hadn't even gone on the date, and still my private life was open for public discussion.

I hadn't spoken to Kip either. It wasn't that I was angry with him for not coming to the game; refusing to contact him had become a game of its own. I would not text him until he texted me. Of course, had he texted me, I'd have flown to his room without hesitation. I had dreams every night of him texting me, of him slipping into my bed. Sometimes, the loss of him come morning would feel so profound that I'd cry. I traced back through our conversations, through the things we'd said; nothing he'd ever said was a promise, but I felt he had promised me something nevertheless. I wondered if he was losing interest. I wondered if I was losing my mind.

Chapin approached and plopped herself cross-legged beside me. "Need help?"

I handed her a string of lights I had yet to work on.

"Excited for tonight?"

I shrugged. "It will be fun, I guess." Across the room, Raj and the twins twirled in circles, wings on their backs and streamers in hand, while Babs hollered about the wasted supplies.

"Is Adam Kipling coming?"

I looked at her; her face was sincere. "I don't know. I haven't really thought about it."

That was a lie. All week long, I'd been imagining this night. I would have Chapin do my makeup, put glitter around my eyes and some bold color on my lips and transform me into something otherworldly. I'd borrow something of hers to wear, maybe that lace-up pink corset top and matching silky pink skirt. Kip would see me from across the room and approach me, in front of everyone, and say in my ear, "Outside. Five minutes." We'd lie down in the garden behind the building and kiss, as the music from the hall fell away and the party carrying on inside was nearly forgotten.

Chapin smirked. "Of course you have."

"Well, maybe."

"This whole place has to look ethereal," ReeAnn was saying across the room. "Like a fairy-tale forest."

"Want to drink with me beforehand?" Chapin asked me.

"Definitely," I said.

— — —

The dance began at eight, but no one other than first years arrived until nine. I stood with the other apprentices by the front door, admiring our work.

"This place looks cool," Raj said.

We all nodded in agreement, even though it didn't. We'd covered the lower windowpanes with green crepe paper—hoping to achieve the effect of sunlight filtered through a thick ceiling of leaves—but where it was already getting dark by four p.m., the paper just hung from the glass, limp and purposeless. Most of the twinkling lights framing the windowsills and tables had already slipped from the tape holding them up and now sagged towards the floor. The tables were scattered with dead leaves—a last-minute addition that looked more accidental than inspired—and covered with dishes of crumbling sugar cookies and watery fruit punch. Nevertheless, I'd drunk just enough vodka in Chapin's bedroom before leaving to make me forget we were in a dining hall, that we were in a place that was familiar to me at all.

While we were drinking, Chapin had played songs that had been popular when we were in middle school, and we danced around her bedroom, me hesitantly at first until the liquor began to grease my joints, Chapin uninhibited from the start. The dancing and the pop music and the buzz made me feel oddly excited for the boys tonight, improbably nostalgic for the school dances of years past. Had I even had fun at high school dances? I recalled taffeta gowns in pastels, dimmed lights and a scuffed gymnasium floor, a DJ commanding us to jump and put our hands in the air. It wasn't any of that I envied or missed—it was the promise of these nights. The promise of a kiss, or a slow dance, or a new crush. I missed youth and its unflagging hope, its infinite excitement.

"Did you like high school?" I asked Chapin.

"No one likes high school," she replied, shaking her butt in time with the music.

Chapin had decided to wear the outfit I'd been eyeing, and so I wore her too-tight bandage dress, the one I'd worn the first night I slept with Kip. I'd felt good as I looked at myself in the mirror, but at the dance, with the other apprentices dressed in matching Elizabethan-style gowns they'd bought at a thrift shop, self-consciousness set in. Even Chapin, in her corset-skirt combo, looked more timely and appropriate than me. My desire to look good had warped my judgment, and everyone could see. I thought to return to the Hovel to change, but that felt like admitting defeat, an acknowledgement of my poor choice. Besides, if I left, even briefly, I might miss Kip's arrival.

As I'd predicted, very few students stuck to the *A Midsummer Night's Dream* theme; save for a few first years who had donned shorts stuffed with towels over tights and oversized blouses, every boy wore a crisp button-down and jeans. Then the buses from Baylor Academy arrived.

As the girls filed into the dining hall, lithe and leggy and unreal, I remembered just why I hadn't applied to the apprenticeship program at Baylor Academy—even the ones that weren't beautiful could easily convince me that they were. Their nails were painted, their hair curled, their shoes strappy, and their dresses tight and metallic and expensive-looking, the kind of dresses I thought only adult women owned. They passed by us apprentices without a glance, giggling behind their hands. They were light as dust particles, elusive as sun-rays, golden wood nymphs I wished to capture between my hands and study and understand. They were women, really, not girls.

Raj whistled. "Wow."

Maggie nudged him. "Please, they're in high school. That's fucked up."

Chapin slid something cool and hard into my hand. I looked; it was a flask. I discreetly bent to adjust my shoe strap and took a quick pull.

Raj noticed. "Let me see that," he said, taking it from my hand. He tipped it into his mouth and handed it back to me, smiling slightly. I smiled back. Perhaps I was forgiven.

Chapin nudged me. I went to hand her back her flask, but she nudged me again, harder. I followed her line of vision. Kip had arrived.

He, Park, and Skeat hadn't spared any expense for their costumes: they wore padded doublets with puffy sleeves, velvet-looking vests, enormous knee breeches, stockings, pointy-toed slippers. Kip even wore a cape and a pilgrim-style hat with a long purple feather spouting from the top.

Raj laughed. "Who the fuck are those guys?"

"I'm glad someone followed the theme," said Babs.

I stared. I willed him to see me, but a crowd had formed around him. Already, a girl with long red hair had slung her arm around Kip's neck and held her phone out in front of them to take a picture.

I poked Chapin in the side. "Can I have some more?"

She nodded and passed me back the flask. I ducked behind her, caring less about discretion this time, and took as long a drink as I could stand.

— — —

The apprentices were expected to circulate the room—to keep the cookies stocked, to make sure no one was sneaking alcohol, to break up any Vandenberg boys and Baylor girls who got too handsy on the dance floor—but I could concentrate on little other than Kip. I followed him around the room, watched him fill a cup with punch, watched him deposit a few pills into the cup and take a long sip. I lurked against the walls as he began to sweat, as he removed his cap and stockings and cape and vest until he wore just his giant breeches and a white shirt, rolled up past his elbows. He danced wildly with his friends, arms thrown in the air and thrashing as though boneless, as though independent from the rest of his body. A group of girls joined them, and he grabbed the wide hips of a blonde, rocking her back and forth to the music. His eyes were marbles, his mouth slack. He stumbled forward once, falling into the blonde, and she laughed; I could tell from the glassiness of her eyes that she was on something, too. I watched him, and couldn't stop watching him, even while the sight of him acting like this made me feel sick.

I was back in college, back across the bar from Zeke Maloney. Maybe he doesn't see you, I told myself, just as I used to tell myself. Maybe he's not purposely avoiding you. But the truth was clearer to me than it was back then: Kip didn't want to be with me, not really. Only at night, when he was lonely or horny, when he could call and know I'd answer. The realization was less devastating than it was satisfying to acknowledge, even if only in my own head. It was a satisfaction with hard edges, a satisfaction that curled my hands into fists and twisted a tight knot of anger in my gut.

The dance ended at midnight. Kip left holding the hand of the blonde, his costume abandoned in pieces all over the room. I was supposed to stay behind and clean, but when no one was looking I tumbled out the door. I didn't look at the buses loading; I didn't look back once until I was halfway to the Hovel, when I heard the sound of footsteps behind me. Even though I knew it was coming, I still jumped when Chapin reached out and touched my shoulder.

"Hey," she said. "I saw."

That was all she needed to say. A sob burst out of me, and she wrapped her bony arms around me. I settled into her chest and cried; it had been a long time since I'd been hugged by a friend. She led me back to her room, grabbing a bag of chips that I was pretty sure belonged to ReeAnn from the kitchen counter, and sat me on her bed.

"Start at the beginning," she said.

And I did. I told her the story of Kip and me from the very beginning, from the meeting between the trees. And like a good friend, she listened, never telling me I was wrong, never saying a word even when we both knew I was leaving the bad parts out. Because even though Kip hadn't crossed the room to talk to me—and how could he, really, in front of everyone?—and probably didn't feel the same way about me that I did about him, a small, tender part of me opened up inside as I spoke, a part that still believed that what I had with Kip was real.

FOURTEEN

I CHECKED KIP'S PROFILE PAGE ALL WEEKEND. I KEPT THE PAGE minimized on the bottom of my laptop screen and pulled it up to refresh it every so often—more often, really, than I care to admit. Finally, late on Sunday afternoon, the pictures from the Ball appeared: Kip, Park, and Skeat with their arms slung around each other; Kip sweaty and manic-looking with his drink in his hand; Kip and the blonde, him holding her tight against his waist. Her name, I learned, was Betsy Kenyon.

I clicked on her profile. She was from Fairfield, Connecticut. She had two older sisters and a teacup yorkie and a fat gray father who looked too old to be her father and a pinch-faced blond mother who wore lots of twinsets. She was a swimmer. She was a third year. Her family had a place in the Bahamas. In her recent activity, she had become friends with Adam Kipling.

It was nearly midnight when I finished looking through all her pictures. My eyes burned in their sockets, and when I shut my laptop, the bluish glow of the screen still seemed to hover before me.

Even after all my investigating, there was nothing to say that something had happened—or was happening—between Kip and Betsy Kenyon. And just because he hadn't come to the game last week—and I hadn't heard from him since—didn't mean I'd been forgotten. I eyed my phone, resting on my chest, and thought through my options. I could be casual: *How was your weekend?* I could be passive aggressive: *Hey there. Remember me?* I could be accusatory: *So who was that girl on Friday?* Or I could say what I really wanted to say: *I would do anything to see you tonight.*

I didn't say any of it. As desperate as I was to see his name on my screen—to have him say something, anything to me—the fear of what I might do if he didn't reply kept me from saying a word. That night, it didn't seem possible to live anymore—not that I was thinking of offing myself, nothing like that, but nausea twisted my stomach and squeezed my head and every nerve of my body felt electrified, and I truly believed that any sort of disappointment could kill me right there and then, just kill me.

— — —

It was November, and everything was dying. The leaves fell from the trees, slowly at first and then all at once, chemotherapy patients losing their hair. The frost hardened the grass into something unrecognizable that crunched beneath my shoes. The sky above loomed heavy and colorless—not even gray, just devoid of color, as though it'd been disregarded. I'd experienced this change every year of my life, but still I feared it. What if this was the year the world didn't come back to life? What if warmth was gone for good and we didn't even know it?

However, on Wednesday morning, amidst all the gloom, I experienced a miracle. As I was heading towards the dining hall from Dale's classroom for lunch—the rest of the day looming even more vacant and frightening than usual due to the end of lacrosse practices—I saw Kip. He took up so much of my mental life that I had nearly forgotten he was real. He was walking towards me—alone, so rare for him—with his hands in his pockets. He saw me. I froze. For a sickening moment I thought he might give me a nod and keep walking or, worse, pretend he hadn't seen me at all, that he didn't even know me, but he didn't. He smiled and approached me. I tried to fight the idiotic grin that was threatening to take over my face.

"Hi there," he called out.

I waved. "Hi."

He came and stood right before me. Something was different about him, and it took me a moment to see it.

"Your face! It's all . . . shaved." He looked so young without his usual scruff of hair, so bare, and I wasn't sure I liked it. My hand rose unthinkingly to touch the exposed skin, but I caught myself in time. The hand fluttered unsure between us until I managed to draw it back down.

"Yeah." He ran his own hand over his chin. "All gone. I had some important shit going on the other day, and I had to look professional."

"What important shit?"

"This dumb contest one of my teachers had me enter. Nothing big."

A beat of silence followed. The air felt thick with unsaid words.

He adjusted the straps of his backpack. "Where you going now?"

"Dining hall."

"I'll join you."

I gestured to the building behind us. "You weren't headed to class?"

He shrugged. "Nah." I wasn't sure if that meant he didn't have class, or if he'd simply decided he no longer wanted to attend.

We walked towards the dining hall. Our hands swung close together, our pinkies touching occasionally. He greeted people as we walked, nodding to and slapping the hands of other boys. Even the ones he didn't directly acknowledge followed him with their eyes. I was dizzy with happiness. I felt loved by association.

"So did you go to the Ball last week?" I asked, feeling emboldened. He was slapping another boy on the back as I asked him, but he still turned to look at me.

"Yeah," he said. "I saw you."

"You did?"

He was grinning now. "And you saw me."

I smiled back, caught. "I did."

There was no one on the path before us or behind us. He wrapped his pinky around mine. "You looked beautiful."

"Really?" All the bitterness and all the doubt of the past few days dissipated, and excuses—work, school, friends—took their place, excuses he didn't even have to provide for me to accept. So desperate was my desire to prove myself wrong that I could have forgiven anything. *Beautiful.*

He looked around quickly to make sure the path was still empty and then put his mouth to my ear. "Come over tonight."

"Why should I?"

I'd meant it as a tease, but his face slipped into an expression close to anger. "Fine. Don't."

"I'm kidding," I said. Then, again, frantic, "I'm kidding!"

"So am I," he said, and when he grinned, the brief glimpse of anger seemed like something I'd imagined.

He released my pinky and waved goodbye, headed into the dining hall. It didn't matter to me that I had kind of thought we'd be eating lunch together; I'd be with Kip that night, and the time that passed until then no longer mattered.

— — —

I got my sandwich wrapped in wax paper so I could take it back to my room to eat. As I was leaving, I looked over to where Kip was already sitting with his friends—laughing with his mouth full of meatball sub—to see if I might catch his eye, if he might ask me to join him. He didn't see me, but I wasn't too disappointed, as I knew to join him and Park and Skeat wasn't an option. How could he possibly explain a teaching apprentice, an interloper, joining their table? What could I possibly contribute to their conversation? Even the idea of unwrapping my sandwich in front of them—chicken salad with honey mustard on rye—made me feel sick with anxiety. Chicken salad wasn't sexy. Eating, flossing, clipping my toenails—those weren't things I wanted Kip to imagine me doing, much less see for himself. That sort of intimacy wasn't desirable to me, and I wasn't sure it ever would be.

As I sat in bed with my sandwich, basking in the freedom of being able to drop bits of chicken salad onto my lap and pick them up to eat with my fingers, I thought more of my interaction with Kip. If Kip had seen me at the Ball, why hadn't he said hello? There was no rule against that. If nothing had changed, as it appeared not to have from our conversation, then why had so much time passed since I'd last been in his bed? I licked honey mustard from my fingers and resolved to ask him that night. I would find out the rules of our relationship, for once and for all, so that I could stop wondering. Then I scrubbed and re-made-up my face, settled into my bed, and waited for night to fall.

— — —

Kip didn't text me, but I assumed since he'd asked me in person that he hadn't felt the need to confirm. I waited until everyone went to bed before I tugged on my sneakers and headed out the door. I knocked lightly, and he grinned when he opened the door.

"You're here," he said.

I felt a spasm of panic. "Do you not want me—?"

He laughed. "Relax." He kissed my mouth and guided me into the room by my waist. "Of course I want you to be here." He kissed me again. "I need you to be here."

I kissed him back. We fell into his bed.

"I want to do something crazy," he said between kisses.

"Like what?"

His erection pulsed through the fabric of his jeans and bumped against my leg impatiently. "I want to tie you up to the ceiling and fuck you upside down."

I laughed. "What?"

"I want to fuck you in the stairwell. Or in the library."

"Kip . . . ?"

"I want you to dress up in some outfit. School girl or something." He paused, thinking. His eyes were crazed and bright. "What if we made a tape?"

"A tape?"

"You know. Record ourselves doing it." He gestured to the laptop on his desk.

I pulled back slightly. "Kip—"

He pulled me back. "I wouldn't show it to anyone. It would just be ours."

I shook my head. "That's not a good idea."

"Oh, come on."

"No."

He was taken aback by the forcefulness of my voice. "Fine." Hesitantly, I kissed him, and we started kissing again. After a few minutes, he asked, "Can I at least stick it in your ass?"

I looked at him. His face was hard, a mask. The light was gone. I had the feeling once again of not recognizing the person before me. "I don't think I want—"

He shook his head. "You know what? Forget it." The room felt cold. We eased down our own pants and fit our bodies together. We fucked routinely, passionlessly. He came with an angry-sounding groan while I stayed silent. Afterwards, we lay shoulder to shoulder, touching only out of necessity due to the narrowness of the bed. Finally, I spoke.

"Why haven't you talked to me?"

"What?"

"We don't talk anymore. This is the first time we've hung out in almost two weeks."

He rolled towards me onto his side. "Are you mad?"

"No, I'm not mad. I'm just trying to figure things out." I paused. "Like, why do you keep disappearing?"

"I'm right here."

"But you're not. I just—I don't know how the rules work."

"What rules?"

"Kip!" There was no keeping the anger out of my voice anymore. "Come on. What are we doing here? I mean . . . what are we? Why do you like me?" I wanted a reaction. I wanted to make him angry, if only to know he felt anything at all. "Am I just a conquest? A Kaya?"

He stared at me, as though trying to register what I'd just said, and then sighed and rolled onto his back. "Imogene," he said to the ceiling. "What the fuck."

"What?"

"We're just . . . having fun, okay?"

"But what—"

"I'm not your boyfriend. I can't be your boyfriend, you know that."

"I know," I spat back, indignant, even while the words stung. I was sure he'd never had to have this conversation with Kaya. She would have known better than to think she had a future with a kid. But Kip wasn't a kid, not anymore. Not to me.

After a minute, he took my hand in his, interlocking our fingers. "You're a sweetheart, Imogene," he said.

I didn't answer. And I didn't want to wait until he fell asleep to leave. I unlaced my fingers from his and he didn't protest. Then I dressed and crept out the door.

I was halfway down the stairs before I began to cry. Loud, indulgent sobs racked my whole body and I crouched to the ground, powerless to stop them.

"Imogene? Is that you?"

I froze. It wasn't Kip's voice; it was Raj's. I heard his footsteps coming down the hall towards the stairwell door.

"Imogene?"

His voice was a hand around my throat. I scampered up the stairs as quickly as I could, though my limbs felt like lead, and back onto the second floor. I heard the downstairs door swing open, saw the lights flick on, and then nothing. After too long a pause, the lights turned off and the door closed with a soft click. I stayed sitting on the hallway floor for nearly an hour before I'd stopped shaking enough to return to my room.

— — —

Ever since the pictures from the Ball had been posted, I'd looked at Betsy Kenyon's profile every day. She began to feel like someone I knew—not someone I admired or even liked, but someone I understood fully nevertheless. I found her accounts on other social media sites, as none of her pages were hidden from the public. She was funny, I discovered; I hated that. I wanted her to be irredeemably stupid, a blithering idiot. She posted pictures of herself with chocolate ice cream on her face and her hair in a dirty knot on top of her head. *I'm a mess!* she proclaimed. *I'm just like the rest of you!* She was falsely self-deprecating; you know she didn't believe what she said for a minute, and she didn't expect you to, either.

No other pictures of her and Kip were posted. On Thursday, however, the day after Kip told me he couldn't be my boyfriend, there was a sign. She'd posted a link to a video on her profile with the caption, *Obsessed. Love good recommendations.* I clicked on the link. It was "For Luna" by Rabbit Foot. And no matter how many times I'd listened to it before, that time it was more beautiful and cutting and unbearable than it ever had been.

On Thursday, Dean Harvey also called a special afternoon chapel for an "exciting announcement." Fourth-year student Adam Kipling had placed first in the regional oratorical scholarship program and would be going on to the national competition in January. Dean Harvey proclaimed how excited we all were, and then encouraged us to rise for a round of applause. Kip was called to stand beside the dean, looking the closest to embarrassed that I had ever seen him. I sat on the side of the room, unable to stand, unable to clap, because the person who I thought I knew better than anyone, the person who a few days before had asked if he could stick his dick up my ass, was being publically celebrated for something I'd known nothing about.

— — —

Raj waited until Friday to text me. Any plans for tonight?

I had no plans, of course. I had nothing to do but to listen to the Rabbit Foot album, to look through Betsy Kenyon's pictures, to search for clips from the oratorical contest only to find grainy cell phone videos without sound that did nothing to satisfy me. Other than Kip on Wednesday, I really hadn't spoken to anyone all week—not even Dale, who had spent the past week barely acknowledging my presence. My bed no longer provided comfort; it was too hot, fetid even. I suddenly wanted—no, *needed*—to leave my bedroom, to be anywhere but there, to get out of my damned head. I suddenly felt I might tear at the walls with my fingernails if I didn't leave that second.

I'd knocked on the wall earlier to no response; Chapin wasn't home. A week ago, as we'd talked late into the night after the All Hallows' Eve Ball, I'd asked her where she went so often. She said her mom lived nearby, in Eastchester. "Are you close with her?" I asked. She shook her head no. "But she's sick," she said as way of explanation. I knew I wasn't to ask any further questions. With Chapin in Eastchester, I had no one to tell me what to do. The decision of what to do with Raj's text message was mine alone to make.

None. Would you like to do something?

He did. I agreed to meet him at his room, and from there we would walk to the Mexican place we had gone to for the twins' birthday. And as soon as the plans were solidified, I tried to quell my anxiety before it could even form. This will be good for you, I told myself. You don't owe Raj anything. You can just be two friends getting dinner. It's okay to not want to be alone.

I started getting ready too early, and I redid my makeup and changed my outfit twice, and when I couldn't stand to look at myself any longer, I sat on my bed and waited. I walked to Perkins Hall slowly, and I walked under the window that I knew was Kip's. There was no reason to lie to myself; I knew the main reason I'd made this date was to have an excuse to go there, to be close to him. I wanted him to see me. I wanted to do anything I could to make him think of me.

Raj was dressed casually, wearing a crewneck sweatshirt with jeans—a choice that, like most things, made me initially relieved and then later disappointed. "You look nice," he said. He leaned in to put his hands on my shoulders and peck my cheek. I tried not to wince. I couldn't decide if I hoped Kip had seen the kiss, or if a witnessed kiss from Raj would induce more pity than jealousy.

"Shall we?" he said, offering his arm.

Regret overwhelmed me, but I had no choice. I gave him my arm and let him take me away from Perkins, away from Kip.

— — —

At the restaurant, Raj was embarrassingly polite. He opened the door to the restaurant for me, pulled out my chair for me, made a big show of spreading his paper napkin out on his lap. This is my second real date, I thought. I looked around, tried to gauge other people's opinion of Raj through their eyes and, by association, their opinion of me. Aren't we a reflection of the people we surround ourselves with, after all? Intelligence, refinement, beauty—I siphoned those qualities from others, from the Darbys and Chapins and Kips who were more intelligent and refined and beautiful than I was but chose me regardless, and I felt these qualities retracted from me when the company

I chose was lacking. I cared deeply what all those people in the restaurant thought of Raj, cared deeply that being with Raj did not make it impossible for them to imagine me worthy of someone like Kip.

After we'd ordered, he laced his fingers together and leaned across the table towards me. "So. I finally got the impossible Imogene to go out on a date with me."

Acknowledging the date while still on the date felt crass, like learning the details of your parents' will while they're still alive. "Hah. Yeah, I guess so."

"You make a guy work hard." He was grinning; we're joking around, his grin seemed to say. It's okay to do this now because we're past all the unpleasantness.

I thought to reaffirm my illness, but decided instead to take his lead. "That's me. Princess Imogen, unable to be wooed."

His smile became uncertain, as though I'd told a joke that he wasn't sure was offensive or not.

"It's from Shakespeare's *Cymbeline*."

Raj shrugged. "Never read it."

"Me neither."

Raj dipped a chip into the salsa, most of the large scoopful falling onto the tablecloth before it reached his mouth. We both stared at the spill. He smiled sheepishly. "Want a drink?"

"Yes," I said.

Conversation was easier after drinks were delivered. We talked about our classes, our students, our sports teams (he was the assistant coach of the swim team, which had just begun practicing for the winter season). I asked him about running, and in a rush of unexpected affection, asked if he would be interested in running together once the weather warmed up. He said he would. Our entrées were delivered, and we liberally picked off each other's plates. Had I been interested in him, I would have said the date was going well.

"I have to ask you something," he said. Our plates were nearly empty, and he'd just started his fourth drink.

"Okay," I said, biting my straw. I was just about to finish my third drink.

"The other night, Wednesday night . . ." He shook his head. "You're going to think I'm crazy."

"Try me."

"The other night in the dorms I heard this noise like . . . like a girl crying. It was coming from the stairwell. And I've never heard you cry, of course, but . . . for the craziest reason, I was sure it was you."

My teeth were still clenched down on my straw. My heart pounded, and I felt weak from the effort of keeping my face impassive.

"So I guess what I'm asking is . . ." He shook his head again, laughing. "Was it you?"

He wasn't baiting me; he truly did not know, I could tell. For an impulsive second I thought I might tell him the truth; he could know that there was someone else and that I hadn't turned down his dates to be malicious, that I wasn't a bad person. And ever since Chapin's reaction to the secret, I was desperate to find someone who might understand. But I knew Raj wasn't that person; all he wanted was for me to tell him that it wasn't me, that yes, he was crazy, and I was more than willing to do that.

"Wednesday night, huh?" I screwed up my face, pretended to think hard. "Hmm, no crying in boys' stairwells as far as I can remember."

He laughed, and I joined him. We had a great laugh at his expense. "I'm hearing things," he said.

"A ghost."

"The Perkins Hall ghost, Crying Christine."

"Bawling Belinda."

Raj paid the check, and we left. He took my hand on the walk back, and I let him because the night had been nice and I didn't want to spoil things. He walked me back to the Hovel and kissed me at the door (which I let him do) but didn't ask to come in (which was a relief). I went in through the back door and watched him walk towards Perkins. I waited ten minutes before following him.

— — —

I'd begun planning it at the beginning of the night. And with each drink, I became more and more certain that the plan was good. I would go to Kip's room and tell him that it didn't matter what we were, that I didn't want him to be my boyfriend. I would tell him anything to make things like they used to be. It was a humiliation I'd never be able to articulate sober. It was only when my inhibitions were down and my basest desires most potent—to fuck, to feel—that it felt okay to act.

I looked down the hall to make sure Raj's door was shut before I crept up the stairs. It wasn't until after I knocked that it occurred to me that it was earlier in the night than I usually went over and that he might not be there, or worse, that he could have someone else in there with him. But he answered, and he was alone. For once, he was surprised to see me.

"Hey?" he said, a question.

I kissed him. I pushed my tongue between his teeth and sucked his bottom lip, open-mouthed and greedy. For the first time in a long time, he didn't taste like booze. It took me longer than it should have to realize he wasn't kissing me back. I pulled away. "What's wrong?"

"It's just . . ." He closed his door behind us and ran a hand over his chin, already sprouting new scruff. "Like, two days ago you stormed out of here all in a huff and now you're back like nothing happened."

"I'm sorry." My voice sounded meek, a little girl's apology.

"It's not something to be sorry about. I'm just . . . confused." He was looking at me with that familiar unnerving intensity.

"I am, too."

He sat on his bed and sighed, looking down at his bare feet. "This whole thing is just kind of fucked up, you know?"

"I know." I sat down next to him. I knew he meant fucked up as in complicated, but still I couldn't help but think it was other kinds of fucked up, too. A fucked-upness I'd spent most of my time in the last few months expelling from my mind. "I know, but I don't want to stop." I paused, hesitating. "I like you."

"I like you, too."

He said this as though it was obvious, but still the words sent up a spark somewhere deep inside me. "Congratulations," I said suddenly.

"What?"

I had meant to say it warmly, genuinely, but it sounded everything but. "For the contest, I mean. The oratorical contest you won."

"Oh, that. Thanks." His eyes drifted to the dresser where, I noticed, a new trophy sat. He flicked his eyes away while I continued to stare. "What was it about?" I asked the trophy. "Your speech."

"I don't know. It was dumb."

"Tell me."

"Jesus." He bristled. "It was about my grandfather, okay?"

I was strangely disappointed by his answer. It was as though he'd told me his college essay was about scoring the winning goal in soccer or a Habitat for Humanity trip to Guatemala. "That sounds nice," I said. I didn't say, *You didn't tell me about the contest.* I didn't say, *What else have you not told me?* I was tired of pushing. He didn't want to talk, and I didn't want to ask him to anymore.

I got up off the bed and knelt before him. I unbelted his pants and tugged them down to his ankles. He watched me solemnly, holding his breath. Slowly, I took him in my mouth and didn't stop until he groaned and rolled his eyes back into his head and came, hot and carelessly, down the front of my dress. "—sweetheart," he muttered appreciatively, stroking my hair.

— — —

I knew he was there the moment I opened the stairwell door; I could hear him breathing. But still I went down the stairs, and at the bottom,

Raj stood from where he'd been sitting on the bottom step and we stared at one another.

"I heard your heels when you came in," he said finally. "An hour ago."

"Oh." I didn't need a mirror to know that my hair was tangled, that my eye makeup smudged, that the front of my dress was crusty with Kip's cum.

Raj shook his head slowly, disgusted. "I knew it. I fucking knew it."

"Knew what?"

He stared at me angrily. "Are you going to try and deny something here?"

I opened my mouth, closed it again. It was exactly what it looked like.

"Right." He turned to leave.

"Are you going to tell?" The question sprang from my mouth without warning, an impulse, a plea.

He didn't turn around. "I don't know, Imogene," he said. I stared after him, even after the door clicked shut, even after his footsteps faded down the hall, even after his bedroom door shut behind him.

FIFTEEN

THE NEXT DAY, BEFORE I'D EVEN BRUSHED MY TEETH, I KNOCKED on Chapin's door. "Enter," she called. I peeked around the door uncertainly, and I found her stretched out on her bed in a pair of simple white briefs and a tank top. I stared at the nearly nonexistent curve of her ass a moment too long, not expecting to see so much of her.

She sat up. "Yes?"

"Oh." I still lingered in the doorframe. "Did you want to, um . . ." I mimed wrapping something around my body, as though it had slipped her mind that she'd greeted me undressed.

"Am I making you uncomfortable, Imogene?" She grinned.

"No! No, I just wanted to make sure—"

"I'm fine if you are."

"Yeah. Okay." I entered the room and shut the door behind me, somehow feeling as though I was the one exposed. I stood by her bureau.

Chapin patted the foot of her bed. "Come here! I won't bite." She loved my discomfort. I knew better than to argue and joined her on the bed. "Now." She folded her feet into her lap and stuck her chin in her hands, assuming a campy telling-secrets-at-a-sleepover pose. "What's up?"

That whole week, ever since the All Hallows' Eve Ball, Chapin had felt like a real friend, the closest I'd come to a friend since my old roommate Darby Li in college. She walked with me to and from meals. She invited me to go skiing with her during winter break. One morning, when I came down the stairs for breakfast, she even said I looked pretty. And it felt like more than her seeing Kip and Betsy Kenyon together at the Ball and finally hearing the entirety of my sordid affair, her kindness born of pity. As difficult as it would have been to believe a few months before, it seemed that Chapin simply liked me.

"Something happened." I fiddled with the quilt at the end of her bed, anything I could do not to look her in the face. "Raj knows."

In TV shows, the minimal explanation always leads to mutual understanding; in reality, my life didn't mean nearly as much to other people as it did to me. Chapin frowned. "Knows . . . ?"

"He knows I've been hooking up with a student. That I *am* hooking up with a student." I'd never said the words out loud before; I didn't like the way they sounded. It was like admitting to a roommate that you masturbated under your sheets after she fell asleep, or to your parents that you used to pee in the pool. Acts that didn't seem so bad in your mind but once made public—once you invited others to express disapproval or disgust—became deviant, forever tainting you.

She looked unsurprised by the fact that Kip and I were still sleeping together. "What are you going to do?"

I looked at her, helpless. I'd wanted a plan, reassurance, comfort. I don't know why I kept expecting these things from others. "I don't know."

"I know what you can do." Chapin looked at me meaningfully. For once, the minimal explanation was enough. "I know."

"Then why don't you stop?"

I wanted so badly for her to understand. I wanted to say, *I can't because I'm in love with him. I can't because I truly believe that after he graduates, we can be together. I can't because I want him to take me out on his boat someday and introduce me to his parents and love me in the way that I know he's capable.* But I didn't say any of that. "I'm going to stop," I told her. "Really, I am. I promise."

She considered me for a moment and then asked, "Why do you do that to your face?"

I immediately put my hand to my chin, to the raw patch of skin I'd struggled to cover with makeup that I knew she was eyeing.

"Sorry, I didn't mean that to sound asshole-ish. I just meant, why do you pick at your skin like that when you know it's going to make it worse?"

I tried to deflect the subject, as I always did. "I spent four years with a therapist while she tried to figure that out."

"But why do you think you do it?"

I contemplated the question for the first time in years. Finally, I said, "I think I do it because I think I can make it better. Only I can't, of course. Then I keep picking, trying to fix my mistake, and it never heals and only gets worse and worse." I lowered my hand from my chin, suddenly conscious that it was still there. "It's disgusting, I know."

Chapin nodded. "I understand, and that makes sense. But that doesn't mean you should keep doing it."

"I know," I said, knowing I didn't really mean it. "I know."

— — —

The next week was the loneliest I'd ever been at Vandenberg. I was so convinced Raj had told the girls that he'd caught me—or at least that I had done something wrong—that I avoided them altogether. I didn't have the energy to win them over. I didn't have the energy to deal with anger or judgment. I didn't want to see any of them—especially Raj—because what I most feared was not the loss of their companionship, but to be told by them that I was in the wrong. They wouldn't understand—no one would understand!—and so that is who I spent my time with: no one. Even Chapin, my confidante, had become someone to avoid. Ever since I'd visited her in her room, she'd hissed constant reminders in my ear ("Have you ended it?") and filled my phone with increasingly frenzied text messages (Do it! Do it!!!). Instead, I listened to "For Luna" over five hundred times. Betsy Kenyon's profile page became the most visited website on my browser history. I ignored my mom's phone calls because, after a few days of this, I became accustomed to the silence. Letting someone else in would destroy that. Hearing a familiar voice would only remind me how alone I was.

I didn't hear from Kip. I alternated between certainty that his name would appear on my phone any minute and doubt that I would ever hear from him again.

Loneliness, I've found, is like drowning: it doesn't matter how stupid you look—how much you flail around or scream for help—because all that matters right then is getting through it. One afternoon at the grocery store I bought a bottle of wine—too-sweet pink Moscato—and I downed it in my bedroom in one sitting; that wasn't something I would have ever done before. The deviance of drinking alone made me almost giddy until my stomach protested and I ended up with my head in the toilet bowl. Another day, after class, I took the train into the city by myself, thinking I might walk around, enjoy some anonymity, disappear for a while, and the moment I arrived I regretted my decision and caught the next train back to Scarsdale. I sat at my window and watched touch football games in the quad. I listened to my roommates laugh and talk in the kitchen and reminded myself they weren't laughing and talking about me.

One night, the night I drank the wine, I even texted Zeke Maloney from college. He didn't answer, and I was upset, but really, what could he have offered me? What could anyone who wasn't Kip offer me? Kip was—inexplicably, unappeasably—all that I wanted. Letting go would be too easy. Letting go was, at the same time, an impossibility.

Around the middle of the week I sent an email to Clarence, asking if he wanted to get coffee and talk. There wasn't anything romantic in my intentions, of course; I wanted company, and I figured he could use some, too. I could edit his papers. I could be his advisor, the big sister I was yearning to be, let him open up to me about his stresses and insecurities. I didn't let myself acknowledge the real reason, the ulterior motive: I wanted to feel competent. I wanted to have something to offer. I was embarrassingly excited when he accepted.

We agreed to meet at the coffee shop on campus Thursday afternoon. He grinned when he saw me and looked nervously at the few tables of boys around us as he took the chair across from me—I felt sure it was his first time meeting up with anyone there. I grinned back; I wasn't used to feeling self-congratulatory, but I did. *This is as much for him as it is for me,* I thought.

Over the course of an hour, a shared scone, and two hot chocolates (neither of us were coffee drinkers, which made my offer of the coffee shop for a meeting place seem ridiculous), Clarence became less player-in-the-drama-I'd-made-of-Vandenberg and more person— only child, Vermonter, oboe prodigy. He told me about the best friend he'd ever had, Lucian Warren, who'd been claimed by leukemia three summers ago. He told me about his dream of working for the refugee services division. He told me about his suspicion that Christopher Jordan, whose dorm room neighbored his in Slone House, was a *marijuana user.* By the end of our hot chocolates, I felt sure that I loved him—a familial love, a love I thought I'd forgotten how to feel. A love without complications.

"You know you can always ask me if you need anything," I told him. "That I'm here if you need me."

"I know," he said, while his face revealed his surprise at the offer. He looked at me, then put the lip of his empty cup to his mouth, pretending to drink. I knew he felt the lopsided nature of our sharing but understood as well as I did that he wasn't to be my confidant. I was the big sister; it was my job to collect his secrets and hold them safe, his to offer them and pretend I didn't have any secrets of my own.

I didn't want Clarence to know my secrets. I liked myself in his eyes: sage, straightforward, beyond reproach or blame.

— — —

Dale asked me to stay after class on Friday, and I almost thought to leave anyway, to pretend to have not heard him or forgotten. By then the idea of Dale's dirty, empty apartment disgusted me; as lonely as I was, a relationship with Dale was never something I fantasized about, never a source of excitement or arousal. Men scared me, I realized—their desires and experiences were too foreign to me. I could never gratify one and would never—at least any time soon, it seemed to me—understand one.

"Imogene." He was unusually somber as he waved me over to his desk. I sat in the chair across from him, wishing the last student out had left the door open.

"Hi," I said; it came out shrill.

"Hi." His voice fell flat, a deflated ball thudding on the pavement. "Imogene, there's something I need to talk to you about."

I willed myself to relax, to appear comfortable. I made my eyes wide as though he had never touched my thigh or said he couldn't talk to a girl who looked like me.

"You're being transferred to another teacher next semester."

That I didn't expect; my façade slipped. "What? Why?"

"It's not you, I hope you realize that. It's . . . well, it's me." He laughed a little, hearing the cliché.

"Did I—"

"It's not something you did," he said quickly. "This isn't about the midterms." He looked to the door, making sure it was closed. "I fear that being around you makes me act a bit . . . inappropriately. You make me forget myself."

He stared at me, waiting for a response. I didn't know what to say; finally, I decided on, "What did you tell Ms. McNally-Barnes?"

"Nothing! Well, no, I told her it was your choice—I hope you don't mind. I just said you wanted the chance to work with another teacher so you could get a fuller experience." Dale looked at me almost sadly. "I've had a great semester with you, and you've been a wonderful help. I just feel this is the best choice right now. For me." He nodded definitively. "Yes. This is for me. I'm sorry if that sounds selfish, but this is something I just have to do."

I nodded, too. "Okay."

"Good! Good." He stood and stuck out his hand. Uncertainly, I took it, and we shook hands across the desk. "Of course, you'll be with me for the rest of the semester still, and it will be strictly professional. And I'll always be happy to provide a reference or offer advice in the future."

We were still shaking hands. I tugged back a little, and he released me.

"This is something I just have to do," he repeated.

"I know," I said. I smiled and wished him a good weekend and left the classroom, wondering why I felt so disappointed.

— — —

Despite the fact that Thanksgiving was less than two weeks away and most of the boys would be heading home to see their families, that weekend was Homecoming Weekend, and alumni—as well as parents and siblings (many of whom, the fathers and brothers anyway, were alumni)—were invited to campus for the last football game of the year. Friday night, a black-tie dinner was held in the dining hall—the most anticipated meal of the year, from what I'd heard. Saturday, after the game, there was a tailgate—or, rather, a disguised networking opportunity—with burgers and dogs. Sunday was high tea. My parents had been invited as well, had received the invitation in the mail—"Should we come?" my mom had asked. "No, no, that must have been a mistake," I lied. "Students' parents only." I didn't want them there, and not just because I was twenty-two and still embarrassed of them—that was something I'd hoped to have outgrown by that point. Every weekend felt like a possibility, a promise, for me to be with Kip, and Homecoming had already stolen one of the last precious weekends before Thanksgiving from me; why unsettle it further with more foreign invaders, with my parents?

The only redeeming aspect of Homecoming Weekend: I would get to see Kip's parents.

After meeting with Dale, I changed into a white button-down and black pants and joined the other apprentices in the dining hall. We would serve as caterers for the event, a choice that felt both debasing and thrifty. "With a five hundred million dollar endowment, you think they'd be able to hire a catering staff," Babs sniffed as the kitchen head—Rube, a flamboyantly gay graduate of the Culinary Institute in Hyde Park—handed out bow ties for us to wear.

The meal, however, was elaborate: three kinds of meat, three kinds of fish, bisques and salads and sautéed vegetables and a dozen dessert options and what I imagined to be very expensive red and white wines. We were allowed to make up a plate before setting up the dining room, and I ate more than I thought myself capable of consuming, ate until I felt sick and sluggish and hurrying around the dining room for the rest of the evening seemed impossible.

"Hungry?" Chapin asked, watching as I dragged one last forkful of dark-meat chicken through mashed potatoes and peas and stuck the whole mess in my mouth.

I swallowed without chewing more than twice. "I guess so."

The truth was I barely remembered eating any of it. All I could think of was the possibility—the desperate hope—that Kip would introduce me to his family. It was, in my mind, pivotal: Introduce me, and he truly cared about me. Fail to introduce me, and he never did.

Though the dining hall was large enough to comfortably seat all the students and faculty and staff during a regular meal, extra tables were brought in to accompany the guests. I aimed a few tentative smiles at the girls as we shuffled tables around the room, but they—even ReeAnn—offered little more than grimaces back. Raj I couldn't look at; we hadn't spoken since he'd caught me in the Perkins stairwell nearly a week before. I knew he hadn't told—I couldn't even be sure that he had told the other girls; perhaps their grimaces were actually smiles distorted by my neuroses, perhaps everything was at once much better and capable of being much worse than I could ever imagine. But then what was he waiting for? Was he giving me a window of opportunity to explain, to save myself, or would anything I said only further incriminate me and convince him to act? I chose to do what I did best: avoid, evade, pretend nothing was amiss and that I would always be safe.

"Cupcake, anyone?" asked Rube, coming out with a tray.

Everyone else demurred. I ate two, first licking off the frosting, then peeling off the foil wrapper and eating soft sugary cake from the bottom to the top, and finally pinching the crumbs from the bottom of the foil. Soon, all my energy was focused on my roiling stomach, as I'd hoped would happen.

— — —

The students and their families and old crabby-looking alumni ("Trustees," Chapin hissed in my ear with something like reverence, sounding strange coming from her mouth) filed into the room at six. I stood towards the back with the rest of the apprentices, waiting for our cue to circulate with wine. Technically, we weren't supposed to serve the students, but if their parents okayed it (and most would; I imagined most of the boys came from households where liquor with dinner was as common as water), we'd have no choice but to consent.

The bottle of Argentine chardonnay that I held perspired in my hands. My dinner had settled in my stomach like viscous lava, churning as I watched the door. I felt ill—Nervous? Humiliated? Who could be sure?—at the thought of serving him, his mother, his father; at the same time, a manic need to be near him possessed me.

Chapin poked me in the hip with her own bottle. "Too many cupcakes?"

"What?"

"You look like you're going to barf."

I shook my head. I couldn't look away from the door. "I'm fine."

She watched the door with me; she knew who I was looking for.

Clarence entered the room, his mom and dad looking exceptionally old, like grandparent-old. His father had too-long gray hair and small round tea glasses, worn without irony. His mother wore a long jean skirt with running sneakers, her gray hair plaited down her back. Clarence eyed the room desperately; unlike the other boys, no one was calling for him to join their table. His father lifted the giant Nikon around his neck and snapped a picture. My heart hurt for Clarence.

"Hey." Chapin nudged me. I turned away from Clarence and followed her gaze to the door.

Mr. Kipling was deeply tanned, barrel chested, surprisingly short. Mrs. Kipling, in a green cocktail dress, had the loose upper arms and faintly distended gut of middle-aged women, but was laughing, dark-haired, beautiful. A taller, fuller, hairier version of Kip held the mother's elbow—Adrian Kipling, visiting from Yale—and Kip followed up the pack, grinning and proud.

"I didn't know he had a brother," Chapin said. "Why don't you go for him?"

I'd known he had a brother, of course. I'd looked up his profile, looked through his pictures. Though he was a senior, he was older than me, having just turned twenty-three—"He was held back in kindergarten for sniffing too much glue, the retard," Kip had told me once. He played football at Yale, was a wide receiver. He'd already been awarded a Fulbright-Clinton Fellowship to study in Nepal after graduation. There was something untruthful in his face. I didn't have any interest in him.

I laughed nervously. "Yeah. Hah."

Rube came up behind us, making me jump. "Perambulate, perambulate," he said, twirling his finger around.

We set off in different directions around the room. I hated this, serving strangers—not because it was demeaning, but because I feared them. The students were intimidating enough; teamed with their parents, they were invulnerable. The parents themselves were even more terrifying. The mothers wore pearls, diamonds, shawls, huge rings on bony fingers, pointy shoes on bony feet. The fathers looked disgruntled, ready to pick a fight. I feared spilling, I feared interrupting, I feared their attention. The trustees looked the scariest, scowling at their empty plates. I stuck to the shabbiest-looking parents, the kindest-looking—"Would you care for chardonnay? Chardonnay, sir? Ma'am?" All the while I worked my way towards the table where the Kipling family sat with the Parks and the Keatings.

Finally I was a table away. The tables, rearranged in a tight configuration to accommodate the new guests, were so close that being a table away meant being close enough to reach out and touch him. Kip's back was to me. Mr. Kipling was telling a joke, laughing prematurely. "So I told him—heh, heh—I told him he could go ahead and stick it up his ass!" Kip and Adrian laughed uproariously. "Frank," Mrs. Kipling chided, but she couldn't hide her smile. Mr. Kipling was red in the face, obviously pleased.

They were happy, I decided. I watched Kip laughing, grinning conspiringly with his father. They were happy and affectionate and close. They were the kind of family to whom Kip could introduce one of the Vandenberg teaching apprentices without further explanation. I took a step closer. I thought about what I could open with, something generous, something teacherly. So you must be pretty proud of your oratorical champion, huh? Hey, how do you feel about potentially having another Bulldog in the family? My tongue felt like a block of wood. I couldn't pretend to be less than I was, not in front of the people who knew Kip best.

I wanted to be at that table more than anything. I wanted to be sitting beside Kip, not as his teacher, not as a guest, but as his. I wanted to be as much his as the fat shiny watch around his scrawny wrist.

"Merlot?" Chapin materialized over Frank Kipling's shoulder, standing between him and Kip. Though less than a foot away, she didn't turn to look at me, didn't seem to be aware of me at all.

"Please." Mr. Kipling gestured to his glass. "Now what's your name?"

She filled it with a practiced hand. "Chapin Dunn."

"Dunn. Dunn. Your grandfather wouldn't happen to be . . ."

"Yes, sir, that's him."

"You don't say!"

I didn't know who Chapin's grandfather was, and I didn't particularly care. I watched her eyes flit over to Adrian as she talked, his eyes zeroing in on the two open buttons at the top of her shirt, the outline of a red lace bra through the sheer fabric. I was being punished, I knew, for my failure to act, for my failure to do as Chapin had advised me. Before Kip could see me, before I could give him the chance to either receive or rebuff me, I slipped back from the table, back into the bustle of the room. I turned to the table nearest me to find Clarence and his parents, sitting with what looked like the families of two first years. His father was taking pictures of the chandeliers hanging from the ceiling, and next to him, his mother was pressing the prongs of her white gold fork into her palm, testing the sharpness.

I approached. "Wine?" I asked dumbly.

The parents all shook their heads. Clarence waved. "Hi, Imogene."

I waved back. "Hi, Clarence."

"Mom, Dad, this is Imogene." He gestured to me, and his parents turned to look at me and smiled, and his mom said, "Oh! Imogene! We've heard so much about you," and I wondered what exactly Clarence had told them about me.

"Clarence told us about all the time you two spend together." Mr. Howell wrapped his arm around his son's shoulder and squeezed, and Clarence blushed, embarrassed and obviously pleased. "We'd love to take you out to lunch tomorrow, if you're free."

I looked between Mr. Howell and Mrs. Howell and Clarence and suddenly, horribly, I knew what was happening. Clarence had led his parents to believe I was his girlfriend, and it was because Clarence himself believed I was his girlfriend. It seemed absurd to me, impossible even, but then the moments that had led to Clarence's presumption spooled before me like a movie reel: the ambulance ride, the drawings, the coffee dates. The shared bus seats (though Clarence's seat was always the one available). The promise I'd made (though I still wasn't sure what exactly I thought I could offer). I felt a mix of confused and indignant; I'd simply been nice to him, a friend, but he had misconstrued my good intentions and crafted a fantasy. "Clarence is a great student," I blurted. "I'm busy tomorrow, unfortunately, but please enjoy your evening."

All three Howell faces fell. Behind me, I could hear Chapin loudly say, "And it was so nice to meet you, Frank." She knew I could hear her; it scared me, suddenly, just how much she knew. I turned my back on Clarence and hurried away.

Back in the kitchen, I grabbed Chapin by her elbow. "What was that about?" I asked.

"What was what about?"

"That." I gestured to the room outside, to the families, to one family in particular. "Why did you . . . ?" The question was too embarrassing to finish. Why did you prevent me from meeting Kip's family? Why did you stop my fantasy from playing out as it was supposed to?

Chapin heaved a sigh and put her hand on my shoulder. "I was trying to protect you, Imogene."

I shrugged her off. "From what?"

"Do you really need me to say?"

"Yes, apparently I do."

Another sigh. "From disappointment."

"You don't think he would have introduced me?"

"I don't think he cares about you the way you think he does."

Rube passed between us, oblivious to the tension. "Perambulate, ladies, perambulate!" he sang.

Chapin picked up a new tray of glasses and smiled sadly at me. "I'm sorry, but I'm right."

I crossed my arms, feeling childish. "I'm sorry, but I don't remember ever asking your opinion." Self-righteousness overrode self-censorship; my disappointment was all consuming, and I didn't give a second thought to my words.

"Real friends don't wait to be asked their opinions," Chapin said. She turned and walked out of the kitchen. After another minute, I joined her, staying as far away from the Kiplings as I could.

— — —

The Homecoming game against Brunswick School was an annual event, the cause of much excitement the next morning. I heard the band playing through my bedroom window, heard happy whoops as boys and their families made their way towards the stadium. I'd gone to the first two football games of the season; I'd worn my blue-and-yellow striped Vandenberg scarf, purchased from the bookstore, had sat with the other apprentices and cheered along with them. Back then, I'd cared about participating, about being seen. But by November, I made excuses not to go. For the Homecoming game, when ReeAnn knocked on my door, I called, "Food poisoning. Sorry."

"Too many cupcakes," Chapin sang back as she passed by my door. Even she was going to the game; I overheard her telling ReeAnn in the kitchen that Frank Kipling, a friend of her grandfather's, had invited her to sit with him. She said this too loudly; she knew, again, that I was listening.

It was unseasonably warm out, a beautiful day. I wished it were overcast, raining, snowing even; it felt wrong to sit indoors when it was so nice out, guilt my parents had instilled in me during childhood. It was the same sort of guilt I felt when I slept past ten, when I napped longer than thirty minutes during the day—any way in which I misspent or squandered my time. Of course, that guilt had become increasingly easier to ignore.

I opened my laptop. I thought to go to Betsy Kenyon's profile page, as I usually did, but instead I went to Kip's. I was surprised to see that his status was active; he was online. Before I could think better of it, I messaged him. I didn't feel the need to be cautious anymore.

Why aren't you at the game?

He messaged back right away. About to leave.

I felt giddy for having received a response, light-headed even. Is Chapin with you guys?

Who's Chapin?

She's another apprentice.

Okay.

It occurred to me suddenly, alarmingly, that the conversation wasn't going well. I felt frantic to save it. I haven't seen you in a while.

My parents are here.

I was talking to a stranger. I figured, it being Homecoming Weekend and all. Haha.

A pause. Then, Gotta go.

His status went inactive. I stared at my screen, feeling the contents of last night's dinner churn in my stomach anew. I'm not sure how long passed before my phone vibrated on my bed. Chapin, I figured.

But it was Kip. My parents are going back to their hotel after the game, before the post-tailgate. You should stop by.

I thought it best to clarify, as nothing seemed clear anymore. By your room?

Yeah.

A moment later, You were right, your friend is here. She's trying to flirt with my brother. Too bad he has a girlfriend.

I lay on my bed and smiled at the ceiling with my phone cupped over my chest, willing the game to go by faster.

— — —

I dozed, and when I woke, it was dark. I felt panicked for a moment before I remembered how early darkness had begun to fall; it was still before five. Off in the distance, the band was playing the Vandenberg fight song, which meant we had won. I didn't care. I pulled on my shoes and brushed my teeth and walked the familiar path to Perkins, to Kip.

I'd never gone during the day, had never been desperate enough to risk it, but with everyone lingering after the game for the tailgate I felt safe. That's why it felt comical, inevitable, a punch line to a joke, when I opened the door and Raj stood before me.

"Imogene," he said.

I didn't speak.

"Please." He didn't look angry as much as distressed. "Don't make me do this."

And because he'd caught me again, because my excitement had made me so unreasonably careless, I felt angry instead. "You don't have to do anything."

"Please, just leave."

I could have. I could have pretended to leave and waited for him to pass before I went up to Kip's room, or I could have actually left, returning to the Hovel without looking back. But I felt betrayed— by him, by Chapin, by all the other apprentices, by all of Vandenberg, really, for trying to keep me from doing what, to me, felt so right—so

I didn't. Instead, I said, "You can't make me," a response so childish I felt sure he would laugh.

He didn't. "You're right; I can't." He opened the door wider, and I pushed past him while he walked away, back towards the stadium.

The panic was immediate, hitting me as soon as I began to ascend the stairs. What if Kip wasn't back yet? What if he crossed paths with Raj as he came towards Perkins; would Raj know it was him? Would Raj say anything to him? What if Kip didn't come at all and this, all of this, was for nothing?

But I didn't worry for long. Kip stood waiting outside his door. He reached out and took my hand once I was close enough.

"C'mon," he said. "We've got thirty minutes, and I want you at least twice."

He kissed me, and it seemed to me that I would do anything, sacrifice anything, go to any outrageous and perilous lengths, for things to always be this way.

— — —

I wasn't surprised, yet was somehow still devastated, when I didn't hear from him the next night. I didn't hear from him the night after that, either, or the night after that. After three nights of silence, I looked at Betsy Kenyon's profile page. Kip had sent her a link to a video, a dog chasing around its tail. Betsy had commented in reply, Johnny! An inside joke, I assumed. As much as it's a cliché, sometimes your blood really does run cold. I'd looked it up once—after I'd seen Zeke Maloney kiss that other girl at the bar and gone stiff with cold, after I'd run to the bathroom to run my arms under the hottest water the faucet could produce, after I'd regained feeling in my achy, tingling arms—because I thought I was dying. Epinephrine and cortisol are released into your bloodstream, and the heart beats faster, and the vasoconstriction of arterioles—required to increase blood pressure—creates the tingly icy sensation. And I felt it then, tingling up and down my arms and legs, my whole body washed in sickening coldness.

I checked my mailbox every day, waiting for a note to appear, waiting for my death sentence. None did; Raj must have been waiting, too.

And then soon enough it was Thanksgiving, and I was packing my bags to return home for the first time in three months, for the first time since I'd met Adam Kipling and I'd become a person I wasn't sure my parents would recognize.

SIXTEEN

MY MOM HAD VOLUNTEERED TO COME PICK ME UP TO TAKE ME back to Lockport, but I wanted to take the train instead. It seemed more romantic to me—the scenery whooshing by, the clacking of the wheels on the track, pretending for a few hours that you were some-one else going somewhere else. "Well, coordinate with your sister, at least," she said. I promised I would, but when I woke Wednesday morning, the day before Thanksgiving, I realized I still hadn't spoken to Joni. I called her—she would be getting a ride home with her boyfriend (a junior from Hunter, I'd learn later, whom she'd been dating for over a month). I called a cab to take me to the Metro-North station, feeling guilty for my relief. More than anything, more than the romantic appeal the trip held, I really just wanted to be alone, to glide home in silence, to spend the time thinking about what I would say to my family.

I can't pinpoint the time that I grew apart from them, because that would imply there was a time we'd been close. Yet my family was not estranged, dysfunctional, broken. I got along well with both my mom and dad, and Joni and I were civil, save for petty fights. My parents had always been great friends—they were pals, really, more than lovers. They were both of medium height with small frames, kept their graying brown hair trimmed just above the nape of the neck, wore similar ill-fitting polo shirts and khakis. Our longtime neighbors, the Castillos, called them the Abney Twins, a nickname that tickled my parents endlessly and made me feel almost unbearably sad. Together the four of us had gone to the Grand Canyon, to Maine, to Florida, once even to Puerta Vallarta as a surprise one Christmas. We were a good family, a happy one, but a family in which the members were acquainted the way coworkers are. We knew one another's birthdays and hobbies, favorite foods and strange quirks, but not, say, what we most wanted, or what we most feared, or who we were after we went home for the night and let our façades fall away.

I wished I wasn't so embarrassed by my parents, so disappointed in them. But I also wished that my mother hadn't worn her gardening shoes and baggy old men's jeans to our mother-daughter book club meetings when everyone else's mothers wore heeled boots and the same jeans as their daughters. I wished that my father knew the difference between "good" and "well" and didn't whistle "Camptown Races" while he sat on the toilet. I wished they didn't treat me like I was fragile, even damaged, one sudden move away from crumbling.

Joni, in turn, was embarrassed by me—her sullen big sister, volatile and strange and perpetually alone. My therapist told me once that I may be projecting, but I was so dissatisfied by the derivativeness of her analysis that I never gave it any legitimate consideration.

On the train, I chose a backwards-facing seat and set my bags beside me. Most of the boys had already left Monday or Tuesday night, as had my fellow apprentices, and my train car was free of them, free of the burden of familiar faces. The train doors snapped shut, and I watched the spire of Morris Chapel, just visible above the trees, grow smaller and smaller until it disappeared. I had expected a feeling of liberation; life at Vandenberg had grown nearly intolerable, after all. My roommates seemed to purposely evade me, Dale to fear me, and all the while I was waiting, waiting, for Raj to decide to turn me in and end it all. But as long as Kip was there, as long as he was close to me and as long as there was hope, Vandenberg was made tolerable. I felt panicked, really, as the train pulled me away. Kip wasn't there, of course—Kip was home— but still I wanted to stay. Vandenberg had become inextricable from Kip in my mind and therefore was the place where I belonged.

Sometimes I read through our text messages. Sometimes I went through the pictures tagged on his profile (though I'd been through them all, at this point, dozens and dozens of times). To pass the time on the train ride back to Lockport, I did something different: I took out a notebook and recorded—from the first time we kissed at the end of September—every time Kip and I had been together. I tried not to confuse myself with the ones I'd imagined, the dreams and fantasies that felt so real I was sure, even days after, that they'd actually happened. I counted seventeen. Three of those times had just been kissing. That didn't seem right; I recounted. Seventeen. It felt like one hundred, one thousand. It felt like I'd been with Kip more times than I'd be with anyone, ever. I tore out the list from my notebook and crumpled it, pushing it towards the bottom of my bag, wishing I hadn't made it at all. Everything seems lesser than it is in your mind when put down on paper.

I wondered how I would possibly have enough to say to my family for the next four days. I feared that if I spoke too little they would see I was slipping back into that precarious place, the one that had made my mom first take me to therapy years ago. Because—though they may not have been able to pick out an outfit I'd like or a guy I'd want to date—they'd learned what it looked like when I wasn't doing well, and it was by more than just the state of my skin. They knew me, and strangely, I wished they didn't.

— — —

Joni's new boyfriend, who I hadn't known existed until that morning, was joining us for Thanksgiving—another surprise. Alex was Canadian, and his parents didn't celebrate Thanksgiving, so he'd bring pumpkin pie, and he would be staying. My mom didn't usually allow guests for extended stays, especially during what was supposed to be family time; while other families loved big parties, loved hosting and having cousins and aunts and uncles and neighbors and friends spilling through the door, we kept to ourselves. "Our house wasn't designed for entertaining," my dad always claimed. But really, it was our family that wasn't designed for entertaining. We liked things small, quiet; we didn't like intruders. But I suppose I can't speak for Joni, as I really don't know Joni at all.

"Hey," he mumbled, shaking my hand. He was extremely tall, the kind of tall most people can't help but comment upon (I didn't), and I had to crane my neck to look up at him. I wondered where he would sleep, if he would be sequestered to the guest room or if my parents would acknowledge that he and my sister had undoubtedly shared a bed before.

Little had changed in the house. The third step still creaked, the downstairs bathroom faucet still dripped. From the walls our faces could be seen in various stages of maturation, trapped and oblivious. Though curtains had been opened and shut and overripe bananas had been replaced with new ones, the house had the feeling of being untouched, unlived in, as though awaiting my return to release its breath. I hadn't lived at home for over four years, and still I felt this way; I probably always would.

My bedroom felt the strangest, like a crypt, like a memorial. I set my bags on the bed where ten-year-old Imogene had slept, and fifteen-year-old Imogene, and twenty-two-year-old Imogene. The books on the shelves, the clothes left in the closet—everything was a reflection of my former selves. Rather than making me feel reacquainted, returning made me feel more distant from myself than ever. Who was the person who read those books, wore those clothes? Surely she wasn't me.

"Dinner!" my mom called up the stairs.

Next door, in Joni's bedroom, I heard the unmistakable wet smacks of kissing.

— — —

Thanksgiving was always at the house of Aunt Carol, my mom's sister, in Buffalo, but the night before belonged to my mom. We ate in the dining room, unused except for special occasions, the table set with the fancy china and the real dinner napkins. My mom had made roasted chicken and lit a few candles. I felt an unfamiliar shame for our shabbiness due to the interloper at our table. Alex was quiet, his reticence seeming more reproving than respectful in my mind. Joni's hand was on his thigh.

My mom beamed. "It's so nice to have both my girls home."

My dad, always quiet, nodded in assent.

"It's nice to be home," I said, wishing I meant it.

"So tell us about school, Imogene." My mom scooped a spoonful of mashed sweet potato onto my plate without asking, a gesture that made me irrationally, childishly angry. "You've been so busy we've barely heard from you since you've started."

I slid the glob of sweet potato to the edge of my plate with my fork. "I'm not in school. I work at a school." I felt bad almost immediately for my insolence but didn't take it back.

"Okay. Tell us about working at the school then."

It was the last thing I wanted to talk about, the preordained subject for me to be asked about. "It's good," I said. Knowing this would not be enough, I added, "Really good. It's been a really good experience. I really like it."

"Alex went to boarding school," Joni volunteered. "He hated it."

My mom was not to be deterred. "What about your class? And the lacrosse team? How are the students?"

"They're all great," I said. "It's all going really well."

"Where did you go again, Alex?" Joni poked him in the ribs.

"The Phelps School," he muttered.

"The Phelps School," Joni repeated.

"I've heard of it," I said, though I hadn't.

My mom was visibly frustrated now. "Do you have anything to tell us about what's been going on with you, Imogene?"

I wondered, when Raj finally revealed what I'd done, how my parents would be informed. Would they get a letter in the mail? A phone call? Perhaps they wouldn't be told at all; perhaps we'd all be able to carry on, continue the ruse, remain tangential parts of one another's lives. "It's all going fine, really. There's nothing much to tell."

A beat of silence passed before Joni spoke. "I finished that art project."

"Oh yeah?" My mom turned to her. "How did it turn out?"

As she continued to speak, describing a project that seemed a familiar subject to all but me, I realized that I'd been wrong. My mom smiled as Joni spoke, my dad nodded warmly. We weren't all strangers. The interloper at the table was me.

Joni mentioned something about birds, and I thought suddenly that I could tell them about the hawk watch field trip to Hook Mountain—something benign, something inconsequential, but something that demonstrated that I was willing to share. As Joni continued to speak, I practiced the story in my head. One of the boys was convinced that bald eagles didn't exist. It was the biggest bird I've ever seen. There would be no mention of the missing boy, Christopher Jordan's peeing over the side of the cliff, Kip waiting for me outside the Hovel the next day. I just wanted to show that I was listening, that I wanted to be a part of things.

"Growing the beard out for the winter, Dad?" Joni asked.

My dad ran his hand along his chin. "Ho, ho, ho."

"Alex tried to grow his out but I wouldn't let him."

My mom laughed. "If only your father listened to me like that."

The moment for telling my story had passed. I tried to smile and laugh along, wishing they just wouldn't ask anything about Vandenberg, wishing there wasn't so much I couldn't tell, still wanting to keep it all to myself.

— — —

After dinner, I retreated to my room to read. Downstairs, I could hear the four of them in the kitchen, talking over decaf coffee. (I'd used my dislike of coffee as an excuse not to stay.) Joni was telling them about Alex's participation on the hockey team, Alex's apartment on the Lower East Side, Alex's parents inviting her to visit Vancouver for New Year's. Unable to read, I set my book down and listened, as though I was sitting down there with them. I should have stayed down there with them. Sitting upstairs alone, I wasn't sure why I'd excused myself at all, but now it felt too late to go back.

I'd never brought a guy home before, but I imagined what it would be like if Kip were there. He wouldn't need me to talk for him; he'd be charismatic, irresistible. He'd pal around with Alex, pull him out of his shell. He'd talk politics with my dad. He'd help my mom with the dishes. Joni would love him.

I sent him a text message. Happy Thanksgiving! I said. I thought to add, *How's home?*, but it felt too chancy to pose a question, to demand a reply. With *Happy Thanksgiving,* it was okay if a reply never came. And it didn't, though I waited up for a while, until the voices downstairs went quiet and the doors shut and the lights went out. Alex slept in Joni's room; through the wall, I could hear them have sex.

After a few sleepless hours, I got out of bed and went to my dresser, where I turned on my lamp, adjusted my magnified mirror, and began picking at my skin. Nearly an hour passed before I finished, my dresser littered with bloodstained tissues, my face red, inflamed, unrecognizable. *Rudolph the Red-Nosed Reindeer,* I thought. The reflection in the mirror felt like someone else's; it didn't seem conceivable that I could have done this to myself.

— — —

When I went downstairs the next morning, my mom was already awake and putting a kettle on the stove. She drew back in horror when she saw me. "Oh my god, Imogene," she said. "What did you do?"

My hand went to my nose. I'd spent half an hour trying to cover the mess I'd made before venturing downstairs, but the effort had been in vain; there was no covering up what I'd done. "I know," I said immediately. "I know it's bad."

She dropped the handle of the kettle without turning on the burner and came around the kitchen island to study my face. "Oh, honey. This looks infected."

"It's not."

"You really shouldn't be messing with your face with dirty fingers," my mom said, and I felt transported back to the dermatologist's office, where each visit I was scolded, regarded with disgust for what I'd done. *Dirty*—the word was so debasing. At least the therapist had tried to help me figure out how to stop destroying my face, rather than trying to shame me into stopping. As if reading my mind, my mom asked, "Do you need to see a therapist again?"

"No." My hand still hovered over my nose, protecting it from her scrutiny. "No, I never do this anymore. I just got carried away." I wished she would understand—that they would all understand— that I couldn't stop. If I saw a blemish in the mirror, it was impossible for me to leave it alone; it was an addiction. *Apply a warm compress,* the magazines said. *Let the pimple run through its life span.* Fuck that— my fingers itched to pick. I could read a thousand articles on bacterial infection and inflammation and scarring, and I would still never stop.

My mom nodded, unconvinced; she knew it was a lie. She retreated back to the stove. I wanted to turn the attention away from my face, to get my mother to look at me with something other than concern. "Mom," I said, "I want to tell you something."

Her hand was turning the knob on the burner but she stopped, turned it off. "What is it?"

"It's nothing bad." I fiddled with the mail on the kitchen island. Credit card offers, catalogues. Her eyes bore into me. "I just want to tell you something."

"Okay."

I was nervous. It was like telling her about my first period. It was a conversation I'd seen countless times on TV, but it seemed that watching it play out again and again had only made it more difficult for me to take an active role in the scene. "I met someone."

"Someone . . . ?" The meaning, which I'd thought would be so clear, was lost on her.

"A guy. I met a guy that I like."

"Oh. Oh!" We'd never talked about boys before, my mom and I. I'd never talked about the boys in my class or commented on a male celebrity's cuteness, had never even explicitly expressed a sexual preference before. Save for the one date I'd gone on the summer before with Robert from Lockport Federal Credit Union, she may have assumed that liking a guy had never even occurred to me. "When did this happen?"

"A few months ago. Back in September."

"Well!" My mom scrambled, deciding what to ask, what could be asked. "Well!"

I helped out. "His name is Adam."

"Okay." She nodded several times. "Is he . . . ? Where did you . . . ?"

"If it's okay," I said, interrupting, "I don't really want to go into details, not yet. Would it be okay if maybe I just told you about him?"

This stumped her. "Of course."

And so I did. I described him, from his dark hair to his skinny limbs, and talked about his sailing and his family and his bedroom and everything I could think of, everything I'd collected over the past few months. My mom didn't ask questions; she just listened. She seemed to know that I had never spoken any of this out loud and that what I was saying needed to be said. How incredible it felt to talk, to purge. No one was there to contest a thing I said. Kip was mine to make into whatever I wanted him to be, whatever I needed him to be. It felt good, to be able to tell my mom something so normal.

When I was finished, my mom smiled. "I hope we get to meet Adam some day." Then she squinted, inspecting my face once more. "Are you sure you're okay?"

"I promise," I said, so embarrassed and relieved at once for finally getting to talk about Adam Kipling out loud that I nearly believed the lie myself.

"Will you leave your skin alone?" she asked.

"I'll try," I said, finding that lie even less convincing than the last.

— — —

Thanksgiving at Aunt Carol's house made me uncomfortable, as most events involving extended family did. I didn't know how to interact with Carol's daughter, Anastasia, who was three years older and had muscular dystrophy. Carol's husband, Fred, never made eye contact. My mom's and Carol's older brother, Steven, always showed up late and visibly drunk. Noni, my last living grandparent, stared at the football game on TV and refused to eat anything. There was always too much food. Knowing it would go to waste depressed me.

The five of us arrived just as Carol was pulling the turkey from the oven. "Hello, hello!" she trilled, scooping all of us into hugs, even Alex. "Welcome, welcome."

Two cats sat on the counter, and a third batted at a dishtowel from the floor. Half-dead plants cluttered the windowsills and table. A stack of old newspapers sat in the corner. I glanced at Alex; his face was unreadable. I felt profound relief that Kip wasn't there.

"Anastasia will be so excited to see you girls," said Carol. "Anastasia!"

We listened for the squeaking wheels of Anastasia's wheelchair, but none came. Carol shrugged and turned back to the turkey, humming. Her black zip-up was speckled with cat hair.

"Make yourselves comfortable," she said.

We filed into the living room, where Fred, Noni, and Anastasia sat transfixed by a commercial for baked beans. We went around and gave out hugs, stiff embraces of people who only touched once a year. Then we filled in the empty seats and turned to the TV, grateful for its glow, its distraction. After another commercial, Fred spoke.

"So you're Joni's new beau, huh?" He nodded to Alex, though his eyes were focused somewhere over Alex's left shoulder.

Joni nudged Alex, who was unaware he'd been addressed.

"Huh? Oh yeah, I guess."

"He guesses?" Fred looked around at no one in particular and laughed, looking for someone to join in on the joke.

"He is," Joni said, patting Alex's knee. "He's too distracted by the turkey to know what he is."

Alex stared at the TV, impassive. I was beginning to suspect he was slow, or at least incredibly boring.

"Well, welcome to the family, champ." Fred grinned and sipped his beer. He turned his body in my direction. "What about you, Genie?"

"What about me?"

"Where's your boyfriend?"

Joni snorted.

"Oh," I said. "Oh, no, I don't—"

"Actually," my mom chimed in from the loveseat in the corner, where she and my dad sat side by side in matching maroon sweaters. I turned to her in horror. "Actually, Imogene has a boyfriend, too."

My dad looked confused. "She does?"

Joni narrowed her eyes at me. "You do?"

Anastasia grunted in the corner.

I felt caught in the act, like the time I'd been ironing a pair of dress pants in the basement laundry room and my dad walked in on me in my underwear. Attention was one of many things that seemed more favorable in theory. I'd rather be unnoticed forever than a victim of overexposure.

"Who is he?" Fred pressed. "What's his name?"

"Since when do you have a boyfriend?" my dad wanted to know.

"I—" I felt naked, panicked.

"Leave her alone." Noni didn't turn from the TV as she said this, and her voice was surprisingly forceful.

Fred argued. "Oh, c'mon, we're just—"

"Leave her alone."

"Fine." Fred finished his beer, crushed it in his hand. "How about you tell us about that fancy school of yours, then?"

"Who's hungry?" called Carol from the kitchen.

I stood too fast and felt light-headed, the TV suddenly too loud and the lights too bright and all of it, everyone and everything there, was suddenly unbearable.

Dinner was better. We passed dishes, murmured compliments about the food. Anastasia was fed through her feeding tube, and Alex openly stared. Noni remained in front of the TV, the cheers and whistles of the game echoing down the hall. Eating trumped conversation. Just when we began to slow, our stomachs taut and angry for our abuse, Steven arrived, a welcome diversion in a stained T-shirt. The meal was passable, and for that we were all relieved.

I imagined Kip's Thanksgiving dinner. I imagined an enormous family, forty or fifty of them, all different ages, all beautiful. They'd all wear dresses and suit jackets and ties and take a family portrait on the grand staircase. The dinner would be catered. Everyone would drink wine.

At one point I excused myself to the bathroom. First I checked my phone; he hadn't texted me, and I was unsurprised and devastated anew. I thought to text him again—maybe he hadn't received it the first time? Maybe he'd forgotten to respond and needed a nudge?—but even I knew when the boundary between persistent and pathetic was crossed.

Then I checked my reflection in the mirror; my nose was a crusted mess, much worse than I imagined, and I wished I hadn't looked. I thought, not for the first time but certainly the most seriously, that I needed to stop picking. It was clear to me and to everyone else around me that I was destroying my skin, but what no one could understand was the release I felt from my prodding and poking; it was too cathartic to feel destructive.

— — —

The weekend passed uneventfully. Joni and Alex walked along the Erie Canal, went out with Joni's friends, lazed in front of the TV lying on top of each other like beached sea lions in a way I thought inappropriate, almost crude, to do in front of our parents. I resented them. It occurred to me that, even with Kip in my life, I couldn't be happy for her, couldn't be happy for anyone who was part of a pair. I wanted to be the only one. I wanted the joy of coupledom to be mine alone, the envy of all. As a result, I spent much of my time in my room. My resentment scared me in a way I wasn't prepared to question.

I thought about calling Jaylen and Stephanie, but knew I never would; I just liked the idea of seeing my old friends, of having old friends. I no longer knew Jaylen and Stephanie. I didn't even know the person I'd been when I was their friend—Had I been silly? Serious? Sarcastic? There was no "Classic Imogene," no "That's-so-Imogene"—I was amorphous, slipping in and out of personalities, changing characters mid-scene. I didn't know what I'd been like as a child any more than I knew who I was then, and I could only imagine who I'd choose to become. The people around me were my gauge; I matched them, mirrored them. I was a smooth, pliable presence that everybody and nobody could love.

Chapin sent me a picture of her socks the day after Thanksgiving, toe socks with little Santa Clauses on each toe. Miss you, she said. It felt good to know that, even if perhaps I wasn't quite forgiven, I could still be missed.

My mom came into my room Saturday afternoon as I lay in bed reading, inculpable and safe in an alternate world. "How would you like to go for a walk?" she said. "It's beautiful outside."

The sun peeked between my drawn curtains, insistent and cruel. As usual, I wished it were raining. "No, thanks."

She sat on my bed. "You've barely left your room since you've been home."

I knew this was more accusation than observation. "I'm tired. This is my break." I kept my book open before me, making clear this invasion wasn't welcome.

She squinted at me. "This Adam," she said slowly, "does he treat you well?"

"What?"

"Adam. Is he nice to you?"

Kip's niceness had never occurred to me; it was as though she'd asked if Kip had allergies, or if he flossed regularly. "Yeah," I said. And then, almost angrily, "Yeah, of course he is."

"Okay." My mom raised her hands in a whoa-there gesture. "I just . . ." She trailed off, stood, headed towards the door. I felt immediately sad, panicked, wanted desperately for her to stay, but I didn't say a word. At the door, she paused and turned back to me. "You know," she said, "it's not healthy, lying in bed all day."

I could have agreed, could have gone on that walk like she wanted. Instead, I said, "This is what I want to do."

She nodded. "Okay." Then she closed my door behind her.

— — —

Joni volunteered to give me a ride to Vandenberg with her and Alex, and I surprised myself by accepting. My bags were heavy, and train travel was a pain, Perhaps, too, I felt guilty for how little time I'd spent with her over the holiday, how cruel I'd been to not join my mom on a walk, and I thought a few hours spent in the car with my sister might make up for it.

We hugged our parents goodbye in the driveway, and my mom made me promise to take good care of myself, though it was hard to say what was best anymore. Alex perfunctorily offered me the passenger seat, but I declined. It was nice to stretch out in the back, where there was less pressure to contribute. The three of us talked a bit about the hairball Joni had discovered in Aunt Carol's pasta salad, a bit about the new bird-watching binoculars Mom had gotten Dad for his birthday with extra-low-dispersion glass that neither of them could figure out how to use. I wished again that I had told them the story of the bird-watching field trip.

Alex and I both dozed, and when I woke to the sound of Rabbit Foot's "For Luna," I thought I was still dreaming. I watched Joni in the rearview mirror, mouthing the words and nodding her head in time to the music.

"You like Rabbit Foot?" I asked.

She nodded, still keeping the beat. "Yeah, they're pretty cool."

"A guy I've been hanging out with introduced them to me."

"Your boyfriend?"

It was strange, having a conversation with the other person's back turned, especially a conversation you never expected to have. Joni and I never talked about boys, not even about B.K., the rock-climbing instructor, though Joni's relationship with him had materialized right in front of me. It wasn't like she would have ever sought my advice on guys; she and I both knew I had none to give. "Yeah. Him."

She paused, waiting for me to continue. I felt cagey; Joni's attention always felt pointed, malicious. When I'd emerged from the shower that morning to find her waiting outside the bathroom door, my hand flew to cover my nose so quickly I nearly dropped my towel. I waited for comment, but she merely asked, "Can I borrow your nail clippers? I can't find mine." If asked, I couldn't have provided an instance where she'd been overtly cruel, but I anticipated nastiness nevertheless, imagined secret ill will. It was impossible to cite what only existed in my head.

"It's only been a few months," I continued, trying to sound bored, unrehearsed. "He's from Hingham. We've just been having fun, nothing serious." I didn't feel the same pleasure I had telling my mom about Kip; doubt had begun to fester in my mind, and it wasn't just a product of the unanswered Thanksgiving text. The distance from Vandenberg, the reminder of how small and ordinary the life I'd come from was—all of it made my relationship with Kip feel like a cruel deception. It no longer seemed that Kip was mine to talk about; it no longer seemed that he had ever been mine at all.

"You didn't tell me about him." Her voice was strange, almost sounding hurt.

"It's nothing serious," I repeated. *I didn't know I was supposed to tell you,* I wanted to say.

Almost at the same time, we both glanced at Alex, who was still asleep. Joni met my eyes briefly in the rearview. "Will you tell me if it gets serious?" she asked.

I didn't know what to say; Joni was assuming a familiarity we'd never had, assuming the expectations of a relationship much closer than ours. It was disorienting and touching at the same time. I wondered, once more, if she imagined our sisterhood to be more than it was, or if my mind had made it less. "If you want me to."

Alex woke up then. "I gotta pee," he said, oblivious. "Can we stop soon?"

"Yes," Joni said, and she looked at me again in the mirror, to let me know that she was answering us both.

SEVENTEEN

I'D CHECKED HIS PROFILE—AS WELL AS BETSY KENYON'S—EVERY day over Thanksgiving break. On Friday, Betsy posted an article entitled "Why Greenland Is an Island and Australia Is a Continent" on his page with the caption, *Told you!* On Sunday, he commented on her latest profile picture, which showed her at a baseball game: *Yankees suck!!!* There was no doubt they were talking, but the nature of their relationship had yet to be pinned down and was therefore mine to construe. Friends, I decided. Good friends. I felt relieved upon deciding this, even while I knew it was probably not true, even while I continued searching for evidence to refute my own theory. I wanted to be right, but wanted—perhaps even more—to be devastated. I wanted my relationship with Kip to end with dramatics, with glorious indignation, rather than have it crumple into something unrecognizable, something grotesque, and slowly deteriorate, leaving nothing in its wake. Because I'd finally conceded that there was no question anymore about it ending; it was now only a matter of when.

Despite all this, I somehow knew I would hear from him again.

No one can ever deny that I knew Kip, really knew him, better than he even knew himself probably.

He waited until Friday.

Early acceptances started appearing in mailboxes on the Monday after the boys arrived back on campus. Harvard was the first to make an appearance; I saw Duggar Robinson in the dining hall, brandishing his letter of acceptance above his head, hollering, "Harvard, mother-fuckers, Harvard!" New sweatshirts and T-shirts boasting college names popped up around the quad, worn between classes or under button-ups to obey dress code. I heard about all the great upsets, like Cole Hokinson, a scholarship student in the top five percent of his class, being deferred by Dartmouth, while widely-known campus coke dealer Cody Hollander, whose grandfather had recently donated a dozen of his prized Monet prints to the Dartmouth art collection, was accepted. Around noon each day, the boys flooded the mailroom and filled the space with cursing or cheers. There I lingered each day before lunch, waiting for him to come, until the Yale letters arrived on Friday.

I never saw him pick up his letter. But when he texted me Friday night—Come over!—I felt certain I knew what his letter had said.

— — —

I hadn't seen him in almost two weeks, since Homecoming Weekend. He opened the door after I'd barely knocked; I'd just touched my knuckles to the door, really. He'd gotten a haircut over break, his dark floppy hair sliced above his ears in an awkward, freshly shorn way. It looked terrible, and I pretended not to notice.

"Hi, sweetheart," he said, grinning goofily.

"Hi," I said, less certain.

He pinned me against the door, shutting it, and kissed me with sloppy aggression. "You're so sexy," he murmured between kisses. I knew then that he wasn't sober. When he tried to pick me up—a move already made difficult by his scrawny arms—and stumbled, knocking my head against the door, I stopped him.

"C'mon. Let's go to the bed."

I took his hand, and he followed. On his bed lay a thick envelope stamped with the Yale crest, addressed to Adam Kipling.

"Kip!" I dropped his hand, picked up the envelope. "Did you open it? Did you get in?"

He took the envelope from my hand and tossed it to the floor. It fell with a heavy thud. He pushed me to the bed and continued to kiss me. I pulled back.

"You got into Yale, Kip! Aren't you excited?"

He tugged my body onto the bed and straddled me on his knees. He looked down at me, his face drawn and slack, the face of someone sleeping, or dead. "Of course I got into Yale," he said. "I was always going to get into Yale."

"Right," I said. The Oratorical Champion, the Yale Legacy. For the first time, though it was only for a moment, I hated him.

We continued kissing, but the mood had shifted. He seemed frustrated, peevish. He grunted as he tugged down my pants, stabbed two fingers inside me with unexpected urgency.

"Ow," I said, more to myself than him.

He pulled off his own clothes, though my shirt was still on and my pants and underwear were crumpled around my knees, as though I was sitting on the toilet. Once naked, his issue became clear: his penis hung flaccid and unresponsive, dangling like bait.

"Shit." He tugged at it. "Fuck!" He slammed his hand into the headboard, making the whole bed shudder.

"Kip, c'mon. It's okay."

He slammed the headboard again.

"Just let me . . ." I crawled towards him, reaching for him, trying to guide him into my mouth.

"No." He twisted away. "Fuck!" He was up off the bed. He

grabbed the Yale envelope off the floor and threw it against the wall. His face was red and contorted.

"Kip, stop!"

Footsteps pounded up the stairs. Kip and I froze and listened. They paused outside his bedroom. I pulled a bed sheet over my lap, knowing it best not to make any more noise.

A knock. "Everything okay in there?" It was Raj.

Kip, on the verge of a meltdown just moments before, had composed himself and now looked chastened, contrite. "Yes, yes, I'm sorry for the disturbance."

Raj did not leave. He breathed nosily on the other side. "Should I come in?" It seemed less a threat, more a legitimate question; even though it always seemed to me that the other apprentices knew exactly what they were doing, perhaps they were all just as lacking in authority and understanding as me.

"I would invite you in, but I'm afraid I'm not decent," said Kip. Only he could pull off saying something like that, "not decent."

"Okay," Raj said slowly. His feet shuffled, hesitating, before they turned and walked away. I stared at Kip, unsure what to do next. He stood in the center of the room, his chest heaving, his nakedness now ridiculous. I pushed the sheet off me, pulled up my pants.

"We don't have to do anything," I said cautiously. "We can just lay here. We can talk."

"Talk about what?" His voice was snappy; he wouldn't look at me.

"I don't know. Just about whatever. Like we used to."

"Why do you say that?"

"Say what?"

" 'Like we used to.' Like we're a couple or something." He was addressing the wall against which he'd thrown the envelope. I willed him to look at me.

"Well, aren't we? Something?"

He finally turned to face me. "No," he said.

"You're my best friend." I hated how my voice sounded as I said it. It was a pathetic shot, the last card in my hand. When he didn't answer, I added, "I really care about you, Kip."

"I care about you, too." He delivered this like an automated message. I didn't even need to look at him to know it was a lie.

Neither of us moved. I was afraid to breathe, lest I set off anything else.

"You should go," he said.

"Okay," I said. I felt robbed. I was supposed to have excused myself; he had stolen my line. I edged off the bed and towards him. "Can I . . . ?" I reached out my arms, a little kid asking for a hug. I just wanted to touch him. I needed to touch him.

Grudgingly, he let me wrap my arms around his skinny, naked body. He didn't hug me back. Just as I was about to release him, his shoulders began to shake. It took me nearly a full minute to realize he was crying.

"Kip?" I held him at arm's length. His eyes were pooling with fat tears, his mouth open in a silent scream. He was an ugly crier, and it was a horrifying sight. "Kip, what happened?"

He didn't answer, just continued to shake and weep, and so I held him close again, feeling strong for once, almost maternal. Strange shushing sounds came out of my mouth as I rocked his body with mine. His skinny body quivered in an unnatural way that made me believe he hadn't cried in a long, long time. Finally, he sputtered, "It's so much pressure."

"What is?" Was it the oratorical contest? Yale? Worried, suddenly, that he meant it literally, I released my hold on him. "What is, Kip?"

"All of it," he said. "All of it." He choked out another round of sobs, and I held him until he stopped, until he had regained composure enough to wipe his mouth and wiggle out of my grasp.

"You okay?"

"I'm good." Already his face was cold, closed, as though he hadn't just wept in my arms.

"Do you want to talk about it at all?"

He shook his head no. "I'm sleepy," he said, and in its second us-age, I found that "sleepy" had lost its charm. "I'm going to go to bed."

"Okay." I backed towards the door. "I'll see you?" It was a question because I didn't know the answer.

"Yeah," Kip said. He had turned towards the wall. He didn't seem to have heard my question or care whether he'd see me or not, and he didn't seem to notice when I opened the door and left.

Just before I closed the door behind me, I thought I heard him say, "Thank you," but I might have imagined it.

— — —

December had arrived, and with it cold unlike anything I could re-member. It would be the coldest winter in twenty years, the weather reporters claimed. Just like every seasonal change that semester, the first hints of winter felt foreign, a frightening glitch in the world or-der. My hands hadn't felt this stiff with cold last year, had they? Had the wind burned my face this painfully? I felt sure that the temperature would just drop and drop and drop until no one could stand it, until we were sequestered indoors, ran out of fuel, froze in our beds. Aren't you scared? I wanted to ask everyone. Aren't you terrified?

I was thankful, at least, that it had yet to snow. The snow, I felt sure, would bring with it the end.

As I sat in my room Saturday morning curled beneath several blankets—the redeeming part of the cold was that it allowed me to do this—I replayed the night before in my head. Where had I gone wrong? What had I done to upset him? It wasn't until nearly noon, when I still had yet to emerge from my nest of blankets to brush my teeth or eat or even pee, that I began to feel angry. I hadn't done anything. I'd never done or said anything other than what he wanted. How had things still soured? How was it possible to have done every-thing right and still not get what I wanted?

I reached for my phone and texted him. Who is Betsy Kenyon?

I felt triumphant upon sending it, haughty and vindicated. He didn't answer right away; I hadn't expected him to. I lazed around for another hour or two before the regret began to settle in.

I texted him again. I just ask because I want—No. I hit the backspace button—need to know if there is someone else.

Another half hour passed. I sent another message. I hope you're feeling okay today.

I set my phone on my nightstand, still uneasy but satisfied. *No more,* I told myself. *No more.*

— — —

Chapin knocked as the light began to fall outside my window. "Hello? Anyone alive in there?"

"Come in," I said. I couldn't say why, but I wished she wouldn't.

She came in and switched on the overhead light, a move that felt intrusive, even disrespectful. I glared at the light.

"It smells in here," she noted. "Like a dead body."

I didn't answer. She came and sat on my bed, another intrusion.

"You look really sick, Imogene. Really skinny, too. Are you sick?"

I nodded. Illness was always the easiest excuse, the best method of avoidance.

"You've been sick a lot this year."

I nodded again. I needed some sympathy, even if it wasn't for the right reasons. I needed someone to care.

"I don't think you really are sick though. I think you're depressed, Imogene."

The gravity of her voice surprised me. I peeked over the edge of my blankets out at her. "I'm not depressed," I said.

"How do you know?"

"I'm just not."

She crawled over my body until she lay on top of me, our bodies separated by a layer of blankets. Her face was too close to mine, but

I was trapped beneath her. When she spoke, her breath was hot, and the words seemed to spill directly into my mouth. "This thing with Adam Kipling needs to stop."

"Okay."

"No, seriously. It needs to stop. It's killing you."

"Okay," I said again.

My phone buzzed on my nightstand, and we both turned to look at it. As I was pinned beneath her, Chapin was able to pick it up before I could.

"Adam Kipling says, 'Don't worry about it,'" she said, squinting at the screen. She looked at me. "Don't worry about what?"

"I don't know," I said honestly.

She dropped the phone back on the table. "What do you want, Imogene?"

I thought about a book I'd read in middle school, a story about a girl with a terminal illness. She'd been asked what she wanted before she died, and she said what she wanted was one last perfect day, a day where everything aligned and everything felt right. "One last time with him," I told her. "One last chance for things to be how they used to be."

Chapin stared at me, curious. "How do you think things had been before?"

"You know." I tried to keep the agitation out of my voice. "I told you. He was . . ." I stopped, started again. "It felt . . . *real* before." My cheeks burning, I added, "It felt like love."

Chapin still stared. "But was it love?"

I felt small, stupid. "I don't know."

She rolled from on top of me and bounced off the bed. "I don't think it was, Imogene. It rarely is." She paused when she got to the doorway and looked back at me. "It needs to stop," she said again. "If you don't stop it, then I will."

"But how—?"

"And shower for Christ's sake." Chapin pinched her nose. "Like, you seriously fucking reek."

— — —

One last time, and then it would be over; that's what I decided. It wasn't about the sex, if it ever even was. The last few times, Kip hadn't even been able to come, and he'd pumped inside of me long after I'd gone dry, growling with frustration, until I felt the pain would split me in two. I didn't like the sex anymore; it would be preferable to me, really, if we didn't have it at all. I just wanted to be with him. I wanted us to undress and drape our naked limbs over each other under his sheets, to touch each other's hair and chests and faces like we never could—and never would—outside of his dorm room. I wanted him to tell me I was a sweetheart. I wanted him to speak elusive words that I had yet to pick out and place on his tongue.

I wondered how things with Kaya had ended, who had been the one to cut ties. I felt pretty sure I knew the answer—a fifteen-year-old doesn't know how to say no, even if he wants to—and it embarrassed me that I had failed to act as the Older Seductress should. I hadn't done the seducing here. I was the seduced, the swindled, the casualty.

I didn't shower; my body felt too fragile to be subjected to the scalding stream of the showerhead, the cold porcelain, the too-bright light. I didn't want to see my naked body in the mirror. I didn't want to be clean. Instead, I dabbed a bit of scented oil behind each ear, applied fresh makeup, took my hair out of its greasy ponytail and smoothed it down my back. I liked that I looked a little rough, a little haggard. I wanted Kip to see what he'd done to me. If he was to understand what I needed—that one last perfect night with him—then he needed to see me like this. He'd cried in front of me, after all. He couldn't have done that if he didn't care.

I crept up the stairs, something I'd been conditioned to do but that had lost its sense of purpose, like washing my hands before dinner, separating my darks and whites. I held my breath as I ascended, listened to the wooden creaks, the shuffling feet, the boys' voices hushed and foreign behind the doors. He was there; I knew he was there. Two doors down on the right, I stopped, tapped my knuckles against the wood, waited.

This is what I imagined: he'd open the door wearing sweatpants and rubbing sleep from his eyes—it was too cold to go out, too cold to have done anything but go to bed. He'd say hello, too groggy to question anything. I'd step into the room without waiting for an invitation. I'd settle onto his bed. "Come here," I'd say. He'd close the door and join me, and we'd fit our mouths together. We wouldn't acknowledge the night before, or Betsy Kenyon, or the inevitable end. We wouldn't think of anything except tongues, fingers, warm skin.

But he didn't answer. I knocked again, and then I put my ear to the door. Silence. He had evaded the power of my will. He had failed to live up to the expectations of my manifested reality. I waited for a minute more before I heard a doorknob turning down the hall. And then I ran.

I was sobbing before I even pushed through the front door. I couldn't help it—the fury burned like acid up through my stomach and throat and compelled me to release it lest I pass out. Outside of Perkins, I fell to my knees on the dead crunchy grass and bellowed. My vision blurred, the campus tilted. I didn't care who heard me. I wanted to make a scene. I slid down so that I lay on my side, cold blades prickling my ears. I'd spend the night there. I'd be discovered in the morning plastered to the ground, my eyes frozen shut. I'm not sure how much time passed before I felt a hand on my shoulder, heard a voice—"C'mon"—and was guided back into Perkins, back into the warmth.

— — —

I'd never been inside Raj's room before. I'd expected books and posters and pictures, but his room was plain, like mine. He sat me on his bed and wrapped a blanket around me. It was a few minutes before I could talk.

"Thanks," I said. "Sorry." I was too tired to feel embarrassed or even upset anymore. I felt nothing except the comforting weight of the blanket.

He sat on the end of his bed and peered at me, not unkindly. "Are you okay?"

"I don't know." I looked at my feet. "I don't think so. No." Then I began to cry again.

"Okay, okay." Raj stroked my hair. His hand was hesitant; I couldn't tell if he was reluctant to touch me or unsure as to whether I wanted to be touched.

"Sorry," I said again. I wiped my nose on the back of my hand, a bad habit from childhood.

His hand fell from my head—I thought at first it was out of disgust, but then he deposited a tissue box onto my lap. I took one, blew my nose with a loud honk.

"Sorry."

"It's okay, Imogene."

We sat for another minute. I continued to look at my shoes.

"You know," Raj began, "I didn't like him from the beginning."

"Who?"

"Adam. That's his name, right? Adam?"

I looked at him in surprise. "How—?"

He shrugged. "I have the dorm room list. I could hear where you were going. It wasn't hard."

I felt a flush of embarrassment at the idea of being heard. What else might Raj have heard? What else may have been heard by anyone? What if everyone had been in on it, had been listening to the creaking bedframe and moans—*my* moans—night after night? Was there anything worse than a spoiled secret, a secret that had perhaps never been a secret at all? I ignored all this, elbowed it back into the recesses of my mind for later investigation. "Why didn't you like him?" I asked.

"I don't know. Just something about him. He seemed arrogant to me. Cocky."

I nodded, unconvinced. I wouldn't expect someone like Raj to like someone like Kip. "He won the regional oratorical contest," I said, a weak defense.

"That doesn't make him a good person, Imogene."

I bowed my head, embarrassed.

"There's something else, too." Raj shifted, eyeing me nervously.

"What?"

"Well . . . he brought girls back, sometimes. After hours."

I felt that horrible, familiar feeling: the increased blood pressure, the tingly, icy sensation, the sickening coldness.

"Not that often," he said quickly. "But he did. I caught him two or three times and sent the girls home. Different girls."

"Was one of the girls blond?"

"What?"

"Never mind." I shook my head quickly.

"Okay." His timid hand crept back towards me, and he touched his fingers to mine. "I thought you should know."

I looked at him. His face was half-hidden in shadow, just long-lashed eyes, parted lips. Raj was cute, I decided. Raj was really cute, and I was a fool for not having seen it.

"And just so you know, I'm not going to tell. I was never going to tell."

"Really?"

He smiled. "Really."

I curled my fingers around his. I felt dizzy from having cried so much, almost drunk. I could kiss him, I thought.

Raj stood. "Can you get back to your room okay?"

I nodded and stood beside him. I was not supposed to kiss Raj; I was supposed to return to my room.

"Goodnight, then." He reached out, stopped, changed his mind again, and pulled me into a hug. It was brief, perfunctory. He released me and looked at me questioningly. Did he want to kiss me, too? It didn't matter. Only I knew how the story was supposed to go.

I don't remember the walk across campus. I don't remember folding myself into my bed, still dressed. I just remember thinking, tomorrow—that's when I'd feel again. That's when I'd allow my pain to be felt in full.

— — —

I woke the next morning with a vague sense of loss clinging to my consciousness like the remnants of a dream. I sat up and traced back through my nocturnal wanderings. I'd had a dream about Kip, something about a boat and a sprung leak—

Kip. The realization sat itself abruptly on my chest, squeezing the air from my lungs. Nothing had happened, really—I'd gone to his room on a Saturday night and had stupidly, tragically pinned my hope on his being home when he was not—but it felt as though something irreparable had happened nevertheless. Life had proved to be unreliable and unfaithful to my whims. It was a loss almost as great as losing Kip himself.

I think somewhere I'd known he wouldn't answer the door that night. Maybe I'd even wanted for him not to answer. A lack of response is better than rejection. I'd rather have my hopes dashed than have been turned away from Adam Kipling's door.

A fleck of reassurance kept me afloat: Raj would not tell, and that meant my secret was safe. Except for Chapin, that was. Her formerly empty threats had turned to notes slid under my door, a wild influx of angry text messages, once even a confrontation as I sat on the toilet. "I will tell, Imogene," she said. "I swear to god I will."

"Why are you doing this?" I asked.

"Because I like you too much to wait any longer," she said.

But like the night I'd walked away from her, the first night I'd slept with Kip, nothing could make me stop. Not even the will of Chapin Dunn.

Sunday became Monday, which became Tuesday. Finals were approaching, and the campus seemed to be holding its breath, ready to burst. It made my head ache. When I forgot a notebook in my room Tuesday morning and returned after breakfast to retrieve it, I slipped into bed for a moment to alleviate the pain. Then I fell asleep. I woke hours later and laughed out loud when I realized what I'd done.

On Wednesday morning, when I stuck my face from my covers to find the room chill and uninviting, I slipped back beneath. Thursday as well. And all the while I sent text messages to Kip. I miss you. Where have you been? Why won't you talk to me? Kip? Kip? He didn't answer, just as he hadn't answered that door. It didn't matter; I was invulnerable from the safety of my room, my bed. My head. I continued to send them, sure I could wear him down, and even if I couldn't, I knew he saw them, knew I was connecting to him, and that pleasure was too addicting to give up.

Dale emailed me Wednesday. Disregarding class two days in a row without explanation is unacceptable. Please contact me. I didn't respond. I missed the days when he'd liked me. I hadn't realized how much I'd relished in his flirtation until it stopped.

And then finally, Friday, the email from Ms. McNally-Barnes came. Report to my office at 3pm today. Failure to do so will require me to take legal action.

I stared at it, dazed. This wasn't about my insubordination, my skipping class. The horror cut so deep, so immediate, that I thought I would give up all of it—anything I'd ever had with Kip, anything I ever would—if only to be small and anonymous again.

EIGHTEEN

MS. MCNALLY-BARNES SAT ALONE IN HER OFFICE, HER HANDS laced on her desk. Her face was tight and intolerant. I peeked around her office door quickly, discreetly, to the chairs opposite her desk. They were both empty. Of course Kip wasn't there. I should have known we wouldn't be brought in together.

"Imogene." She gestured to the empty chairs.

I sat. I felt close to tears already, just from the cold way she'd addressed me. I would not cry, not yet. I was too old to think tears were still endearing.

"Imogene." My name again—I shuddered at the sound of it. I hoped she wouldn't say it again. "Are you familiar with our policy on maintaining appropriate student–apprentice relationships?"

It was a classic confrontation: the asking of rhetorical questions, the steady exposure of my obvious transgression. This was supposed to be painful and slow, the peeling off of a Band-Aid, the wrenching out of teeth. This was supposed to humiliate me. Any doubt I had about the nature of the meeting crumbled. "Yes," I said, unnecessarily. "I am."

"So you're aware that text messaging with a student is inappropriate?"

"Yes."

"And visiting a student's dormitory room is inappropriate?"

"Yes."

"And that having a sexual relationship with a student is entirely inappropriate?"

She said it; I'd so hoped she wouldn't say it. That term, "sexual relationship," clouded the room, choking the air. I might as well have sat before Ms. McNally-Barnes with my legs spread. What a humiliating thing it was, sex. I sank back into my chair, wrapped my arms around myself, willed myself to be swallowed by the fabric. "Yes."

She held up a piece of paper—an email? A written testimony? An explicit tell-all? She was too far away for me to tell. "You understand then why these allegations are so serious?"

I contemplated whether it would be better not to answer at all. "Yes. I do."

"And do you know the nature of these allegations?"

A trap. I hesitated. "Well, I'm not sure exactly what you may have—"

"How about you tell me your version of events then? You seem to be familiar at least with why these allegations were made."

For the first time since I'd received her email the day before, the injustice of it all took hold of my skull, blurring my vision. Raj said he wouldn't tell. He'd promised he wouldn't tell. Unless, of course, it wasn't him. Could it have been Chapin? Could my friend really have done this to me? Why would anyone do this to me? It was Kip that had hurt me, it was Kip that had destroyed me, it was—

I couldn't help it. I started bawling. I bent over in the chair and clasped my hands to my face. After a minute of this, I collected myself a bit, peeked up at my supervisor. She sat staring, unmoved. Her indifference felt like a perversion. My tears had failed to illicit sympathy, and once again, I'd been stymied by my inability to predict human nature.

"I'll give you a minute," she said. She stood, started towards the door, and then thought better of it and snatched up the papers on her desk. "I'll be back."

And I was left alone, as I'd never really been before in another person's space. I was afraid to touch anything, afraid to even look at anything. This place didn't belong to me, but then again, I wasn't myself anymore. I was someone who had had a sexual relationship with a student and who no one cared about if she cried.

After ten minutes, Ms. McNally-Barnes returned. "Monday," she said.

"Sorry?"

"Monday is when you'll have your disciplinary hearing. We'll review the allegations and decide on a course of action."

I felt stupefied, submerged underwater. I wondered when I would return to reality and this all would begin to sink in. "Monday."

"Nine o'clock in Dean Harvey's office."

"Nine o'clock."

"Imogene?" She peered at me, looking concerned for a moment, almost sad, a reminder of the person she'd been to me when I was still good.

"Yes?"

"I'd return to your room now, and I'd try and stay there as much as possible this weekend."

"Yes."

"And this probably goes without saying, but you are not to contact the student."

The student. I wished she would use his name. I needed confirmation that she knew my alleged sexual relationship had been with Adam Kipling—an adult, an equal, not really a student at all—and not, say, Duggar Robinson, or Christopher Jordan. "Right."

"Okay, then." She crossed the room, opened the door. Her face softened—pity, perhaps? "Will you be alright?"

I wasn't sure what was meant by this, and I also wasn't sure that I would be. "Yes," I said. And I left to return to my room, the place that had so long felt like a sanctuary but had now been transformed—condemned—into a prison cell.

— — —

The night was endless. The night was an immitigable horror. The reality I'd been waiting to set in while I was in Ms. McNally-Barnes office finally did, and with it, shame unlike I'd ever felt. With Kip, I'd loved my body—its dexterity, its dampness, its alternative softness and strength, its ability to provide unimaginable pleasure, the hold it allowed me to have over Kip. Now it felt like a source of disgust. My breasts, conical flesh baggies. My thighs, uncontrollable dimpled and wobbling masses. My feet, my stomach, my arms—it was all disgusting, all contemptible. Why had I thought this body deserving of anyone's love? Why had I thought this body worth sacrificing everything for?

But still I believed Kip had been worth it. I imagined his smile as he pushed into me, his laughter. I wondered if he knew that I loved him.

The Hovel had been quiet when I'd returned, for which I'd been unspeakably grateful, and had remained quiet throughout the day into the night. I didn't wonder where the other apprentices were; I wanted them to stay away. I'd always been a bit of a loner, had enjoyed my own company more than that of others, but my desire to be alone felt profound then, almost insatiable—I didn't even want to be with Kip. I wanted to be in the mountains, on an island. I considered a life of complete isolation. Never having to justify, never having to speak—what a life that would be.

I wondered if the other apprentices knew yet.

Outside, it began to snow.

— — —

I woke fully dressed and sweating, tangled in my sheets. Downstairs in the kitchen, I heard cabinets open and close, the sound of something frying. I smelled bacon. The voices of the other girls intermingled, barking, seeming almost purposely irksome. For the first time in a long time, I was hungry.

I listened to their conversation: final exams, winter break, the snow. Remembering, I hopped out of bed and went to the window. The sun reflected off the thick white carpet that covered the campus, a blinding white light. Sparkling flecks continued to fall. Despite having dreaded the snow, the sight filled me with childish glee. Snow, beautiful snow! I watched it fall another minute before the light began to hurt my eyes and I drew the curtains shut.

I heard a flush, the creak of the bathroom door. Chapin's feet padded down the hall. I held my breath, but her feet stopped at her own bedroom and the door closed behind her. My disappointment surprised me. Perhaps I was tired of being alone.

I waited a minute, hesitating, before I knocked on the wall behind my headboard. No answer. I knocked again.

"Yeah?"

"It's me."

"I know, Imogene."

There was a pause. It was mine to fill, but there were too many things to be said. "What are you doing today?"

"Work."

"Oh."

Another pause. "Did you want something?"

"Oh. No."

A few minutes passed before I knocked again. She must have put on her headphones because it took three knocks this time.

"What?"

"They know. They found out about me and Adam."

"Who did?"

"Ms. McNally-Barnes. The teachers. There's going to be a hearing."

Silence.

"You didn't tell, did you?"

She didn't answer. I was about to knock on the wall again when she burst through my door. She looked as though she might cry.

"What—?"

Chapin came to the bed and hugged me. "Oh my god, Imogene," she said.

"So you didn't—?"

"No, you dumb shit, of course I didn't tell." She hugged me harder. "Oh my god, Imogene. Oh my god."

For the first time it occurred to me that my career at Vandenberg was over.

— — —

Chapin stole me a plate of bacon from the kitchen, and I ate in my bed, wiping my greasy fingers on my duvet. I felt as though I'd been told a relative had died—my parents, Joni, all of them at once in a fiery car explosion—and I was trying to understand what that meant. How long did it take to digest unthinkable tragedy? Was the body even capable? I could say the words aloud—*I am going to be asked to leave Vandenberg. I will never see Adam Kipling again*—but they meant little to me. Perhaps because, really, I didn't believe them to be true. My parents, Joni, they didn't die. I couldn't be fired. Kip wouldn't let me go. Tragedy was something that happened to other people. I was too ordinary, too inconspicuous, to fall prey to the universe's wrath.

I tried to read, tried to watch TV, but my mind felt too sluggish to concentrate. Knowing I was imprisoned made me antsy. I paced my room. I watched the snow fall. I pulled a duffle bag out from under my bed at one point and began to pack, but I stopped myself. I wouldn't know—couldn't know—what would happen until Monday, and preparing for the worst felt unproductive and cruel.

I imagined instead an alternative ending. I imagined a court-room, Dean Harvey acting as the judge, and Kip on the witness stand.

"Did you have sexual relations with Imogene Abney?" Ms. McNally-Barnes would ask, pacing the floor.

Kip would look at me briefly, sitting alone before him. "No, ma'am, I did not."

"Would you say there was anything inappropriate about your re-lationship with Imogene Abney?"

"No, ma'am."

"So you're saying that any claims that have been made about a sexual relationship between you and Miss Abney are false?"

"Yes, ma'am. She didn't do anything wrong."

I looked at my phone on my nightstand. It had been silent all day. I knew I couldn't text him, and sending an email would also be un-wise. Perhaps I could leave a note in his mailbox—BURN AFTER READING, it would say, like in the movies—but he wouldn't check his mail between now and Monday. My desire to speak to him was physical, a numbing pain that caused my whole body to ache. Little was more agonizing than being denied what you once had.

The worst part: I wasn't even sure what I'd had anymore. It'd been less than a week since I'd last touched him, and it felt like a lifetime. The memories were already tremulous, fleeting, wavering in my con-sciousness like the surface of water. If I couldn't have him, I'd give anything to have something physical to hold on to—A picture! A letter! For a desperate moment, I wished we had made that video together like he wanted. All I had was our text-message exchanges, which I read over and over, the words as familiar to me now as lyrics of a beloved song, as the lyrics to Rabbit Foot's "For Luna."

How do you prove something that no longer exists? How could I ever explain to anyone what Kip and I had been, what Kip and I had shared? We were accomplices, the sole witnesses, Kip and I. And because I'd failed to retain a tangible keepsake from what we'd had—a stolen T-shirt. A hickey, even—I'd always have doubt, always suspect that it'd all been in my head.

That was the most agonizing thing: not being sure that what you'd once had was even real.

— — —

I tried to will myself to dream of him that night. I thought of a conversation we'd had back in mid-October, back when things had been at their best. He'd just come, and he lay still on top of me, his heart hammering into my chest.

"Imogene," he said. "What are you going to do?"

"What do you mean?"

"I mean, after this year. It's just a year that you're here, right?"

We never talked about me. We talked about him, and Hingham, and sailing, and his family, and Yale. There had never been a reason to talk about me. "I don't know," I said.

"You don't know?"

"Well. I'm going to get my master's."

"In teaching?"

"Yeah, in teaching."

He rolled off of me, so we lay shoulder-to-shoulder. He spoke to the ceiling. "Where are you going to go?"

I turned so I could see the side of his face. "Go?"

"To get your master's."

"Oh. I don't know."

"Where have you applied?"

"Nowhere, yet."

"Do you even want to teach?"

He caught me off guard. "Yeah. I mean, I guess so. Yeah."

Still speaking to the ceiling, he said, "Well, if you do, and when you apply, maybe you'll end up somewhere in Connecticut."

"Connecticut?"

"Yeah. Like New Haven?"

"Why?"

"Because." Kip turned and smiled at me, almost shy. "That's where I'll be."

I didn't dream of Kip. I dreamed instead of a bathtub with a broken faucet that wouldn't stop running, and it filled the tub until water spilled over the edges and leaked onto the floor and no matter what I did, I couldn't get it to turn off.

— — —

I awoke Sunday morning to the sound of shouting. It was happy shouting, the yelps of children. I went to my window and drew aside my curtain. The snow had finally stopped; dozens of boys tumbled and scrambled through the giant white banks, hurling snowballs and throwing powder into the air. I watched them for a while, smiling. I loved them all, I really did.

I thought, for the first time in a few days, of Clarence. Since I'd humiliated him in front of his parents at the Homecoming Weekend dinner, we'd emailed intermittently. I'd proofread his art history final, a stammering review of the Italian Renaissance that I'd attempted to shape into something passable. He'd told me about Thanksgiving in Vermont, a sullen affair for an only child with elderly parents and no other family to speak of. He hadn't once mentioned what happened at the dinner, and I began to think that I'd misunderstood the whole interaction—that perhaps he hadn't made his parents believe I was his girlfriend, that he'd simply told them what I really was: the only friend he'd made during his three years at Vandenberg. I was ashamed of the way I'd treated him, but it was a relief to know he liked me enough to absolve me, that I'd been so easily forgiven.

I thought about asking him to do something that week—I hadn't heard from him in a few days and I was starting to worry—but I was too ashamed to face him. I felt sick at the thought of him finding out about Kip, and it felt only a matter of time until he did. His finding out felt worse than my parents, worse than my fellow apprentices, worse than anyone. That, I couldn't be sure he could forgive.

The Hovel was silent. I looked at the clock; it was already past eleven. They were probably already at the library preparing their final exams, or perhaps they'd also gone out to play in the snow. I felt an unfamiliar ache, one I hadn't felt since high school, of having not been included. I'd been given an opportunity, and I had scorned it. I mourned momentarily the death of friendships that never had been and never would be.

My phone buzzed on my nightstand. My heart leapt into my throat. I'd been conditioned to believe that a phone notification meant Kip. Who else could it be but Kip?

I retrieved my phone, mind racing. It wasn't Kip. It was Raj.

Hi. Chapin told me what happened.

I stared at the phone, still disbelieving that what I'd felt so certain of hadn't been true.

The phone vibrated again. I just wanted you to know that it wasn't me who told. I promised you I wouldn't, and I didn't.

One last vibration: I'm sorry this happened to you, Imogene.

I sunk onto my bed, phone in my hand, messages unacknowledged. It hadn't been Raj who had told, and it hadn't been Chapin. It could have been anyone, I told myself. Anyone could have known, anyone could have told. But even while I thought these words, I knew they weren't true. I didn't allow myself to dwell on this, wasn't even prepared to approach this. I pulled my legs into the bed and slid them under the covers. I had nothing to do but wait for the next day to come.

— — —

I woke again at twilight, the light outside waning and sad. I felt suddenly, painfully lonely, lonelier than I had ever been perhaps. I reached for my phone.

My mom answered on the second ring. "Imogene?"

"Hi, Mommy," I said. I hadn't called her Mommy since I was six.

"Imogene, is everything okay?"

"No, it's not."

"What's wrong?"

I wanted, for one last day, to have unremarkable problems. I wanted what I felt to be my real loss mourned before it was muddled with indecency, before it was delegitimized and shamed. "It's over."

"What's over, Genie?"

"Adam and me." My voice broke. "It's all over." And then I sobbed. I clutched my phone to my wet cheek, wailing into the mouthpiece, finding no comfort in its cold screen but feeling release nevertheless. I was in pain. I had every reason to be in pain, and it felt so good to express it. When I finished, I sniffed and sat up, waiting for kind words.

"Well," my mom said. She cleared her throat. "Boys come and go."

There was a beat of silence. "What?"

"Genie, it feels terrible now, but you'll meet someone new. Don't let this one get you down."

I must have heard wrong. "What?"

"What what?"

"This wasn't nothing." My hands trembled. "This was real."

"I never said it—"

"I loved him!"

"Okay, okay, I'm sure—"

"I really did. I really, really did."

"Imogene—"

I ended the call. I threw the phone across the room, and it landed on the carpet with an unsatisfying thud. She didn't understand—nobody could understand! She'd never been wanted by someone who had everything. She'd never had so much to lose. I pulled on my jacket and a pair of sneakers and flew out the door.

The campus was still and eerie, a world locked in a plastic snow globe. The snow instantly soaked through my sneakers as I trudged down the paths, but I didn't even notice. All I could see was my destination before me, a clear path, at the end of which I'd find the answer.

I tracked snow up the stairs of Perkins and down the hall, and it melted in puddles under my feet as I knocked on his door. His friend Skeat answered.

He peeked out and looked at me. "Oh, shit," he said.

"Kip?" I pushed the door open, catching Skeat off guard so that he stumbled backwards. I peered around the room. Park sat at Kip's desk, a book open before him.

"Oh, shit," Park said.

"Where is he?" I looked first at Park, then Skeat. "Is he here?"

They looked at each other.

A toilet flushed down the hall, and then Kip emerged from the bathroom, wiping his hands on his shirt. He froze when he saw me.

"It was you," I said.

He trained his gaze somewhere past my shoulder, avoiding my eyes. "You should go."

"What did you tell them? Who did you tell?"

He walked past me, still coolly brushing his hands on the hem of his shirt. He stepped into his room and closed the door.

"Kip!" I raised my hand to bang on the door, lowered it. "Kip," I said softer. "Why would you do this?"

Skeat stuck his chubby face back out the door. "You need to leave," he said.

"I just want to talk to him." My voice was dangerously close to a whine. What was it that I wanted to say? That nothing had ever made me feel so powerful, so important, as being his? That nobody had ever made me feel as precious, as loved? That I'd give up anything, everything, to be a part of the world he'd offered me?

Skeat shut the door. "Sorry," he called out, the apology muffled and flat.

I stood there another moment, listening to their whispers on the other side of the door, before I left. He had left me with no choice but to walk away.

NINETEEN

IT MAY SOUND STRANGE, BUT I WASN'T WORRIED ABOUT THE
disciplinary hearing. My thoughts were too consumed by Kip, my
mind a muddle of eroticized revisitings of our best fucks, aching re-
membrances of his wiry hair and harmlessly sour breath, solemn
cataloging of every look he'd even given me, every smile and furrowed brow. I didn't think of the bad times—the fits, the disappoint-
ments. I didn't want solace, and I didn't want to think about how
better off I was. I wanted to be miserable, wretchedly miserable, and
the only way to indulge fully in my misery was to continue to believe Adam Kipling was the best thing that had ever happened to
me. And so I did, and I thought of him and dreamed of him and
alternatively rubbed myself between my legs and sobbed until snot
dripped down my chin. It didn't seem possible that I would ever think
of anything else. I wasn't sure I wanted to think of anything else.

But really, I didn't think about the disciplinary hearing because
I didn't think it would actually happen. It loomed ahead as inevitable
and preposterous as death. Yes, I would die someday, of course I would,
but until then I was immortal; until then, nothing could touch me.

When my alarm went off Monday morning, its angry bleating pulling me from a hazy dream, I couldn't remember for a moment what that sound meant—it had been a while since I'd had a reason to wake up. Was there a fire? An emergency? But the realization reached my consciousness and shuddered down my body like cool viscous goo: my affair with Kip was about to be publically dissected. I was about to be undressed and shamed, never again able to consider myself good.

I dressed quickly in the pale pink ruffled blouse and shapeless gray slacks I'd worn for the first day of classes, and when I stood before the mirror, I nearly laughed out loud. There was my cotton bra, on full display through the sheer fabric. Had I learned nothing from my mistakes? Had I really learned nothing at all?

— — —

The building of Dean Harvey's office was too warm, almost suffocating, and I immediately soaked through the armpits of the sweater I'd thrown on in lieu of the see-through blouse. A secretary sat outside his door, texting intently on her phone.

"Hi," I said, offering a wave.

The woman blinked at me. She looked too old for this job, too old to have her dress pants tucked into a pair of Uggs, too old to not address me. I decided that she hadn't graduated high school, that she'd earned her GED instead and spent her free time uploading pictures of her manicures and pretending not to feel bitter that her ex had a new girlfriend. She'd probably stay there outside Dean Harvey's office for the next thirty-five years, the dumb piece of shit. The viciousness of my thoughts startled me. I hadn't even known I'd become mean.

"I'm here to see Dean Harvey."

"Why?"

"I have a meeting with him."

She sighed, lowering her phone. "Name?"

"Imogene. Imogene Abney."

She went back to her phone. I stood, waiting, rocking on my feet. I checked the clock nervously. After another minute ticked by, the secretary looked up at me. "Well?"

"Sorry?"

"Are you going in?"

"Oh." I stumbled past her, reaching for the doorknob. "Thanks."

She didn't respond. I hated her, hated her for exacerbating my unease, sure that horrible bitch was the reason my hand shook as it turned the knob.

Just like the Friday before when I met with Ms. McNally-Barnes, I wasn't sure what to expect, but what awaited me on the other side of the door was worse than anything I could have imagined. Five teachers sat in a row against the side of the wall, among them Ms. McNally-Barnes; Ms. Moore, the supervisor from the field trip; and Dale. At the sight of him, my stomach twisted like a wrung-out rag, and I feared my bowels might fail, spilling my horrible, stinking insides onto the floor in a crushing mess. Dean Harvey sat before me behind an imposing oak desk.

"Ms. Abney," Dean Harvey said, his jowls jiggling. Up close, he was almost unfairly ugly. It startled me for a moment that he knew my name—the name of a lowly apprentice, someone he'd never had a reason to speak to or know before—but I reminded myself that of course he would. A name is known for one of two reasons: its owner has succeeded or failed, and I had failed at remaining anonymous. He gestured to the chair in the middle of the office, placed at an angle so I could face both him and the wall of teachers simultaneously.

I sat. I felt wet and unclean, sweat pouring uncontrollably from all parts of my body. It now seemed insane that I hadn't feared this meeting all weekend. But really, nothing could have prepared me for this horror.

Dean Harvey quickly went through introductions of the teachers—the Disciplinary Committee, he explained—but I missed the names of the two unfamiliar faces. How strange, that they knew whom I'd had sex with, and I didn't even know their names. My mind was racing too fast to retain anything new. Dean Harvey went on to explain that we were "just going to talk," that "nothing was decided," and that I had "no reason to be nervous." I sat on my shaking hands, forced a small smile. The wall of teachers remained stone-faced. Dale looked out the window.

"Do you have any questions for us before we begin?" Dean Harvey asked.

I looked at him, then at the teachers, then back at him. I'd never had so many eyes focused on me—not even in the classroom, where eyes tended to wander. "Did you . . . ?" I hesitated. "Have you already spoken to . . . ?"

"Yes, we spoke to the student in question when he first came forward."

The Student in Question. Say his name, I wanted to beg.

"He's here actually, and we're going to have him come in and give his testimony before we get started." Dean Harvey nodded to one of the teachers I didn't know, and she went out into the hall.

My body went numb. Adam Kipling was here. Then the door re-opened, and the last person I'd ever expected to see entered the room.

"State your name for us, son," said Dean Harvey.

"Clarence Howell, sir."

He didn't look at me. He planted himself in the chair a few feet away from mine that Dean Harvey directed him towards, and he kept his eyes trained on the disciplinary board as though he didn't even register my presence.

"Tell us what you told Ms. McNally-Barnes, son."

Clarence nodded gravely. "I heard these two fourth years in my math class talking," he started. "Max Park and Sam Keating. They were talking about their friend, who was seeing one of the teaching apprentices. I heard Imogene's name, but I didn't believe them, because I knew Imogene, and she wouldn't do that."

For the first time, he chanced a look at me. His eyes were red; he'd been crying. I felt suddenly, violently, that I wanted to hurt him.

"But then I was sitting outside by Perkins Hall last Saturday, about a week ago, and I saw her. Imogene. She went in, and she came out crying. And I knew Max and Sam were right."

"You were spying," I said, unable to keep the words in. "You were spying on me."

Dean Harvey ignored this. "And then what happened, Mr. Howell?"

"I went to Ms. McNally-Barnes, and I told her."

"Can you confirm this, Ms. McNally-Barnes?"

"Yes," she said. I didn't see her; the whole Disciplinary Committee had blurred before my eyes, faceless as a Greek choir, speaking as one. "I spoke with the student, and he confirmed everything."

Dean Harvey excused Clarence, and he left. I'd never known anyone could be possible of such betrayal, and certainly never would have expected it from Clarence Howell—my friend, my partner in solitude. And it wasn't just him, I realized; it was Kip, too. *He confirmed everything.* It was difficult to say whose betrayal was more unforeseen, whose hurt worse.

Dean Harvey had me start with our first meeting. I described my late-night walk, my encountering Kip and his friends in the woods. I didn't mention the beer, or the breaking of curfew, or Kip walking me back to the Hovel. I would not lie, I'd decided; I would just omit the more incriminating details, the details that didn't really matter to the story anyway. And I didn't call him by name; I referred to Kip only as "him" and "he," a pronoun without a face, without an identity. An unwritten rule seemed to exist that Adam Kipling's name could not be spoken in the office and certainly not by me; I was almost reluctant to say it—scared, ashamed. His name didn't belong in the room, I realized; nothing that had passed between us belonged in this room.

"And how did your relationship develop?" Dean Harvey prodded.

The word, "relationship," gave me a sad thrill. The teachers, silent and stern, continued to stare. Even Dale had turned away from the window to watch me.

I told them how Kip had anonymously left me his phone number, how curiosity had prompted me to contact him, how I'd stopped when I realized it was him.

"And you never responded to the text messages after you realized they were coming from a student?"

My head was a whirl, my thoughts too quick for my mouth to relay them. I explained how he'd continued to text me, how he wouldn't stop. It seemed suddenly, comically obvious to me: It wasn't my fault! He'd pursued me! Couldn't they see that none of this was my fault?

From there I went on to how Kip had showed up at my doorstep, uninvited. I became almost giddy, the realization continuing to dawn on me, my faultlessness even further supported. I'd done nothing to encourage him. It was him! It was all him!

"Did you ask him to leave?"

I paused. I felt intolerably hot under their stares. I was sweating profusely by then, my skin drenched beneath my too-heavy sweater, my hair stuck to my neck and face in wet clumps. "I tried to."

"You tried to ask him to leave?"

"I did. But he wouldn't."

"Did he threaten you?"

"No," I said slowly. "He just . . . wanted a drink of water."

Dean Harvey looked skeptical. He made a motion for me to continue.

I did. I realized, as I spoke, that I had never told this story before, the story of Kip and I—not since I'd told it to Chapin the night of the All Hallows' Eve Ball, and even that hadn't been the full tale. I'd never had the audience, the interest. It may not have been the audience I sought, but it was thrilling nevertheless, to finally get to say it all out loud. I told them about the kiss, and how it happened again, and how eventually—I reddened then—things became more intimate. I left out the visits to his dorm room, the extent of our intimacy, the unnecessary sordid details. All they needed to know was that Adam Kipling had wanted me and had worn me down. He was the one in control. I'd been helpless to resist.

"And what happened when the student decided to discontinue to relationship?"

I froze. "He didn't."

"He never tried to break things off?"

"No," I said, confused. "No, never."

"And you never harassed the student?"

"Harassed?"

"Sent multiple text messages? Showed up at his dorm room uninvited? Hung around his residence hall?"

I was going to be sick. I clutched my stomach and tucked my chin into my chest. Was this what he'd told them? Surely he couldn't have made it seem like—

"Ms. Abney?" I felt Dean Harvey's eyes on me.

I snapped my head back up. "Why wasn't it harassment when he did it?" I asked, startling myself. "Why was he allowed to text me and show up at my room and that wasn't harassment?" I was met with a group of blank stares. I felt panicked, desperate. "I didn't do anything!" I cried.

"This isn't about getting anyone in trouble, Ms. Abney," Dean Harvey said, the softness of his voice more disparaging than soothing. "We're just trying to find the best solution to a problem."

Alarms rang in my head. "What did he tell you?"

"That doesn't matter."

"What, is he going to file a restraining order?" I paused, mind still reeling. "Am I going to get arrested?"

"That's not something—"

"Oh my god." I buried my face in my hands, the tears finally coming. "Oh my god." The injustice of it all threatened to choke me. I couldn't be left with all the blame. I wasn't the one to blame at all. "This isn't the first time he did this, you know." I didn't know I'd said the words out loud until six faces swiveled at once towards me, suddenly rapt. "It's true," I said, less certain this time.

"What are you referring to, Imogene?" Ms. McNally-Barnes asked.

"Kip—er, Adam." I'd said his name; the spell was broken, the jig was up. "He used to, um, see another apprentice before me." I sidled to the edge of my seat. I nodded to Ms. McNally-Barnes, close to pleading. "Remember, at orientation, you told us about those apprentices? The ones who sometimes developed too-close relationships with the students?"

"I'm not sure what you're getting at, Imogene, but I can assure you—" Ms. McNally-Barnes fixed me with a look so ashamed, so repelled, that I knew I wouldn't be able to feel like one of the good ones ever again. "—nothing even remotely close to the level of involvement you engaged yourself in has happened or will ever happen again at Vandenberg."

I fell back into my chair as though slapped. It was so obvious I would have laughed if I weren't so close to tearing my hair out. Of course Kaya had gotten away with it. Of course Kaya had known exactly when to walk away.

"Imogene." Dean Harvey's voice was stern, and I turned to look up at him. "Why don't you wait outside for a moment?"

I sniffed, tried to compose myself. "Okay," I said, as though I had a choice.

Outside, the secretary was still on her phone. She glanced up at me as I took a plastic chair against the wall, and then looked back down at her phone. "You okay?" she asked the screen.

"I'm fine," I said. I flipped her off beneath the seat.

Fifteen minutes passed before Ms. McNally-Barnes came out to call me back into the room. She took her seat with the teachers, and I took mine in the center.

"Ms. Abney." Dean Harvey smiled at me, strangely, and I offered an uncertain closed-lip smile back. "This is a messy situation."

I nodded.

"And we don't want this messiness becoming public knowledge, right? Vandenberg is a proud institution, and I'm sure you have a bright future ahead of you."

I nodded again, waiting for him to continue. He didn't; he only smiled wider. I mirrored his smile, my mouth aching.

"Do you see what I'm trying to say?" he asked.

"I'm not sure I do."

"We're not going to fire you, Imogene."

"You're not?"

"No. But I'm afraid you're going to have to leave this school."

A beat of silence passed. "I don't understand."

"We want you to leave of your own volition," he prodded.

"You want me to quit?"

He smiled sadly in answer.

"Oh." All eyes were still on me, waiting for me to deliver a line. "Um. I guess I quit then?"

Dean Harvey stood, extended his hand. "You will be missed here."

I stood on wobbly legs and shook his hand. I felt like a puppet, guided by strings. Ms. McNally-Barnes stood and extended her hand, and I shook it as well. Dale glanced up at me, and unsure what else to do, I offered him a shy smile. "'Bye, Dale."

He looked away, busying himself with his briefcase.

I headed towards the door, then turned back. "So do I need to sign anything or . . . ?"

"Just be packed up by tomorrow." Dean Harvey sat back in his chair. "We'll take care of the rest."

"Okay." I reached for the door handle. "'Bye," I said again, lackluster parting words worthy of a lackluster parting.

No one responded, but I hadn't expected a goodbye.

– – –

I left in a daze. The sky that day was radiantly blue, the sun a mighty beam; it reflected off the banks of snow, and I walked blindly into the light until my eyes adjusted and the world returned. I remembered after a moment that I'd forgotten my jacket in the waiting room of Dean Harvey's office, but there was no way I was going back to get it. It was a J. Crew peacoat, last year's Christmas gift, one of my most prized possessions, but nothing could make me go back. His secretary could have it, I thought. No doubt it was nicer than anything she owned, the cheap slut. I laughed to myself. She'd probably sell my coat on the black market for crack, the whore! Hostility burned within me, and I fed it greedily. I hated that secretary more than anyone. I wished that secretary would skid on black ice and crash her piece of shit car into a fucking tree.

A bell tolled. It must be lunch. As the building doors opened and students spilled into the quad, I felt a wave of panic, like nausea. I was an escaped convict, a mass murder on the loose; I needed to hide. What if a warning had been sent out among the student body? A word popped into my head, a word I'd never once connected with myself but that, while never voiced by anyone around me, had been implied by everyone's eyes and tones and stares ever since this thing—this mess—with Adam Kipling had begun: Pedophile.

"Boys!" a disembodied voice called in the distance, a teacher's voice. "Boys, settle down!"

Boys, boys, boys. I couldn't let them see me, and I certainly couldn't look at any of them. I quickened my pace. Of course they'd want to protect the school, the proud institution. I imagined "they" as the investors and the alums, the faceless higher powers behind the well-bred boys of Vandenberg, all standing in a line. They all knew that I didn't belong. They all had so much more to lose than me. I turned on my heel and strode in the opposite direction. I had twenty dollars in my pocket. That was plenty to take me away from there.

At Metro-North, I got on a Grand Central Station–bound train. My phone buzzed in my pocket. I jumped, still hopeful—for whatever insane, twisted, tragic reason—that it could be him.

It was Chapin. What happened? What did they say?

I ignored her. I stuffed the phone back into my pocket. It buzzed again.

What's going to happen to him?

Nothing, I thought. I switched the phone off altogether. Nothing would happen to Kip, and she knew it. And Kip, I was sure, knew it, too.

— — —

I walked to Bryant Park because it was close, I knew how to get there, and I had nowhere else to go. I'd never been in the city alone, and being pushed along the crowded sidewalk, big buildings all around me, gave me something like a high. It was strange to me that I'd been into the city all of two times in the nearly four months I'd been at Vandenberg—a whole world that I'd neglected to explore because I'd been so comfortable with the smallness, with Kip. It was foolish, I realized; so much had been at my disposal, and I didn't even see it.

The ice rink had been set up for the season, and skaters with clasped hands glided around the perimeter in dizzying circles. I had enough money to buy myself a hot chocolate, and after a moment of hesitation, I bought myself a cup. Emboldened, I even asked for a dollop of whipped cream. Fuck it! Fuck it all! I'd gain fifteen pounds, maybe thirty. I'd become an alcoholic. I'd move across the country and work at an ice cream parlor. Very little seemed to matter anymore. It was a fleeting but thrilling feeling.

The hot chocolate made me think briefly of Clarence, of how perhaps I was deserving of his betrayal, but I pushed the thought away.

I'm not sure how long I stayed to watch. One couple caught my eye—high schoolers, it seemed—and I tracked them as they did twelve, then thirteen, then fourteen laps around the rink. The girl had flushed cheeks, the guy braces. I wondered if they'd kissed yet. I wondered if they'd fucked. I couldn't imagine anyone that age wanting or knowing how to fit themselves together with another person, how to position themselves, how to thrust. How did anyone know, really? The hot chocolate scalded my tongue, even while I shivered all over, jacketless. I was ashamed of myself for speculating about the sexual experience of strangers, of kids. I was ashamed of the way my shit stank and of the stray little hairs around my nipples and the ugly blue veins on the back of my hands and down my thighs and on my eyelids. I drained the rest of the hot chocolate in one sip; it churned in my stomach.

What a waste, I thought. The hot chocolate, the round-trip train ticket from Scarsdale to Grand Central, the loss of my jacket. What a waste that I'd lived forty minutes outside a city that I didn't allow myself to explore, that I'd had a career opportunity but hadn't given myself a chance to succeed.

I waited for the two teenaged skaters to make one last loop before I stood. Then, on a whim, I fished my phone from my pocket, powered it back on, and called Joni.

"Imogene?" She answered with the trepidation of someone expecting bad news, and I realized that I'd probably never called her before.

"I'm in the city," I said.

"I'm in the art studio. Is everything okay?"

No, I wanted to say. Everything is over. But I wasn't ready to say it out loud, not yet. I wasn't ready to tell my sister that I needed someone, that right now I needed her, because I didn't know what happened next, and I was afraid. "It's fine," I said. "I'm fine. I just wanted to say hello."

"Hello, then." She sounded skeptical and a little amused, unsure of why I'd really called, perhaps wondering, as I was, why we were strangers to each other. I hoped she knew that I called because I was trying to change that. I hoped she picked up because she wanted to try, too.

"Hello," I echoed.

— — —

On the train ride back, I looked up Kip's profile, something I'd resisted doing for longer than I'd thought possible. His relationship status had changed. Adam Kipling was in a relationship with Betsy Kenyon. I knew then why I'd spent so long away from his page. The only way to make reality bearable was to construct my own.

"That fucking bitch," I said aloud. "That slutty little cunt."

The insults felt delicious, a temporary relief, the forbidden "c-word" like licorice. I clicked over to her page, stared at her for longer than I should have. Forget Dean Harvey's secretary; it was Betsy Kenyon who made me feel dizzy with hatred. And I held tight to that hatred like a rock in my hand, knowing the moment that I let go, all that would be left was a dull ache.

— — —

Back at the Hovel, all the apprentices except for Chapin sat around the kitchen table. They turned all at once when I walked through the door, instantly hushed. They'd been talking about me. I stared at them, and them at me. We hadn't been trained for this situation. There were no words in our guidebooks for what I had done.

Raj finally broke the silence. "You okay?"

"Why wouldn't I be?" I said. I didn't mean to sound cruel, but the irony was too great for it not to come off as insincere, angry even. I tried to smile to offset the sarcasm, but it felt strained.

"Ms. McNally-Barnes told us what happened," ReeAnn said, hesitant.

I nodded, still paralyzed in the doorframe. I started past the table to the stairs.

"Is it true?" It was Meggy that said this, calling out after me. "Did you really do it?"

"Meggy!" I heard Maggie swat her, my back still turned. "You can't ask her that!"

I didn't answer and began up the stairs.

"I'm going to take your room, if that's okay," said Raj.

I still didn't look back. At the top of the stairs, I heard one last snippet of conversation ("—honestly really disgusted—" Babs muttered) before I closed my door.

I lay facedown on my bed. It was dinnertime, and all I'd had all day was a hot chocolate, but the thought of procuring food was exhausting. I couldn't go down to the kitchen. I didn't want to order anything, didn't want to talk on the phone or exchange money at the door—plus, I would have to leave my room, which wasn't something I was planning on doing for the rest of the night. Maybe I could starve myself. I could get skinny—scary-emaciated skinny—so that everyone who saw me would think, *Well, clearly she isn't well. She can't be blamed for what she's done.*

Chapin came in without knocking. I could tell it was her without having to look. "You're back."

"I'm back," I said.

She sat on my bed. "When do you have to leave by?"

"Tomorrow."

"Where are you going to go?"

"Dunno. Home, I guess."

Just then, my phone vibrated on my bed. We both looked at the screen. My mom was calling. I ignored it.

"Does she know?" Chapin asked.

"No."

After a minute, the phone rang again. A voicemail. Then she called again.

"I think she might," said Chapin.

"Yeah."

I nudged the phone so it dropped off the end of my bed, its buzzing muffled by the carpet. I'd thought about how my parents would react, of course, but up until that point I'd been thinking that perhaps they wouldn't have to know at all. They didn't know when my winter break began. And I could get a new job and an apartment before the next semester started up again, apply for graduate programs in the meantime. It was only for a few months. Or maybe I could just tell them I quit—that was the truth, after all. I could say the job wasn't a good fit for me. They would understand. What they wouldn't understand was my relationship with Adam Kipling. No one could understand it, because now that it was over, I no longer understood it myself.

I looked at Chapin. "What am I going to do?"

"What do you want to do?"

"I don't know." I rolled onto my back. After a moment, I asked, "Do you like teaching?"

Chapin peered down at my face. She really wasn't very pretty; she had acne scars along her jaw and dark circles under her eyes. I wasn't sure why I'd ever been so afraid of her. "Of course I like teaching," she said, surprisingly sincere. "That's why I'm here."

I closed my eyes. "I don't think I do."

"Do what?"

"I don't think I actually like this. Teaching, that is."

A beat of silence passed before Chapin burst into laughter. "Are you serious?"

I laughed, too. I couldn't help it. "Yeah."

"Jesus, Imogene. Then do something else."

How simple it seemed, how simple it all suddenly seemed. We laughed until our stomachs ached, and then we went to go get McDonald's because, fuck it, why not? Why not enjoy things while we could?

— — —

On Tuesday afternoon, Chapin volunteered to drive me back upstate; it was nearly winter break, and she could get away with leaving a few days early. We could rent a car, she said. We could stop over in the city and crash with a guy she knew, party for a few days. We could drive up to Canada. We could go anywhere. She was so thrilled with her plan that I became excited, too. A road trip! An adventure! But I didn't deserve an adventure. Adventures are for those who have accomplished something. I knew that I needed to stay and contend with what I had done, that dodging reality was over for me.

"Who am I supposed to hang out with next semester?" she asked. She nodded towards my bedroom door; downstairs, we could hear the other girls and Raj watching the show about the mismatched couples raising the puppies, laughing too loud. "Them?"

I smiled. Finally, she had confirmed it; it was us versus them. I was in the cool group, with Chapin. I wasn't one of the dorky girls. Feeling emboldened, I said, "Well, if you get bored, I hear hanging out with students is fun."

Chapin blinked, confused, and then laughed. "Oh my god. You made a joke. That was so cute."

She pulled me into a hug, her clavicle bones pushing hard against my chest. Like most friendships, I imagined ours was one of proximity. We'd talk for a month, maybe two. We would not stay friends. Our relationship only existed because we were both there, at Vandenberg School for Boys, and we were each other's best option. I felt sad for a moment, but it quickly passed. There was no reason to mourn; I'd always known it wouldn't last.

A cab delivered me to the Metro-North station, and after hauling my bags onto a car, I pulled out my phone. My mom had left three voicemails. I listened to them as the train pulled away from the station, my four duffle bags stacked around me like a barrier.

The first was relatively calm. "Imogene, someone called the house today who said he was representing Frank Kipling. Something about you and his son. Do you have any idea what that could be about?"

The next wasn't. "Imogene, I just called that man back. He said his client is deciding whether or not to press charges against you. Frank Kipling's son is a student at Vandenberg, but he couldn't say anything more. Call me."

Finally, the last message: "Imogene, I just got a call from your school. I need you to call me back right now."

The messages had all been left the night before. I turned off my phone, tucked it into my pocket. I closed my eyes and leaned my head back against the seat. I thought back to my cab ride through campus to the train station, my last one. I know it was all in my imagination—or at least it probably was—but it seemed everyone I passed turned to look as I glided by, a celebrity escort behind tinted windows, an infamous prisoner's convoy. I imagined the popping flash bulbs of old-timey cameras. "There she goes!" I imagined them all whispering. "She's leaving; she's gone." I looked for one face among the many I passed. He wasn't anywhere to be seen. It hit me then, for the first time, that I would never see Adam Kipling again.

— — —

I didn't call home right away when I arrived at the Lockport station. I arranged my four bags around me, bought a slice of pizza, and people-watched. An old man hacked and spit phlegm into a garbage can. Two kids kicked a vending machine. I'm not sure how long I stayed. I nodded off at one point, first lacing the straps of my bags over my arms and clasping my hands together so I could protect them all at once. As it grew dark outside the windows, a police officer approached me. "Do you need a ride, miss?" he asked.

I smiled. To him, I was not a criminal for hanging out in a train station. To him, I was still pretty, small, blameless. "That's okay," I said. "My boyfriend is coming to get me." I didn't plan to say it; the word escaped from my mouth as easily as my own name.

He nodded. "Have a good night," he said.

I felt giddy as he walked away; I forgot, momentarily, that my boyfriend wasn't coming to get me, that I didn't have a boyfriend at all. Another half hour passed before I finally called my house phone. My dad picked up.

"Genie?" He never answered the phone, and I was startled to hear his voice. "Why haven't you been answering your phone? Where have you been?"

"Will you come get me?" I asked. I kept my voice low, as the police officer was still nearby, and I didn't want him to know my boyfriend wasn't coming.

"Where are you?"

"I'm home," I said.

— — —

They were afraid of me at first. They let me stay in my room, knocked timidly on my door for meals, didn't protest when I said I wasn't hungry. They didn't know what to do with their daughter, the pedophile. They hadn't raised this person, and they didn't know how to approach her without getting hurt.

The story came out slowly, in pieces. On the car ride home, I explained to my father that I had had a relationship with Frank Kipling's son, and that Frank Kipling's son was a student. My dad stared ahead out the windshield. We didn't talk again until he pulled into the driveway, the headlights like two big eyes on the door of the garage. He turned off the ignition and looked at me.

"You could get into some serious trouble here," he said.

I nodded. "I know." The most personal moment my dad and I had ever shared before this was when he taught me to drive. He'd never even seen me in a two-piece bathing suit before.

"You could be arrested."

"I won't be. He's seventeen. That's legal in New York."

He blinked at me, uncomprehending. Then he left the car and went into the house. I followed him, my bags in tow.

My parents talked late into the night. I didn't listen to them; I didn't want to hear what they were saying. I played the Rabbit Foot album instead. Between each song, I went back to "For Luna" and played it again.

Mr. Kipling dropped the charges. He didn't want to make trouble; he didn't want to taint his son's future. A proud Vandenberg alum himself, he also didn't want to discredit the school with a scandal. My record was wiped clean.

"Isn't that wonderful news?" my mom asked. She'd gone from stony anger to helpless enthusiasm; my catatonic state was beginning to frighten her.

"Sure," I said.

A few days later, I read online that the Marshall Huffman Library would be expanded and renamed the Kipling Library. It would have a new branch for Chemistry, Earth, and Space Sciences, set to open in the fall of next year.

My dad wouldn't look me in the eye. My hair had become so greasy I could slick it up on top of my head, stand it up straight like a troll doll's. After five days of this, my mom finally marched into my bedroom and threw open the curtains.

"It's over," she said.

I blinked stupidly at the light.

"No more of this. It's time to get up."

I looked at her, and she looked back at me. I never had to tell her that Frank Kipling's son was Adam, the guy I'd told her about, the guy I'd loved, the guy who had broken my heart. She always just knew. I slid one foot to the ground, and then the other. I wore only a T-shirt and underwear, no shorts, but I wasn't embarrassed. I had no pride left. "I'm up," I said.

She nodded. "That's a start."

TWENTY

THAT WAS YESTERDAY. I HAD SHOWERED, I HAD DRESSED, AND I had gone downstairs to have breakfast with my parents. My mom had even taken me to the mall so I could begin my Christmas shopping. I'd spotted my old friend Stephanie and her twenty-eight-year-old boyfriend in the food court eating Chinese food, and I didn't say hello. "You're being silly," my mom told me. "Why can't you just say hi?" I couldn't explain that no "hello" could circumvent the time that had passed between the summer before college—when we'd last seen each other—and now. Stephanie didn't know the Imogene I was now.

I'm not sure I know who she is either.

From my bedroom now I can hear my parents in the kitchen, their voices soft. I imagine I have another two hours until I'm forced to shower and dress and "participate," as my mom says. The joy of having retired parents—it seems I'll never be alone again.

Since my first night back, we haven't talked about the reason I'm here, the reason I've returned home. When necessary, it's referred to as "the incident"—and Kip "the student"—but rarely is it necessary. They avoid the topic, and I do, too. My sexuality, my desires, my perversion—these are things we cannot touch under any circumstance if we are to continue our relationship as parents and child. It is all too cringe-inducing, too intimate. Largely, my parents have acted as though I never left Lockport, a narrative I'm starting to believe myself.

Jangling keys, the opening and closing of the closet door in the hallway—it seems my parents are getting ready to go somewhere. I listen closely to see if I can discern where. Steps approach the bottom of the staircase. I brace myself, waiting for a voice to call up to me. It doesn't come; the steps pass. The car starts up and drives away. Rather than the relief I expected to feel upon finally being left alone, I start to cry. My parents no longer care whether I wake today or not. I decide that the only thing worse than constant surveillance is to be forgotten. Maybe they've forgotten I'm home; maybe they think the past week has just been a horrible nightmare. I feel bad for myself a minute or two before I find my resolve. *It's over,* I tell myself. *No more of this.* I push aside my covers and get out of bed.

Some mornings are better than others—this is a good morning. *French toast,* I decide. I make four slices, drown them in syrup, and sit cross-legged with my plate in front of the TV. I eat with my hands. I laugh out loud at the TV, something I've never done before. Outside, it begins to snow. For a horrible moment, I imagine my parents getting into a car accident, sliding off the road and crunching their car into a tree. They'd both die instantly, painlessly. I'd get the house and everything in it. I could sit here for the rest of my life, licking syrup off my hands and laughing along with the canned laughter of the TV audience. I languish in that fantasy longer than I should.

They return in the afternoon with Joni, who is home for winter break. The three of them are laughing as they come through the door, Joni telling the end of some story about school. I have no idea if she knows. I peek my head around the doorframe.

"You're awake," my mom says, surprised.

I wave. "Hi."

Joni drops her bag and stares at me. She knows. Oh Christ, she knows.

"Why don't you get dressed?" my mom says, not unkindly.

"Why?"

"You just should," she says. My dad stands behind her, saying nothing.

It is only when I return to my bedroom that I realize I am wearing a T-shirt and underwear, still no shorts. The pan and bowl and spatula I used to make the French toast are still sitting in the kitchen sink, my syrupy plate on the living room floor. I look in the mirror. My face is waxy, sunken, horrifying. I didn't even think to apply makeup before leaving my room. I sink to the floor and sob. I think it would be best if I were never to leave my bedroom again.

— — —

In the past week, I have received two text messages—one from Chapin, one from Raj. Chapin sent me a picture of the boys exiting Morris Chapel after the Christmas mass, their arms raised in celebration for the beginning of Christmas break. I scanned the tiny pixelated picture for his—Kip's—face, wondering if there was a greater reason for her having sent it, but I could not find him. A few days later, she sent me a smiley face. I replied to ask about her plans for winter break, but I haven't heard back from her. Perhaps the expiration date of our friendship has come sooner than I'd expected. I wondered if she had forgotten about our ski trip.

Raj simply asked if I was doing okay. I said that I was. He asked if I was sure. I said that I was. He reminded me that he was moving into my bedroom next semester. I said that I hoped he liked it.

I checked my old Vandenberg email inbox—*to make sure there were no follow-up messages from Ms. McNally-Barnes or Dean Harvey,* I lied to myself—and discovered an email from Clarence Howell, sent the day after the disciplinary hearing. *I'm sorry,* it said. *I shouldn't have followed you, and I shouldn't have told on you. But it didn't even feel like I was turning you in, because the you I knew wouldn't do what you did, and I realize now that I don't really know who you are. I wish I had known, but then again, maybe I would have liked who I thought you were better.* His words stung because they were true; he liked the Imogene he'd crafted in his mind more than he would have liked the real me. After the hearing, after my resentment had faded, it occurred to me that I had betrayed Clarence, too. I'd made him believe I was his friend, that he wasn't the only one who was under-prepared and out of place at Vandenberg, and then I had abandoned him the moment I felt I belonged. And if I was honest with myself, I knew I'd led him on romantically as well; I could pretend that I didn't mean to, but I did. I loved to be loved, and I never once thought that someone could get hurt besides me.

Neither Raj nor Chapin—and obviously not Clarence—mentioned anything about Kip. I knew better than to ask. I wanted to more than anything—I wanted a report of a sighting, a picture, a rumor, any sort of evidence that he was still alive and well and hadn't vanished from existence—but still I didn't ask. I checked his profile page instead. Every day, twice a day, I took an intimate look into a life I was no longer a part of.

The last day before winter break, he'd updated his status: *Half-way done with senior year, baby!!!* A few days later, Betsy Kenyon posted several pictures: Kip struggling to pick up a piece of sushi with chopsticks; Kip caught off guard, laughing with his head thrown back; the two of them in front of the Rockefeller tree, their faces pressed together. Soon after that, Park posted an article on Kip's page. I clicked on the link. It was a list: "The Hottest Teachers Caught Sleeping with Students." I stared at the screen a moment, perplexed, before I began to laugh, my teeth chattering uncontrollably. I was remembered. I was here, I was acknowledged, on Kip's profile page. I kept checking back throughout the day to see if Kip had commented on the article, but by that night the article had disappeared. I guess Kip knew better than to keep any trace of me around.

I did an online search later—"Imogene apprentice Vandenberg." No results. I was gone.

I know I will never hear from Kip again. I spend a lot of time thinking of things I'll say to him if I could. Sometimes they're jokes; after the renaming of the library was announced, I thought to say, *Immortalized forever in the library. Could you think of a greater honor?* When Rabbit Foot's first single began to play on the radio, I thought, *They've gone mainstream. How could they?* But largely the things I want to say are angry, resentful, pitiful. Sometimes, *I hate you and your stupid little prick.* Sometimes, *You have no idea what you've done to me.* But I never send them. The person I want to send these messages to doesn't exist, at least not as I imagine him. I delete his number from my phone, and all of our messages, too—a decision that I regret immediately and agonizingly but that I know, ultimately, will be for the best.

The last time I ever look at his profile page, there's a new status update: *I love dick in my butt!!!* I recognize, of course, that he's been hacked—he'd accidentally stayed logged on to a friend's computer, or left his laptop open and unattended, and someone had posted this as a joke. But strangely, it doesn't matter to me who wrote it or why. For the first time, I feel embarrassed by my relationship with Kip, embarrassed that I'd imagined him better than this, capable of more than his years could even allow. It's as though the curtain has been drawn back, the trench coat opened to reveal a child standing on his friend's shoulders.

I don't fault him for this deception. Adam still has many more years of growing up to do. But me? My time is up. I am not a child anymore.

— — —

I listen to the three of them downstairs, my parents and Joni. The sink turns on, and I hear the scratchy sound of a scrub brush against a pan. My mom is doing my dishes. She is cleaning up my mess. Shame roils through me. I sink onto my bed and listen.

They are talking about the garden my dad is planning outside, my mom's recent joint pain, Alex the Canadian, whom I'm surprised to learn my sister is still seeing. Never before had I considered any of her relationships legitimate; she had just turned eighteen, hadn't she? How could she possibly know what she wanted? To me, her relationships were postured, semblances of real intimacy, nothing more than indulgent experiments in claiming another person as her own. But perhaps it was no longer a performance, no longer just the fleeting thrill of holding hands and touching lips. Perhaps my sister had found love before me.

I wait for the subject to turn to me. They have to talk about me eventually; how could they not talk about me? I am the pitiable, the shamed. They have to decide what they're going to do about me. They have to wonder how they can help. But my name isn't mentioned. It is as though I do not exist, as though I do not merit any sort of acknowledgment. Before, I had dreaded that, the being discussed. I imagined talk of medications, of mental facilities—therapy is not a question; I will surely be returning to therapy. But now that it doesn't come, I feel even more pathetic. I am a problem too unpleasant to contend with. Or, worse, they don't even realize how big of a fucking mess that I am.

It occurs to me for the first time that it is not disinterest or a lack of understanding that keeps my family from knowing me. It is me who has never let them in. It is me who has barely stepped out of my own head.

I cry. I have cried so much in the past couple of months that is a wonder I have anything left, but I do. I cry, and when I hear no acknowledgment of my crying downstairs, I cry even harder. Can they hear me? Can they even fucking hear me?

"Can you hear me?" I scream it at my closed bedroom door. There is no response. I cross the room, vision blurred, and pull open the door so quickly it slams against the opposite wall.

"Can you hear me?" I yell again. I stomp down the stairs into the kitchen. The three of them sit at the table, and they all turn to look at me.

"Imogene, are you crying?" My mom stands. "What's wrong?"

Her face, an unfamiliar hardened mask for the past week, is concerned, kind, and I collapse into her arms. She sits again, and I curl up in her lap as I haven't done since I was a kid. I'm probably hurting her; I'm probably too big for this. But her arms are wrapped around me, and it feels too good to let go. I feel a hand on my back— my dad's. And then there is another in my hair—Joni.

"I don't want to be alone," I sob.

"Imogene." My mom says this softly, sadly, into my ear.

"I don't want to be alone, I don't want to be alone." It is a realization so profound, so suddenly and intensely true, that I cannot help but say it again and again. "I don't want to be alone."

"Imogene." My mom's breath is warm and wet on my ear. "You're not alone. You're not, you're not."

She holds me until the pain subsides—not entirely, but at least a little bit.

— — —

I don't know when it will stop hurting. I don't know what I will do tomorrow, much less a month from now, or for the rest of my life. It feels good to know for certain, at least, that I don't want to teach. I look at job boards online sometimes before bed. I haven't found anything that excites me yet, but I am amazed by how much is out there. Two days ago, when my mom sent me to the store for milk—a transparent attempt to get me out of the house—and I was driving through town listening to "For Luna," suddenly, unexpectedly, I couldn't recall Kip's face. I could see eyes, a nose, a chin, but I couldn't quite fit it all together. My brain reeled, and I pulled over to the side of the road. I rested my forehead on the steering wheel and tried to concentrate. My head hurt from the effort. It was no use—I could not see his face.

I would be able to go home later and pull up an image of him, but in that moment I could not remember what Adam Kipling looked like. In the same way that I can't really remember what my old friends Stephanie's and Jaylen's voices sound like anymore, or the scent of the perfume my roommate Darby used to wear, or what it felt like to have Zeke Maloney inside of me, Adam Kipling has started to become a part of my accumulated unconsciousness.

I'd pounded the steering wheel with frustration, wondering how I could possibly forget his face, how it was possible that someone who once felt so important could already be gone. But now I wonder if it had ever really been about Adam Kipling. Perhaps it was never really about Adam Kipling at all.

ACKNOWLEDGMENTS

My gratitude is too deep to encompass succinctly and too over-whelming to express wholly, but I will try my best to acknowledge all of those who have helped me make this dream come true.

To the entire InkWell Management team, especially Stephen Barbara and Claire Draper: thank you for being the best colleagues and some of my biggest supporters. It's an honor to have you represent me, and it's a mystery to me why you trusted me to handle your royalties and accounting.

To Sara Goodman, Olga Grlic, Jennie Conway, Nancy Sheppard, Brant Janeway, Brittani Hilles, Will Rhino, and everyone else I've had the pleasure of working with at Wednesday Books: thank you for investing in my story, for sharing my vision, and for making it all come to life. You've made *Indecent* better than I could have ever imagined, and I am forever indebted to you all for that.

To the incredible professors who mentored me during my time at Boston College and Sarah Lawrence College: thank you for helping me become the writer and the person I am today.

I can only hope to impart the wisdom you have gifted me onto someone else someday.

A special shout-out to Elizabeth Graver, who I forced my presence upon for three semesters and who exposed me to authors and opportunities I may have never discovered otherwise, as well as to David Hollander, who was the first person not related to me or dating me who told me I was a real writer.

David, thank you for believing in me, and for assuring me that it was okay to believe in myself.

To the ladies of Helene's Kitties: thank you for always reading and always supporting. You all are the source of endless inspiration and laughs, and I'm so lucky to have you in my life. Extra thanks go to my favourite teacher, Katherine Granger, who has read everything I've written since my freshman year of college and who inspired this novel (but thankfully has not slept with any of her students). To Mickey, my sweetheart: thank you for challenging me, encouraging me, and keeping me (mostly) sane. I am a better and stronger person because of you. Thank you for making my dream your own and celebrating my successes with me. I love our life together.

And last, but certainly not least, to my family: thank you for loving and accepting everything that I am. Mom, Dad, and Kat, you are my best readers and most loyal fans. Thank you for your feedback and enthusiasm and for only being slightly mortified by the gratuitous sexual content. Thank you for giving me a life where everything is possible. I don't know where or who I would be without you.

ONE PLACE. MANY STORIES

Bold, innovative and
empowering publishing.

FOLLOW US ON:

@HQStories